ALL GREEN
SHALL PERISH

ALL GREEN

SHALL PERISH

and other novellas
and stories

❦
❦❦❦
❦❦❦❦❦❦
❦❦❦❦❦❦

EDUARDO MALLEA

EDITED, WITH AN INTRODUCTION, BY
JOHN B. HUGHES

Translated from the Spanish by the editor and others

19  *66*

ALFRED A. KNOPF : NEW YORK

L. C. catalog card number: 65-11113

THIS IS A BORZOI BOOK

PUBLISHED BY ALFRED A. KNOPF, INC.

FIRST BORZOI EDITION

Fiesta in November was first published in Spanish, under the title *Fiesta en Noviembre,* by Club del Libra A.L.A., Buenos Aires, in 1938. It was later published in Spanish by Losada, Buenos Aires, in 1944 and again in 1949. It first appeared in English in an anthology entitled *Fiesta in November,* published by Houghton Mifflin Company in 1942. It was later included in the anthology *The World's Best,* published by The Dial Press in 1950.

All Green Shall Perish was first published in Spanish, under the title *Todo Verdor Perecerá,* by Espasa-Calpe, Buenos Aires, in 1941, and reissued by them in 1945 and 1951. It was published by Aguilar, Madrid, in 1952. A Brazilian edition was published in Portuguese by Editôra O Globo, Pôrto Alegre, in 1949; an Italian edition, by Bompiani, Milan, in 1956; and a German edition, by Nymphenburger Verlagshandlung, Munich, in 1964.

Chaves was first published in Spanish by Losada, Buenos Aires, in 1953. A French edition was published by Librairie Gallimard in 1964.

Anguish was first published in Spanish as *La angustia,* in the magazine *La Revista de Occidente,* numbers CXXX and CXXXI. It then appeared in *La ciudad junto al río inmóvil,* a collection of short stories by Mallea published by Sur, Buenos Aires, in 1936. This volume was published again by Anaconda, Buenos Aires, in 1934, and by Editorial Sudamericana, Buenos Aires, in 1954.

The Lost Cause of Jacob Uber was first published in Spanish as *La causa perdida de Jacobe Uber* in *La ciudad junto al río inmóvil.* It also appeared in the volume *Todo Verdor Perecerá.* It was first published in English in the *Kenyon Review* Vol. 6, No. 4, Autumn 1944.

The Heart's Reason was first published in Spanish as *La razón humana* in the magazine *Realidad.* It was included in the volume *Todo Verdor Perecerá* and then appeared in a collection of stories by Mallea entitled *La razón humana,* published by Losada, Buenos Aires, in 1959. It was included in the anthology *Veintidós Cuentistas,* published by Centurion, Buenos Aires, in 1963. The English version was included in *Spanish Stories and Tales,* edited by Harriet de Onís and published by Alfred A. Knopf in 1954, by Pocket Books, Inc., in 1956, and in a Spanish version of this anthology published by Washington Square Press in 1961.

The Shoes was first published in Spanish as *Los Zapatos,* in a collection of stories entitled *Posesión,* published by Editorial Sudamericana, Buenos Aires, in 1958.

INTRODUCTION

"A sweet immanent charity illumines the lives of men; all the rest is uncertainty, pettiness and betrayal." This tightly balanced, doubly divided sentence synthesizes in its most poignant form the theme, tone, and "message" of Mallea's fiction and of his work as a whole. The elegant containment of the sentence serves only to heighten and dramatize its irreconcilable inner conflict, its division into two warring halves. The order in which the statements are given tells us more. For Mallea "uncertainty, pettiness and betrayal" occupy the larger sphere, usually and ultimately triumph in life; but what draws and holds the reader's attention, beyond and in spite of the "closing" of the sentence, its perverse summation of man's worst fears, frustrations, and doubts, is the point of departure, the defenseless lyrical affirmation of the beginning.

Mallea's fundamental concern as a writer and the core of his art are based upon man's conflict with himself, his "inner drama"; what he has called in a recent essay "the inner war." This is extended from within the individual, to man's conflict with nature and society, the battle of the sexes, and the writer's struggle for meaning and expression. Baldly stated, the effort to communicate, to go beyond oneself, to love, is committed to a "losing" battle with spiritual isolation and stagnation, man's capacity for self-destruction and the destruction of others in an "alien" and corrosive world.

Like their creator, the central characters of Mallea's fiction struggle with all the means at their disposal to transcend their "fate": *themselves*. In each, hope is pitted against despair, life against death, "immanent charity" against "betrayal." The final outcome is never really in doubt. Sooner or later, "they," and by implication "we," are all "losers." Individual "losses" along the way may be large or small but they are nonetheless "losses."

"Victories" are won at great cost, are in some obscure way defeats. Mallea's characters are alive to the extent that they are aware of their plight and struggle against it. Above all, they are alive to the extent that they are capable of suffering. The capacity to suffer as men and women is equated with authenticity and, as such, emerges as the supreme human value in Mallea's art.

This is a grim "truth" for a writer to confront honestly, hopefully, and with compassion—in the best sense, *naïvely*—over a period of forty years. But this is precisely what Mallea has done since the publication of his first book of stories in 1926 through the more than thirty volumes—novels, essays, plays, stories, and novellas—which go to make up his published works thus far. It is this specific moral-aesthetic commitment which makes him unique in Argentina and in contemporary Latin American literature.

The "isolated conscience" and the "divided self" are, of course, themes of all times and particularly of our time. In one form or another, they have been central preoccupations in most modern and contemporary writing, from the Romantics through the Existentialists. The American reader may find in this selection of Mallea partial affinities to the "tragic sense of life" of the Spaniard Miguel de Unamuno; the controlled passion, courage, and grace of Camus; the sensual "this-worldly" pessimism of François Mauriac; the intensity of "interest" and aloof, polished surfaces of Henry James; the inner doubt, frustration, and momentary expression of love for his fellow men of Sherwood Anderson; even something of the stammering "near-poetry" and stark, symbolic drama of Eugene O'Neill. One could go on. Such comparisons are suggestive; but they fix upon aspects of Mallea, not on what is most characteristic and alive in him.

More to the point, they take him out of the only valid context within which his work can be understood. Mallea is a Latin American—specifically, an Argentine writer. What may be mistaken for European or North American overtones are coincidental, not derived. They spring directly from the culture of the River Plate and are only fully appreciated in terms of that culture.

Argentina and Uruguay, the countries on either bank of the

estuary of the River Plate, occupy a unique position in Latin America, within the Hispanic world, and in the larger context of "Western" and contemporary civilization. The two countries speak a similar unmistakable *rioplatense* Spanish and share a folk nationalism and mythology whose most original creations to date are the gaucho and the tango. In short, they resemble each other and differ in the same ways from the rest of Spanish America. Taken together, they have the most clearly defined cultural personality in Latin America. Leaving aside local crises, forms of government, and national pride, whatever is said of Argentina is equally true of Uruguay. If there is a significant cultural difference, it is the more aggressive nationalism, the sense of manifest destiny of the Argentine. Like the United States, these are countries with a population largely drawn from the European immigration of the nineteenth and twentieth centuries. They are the most "modern," prosperous, "progressive," and literate societies in Latin America.

Here, the Spanish colonial structure was first successfully challenged from within. Here the most original and ruthless of the caudillos (the kind of personalist leaders peculiar to Iberian culture), Juan Manuel de Rosas, created the first popular dictatorship of Latin America. Here, in opposition to the tyrant, was born the first original literature in Spanish America since Independence, a literature springing naturally from the historical drama of Argentina, one whose vigor and style were rooted in the inner contradictions of the new nation. Here Latin America's greatest educator, Argentina's greatest President, incidentally a great writer, Domingo Faustino Sarmiento, preached a government of law, democratic institutions, immigration, and change, and imposed his "civilization" upon the "barbarism" of Rosas, fighting Hispanic tradition, the caudillo, and the gaucho in terms of that tradition, as a caudillo in spite of himself, and as an intellectual gaucho whose principal weapons were ideas. Here, against the "barbarism" of Sarmiento's "civilization," Argentina's greatest book and national poem, José Hernández's *Martín Fierro*, written in the idiom of the defeated and disappearing gaucho, told the story of the man on the bottom, the victim of all governments in Latin America, and etched the profile of a gaucho singer and the virile melancholy and humor of his song upon the memory and conscience of his countrymen.

From the perspective of the post-Perón era, it is evident that the conflicts of the past have merely taken on more subtle and inward forms in this century. Today Buenos Aires, cosmopolitan metropolis of the Spanish-speaking world, continues its dialectic with the stately colonial cities of the North and West, while both are nurtured and challenged by the fertile void of the Pampas. Here Hispanic tradition, intense and dynamic in the integrity of its personal and artistic expressions, static and closed in its dogged resistance to ideological, scientific, and social change, periodically opens and closes to the innovation and mobility characteristic of modern mass societies. Here a generous new society, unlike any other in the Americas, strives to penetrate its masks of pretension, self-denigration, and nostalgia in order to recognize itself for what it is.

In what is perhaps his most personal book, *History of an Argentine Passion* (1937), Mallea wrote: "If Argentina has a rhythm, it is the inner oscillation of her deepest unfulfilled aspiration." It is not accidental that Mallea should characterize Argentina in terms of a rhythm, nor that his description of his country should serve so well to characterize the special quality and rhythm of his own prose, with its tense inner balance, its persistent "muffled song," its "hopeful despair." For to all the other levels of conflict mentioned at the outset must be added Mallea's personal identfiication with his theme and the identification of his characters with the "destiny" of Argentina. Mallea sees Argentina as a country divided against itself, in search of its true identity.

He expresses the division he sees among Argentines in terms of *visible* and *invisible* Argentina. Visible Argentina is pretentious, prosperous, superficial, *inauthentic*. It plays a role; *represents*, as opposed to *being*; adopts bits and pieces of foreign ideas and phrases for use at fashionable cocktail parties and turns its back on Argentine reality. It is characterless, flat, neither true to itself nor to the foreign models it chooses to imitate. Its sole goal is to acquire wealth and appear important in the eyes of others. This is the society depicted at the house of Eugenia Rague in

Fiesta in November. Because it is powerful, unscrupulous, and without direction, this heterogeneous and inauthentic oligarchy is dangerous. In opposition to it, Mallea poses a submerged, *invisible* Argentina—true to itself, which consciously rejects this superficial society and looks inward to find its true roots and meaning in life. Its "creative discontent" and voluntary "'exile'" from visible Argentina is the basis for self-discovery, and genuine not spurious achievement, as well as for its ultimate "return" to society. The *solitude* of the individuals who comprise *invisible* Argentina is seen as the essence of their humanity.

"Every mystique has its origin in the solitude of a human heart and that solitude, far from isolating us, is our profoundest link with one another. . . . There is nothing more powerfully universal than a fertile solitude."

Although Mallea's concern is fundamentally "moral" or psychic, there are unmistakable political overtones, directed against those in power—the irresponsible oligarchic financial interests which had subverted democratic institutions and the structure of Argentine society from 1930 on.

Mallea's view of life is essentially a religious one. In Unamuno's sense, he is one of those who *wants* to believe. In *History of an Argentine Passion* he seeks to create a secular literary rite, adequate to his time and his country. Mallea is his own character who both confesses and narrates his own discontent, his own "passion." In his novels and stories the sacrificial victims are his characters; but in *History of an Argentine Passion*—and in his other essays—Mallea created the discipline and symbolic form of his "ritual-narration."

There is something here which suggests the contemporary European Existentialists, whom Mallea anticipated, and also overtones of a dispossessed and inoperative Christianity. But Mallea's closest spiritual kinship is with the lyrical search for self of the Americas, North and South, the tradition which in the United States derives from Walt Whitman and has been continued in the twentieth century by Waldo Frank, Sherwood Anderson, and Thomas Wolfe, and still more with the anguished personal and national confessions of the Hispanic world from Unamuno through the Mexican Octavio Paz. This last is by far the most important. Mallea's preoccupation is rooted in the Catholic culture which Spain brough to America and which survives—if only as custom—in Argentina.

History of an Argentine Passion is a work belonging to no specific genre, a "man-book," part analysis, part autobiography, a lyric confession of self-alienation and self-discovery. Mallea begins by sharing with the reader the earliest recollections of his childhood in Bahía Blanca. For the young Mallea, the cold landscape was matched by the inhospitable and impersonal modern port city on the Atlantic, the southernmost of the hemisphere. "It was terribly hard to live in that frozen, changeless climate. Not a single green field around the city; there were no shadings of color and no sunlight for days and days, only the gray stone, the gray wind, the gray sand; the hostile atmosphere, the endless afternoons, the sudden and total blackness of the nights." In his novels and short stories Mallea will evoke again and again this desolate landscape, which symbolizes for him the gray horizontal Inferno inhabited by the Argentine middle class.

Argentina is a melting pot. Although Mallea himself is descended from an old Creole family, he attended an English school in Bahía Blanca where the majority of his classmates were the sons of immigrants. Although he felt somewhat ill at ease with his fellow students, he came to respect them. If they were not yet fully Argentine, they had much to give and should ultimately become an integral part of a new and vital Argentina of the future. He also came to respect the discipline and justice of the school, which he was to compare favorably with the Argentine school to which he transferred, and later with the University in Buenos Aires.

At the age of thirteen he moved to Buenos Aires with his family. He was at that time a timid and withdrawn adolescent. Buenos Aires was an overwhelming revelation for Mallea. Here the essential part of his education took place outside of the classroom, in his walks, in contacts with other young peoople, in his gradual awakening to the world around him and to himself as an individual. He describes himself in the following terms: "Life has only two sources of sustenance and mine was not precisely action. When action does not nourish a human existence, that existence is nourished by passion in the sense of suffering and sacrifice . . . this passion can be conscious or blind in the one who suffers it. If it is blind, the torment is unbearable, the misery becomes almost physical. But when it is conscious, a passion of the imagination, it allows the individual who suffers it to experience life in the raw, without defenses . . . and that somber boy, more sensitive than intelligent, with a small desperate spark in his eyes, precociously rid of joy, was the logical offspring of a family made up of sensitive but silent human beings." Mallea's youthful attitudes are closely related to the painful silences of his characters in whom the absence of dialogue is allied to introspection and alternates with extended lyrical monologues. The problem of communication between people, the precariousness of all human contact, is central to all of Mallea's work. His characters reach out clumsily and are "rebuffed" either by others or by their own inability to go beyond themselves.

It did not take long for Mallea to seek out and be sought out by the most intelligent young people of his generation. His first published stories won immediate recognition and ultimately led into transforming the shy, discontented youth into an acclaimed public figure, a spiritual force not only in Argentina but wherever Spanish is spoken. The visible signs of success came relatively early, in the thirties and forties. As director of the literary supplement of *La Nación*, a post he held for some thirty years, he was the most influential single figure on the Argentine intellectual scene. During these years, he was also one of the editors and contributors to *Sur*—probably the outstanding literary review in the Spanish language. A parallel in terms of American literary and intellectual life would be the combined editorships of *The New York Times Book Review*, *Partisan Review*, and *The Reporter*.

During the thirties Mallea, like other intellectuals of his generation, protested the curtailing of political liberties, corruption, and control by the oligarchy which followed the overthrow of President Irigoyen by the military in 1930. He sympathized with the Allies in World War II and was a steadfast opponent of the Perón regime (1945–55). In the wake of the revolution which overthrew the Perón dictatorship, he was named Ambassador to the United Nations Educational Scientific and Cultural Organization in Paris by President Aramburu. In this capacity, he later went to India to attend a UNESCO conference. Since then, he has returned to private life in order to devote himself exclusively to his writing. He has lectured at leading universities and centers of knowledge in Europe and in the United States, and it should be emphasized that for Mallea the decision to devote his life to literature has never meant a withdrawal from the problems of life but precisely the reverse: for him the only meaningful "action" has been and is the confrontation of human conflict in all its complexities within the framework of literary creation.

Above all, Mallea is a moralist—in the broadest sense of the term. That is to say that he is a moralist in the same sense that D. H. Lawrence, Unamuno, and Camus are moralists. For Mallea, life has always come first and art second. Or, to put it another way, the most meaningful art can only be born out of an intense experience of life, one which seeks out and requires that human experience be meaningful. We are dealing with an author whose sense of mission, whose vocation as a writer, did not allow him to accept the convenient niches of easy "success," the professionalism of our day which is so often the mere mastery of techniques, genres, or topics "in demand." Mallea has never succumbed to the basically similar temptations of assiduously writing down to a supposed mass public nor of writing "up" (?) to the supposed intelligentsias of Bohemia or Academia.

The principal qualities of Mallea's fiction are his primarily musical, thematic conception, a cyclic, "cumulative" style, charged with great lyric tension, and finally, the capacity to transform an apparently insignificant individual life into the very essence of the human condition.

In his taut control of the conflict between the static and the dynamic elements within the human psyche, we find the basis for the lyric-dramatic intensity of Mallea's prose, which carries the author's meaning as much in its rhythm and tempo as in its "content" of plot or idea. This conception and style are perfect vehicles for Mallea's "inner dramas," which are never resolved but intensified at a slow and rhythmic pace, moving fatally from climax to climax, and ending only with the sounding of the finale which exhausts the theme.

One could say that *Mallea is a poet who conceives the novel-istic content of all his works in musical terms which he controls thematically like an essayist.*

Mallea's gifts as a writer are peculiarly well suited to the essentially poetic forms of the short story and the novella. Here he achieves a concision, a tonal control, and, most important, a "ritual meaning" which is immediately communicated to the reader, giving him the impression of having been a participant with the author in a sacramental ceremony in which both have undergone a kind of "communion" through the sufferings of the exacerbated conscience of the principal character, a propitiatory victim whom the author "sacrifices" to the order of the universe. The closed framework of the shorter forms of fiction makes possible these advantages of composition and intensity.

"The Heart's Reason" allows us to capture the qualities of Mallea's best work in miniature. The plot could not be simpler. Celedonio Montuvio, an unimaginative insurance agent, becomes jealous of his wife, Alicia, and suspects that she is having an affair with Valentín Bordiguera, a "man of the world" whom Montuvio had originally invited to a party in order to impress his friends. He has been slow to suspect his wife, but one day as he travels to work, he goes over all the evidence which could justify his suspicion. He tries not to think about it but is unable to do anything else, and finally places himself at a spot where he can surprise the lovers at the entrance of Bordiguera's apartment. After waiting for hours, he sees Bordiguera leave with a woman who, at the moment when they are passing directly in front of him in a taxi, he identifies as *not* being his wife. His relief is so great that Montuvio resolves to confess the whole business to Alicia and ask her forgiveness. However, a few hours later, in spite of what he has seen with his own eyes, he comes again to believe that the woman he had seen *might have been*, and at a given moment *was*, Alicia. This uncertainty leads to his total confusion. He is unable to resolve the question, and we last see him paralyzed and destroyed, "without knowing what to do or which way to go, his lower lip hanging idiotically, terrified . . . as if struck by lightning."

In terms of externals, virtually nothing has happened in this story. The plot, as I have given it, is of little or no interest, but for Mallea and his readers the real action of the story is what takes place in Montuvio's mind. His doubt is a leitmotiv, which, as it is repeated, gains in momentum until it leaves Montuvio at the end objectively situated from the outside and totally lost within. The reader is caught up in the web of Mallea's prose. We will always remember Montuvio this way, just as we remember that other "small lost soul," Akakii Akakievich of Gogol's *The Cloak.* Montuvio's pain is authentic and could be our own. He has become the embodiment of his misfortune. It is inevitable that the story should end here, once the theme and the rhythm have been fully exploited.

Fiesta in November is a work of larger proportions, but the literary qualities encountered in miniature in "The Heart's Reason" are present, although the theme and subject matter are much more complex. The musical conception of the work is still more evident in its structure. Two apparently independent stories are woven together contrapuntally. In one, we witness the momentary coming together of two authentic but incomplete and ineffectual individuals, Marta Rague and the painter, Lintas, who are naturally drawn to each other by their mutual rejection of the vacuous and vicious guests attending an ostentatious dinner party in Buenos Aires. The other story describes the arrest and execution of a poet by a firing squad composed of "undifferentiated," nearly faceless soldiers. The two fiestas—the one social, the other of blood—are linked thematically by Lintas's account to Marta of the fatal beating of a Jewish book dealer in Buenos Aires by a group of Argentine fascists, and by the sinister undercurrent of violence which lies behind the conversation and actions of the guests in the house of Eugenia Rague. The poet's anguish and creative conscience, although more developed, parallels that of Lintas and the as yet unformed but acute intelligence of Marta. The two stories serve as commentaries upon each other. The essence of the art of *Fiesta in November* is in the tone or mood it evokes. The musical structure is seen not only in the repetition of phrases and motifs, the punctuation which carries and measures the beat, but in the way the two narratives intertwine. *Fiesta* begins with a fragment of the poet's story written in italics, signifying that in spite of its shorter length, it is the

more important of the two and carries the larger burden of meaning. Its somber tragedy is thus projected on the longer story,
which gains in suspense and intensity. The fragments continue to
interrupt the longer narrative until the end, only to be repeated
verbatim, followed by the inevitable fatal conclusion. Lintas and
Marta, the most sympathetic characters of the longer story, strive
desperately to communicate with each other, and Lintas succeeds
imperfectly in awakening in Marta an awareness of the need to
choose definitively between the forces of evil and those that are
authentic and creative, while Marta, again imperfectly, brings
home to Lintas the sterility and negativism of his need to fight
against what he dislikes, before he is able to fight *for* what he
truly believes in. Both are held back by their pride from attaining
the semi-mythical authenticity of the poet.

Behind *Fiesta in November* are many historical circumstances
which no longer hold true today—the Second World War, the
Nazi persecution of the Jews, the end of the Spanish Civil War,
and the fresh memory of the execution of Federico García Lorca,
the unmistakable signs in Argentina of the new order which was
shortly to become the Perón dictatorship. But no special historical knowledge is needed to understand and appreciate Mallea's
novel. As the author tells us at the outset, "the people who appear
in this book are fictional," and the theme is universal. The reader
experiences, participates in the rite of sacrifice. The sacrifice of
the authentic, the personal, and the creative by the false, undifferentiated, and sterile—of the best by the worst. The passion
of Christ still holds a universal message for many who are not
Christians.

All Green Shall Perish is Mallea's best-known work of fiction
in Spanish and perhaps his greatest artistic triumph. In *Fiesta in
November*, fatality is suggested and evoked; in *All Green Shall
Perish*, it reigns unchallenged, unalleviated. This is Mallea's most
somber work. If the majority of his "causes" are "lost" in the
first instance, there are also occasional glimmerings of light and
hope. Here the reader is overwhelmed from the outset by the
inevitability of events and by an increasingly oppressive atmosphere. A sense that the world is forever hostile and alien to man
is evoked from the first sentence on, never to leave the reader

until the final catharsis. This closed horizon gives this novel, more than any other of Mallea's, the literary equivalent of a "sacrificial rite":

> Forty-four successive days of drought and fire laid waste the hills, the valley, the wild scrub; the earth's sparse head of hair bare to the sun. In the daylight hours, boundless and distant from the sky, stretching as far as the eye could see, the countryside seemed an endless ashen surface, vast and white. White was the dry earth; white the pastures; white the pampas grass and the skeleton elm. White the *carob* and the *tala*, gnarled and knotted and rigid like dead nervous systems drawn from the earth into the burning air. The fields everywhere revealed the earth's spectral hungry face and parched mouth, its squalid paw, stretching limply for miles on end. Below, cleaving its way through the valley among the *yuyos* like a twisting fissure, the bed of the stream held only stones and a thin thread of clear water, as white as the land around it. From time to time, a lean stray animal approached to drink; then made its exhausted way through the thorny bushes. In all that region of desolation and drought hardly any cattle remained. Sometimes a solitary horseman would appear against the skyline above the deserted house, or a fleeting automobile, covered with dust, or, on the slope, a lost calf. All else was barren; stony hills and ridges to which nightfall alone brought the respite of shade.

These repetitions are overwhelming. There can be no salvation in this land of death. And the sense of isolation and death within the characters themselves determines still more the course of fate than this desolate landscape. It is impossible to separate meaning from sound and rhythm, the fatal overtones of Mallea's prose. Indeed, one could not exist without the other.

The novel's title could have been *The Passion of Ágata Cruz*, or, better still, *Requiem for Ágata Cruz*. Ágata's story is divided into two parts. The first takes place in the terrifying countryside of the beginning and ends with the death of her husband, Nicanor (Without Song) Cruz, and Ágata's frustrated attempt at suicide. The second is situated in the barren urban landscape of Bahía Blanca, where Ágata, after possessing an illusory moment of happiness in the arms of her lover, Sotero, loses all hope of happiness when confronted at last with the certainty of inevitable solitude. Mallea describes her in terms of death, recalling the parched landscape of the beginning: "While in bed, her slender body at rest, her face white against a bedspread a thousand years old, her eyes devoid of inner scenery, her limp fingers relaxed over the material they rested on, everything in her suggested a corpse, with the exception of that knot which from the depth of her being still insisted on having hidden rights." Inadvertently Ágata reveals to us her inner awareness of futility in the description of herself she confides to Sotero: "I thought the world was an enormous flight of birds, and that I had only to stretch out my hand to stop the one I wanted. Then one sees that the bird is oneself, and that the world is the hand that claims one."

Ágata's inner drama is symbolized in her name (Agate Cross). Thus she is condemned by her own nature which is gradually revealed to her and which she analyzes pitilessly, wounding herself at every step along the way. According to Ágata, "each being is not like the water or the wind, subject to influences and change. Each being is a single, unmodified tendency. Each being *is* its tendency."

Thus the Mallea character—an isolated and desperate self-awareness—destroys itself with the discipline of its own logic. This is a process found in other Mallea novels. It is what happens to Celedonio Montuvio, Ana Borel, and Jacob Uber. This self-contained, closed perspective and character form the very basis of his stories and novellas. The novelist in Mallea has made his characters appear real and we empathize with them; from this point on, the essayist and his theme, and still more the poet, whose interest is in the rite that is being fulfilled, take over, closing off the possibility of the unexpected, or of further development. The view of life which Ágata's introspection evokes in her brings to mind another terribly withdrawn Mallea character, Gloria Bambil, from his novel *The Bay of Silence*, for whom each individual life is symbolized, contained, within a closed room.

Mallea has chosen to enclose the sources of "disenchantment" within the intensely private domain of man and woman. For him this limited stage becomes the prototype of feeling for all human experience. The apparent way of escape out of loneliness—love, tenderness, sexuality—is for these characters a disappointing source of frustration: they are like birds trying to force their way through a windowpane. Mallea is brave about this. He insists upon running the risk of annihilating the whole man or woman. He writes out people to the most abstract, tenuous, unvibrating dimension of human figures, barely visible, alone, and only slightly more so because of the presence of one to the other. *All Green Shall Perish* offers the eye just enough to hold on to, not one detail more. All superfluous delineation is sacrificed to the distillation of terror that takes its shape from the accrual of the experienced moments of the central characters until finally nothing is possible. Time moves slowly about his characters; their lives endure the minute abrasions of one despairing moment finding its hold upon the next. One can only look inward to find truth—and spiritual death. In *All Green Shall Perish* Mallea has unleashed upon the unsuspecting reader all the pressures that reduce individual life to paralysis.

We leave Ágata, as we had left Celedonio Montuvio, bearing her cross, at the maximum point of exacerbated suffering, when there is no hope left: "She had no notion or sense whatever of what was around her, of the town, of the enormous Sunday calm or of the image only a few steps away, the bulk of wood which stood in front of the chapel and at the foot of which it was written: *Ego sum via, veritas et vita:* 'I am the way, the Truth and the Life.' It was very late when she got up suddenly, as if called by a scream, and, without direction or discernment, started running against the darkness."

The closed system of life, most fully elaborated in *All Green Shall Perish*, has its antecedents in two of Mallea's earliest stories, "The Lost Cause of Jacob Uber" and "Anguish." In the first there is no possible relief; this is truly Mallea's most closed and conscious statement of hopelessness. Jacob Uber is a person totally withdrawn in his self-made "well of loneliness," or *ensi-*

mismamiento (a Spanish word meaning one who is totally enclosed, totally wrapped up within himself).

Mallea wastes no words: "One thing alone kept people from hating Jacob Uber: the undeniable fact that his entire life was overshadowed by suffering, a suffering so intense that in the end it destroyed him." His moral cowardice and timidity are such that "he had never confided anything to anybody, never had become sufficiently intimate with any human being to feel like unburdening himself of what he considered the vapid story of his life. . . . For years and years all his yearnings had centered on ridding himself once and for all of this vitiated atmosphere which so weighed him down. But the wretched man could never sufficiently destroy the evil spirit within to achieve this reformation, and there were periods when he felt as though he were trailing his hated self around much as a serpent drags his cast-off skin. . . . He took a melancholy view of himself as a human receptacle containing its own world, one with no outlet, a stagnant world where one mirage after another moved slowly by." Yet the reader sympathizes with Jacob Uber because he bears within him a "seed of tragedy." It is only this, the intensity, the humanity of his suffering, which allows the reader to forgive his inertia, his unconscious cowardice and resignation, the hypochondria that destroys him.

Jacob Uber comes close—as close as he can—to the most intimate of human relations. In the love he feels or *thinks* he feels for Carlota Morel, the language teacher whose intense but fumbling attempts at intimacy with him are nearly as stifled as his, although she at least is capable of confessing her unhappiness to him, he might have found a release. But Mallea denies him this possibility. The girl talks incessantly about the madness of Hölderlin. And one night Jacob Uber breaks off the relationship. He is himself sinking into madness. The remainder of the story documents in minute detail, stage by stage, the hero's disintegration. At first he is exhilarated, liberated, by the fact that he no longer needs the real Carlota Morel but can closet himself in his apartment with the image of Carlota his fantasy has shaped. Later on he is overwhelmed by despair and idealizes their past relationship, even in its most sordid details. But he makes no effort to contact her because of a growing numbness and lethargy. He goes to a cemetery.

There is only one release for Jacob Uber. "Suddenly, as if he heard a voice calling, or perhaps because he was overcome by a horrible wave of fear, he got up and began to run, his eyes fixed on the distant horizon, as if entranced. Reaching the edge of the water, he flung himself into the river, producing a noise like applause in the water . . . Death was one place where at least he could enter and find rest, find something real, inexorably real. Suddenly he stopped swimming and began to shout. His cry echoed far. The water opened for a second, then once more presented to the supreme calm of falling dusk its normally motionless and colorless surface."

"Anguish," which, when it first appeared, attracted the admiration of Miguel de Unamuno, is the genuine forerunner of *All Green Shall Perish*. Here a withdrawn, prematurely wounded girl, intelligent but frigid, is driven and drives herself to a state of mental anguish, finally revealed as insanity. As in the case of Ágata Cruz, the roots of her ultimate destruction are found in a lonely, emotionally starved childhood. Her situation is brought to a crisis through her unfortunate marriage to Jaime Benes, a buoyant, childlike enjoyer of the superficial pleasures of life, and the companionship of a vacuous circle of friends which becomes the center of the couple's social life. His inability to concentrate for long on anything, and his absorption in constant selfish diversions, make him oblivious of his wife's increasing terror and latent hysteria. A typical party given by the Beneses for Jaime's friends brings on what may be the final, irrevocable attack of madness. Her husband, who has never understood her before, is shocked into a recognition of his lack of comprehension: "Now it seemed to him that he had been conversing with her constantly and that she had abandoned him in the middle of a conversation, betraying him in his will for happiness, inflicting something on him which he didn't deserve." However, his confusion is not total. In his way, this seemingly empty man had always cared for her, and at this moment his tenderness and devotion come to the fore: "Suddenly he felt a strange wild tenderness for that woman who was lying upstairs with her forehead burning under the ice. He wanted to be near her. To speak to her, to flood her with words, to call out to her even if she persisted in her absence, in her deafeness toward him."

There are more characters, and fully realized ones—among them, Señora Saliciano, theosophist and semi-hysterical owner of a dressmaking shop—in this story than in any other of Mallea's early stories. In this sense it can be said to anticipate the larger world of his later works. Another Mallea "character," fully treated here, omnipresent in detail, mood, and atmosphere, is the city of Buenos Aires, whose special flavor is evoked in so much of Mallea's best prose.

In *Chaves* and in "The Shoes" the anguished tension and sense of inner conflict remain constant but move on to other areas of life. The basic problems have not changed: men do not communicate with themselves or with others. But here it is the others who will have to bear the brunt of responsibility.

Chaves is the love story of a man who cannot express his feelings adequately through words. But because words are part and parcel of the essence of love, he "sacrifices" himself gladly, although at great cost, in order to win and hold Pura, his beloved, when she arouses his jealousy by showing interest in another man. Although by nature the closest thing to a mute in all of Mallea's fiction, Chaves forces himself to talk to Pura, and when he is not with her, seeks out themes and subjects for conversation. His love enables him to talk as garrulously as possible in order to win her. He continues this technique of love through words, a medium which is foreign to him, until her death plunges him once more into silence. Of all his novels it is here that Mallea makes the most effective use of flashbacks, reminiscences, fragments of memories: these are invariably sparked by Chaves's other "communion," his sense of intimacy with the world of nature. Here he is at home, not in the world of men. Indeed he refuses, voluntarily and involuntarily, to say to his fellow workers in the lumber mill more than is absolutely necessary. The other workers mistrust and fear him: "Man is always saved in some way, through some weakness or intention; but myth . . . never," and Chaves, by dint of his silence, his refusal to reassure and assuage the fears of the insecure, has become a walking myth. At the conclusion of the novella, only the intervention of the foreman, Molers, saves Chaves from a beating by a crowd of angry workers. "In a confidential tone he [Molers] said to Chaves, imploringly: 'Aren't you ever going to tell them what they want to be told? Something . . . anything . . . Aren't you ever going to say anything? Won't you ever talk with them, speak to them?' The larch trees were beginning to take on a tint of blue shadow from the evening slowly covering them. From the distance came the murmur of the river, the perceptible whisperings of the woods, the delicate brushing of the barges in their slow advance, all the sounds gathered in by the growing silence. 'No,' Chaves said."

Paradoxically, Chaves's "no," as well as his love and the force behind that love, make him the most heroic figure in Mallea's world of victims and anti-heroes.

In "The Shoes" (1959) Mallea returns to the gray, impersonal, and dehumanizing world of a modern metropolis. Federico Morales is an employee of a large corporation. His life consists of monotony and routine. On the surface, he is merely another member of the "lonely crowd" or the "sane society," but Mallea seeks to show us what is most human in Morales—his inner drama, however moderate, however trivial it may appear, and his capacity to suffer. One day Morales catches sight of an "imposing pair of shoes" in a shopwindow: "It was a beautiful pair of walking shoes, brown, bordering on the red, well-fashioned and delicately stitched, with tapering toes; unquestionably the work of a master craftsman. They were displayed on shining shoe trees, over which hung a ticket flaunting the word: IMPORTED." Without his suspecting it, these shoes will transform his life. He is tempted to buy them, but is convinced that they will be too expensive for him. After much thought—for him the beginnings of mental anguish—he decides to buy them. The price is fabulous, the equivalent of one entire month's salary. But with the encouragement of his wife, Leonor, he acquires the shoes. At first he doesn't wear them in public. On a special occasion, he decides to display them before his three most intimate friends. They cannot restrain their curiosity and demand to know the price. When he tells them, they are profoundly shocked. Gradually, as the story progresses, the reaction of his friends is expanded and distorted by all those with whom he comes in contact. It is felt that in buying the shoes he has committed an act of treason. It is as if he thought himself better than the others. He has failed to conform to public opinion and must pay the price. Rumors are spread about him so effectively that he loses, first, his position as a secretary of a cultural society, and finally, is asked to resign from his job. He encounters nothing but hostility in those who knew him slightly, and veiled coldness from his former friends. He is retired on a pension and he and his wife are forced to look for a smaller house in the suburbs. Morales is a changed man. His genuine modesty and decency have been placed on the defensive but he has been able to bring forth a modicum of self-respect in his heightened self-awareness and new insight into the nature of life itself. The conclusion, their move to the suburbs, has a bitter-sweet flavor about it in which the forces of good and evil are seen to be struggling with each other beyond the confines of the couple's new home.

Inevitably something is lost in translation. Not only the translation from Spanish to English but also the subtle shifts in the cultural frame of reference from Mallea's Argentina of the thirties, forties, and fifties to the contemporary American reader. The remarkable thing, however, is not how much is lost but how much remains—the authenticity and universality of Mallea's message in English. Above all, the honesty, courage, and compassion of his conception remain. Mallea is a great Argentine writer; a great writer because he writes for all men, and about what he knows best. His characters are unmistakably our contemporaries and the ever-present sense of alienation of modern man finds in his writings a badly needed note of muted tenderness. If K. in Kafka's *The Trial* and Meursault in Camus's *The Stranger*—ritual sacrifices beyond a shadow of a doubt—are eloquent symbols of the human condition, they are somehow more abstract, less our *brothers* than Celedonio Montuvio and Ágata Cruz.

JOHN B. HUGHES

August 1965

Contents

Fiesta in November
(translated by Alis De Sola)   *1*

All Green Shall Perish
(translated by John B. Hughes)   *109*

Chaves
(translated by Maria Mercedes Aspiazu)   *253*

Anguish
(translated by John B. Hughes)   *305*

The Lost Cause of Jacob Uber
(translated by Helen B. MacMillan)   *345*

The Heart's Reason
(translated by Harriet de Onís)   *371*

The Shoes
(translated by Maria Angelica Deulofeu)   *393*

These translations from the Spanish
have been approved by Eduardo Mallea.

FIESTA
IN NOVEMBER

*. . . And he felt in himself a need to give thanks for having been
made of that particular clay—Argentine clay, American clay—
and of no other. And, at the same time, a secret, an insistent and
powerful dread, as though in foreknowledge of certain dangers,
certain poisons in the very air, miasmas come from afar, bloody
misfortunes from beyond the sea. . . .*

*. . . It was eleven o'clock at night. There was a violent, pro-
tracted pounding at the door, blows that sounded as though they
were made by the butt end of a Mauser. Opening the door, he
saw a patrol of armed men, filthily clad, with unkempt hair and
beards, their rawhide belts smelling of sour cheese. One of them,
the one in front, said, roughly but without conviction: "We've
come for you."*
He stared in horrified astonishment at that brown heavy face in

*which weariness clashed with a profound and nervous irritability;
he saw the cruel mouth, the furious eyes, the powerful soldier's
body. . . .*

*In his hand he still held a bit of white bread, homemade bread
which he had picked up a few minutes ago from the carving table
in the dining room. He remembered suddenly that he was alone
in the house, that neither his mother nor his sister was at home.
He remembered, too, the scrap of paper which he had left lying
carelessly on the table. On it were the penciled beginnings of a
poem. . . .*

On the thirtieth of November, at exactly eight in the evening,
the jalousies were drawn on both sides of the house where it
fronted the streets. It remained thus an isolated continent with a
climate far less intemperate than that of the increasingly breathless city outside. Besieged from without by that tidal wave of
heat, it held as it were in concentrated form its own expensive
and lordly atmosphere. All its rooms were permeated with the
cool fresh scent of flowers, of magnolias, geraniums, freesias,
roses, carnations, and early jasmine.

The hoarse notes of the Tchang clock on the upper landing
were still striking eight when Eugenia Rague came down the
stairs into the shadow of the great drawing room, the stiff silk of
her gown rustling rhythmically in the still, close air. On the last
step she paused, one clawlike hand clutching her lorgnette, the
other rigid on the dark rail of the stairs. Her face had a sort of
sour austerity, a look in which violence and apathy were incon-
gruously blended, forced to use the same mask for disparate ends.
Her eyes, cold, uncompromising, swept the twenty square yards
of the Renaissance hall, seeking some dissonant detail, some alien
note in the perfection of its order. Had she found even a single
vase out of place, it would have been sufficient to release her
fury, that fury whose scope and peculiar ingenuity were well
known to every person in the house, her husband, her children,
and her servants alike having suffered its disastrous impact.

This room was her church, and her vigilant inspection of it was
a sort of ritual. Standing there in the half-darkness, her lips
moved soundlessly, enumerating her treasures. They were fine

cruel lips, the lips of a puritan, harsher than any God would be in exacting vengeance upon the sinner. Forty years of impassioned aridity, of empty prayer and inert ambition, had resulted in this cult of the antique whose taciturn priestess she was. She had collected things everywhere, torn them from their native setting and set them up here in unnatural proximity: a huge tapestry depicting a hunt, the dark splendor of a candelabrum, statuettes of ivory and bronze, paintings, vases, glass coffers, bric-a-brac of every conceivable description.

From the stairs, her glance raked them all and then returned to the portrait which faced her across the cleared space of the room. It was a portrait of Cardinal Wolsey, painted by Raeburn's disciple, Garnett, badly preserved, full of dust and germs, the canvas rotting under its film of oil. But it challenged her as always, it compelled her attention. The fleshly nose, the vermicular brows, the whole face, so old, so weary, gave her an impression of mysterious disdain as though survival in this form were another death to the spirit, inexpressibly worse than the fact of death itself.

She would spend hours brooding over the meaning of that look, feeling in it a subtle mockery directed at her alone. The painted image forced her to speak, to justify herself: "You, Wolsey, old prelate, rector of Limington, counselor of Henry the Eighth, enemy of Anne Boleyn, protector of England, you were strong because you knew what you wanted—an England made in your image, rich within and independent of the world. But I am stronger than you. Yes, I, Eugenia Rague, native of Yorkshire, English by birth but Argentine by adoption, installed by my own will in this land which I detest but whose strength I have absorbed into myself. You dominated lives; I dominate the very source of power. One word, said at the right time and in the right place, that is all I need. Because of this word of mine, the shape of things is altered, the entire world seems to tilt only at my command. . . ."

Every morning, when she came down the stairs, the muscles in Mrs. Rague's throat strained and shook with this silent defiant greeting. Every morning she crossed the great room as she did now, noiselessly but for the rustle of her silks, and stood before the portrait of the Cardinal, her eyes lifted to him in what was almost reverence. Though that painting was the only thing in the room for which she professed no devotion, which she regarded, indeed, with resentful animus, still she could not withhold her tribute. Every day her resistance to that old dark face became weaker. In a queer subterranean way she was being conquered by weary eyes, a fleshy nose, and those long vermicular brows.

She stood for a moment immobile with that feeling of exhaustion which the portrait increasingly induced in her. Then, drawing back a little the heavy curtain of a window, she turned to observe the effect of the slanting light on the ancient features. Her voluptuous absorption was shattered, however, by the sudden brutal sound of a gong from the distant pantry. She would have to speak to Rickert, she thought with annoyance, moving away from the Cardinal, letting her attention rest lightly on other objects, barely discernible in the shadows of the deserted room. In passing, she glanced at the three sacred knockers of St. George and the Dragon, feeling in her mouth the bitter taste which still lingered from her unsuccessful attempt to sell them. It was the fault of her husband, who had been stupid about the whole business, allowing himself to be persuaded that they were mere copies of the ones in the National Museum in Florence. Three thousand dollars for each should not have been a difficult price to obtain. She had paid several times as much for that anonymous prayer book of the Italian Quattrocento which lay beside them.

A light flared at one end of the room where a door led to the butler's pantry. Rickert appeared in full dress, carrying a tray heaped with silverware. . . . That stupid head of George Rague's, stupid head and ridiculously tender heart! Why, this very evening, his incurable levity might have resulted in spoiling her party. He had been at the point of inviting to it his secretary, Brian, though he knew that the entire German embassy was coming, including Gerta Rustyg, who had been involved with the young man in a spicy affair. And his excuses—what an infantile candor they displayed! He had no idea that Brian's adventure with that faded and insipid creature could possibly be regarded as an international incident. Absurd improvidence! Either one had an instinct about such things or one had not. She flicked her bony freckled hand impatiently and became aware of the servant who was passing nearby.

"Rickert!"

"Madame?"

"What are you doing here?"

"I'm bringing the silverware which Madame ordered placed on the little table."

"Very well, but go now. Nobody is to enter this room, nobody at all."

The servant bowed and slipped away silently. But, before he could make his escape through the door, she called out to him sharply, "Rickert!"

"Madame?"

"There is to be no noise, no confusion among the servants," she said in her dry and acrimonious voice. "If anything is broken, it must be reported to the housekeeper tomorrow and charged to the one responsible."

"Yes, Madame."

"When the guests have left, come to me for instructions." And, as the man still hesitated in the doorway: "Go. That's all."

She was alone again in the deepening shadow of the room. Tall, languid, as laden with jewels as an idol, she stood contemplating her spoils with the air of one who listens attentively to the complex harmonies of an orchestra. They were music to her, these pieces so minutely accumulated, the swelling chords of her own avid spirit. Gems from England, Italian ceramics, porcelains of the Ming Dynasty, rare sixteenth-century choir seats, gilded icons, a magnificent carved lectern, a Tudor armoire belonging to the counts of Essex, the filthy black hat used by Nelson before going to his death at Trafalgar, an ancient prie-dieu from St. Paul's, rich cloths still faintly odorous with the blurred, musty smell of dead civilizations. Her thin high-bred nose sniffed it in with measured and deliberate sensuousness, the nostrils first delicately pinched, then flared with satisfaction.

All this spelled power. Nobody thought of this missal or that lectern simply as objects in themselves. They were invested with an invidious significance: they were coveted for what they meant rather than for what they were. Certainly her magnificent collection—the loot of five continents, gathered piece by piece with ardor and perserverance—was the most envied in America, with the possible exception of the one belonging to Patiño's relative in which she had never really believed. (She was inclined, indeed, to regard it as an out-and-out fiction, a malicious fraud perpetrated by persons hostile to herself.) Well, she thought fondly, directing a glance of sprightly intelligence at the Admiral's hat lying on its silken cushion, tonight my collection will do its duty.

Again, with a kind of furtive delight, she breathed in that strange odor, redolent of sandalwood and lavender and death, which her antiquities gave forth. It was mingled now with the strong concentrated aroma of the flowers—blue flowers in blue pots, great superb masses of them!—and with a certain intrusive exhalation drifting in from the street on that hot November night. The vast residential district which formed a rectangle around the north plaza had its own distinctive smell, compounded of fresh asphalt, of trees and bushes and grass newly sprinkled, sharply green; it held a little, too, of the breath of the river, winding casually from the northeast, giving as it turned the merest wave, a just perceptible breeze.

Some queer association led Mrs. Rague's thoughts back to her husband. If only he were more capable! If only, for this one evening at least, he could overcome his irresolution and conclude with Ráices that ticklish business involving the Rosario-Liverpool stock. Then, then at last the dream might become reality and this scent of early summer come to them from the Thames Embankment, rising heady and sharp from an earth and a river she loved. And a people . . . ?

Her bony hand clutched the silk folds of her dress. That Lord Burgley! Insolent man, he had hardly deigned to look at her while being introduced. London . . . a winter afternoon . . . the Savoy. . . . And that other one, Lady Gowers, with her loud, noisy, exuberant laugh, her head like a flower lifted in laughter above the shabby broadtail coat. Laughing, laughing while Mr. Alvan, the good-natured fool, kept insisting, "But they're the Ragues of Buenos Aires, the George Ragues, don't you know . . . ?" Lord Burgley, Lady Gowers, Mirabeau Leicester, and the other, Atkinson, Denis Atkinson, drunk and disorderly on Regent Street at midnight, head bare and swallowtails flying. . . . Oh, they would see, all of them, they would choke on their own saliva when her wonderful collection was transferred to Pall Mall. Forty pounds for one solitary item, and that a trivial one! How do you like that, Lady Gowers, my fine lady, Patricia Gowers?

As though suddenly recalled to reality, Mrs. Rague drew a deep breath and unclenched her hand. She called out in a voice intended to be peremptory but which sounded almost broken, "Rickert!" But Rickert was no longer there, so she simply stood with puckered brow, bust high and head thrown back in her preferred attitude, bitterly angry and unable to vent her spleen. She did not, she would not, tolerate in herself cheap complacency of this kind. She had thought once: We all carry within us two creatures, one of the city and another. It was the other she hated, the provincial creature lurking like a poor relation in the dark corners of her mind, taking advantage of her abstraction to show its ugly head.

She took a few steps and yanked viciously at the missal cloth hanging from the lectern. She could not endure hating herself as she had to at moments like this. She would have lashed about her recklessly, destroyed without mercy if it had served to silence forever that stupid creature. Her jaws set tight, her blood pounded in fury against her skull. *Power without implies power within. The happiness of the claw is to be the claw.* She swept up the stairs, still without any noise except the soft rhythmic rustle of her silks, rustling in time with the furious obsession of her thoughts. . . . Well, what of it, Lord Burgley, what of it, Lady Gowers? Power is power, and damn all the rest.

As she was crossing the hall of the second floor, she met the children's former governess, now vaguely acting as lady's companion. It was a quite useless function, and Mrs. Rague detested her as she detested everything which had its origin in sentiment. "Has Miss Brenda come in?" she asked coldly. Receiving a negative reply from the woman, she pushed past her into her own room, slamming the door and locking it behind her.

. . .

Under the steeple of the Tudor portico the girl stood and laughed, the basket of fruit dangling from her arm. Heavy lids half covered her greenish eyes and her lips were red, brutally red and hot in the gathering night. "I don't want to know anything." She laughed, biting her lips so hard that their blood stained her teeth. "I don't want to know anything," she said, shaking her head from side to side with comically childish passion. Her red muslin dress had white dots, her shoes were buckled, and she wore no stockings on her tanned bony legs.

The servant's round glassy eyes gloated upon her over the plate of fruit he had just selected. "Someday I'll have you," he said. "You'll know something, then."

"How bold you are!" The girl stuck her tongue out between the little bloodstained teeth. "How very sure!"

"Someday you'll come to me," he insisted. "You'll come with your basket and say, 'Here I am, today I bring no fruit, my basket is empty.' "

The girl burst into a peal of laughter. "Yes, yes . . . !" she cried. "Someday."

Summer Season, read the large placards on the walls. Everybody seemed to be abroad that night, crowding the streets and the streetcars, seeking in the heated darkness of the city a breath of alleviating air. Young men gay with bright ties, unattached girls, the gentleman perspiring in the depths of his Minerva—all of them had the same goal. But there was no relief in the streets. The air was so dense that it clogged the thin nasal passages. Mouths opened, panting. Would the sultriness never cease?

The victrola was made of a too brilliant mahogany. It stood against the wall, near the french window with its flying curtains. The old man went up to it and started the disk moving again. He was in shirt sleeves and black dress trousers and he had an apoplectic-looking neck. The needle was set badly, so that it screeched recurrently against the record, but the old man paid no attention to this defect. He returned to the middle of the room and, standing with widespread legs at some distance from the mirror, began to adjust his tie.

If Ráices won't do it, he mused, if he refuses to sign the contract until he can get more for his stock, a convincing and concrete guaranty—if he stands pat, in other words—what am I going to do? It's no use offering him new pledges on our part; if he feels that way he won't accept them. And bringing a third party into it, to arbitrate confidentially, would mean a loss of time. I can't afford that, I've got to get on with the business. . . . His mouth contorted violently as he stretched his neck and pulled the stiff formal collar into place. His arms were rather short for this task, but he persisted heroically. . . . I've got to work without losing a second; the slightest delay and everything's lost, absolutely everything.

He lowered his arms and looked attentively at himself in the mirror. Dissatisfied with his inspection, he untied the knot of the white piqué tie, took off the collar, and sighed aloud, "Everything?" As though only now becoming aware of the discordant noises from the victrola, he walked over to it and corrected the position of the needle. Then he waited. A voice that was at once grave and majestic and singularly twangy rose from the instrument. It might have belonged to some dogmatic robot; its penetrating monotone was designed to engrave itself deeply upon stubborn and unreceptive minds.

The enormous wealth and power of the nobles were beyond the Crown's reach, and the danger that these great ones might confederate was not altogether illusory. The War of the Succession had demonstrated just this possibility; on that occasion a small group of them had almost succeeded in imposing their will upon the country as a whole. The first countermeasure adopted by the kings was to reduce and humiliate the nobility, a step facilitated by their internal discords and squabbles. The great ones had previously managed to snatch from Henry the Fourth almost his entire inherited estates, annexing the Crown's lands to their own and failing to respect even the holdings of the various municipalities. Moreover, they had exacted enormous pensions in payment for these public leaseholds. It had become by all means necessary . . .

The old man's eyes remained glued upon the whirling center of the disk. Meanwhile, the blowing white muslin of the curtains slapped lightly at his head, a head almost bald, covered with sickly yellowish parchment-like skin. His eyes were small and green, somewhat protuberant, slow to react. Above them the forehead, broadened long since by his premature baldness, was wrinkled in regular horizontal folds. The mouth was large, with fleshy lips which still retained a certain freshness of texture. . . . If Ráices is willing, but wants me to pay for the title ahead of time, that won't be possible either.

He was not really tired, but all these worries made him a little nervous. He had never been able to give his imagination the scope it demanded; he had always had to enclose it in a strangling web of calculations, numbers, plans, and conjectures. These, on the other hand, betrayed his native propensity by wandering in a sort of fantastic circle which bore little relation to the circumstances involved. Life had pushed him around, forced him, every day more tyrannically, into a sort of dreary treadmill. His career as an active speculator involved him not only in a maze of ever-multiplying interests, but in the lives of the people linked to those same interests. It was time now, he thought, to rest, to take advantage of these last years in his personal history, and to concede to his spirit, so enfeebled by its underground existence, the chance of recovery.

He would have liked simply to sit in a chair and devote himself, passively and serenely like those ancient bearded philosophers of whom he had been told, to the evolution of his dreams. But, if he had even begun to put this harmless idea into practice, his wife, Eugenia, would have checked him at once. She would have appeared in his room, confronting him with her harsh irony, her buzzing and exasperated tone, just as she had always done when he appeared to stray, however slightly, from what she considered the normal condition and necessary objectives of masculine existence—the pursuit of gold, including its more elusive and abstract manifestations. Mr. Rague would never be able to blot from his memory the recollection of the many sleepless nights he had spent with his eyes fixed upon the ceiling, his brain obsessed by serried ranks of figures, while, in the bed beside him, his wife slept on peacefully like a keeper who knows her ward is safe.

He went back to the middle of the room and began again his

struggle with the tie. He stood in the same position as before, his neck straining and congested, his legs a little apart. Pausing in his labors, he went over to the night table and poured himself a glass of water from the cut-glass pitcher. Both the pitcher and the glass were far too opulent, too heavy; it was a job to lift them at all. Besides, the water was lukewarm, stale; it had not been changed since morning. The old man made a gesture of disgust and resumed his stance before the mirror. . . . According to the considered opinion of the Directorate, all the documents should be transferred by tomorrow afternoon. I think a few more hours might be conceded, till the next morning, perhaps. Obviously. But no more. Not a second more. The phrase "not a second more" seemed to have a magical effect upon his manipulations. The end of the tie slipped neatly into the knot. "Not a second more," he repeated firmly. "Not a second more."

Standing quite still, he examined with candid satisfaction the result of his effort. Meanwhile, his lips kept on moving soundlessly. At that instant he became aware again of the voice from the victrola, which had kept on moving, too. "*Thus the ambitions of the monarchy became clearly defined, toward the clerical establishment as well as the nobility. . . .*" His brows puckered, he approached the instrument, listened for a moment in confusion, and finally replaced the needle at the beginning of the record. The grave professorial voice did not falter. "*The enormous wealth and power of the nobles . . .*"

"Well," he said—and his tone was resigned—"I won't be able to learn a word of history today."

Forcing himself to pay attention to the lesson, he began to hunt for his evening vest, first on the bed, then on the chairs, finally inside the wardrobe. With the garment in his left hand and his right on the knob of the wardrobe, he listened closely, even repeating the name of Henry the Fourth a couple of times. After that, he returned to the mirror. He noticed, with some surprise, that there was a slight stain on the white expanse of the shirt front, a small, almost imperceptible gray spot. He went closer to the mirror and examined it minutely. "There's no doubt of it," he sighed. He fiddled around in the wardrobe for some time, without any success, however; made a useless trip to the adjacent bathroom and stared at his empty hands in perplexity. After a period of vacillation, he dug in the wardrobe again, emerging with a pigskin bag. Out of this he took a glass vial. Posing purposefully in front of the mirror, he moistened a handkerchief with the contents of the vial and began to rub it on his chest. The small gray spot disappeared. He felt extraordinarily pleased.

"Later on, the gentlemen took part in a third rebellion . . ." He had missed everything in between! Running to the victrola, he started the record again. Again the professor droned on about the enormous wealth and power of the nobles.

This time he was determined to listen without interruption, but he had left his vest in the wardrobe; he had to retrieve it. He did so, muttering recriminations to himself. *"The War of the Succession had demonstrated just this possibility . . ."* The old man nodded in approval. "Very well said," he murmured. "Excellent order. Excellent method." At that moment, inopportunely, he began to be worried by the thought that Ráices might not show up for the dinner at all, that he might send some last-minute excuse. What a calamity that would be! He would then have to change the political complexion of the Directorate from head to foot, reopen the whole business, set his traps anew. And there would be his impatient wife to deal with. And the needs of the company to consider. . . . But, after all, what was the point of being so extremely pessimistic? He slipped on his swallowtail coat, delicately arranged the white linen handkerchief, placed the small green button of the Belgian decoration in his lapel. . . . Clearly, there are many ways of not being present, not counting actual physical absence. Such as rejecting the conversational gambit, turning it off in another direction. Nevertheless, one had to put things in logical terms, logical and normal terms. . . .

Knuckles rapped at the door. "Come in," he said absently, while the voice of the record twanged on louder than ever: *". . . in this way the grave situation existing in the political domain . . ."* The servant had come in with a small silver tray.

"Some letters for you, sir. They arrived this afternoon."

Sudden rage choked the old man. He hurled the tweezers he had been manipulating upon the floor. "God of all gods!" he shouted. "Have you decreed that I'm never to have any peace?

This won't stop till I dismiss every servant in the house. All of you falling on top of me with that idiotic victimized look on your faces. Leave me alone for once. Go on now, close the door, close it, I say!" He flung himself down on the sofa and rested his head against its back. "Night after night, and I don't get in one blessed word of history! It's enough to drive one mad."

The butler hurried precipitately down the service stairs. The roar of the nearby street reached him through the large windows with their panes of frosted glass; he heard buses, taxis, delivery trucks rushing by in an unregulated and savage stampede. Looking out, it was strange to see among all that clatter the old tranquil tower of Pilar, so anachronistic here, so definitely of another age, with its rudimentary cupola, its colonial belfry, and simple sturdy arches.

The strong green young branch of a hardwood tree reached almost across the street, its naked trunk stark above the asphalt. From the east came the sound of the twilight siren, singing to the oblivious ear of those who passed by, seeming to fade if one listened too attentively. The door of the outer kitchen slammed behind the butler, Nicholas Morla, beating the air into wind. He hesitated, confused: "Isn't Miss Marta in?" he kept asking of everybody. Miss Marta was not in. "She's not in," he repeated, mysteriously crushed. What was he to do, how was he to deliver that urgent message, that entreaty which had come over the telephone?

"Nicholas Morla's lips are as white as ashes," was the interested comment of the assistant cook.

She was not at home; Miss Marta was not at home. What should he do, burdened as he was with that message? It was useless to give it to any of the others. He peered out of the small square kitchen into the heat of the street. The wide avenue was far away.

She had left the door of her bedroom open, the lamp lit, and had fallen at full length upon the bed. She was a tall girl; on the bed lay five feet seven inches of firm, slender, elastic flesh. Her legs were long, finely muscled, her breasts delicate and hard.

(Yet, small as they were, almost epicene, they vibrated with her when she walked.) She was twenty-seven years old: twenty-seven years without a dead day in them, not a single dead day, twenty-seven staunch years of restlessness and curiosity. Passionate curiosity, hunger to see, smell, hear, feel—that was what she had. Twenty-seven years of asking herself: What is this strange thing, life? Life, things, places. A sudden wonder about people, about geography, about natural facts, ideas, books, everything. And, with it all, a weariness, a boredom, a need *not* to know.

Was it she who changed, who suffered alteration, or things themselves? That nose, that brow, that glance, that particular way of being a man—was it the same yesterday, the day before? Or had he changed? Those features which sparkled with intelligence became stupid; that silent and beautiful shape, once comprehending in itself the whole world, was an empty shell, holding nothing but a vast, an irremediable boredom. The way he had of caressing the skin, the tact, the virile tenderness, the wisdom she had sensed in it, into what had it been transformed that it seemed merely a routine now, the outward manifestation of a native indifference?

A wave of disgust swept over her. Enough of him, of man; the books were still there. One arm, stretching languidly, picked a volume at random from the night table. *The Anatomy of Melancholy*, Burton's *Anatomy*, an admirable work, particularly at first reading, when one first savored, deliciously, its profound acumen. Life was strong in it; that singular creature, Burton, sprang vividly out of the gray text. Democritus, Jr., physician of the soul. "Give not way to solitariness and idleness." Good. "In moderate exercise is a most forcible cause of melancholy." Yes, and in vaingloriousness, too, in pride, pleasure, ambition, study, education, poverty, desire, and cupidity. All of them were causes of melancholy, all means to the same end. The book itself was melancholy, it had a depressingly monotonous cast. No, Mr. Burton wouldn't do. A novel, perhaps, D. H. Lawrence, Huxley, Garnett, Hemingway—what were they but turns of the same wheel, the persisting ineluctable wheel? Paintings, men who painted. Three, at most four, washed up by the mediocre tide. One Pascin, one Picasso, one Braque. It seemed worthwhile to buy them, so they were bought. Then, slowly, they began to disintegrate, to distill their poison. The lie, the commonplace technical calculation upon which the entire plastic mass rested, seeped through to the surface.

But what else was there? The planet is not large, there are only a few streets which the feet long to tread, the rue Saint-Honoré, Bond Street, the Via dei Condotti; only a few faces rare with wisdom, a few books, and those already read, a few places the heart remembers. Beyond these, nothing, nothing except ugliness, vulgarity, stupidity. The same gestures, the same words, the same tricky self-justification. Here is one attached to his little automobile, another who cherishes his little vices, both insisting that society be regulated in their favor in order to secure for themselves permanently that little automobile, those little vices. Nothing else is of any importance to them, they bend their knee to no other idol. . . . Humanity! She was sick of humanity. Men, women, and children, they all sought only their private ends, and the lot of them together would never be worth more than the sum of their appetites.

She stretched uneasily, her eyes fixed on the ceiling, her whole body tense with fatigue and a deep repugnance. She would have liked to turn away finally from everything in her surroundings, everything that bore, like a fraudulent trademark, the inaccurate designation of life. It is not life, she thought drearily, none of it is life; the vital impulse has escaped from it and gone on elsewhere. . . . Her head moved painfully from side to side; she was trying to avoid thought, too, wanting in this moment of disillusion to be only a mindless animal, a creature burrowing for rest into its hole. But she could not relax. In spirit she still wrestled with the image of that man, now so odious, who had stirred in her, briefly, a faltering hope.

Her arms open, as though spread on a cross, she remembered how crudely he had tried to pass his base metal for gold. Then a sudden access of laughter swelled her throat; she was shaking with laughter on the bed. The scene played itself out before her, vivid and detailed as a moving picture: her hands cupped around that face, so puzzled and immobile, like an inhuman mask in its greediness of the flesh, her voice speaking to him in the calm precise tones one uses to a child. "But . . . is this really the way to make love? With words, with clever little plots and stratagems? If you hadn't said anything, I might have turned to you out of the need, which we all have sometimes, to surrender ourselves, to come near to another. But you talked too much, you didn't leave any shadows. No, you didn't leave a single shadow in that body of yours, nothing, only emptiness. . . ." And that mask, confronting her, remained immobile and puzzled. He allowed himself not even the least gesture of surprise, though his system, his infallible, terrible, and premeditated dialectic, for once had come to naught.

And now, thinking about it, she too was quiet, she did not laugh any more. She lay on the bed, exhausted, a copper-colored body, gray eyes: Marta Rague.

Yes, now at last she could rest, but in half an hour it would all begin again. She would have to get dressed for her mother's party and be polite and approachable as ever. That was society: to be by nature neither polite nor approachable nor brilliant nor sociable nor happy, but to behave toward the world as though one were all of these, polite and approachable, brilliant and sociable and happy. To be for others what one could not be for oneself. To betray first oneself and then them. That was her life: a perpetual betrayal, a falsifying of her own nature.

She was thinking about emptiness again, not that of others this time, but her own, the great void which was Marta Rague. Was it, after all, enough merely to move, to occupy space, to have a taste for this or that? Did these small predilections add up to make a person? Or should she listen to the murmur, confused but subtly disturbing, of her tyrannical inner self?

She was thoroughly fed up. Fed up with her very reluctance to question further, with her unwillingness to start the avalanche rolling. The world was a mass of illusions, but, belonging to it, to that system of customs and prejudices, how could one stand, how maintain oneself once the rocks began to move and the earth to shiver under one's feet?

There was in her, in the somber depths of her spirit, a tragic dream, a need to be used utterly, to immolate herself in flame. It was almost dead, stifled by the daily comedy of existence, the laughter, the prattle. Years ago already, traveling back and forth to the provinces—her father was then involved in railroads—looking from the windows of the train at the flat passive country-side, she had seen in it a parallel to her own submissive nature. As the prairie awaits the rain, just so, stupefied, obscurely wounded, she awaited her destiny.

But her love, that single terrible drop of love in her being, that was not resigned; it ranged itself on the side of those who kept in step with things, who sought them out, defied them if necessary. Thus she was inclined to despise herself, lacking the courage to be uncompromising, unable to take the bold step which might have led her to glory or sent her crashing into the abyss.

Lying there, Marta Rague bent her arm at the elbow and lifted it to cover her face.

Suddenly, unexpectedly, as at a magical word of command, the lights flashed on, flooding the drawing room with what was al-most a lunar radiance. The fleshy yellowish face of Cardinal Wolsey, so moribund among the shadows, became transformed into something brilliant and alive. Every corner of the room was illuminated, bathed gloriously in light. The innumerable prisms of the Louis Seize chandelier shivered with it; it was caught and tossed back by the shining black tile of the floor. Mrs. Rague's treasures were dazzlingly displayed, with such ostentation, in-deed, such regal splendor, that the scene might have been laid for a court reception instead of an ordinary private party.

Between all these fine objects, so haphazardly collected, so alien to each other, a sort of *entente* had been established. They seemed, in a way, to speak together as do guests who meet in the same home and derive from the unity of their background a certain communal understanding, a fleeting but genuine warmth. There were singular and yet effective conversational units: the freesias strewn, like a thousand starry faces, over the length of a carved Greek bench with a *Dolorosa* made of jade; while, from the wall nearby, the effigy—attributed to Hieronymus Bosch—of a Knight Templar, fiery and tortured, seemed to appeal, with bloodstained mouth and an anguished gesture, to the cool white flowers for surcease. Another dialogue, of marked though discreet tone, obtained between three small coffers of the Ming Dynasty and a pure cone of Aztec gold.

It was nine o'clock. Dignified, severely smiling, Mrs. Rague came down the stairs, ready to take her position by the door. The shadow of a great white orchid lay over her bare, freckled, and somewhat sunken chest. With a slight motion of eyes and chin she beckoned to her husband, who was following her down at a meditative and unhurried pace. It was, as he well knew, a minatory gesture and he hastened to get into place beside her, imitating at the same time her formal smile, like one who takes part in a ceremonial rite.

At this moment the doorman came up to Mrs. Rague for lastminute instructions. Having received them, he bowed and turned on his heels, but she checked him with her dry and acrimonious voice: "Have you understood?" The servant's glance shied away from those icy eyes. He nodded timidly and went back to his post.

Mrs. Rague embarked on a low-toned and desultory conversation with her husband. Fulano had said he would come, Mengano that he would not. It would have been preferable to have Mengano rather than Fulano. Nevertheless, though the latter was unquestionably an idiot, it was important to have him see the three famous knockers of St. George and those choir seats she wanted to dispose of.

From the winter garden next to the dining room came the broken yet harmonious sound made by plucking a stringed instrument. The members of the orchestra were tuning up, the delicate *ping* of the plucked strings giving way occasionally to a more full-bodied tone as the bow was swept across them. The pianist was leaning over the keyboard. He had a hungry face paled by powder and he scanned the score anxiously with his myopic eyes.

Like a vaudeville number which must be punctually timed, the first six guests made their entrance together: four women of various ages, all smelling of the same fashionable perfume, their heads sleek and shining with brilliantine, and two elderly diplomats. One of them had lyric hair, curling thickly and parted in the middle in the Southern style. The other's features were lean and unhealthy; he looked like an Erasmus devoured from within by doubt and worry but not unmindful of worldly pomp.

"Jílgoles!" Without paying any attention to protocol, Mr. Rague clasped in both his own the milky-white hand, like an abbot's, of the curly-haired diplomat. The other he greeted with greater reserve, feeling almost instinctively that, at a certain time of life, one has already taken sides, chosen one's friendships according to a private system of values.

Mrs. Rague, meanwhile, touched lightly the hands of the four women, giving each the same regimented smile, the same lift of her brows, crinkling the high forehead. She was far less influenced by personal predilections than her husband, but she knew that there were unfailing ways to limit a too confidential approach or cut short an excess of temperament. An opportune hoarseness, a calculated distraction, and everything was under control again.

"I thought I was going to be late," one of the women was babbling. "I was so absorbed, one of those quite unexpected enthusiasms. Ruskin, you know. He's too delicious, I couldn't stop reading." She gurgled lusciously and went on without stopping for breath: "I suppose I'm awfully impressionable. Things come home to me so. . . . Oh, it isn't just books. A flower might do it, a lovely animal, the configuration of a cloud. All I know is that suddenly I'm caught by a sort of enchantment, almost paralyzed. It's just the way a cobra . . ." Her voice faltered, trailed off under Mrs. Rague's unvarying stare. She laughed abruptly: "How silly I am!" A purplish stain dyed her cheeks; the brilliant sensual eyes shifted uneasily. The other women looked at her with barely concealed curiosity.

A brazen clangor sounded from the winter garden, where some metallic instrument had fallen to the floor. The women jumped. But Mrs. Rague showed no sign of disturbance; she merely stepped forward a little to greet newly arriving guests. Meanwhile, her husband ended his conversation with Jílgoles and proceeded to devote himself to his duties. The old diplomat followed the four women into the interior of the drawing room, embracing them lightly with his greedy connoisseur's glance.

"You were talking about Ruskin," he purred pleasantly. "Certainly, he is always the modern, the eternal modern, I might say."

Lucrecia Batros derived no comfort from this recruit to an enthusiasm hours old and already stale, an enthusiasm, moreover, which had caused her to suffer embarrassment. Emitting the pretty coquettish shriek of the overcivilized female, she pounced upon a beautiful crystal sphere which stood in elegant solitude upon a table nearby. Jílgoles smiled at her like one who understands all. "As Góngora remarked," he said, "a serpent lurks in rock crystal." The other man, the one with the meager intolerant Erasmian face, was obviously annoyed by this literary ostentation. He took his wife's arm and led her to another part of the room, to that point, exactly, where the effigy of the Knight Templar hung on the wall and sent its tortured appeal into space.

In the few minutes the room was full of people: frock coats, bare backs, white throats, ringleted and silky heads. The play of light lent a deceptive glow to the grayest skins, invested the most vulgar attitudes with a luminous enchantment. It was as though some generous power were disposed to be indulgent toward that sorry assemblage with its precautions against time and debilitating ignominious age, as though it wanted to perform for some hours an act of forgetfulness and renewal.

At the same time little rivulets of conversation were forming and flowing together, like streams that feed a major river, into a mighty torrent of talk. All of them vied with each other, seeking, with whatever competence they could muster, the nimble phrase, the expressive gesture. They might have been competing for ultimate glory, so fiercely did the battle of words rage between man and woman, between one group and another. "If this one pretends to know something, I'll pretend to know something else," was the general attitude. It resulted in a superficial display of intelligence in which no subject, whether art or world events or philosophy, was at all adequately explored.

The crowd surged into every nook and corner of the great room, settling on the couches which were ranged along the wall under the tapestries, the silk cloths and the medieval banners.

With the circular movement of the viper which swallows its own tail and ends by devouring itself, the latecomers served those already present as a topic for praise or disdain. While Mrs. Rague, somewhat humanized by the increasing social importance of the arrivals, was extending her welcome to the ambassador, Marco Portinori, two of her guests embarked upon an amusing project. They were the rich magistrate, Constantino Esegovio, with his almost beatific indolence, and the astute and rapacious-looking Dr. Olandir. Together, in a procedure reminiscent of the game in which blindfolded participants try to pin on the donkey's tail, they were attempting to involve their corner of the room in a general examination of the prevailing morality.

Every eye was fixed on them. The important thing, they insisted, was to classify, without wounding, in a simple yet elegant way. Not to say, crassly, "He diverted the funds of an estate entrusted to him," but, with more finesse and verbal caution, "He diverted himself with the funds of an estate entrusted to him." Could anybody, for example, believe such a thing about the magistrate, Esegovio? Obviously not; in his case it should be considered a question not of criminal but of merely personal diversion. . . . It was enough to look attentively at that face, soft, tranquil, of an almost poetic fullness, to realize that here was a man justly chosen for honorary burdens, such as presiding over a cultural commission or administering an historical collection, a man who deserved to be publicly recognized as one of the pillars of society.

It would be worthwhile to study sometime the psychology of this strange species peculiar to our societies: the professional sustainers of civic virtue. The more private interests an individual of this type amasses, the more strident and intransigent is his cry for public purity. It is an odd compensatory faculty, one which the magistrate possessed in abundance but of which Dr. Olandir did not show the slightest trace. To him, if one was to believe the prevailing opinion that evening, glory was of no more value than a copper coin. Just as this comment was being expressed, the Ragues approached the center of the room. With them was a French couple, descended by an indirect line from the dukes of Enghien.

"Dr. Olandir is the typical cynic," observed a tall thin gentleman with a beautiful watch chain. "Esegovio, on the other hand, is as prudent and sagacious as an old prelate. He even thinks in a dignified way. 'What does my conduct matter?' he seems to say to himself. 'I profess a moral standard, I urge others to take the right path. . . . If I help to sustain a stainless white edifice, is it important that I, myself, happen to be a rather black brick?' " The gentleman lifted his brows and smiled pointedly.

A merchant from the North broke into the discussion. "Disgusting!" he cried with exaggerated vehemence. "In my opinion, both of them are equally cynical."

The gentleman fingered his handsome watch chain. His glance dismissed the other from consideration as though he were nothing but a cloud of dust forming in the distance. "Ah, yes," he murmured. "But you shouldn't forget that cynicism is a form of aristocracy. And one of the least easy, my dear sir, one of the least easy."

Marta came downstairs spiritlessly. She had put on a very light dress which harmonized with the freshness of her coppery body and with the expression, at once inhibited and savagely desperate, in her great gray eyes. (One would believe her won, and suddenly those eyes revolted, became desperate. . . .) Her straight short shining hair was brushed back smoothly from the temples. It was still very wet; she had not felt like drying it after her bath. Before hurrying downstairs, she stopped before a mirror in the hall, stared at herself, and gave a quick pat to her hair. Then, almost precipitately, but with her mind far away, she made her descent.

What, after all, did that sea of faces mean to her, that sea into which in another moment she would plunge? Faces, minds, souls—could one dare to expect that, hidden in one of them, there might be a human message, some trace, not corrupted but pure, of an instinct beyond dull cupidity and the desire for an easy and sheltered life? No, that was asking too much. Animals react with a quick candor which resembles intelligence; they leave no doubt of what they like or detest. But these people were always on guard, mannered, egotistical, ready to put on a show. Their outward fervor was accompanied by an inner apathy which was comparable only with death.

She shrugged, herself indifferent. Two years ago, when she had first begun to see through them, they had filled her with loathing. That feeling was gone now, replaced by a sort of passive contempt, a dry, hard pity which it was hardly worthwhile indulging since what caused it was so fundamentally inert. It was enough that she had been able to rid herself of the slow and deadly poison which had filtrated into her from years of contact with that type of mind. Now she was immune to it, even to having them beside her, even exchanging with them the arid and conventional words which formed the acknowledged code of their kind.

She entered the drawing room. Immediately there was a buzz around her and three young men approached her with demonstrative enthusiasm. The youngest of them, who stammered, held his cocktail glass high in greeting. Soon all those obliging male hands were offering her other glasses and Marta took one without looking to see from whom it came. Her lips were dry with thirst. The mixed odor of lemon and gin was as revivifying as smelling salts, and she breathed it in before drinking. Glass in hand, she went on greeting people, giving each a smile, a word, glancing now and then at a rose, at the freesias, the native jasmine.

That quick and sidelong glance did not fail to take in, meanwhile, a general picture of the elegant creatures who crowded the room. Isolated at one end of it was a little group of visitors linked to each other by the noble affinity of birth, bearers of illustrious names: the Pieláride, the Muniagurri, the Ugué; at the other end were the diplomats, from the ambassador himself to the discreet secretary of the chancellery; in between—listening to Mr. Rague, who was at that moment involved in an enthusiastic but rather vague description of a vase which he claimed had been saved from the ruins during the notorious massacre on St. Bartholomew's Eve—were the opulent bourgeoisie. The worst of them were dressed by the best tailors, plump painted ladies who were expiatory victims of Patou and Cocó Chanel, and men who seemed too large for their brief frock coats, none of them, however, despised by Eugenia Rague.

"Marta! My treasure!" Mr. Rague, with the air of a victim, appealed to his daughter for assistance in these ceremonial duties.

"Isn't everybody here?" people were murmuring. It was time to go in to dinner. "We'll wait a while longer," Mr. Rague muttered. His worried eyes wandered from the door to the place where his wife was standing. If Ráices shouldn't come, he thought, but his lips were saying something entirely different: ". . . of course, politics require one to look at things from a radical point of view, radical in the sense that it goes to the heart of the matter, leaving no doubt. The moment a man hesitates he has stopped being a politician. . . ." His face, greenish by now, was nevertheless perfectly composed; nobody could have denied that, at the moment, he was the very incarnation of prudence and good sense, even of sagacity. He felt a slight moisture on his forehead, his upper lip, and wiped it off with the white linen handkerchief.

"In conclusion . . ." One of the blue-blood contingent was holding forth, with measured sententiousness, to an audience composed of three young girls and two serious-looking men. Behind his head, a quite accidental background, hung a tapestry depicting the *Descent from the Cross.* "The only action worthy of these times is extermination. Sweep out, purify . . ." He paused, took a swallow of gin and tonic. "The world belongs to the elite. To become better it should belong altogether to those races which have been purified by their history and their private tradition. We should apply—indeed, we are backward if we do not—the excellent solution of the Tarpeian Rock: whoever does not carry his letters patent in his blood must pay for his bad luck. Destiny is not made, one is born with it. Everyone not born to lead is born to be exterminated. *À bon entendeur . . .*"

Marta rolled her eyes and saw Drabble nearby, standing alone and drinking with concentration. She remembered the night, three months ago, when a poor unfortunate woman had tried to kill herself outside the nightclub. They had struggled with her heroically, she and Drabble, and had finally brought her to her senses. Seen in the light of that fugitive episode, Drabble seemed to her a man of honest mind, sane and mature. She would have liked to join him now, but, before she had finished collecting her thoughts, she was again surrounded by garrulous idiots, laughing with them over some stupid anecdote.

Black shining heads and blond ones, perfumed and waved. Springy waists, gracious lips, teeth dazzling white under the lights. Men who argued, women who laughed, girls of a disturbing restless charm. Old protruding bellies adorned with linked chains and the two inevitable pearl studs. Insidious faces, faces of frigid women, glances that went hunting through the room with a kind of desperate reserve. The waxed black floor had almost disappeared, lost in the continuous movement of black trousers and trailing silken skirts.

Here a general was haranguing three ministers of state who listened to him in silent disapproval; every time his upraised hand emphasized a point, their intolerant expressions grew more marked. A little farther on, a learned lawyer expounded his views on the new school of painting: ". . . there's already something morbid here, an obvious degeneration of taste, a quite abominable penchant for the deformed. Of what use now is the study of anatomy to which classic painters attached so much importance? Years of study, of empirical observation, all wasted. A cartography of the diseased mind would be far more to the point these days."

"Yes . . . Yes . . . Yes . . ." These vague murmurs of assent came from a group of merchants and industrialists, circling, like planets around the sun, a ponderous politician who was advocating protection for what he claimed were forgotten native industries. "Gentlemen, this would mean renewal on all fronts of our national power." Not far away, a widow, only recently out of mourning, squandered with a sort of weary prodigality her fresh stock of smiles. Among the oblivious recipients of this largesse was an elegant and amiable official who was using a small statuette which he had picked up from the table as the subject for an erudite discourse. "Already in the thirteenth and fourteenth centuries," he said, "there was this exultation of the purely spiritual aspects of the human figure. I've seen the faces of page boys, engraved crudely by some obscure artist of the time, which could be mistaken for those rapt and innocent ones by Fra Angelico in the small inner rooms of the Vatican galleries." Phrases, bits of phrases, isolated words. Marta kept hearing them as she moved through the room, her ears tuned unwillingly to that absurd siren song. It brought to mind so many familiar things—books, art, endless talk—and it aroused the familiar feelings of boredom, of uselessness and pain. All her life now seemed to her a dull and trivial sacrifice to what was essentially a stereotype, one, moreover, which had no chance of survival. The thought of it pounded in her brain like a discordant and increasingly strident march, chords swelling and breaking and incessantly beginning again. A great march of doom, grimly sonorous and at the same time cloyingly, ineffably sweet. Childhood and youth, perhaps even old age; the sticky sweetness held her fast, she was caught in it as a fly is caught in flypaper. With anguished effort it may lift a foot, but the attempt to free itself is useless, body and wings remain glued to the paper, and finally the foot drops back again, the fly is finally conquered by the thick sweet force of the molasses.

She saw her father run and throw his arms joyously around Ráices. Good! they could go in to dinner at last; it would mean a little less contact with all these people. She remembered how, when she was a little girl, her mother had made her sit, dumb and solemn, at the dining table and how she had thought longingly of the children playing outside in the street, the flowers, the fish in the pond, the rustle of leaves in the afternoon wind. The whole world outside was alive and free. There were the passions: fear, pleasure, true pain; the cities and people; fire, water, earth, and air; there was experience in all its fullness.

Now, with the glass in her hand, brooding and silent among the lights and rich draperies, the garrulous, laughing throng of people, she thought again of that other world "outside," of the universe which was not molasses, not just pretentious decay. The stupidity of her days, past, present, and future, seemed to her appalling; it aroused in the unfree intimate center of her being a curious obsessive rage.

This day, for instance, this day which was already beginning to end, how dull and quite horrible it had been. She had opened her eyes to magnificent sun, invading the high-ceilinged room in a shaft of light that was like a mighty sword, brandished from on high. Coffee and fresh cream were waiting for her on the little portable table which had been drawn up beside the bed. (Yes, of course, she said absently to the young man arguing with Rebecca Lagos, of course she agreed.) The air was crystalline, a pure blue;

it filled her with unmotivated joy. She sucked it in, stretched, got
up, and took her bath. At ten she was crossing the little garden in
front of the house, stepping over wet green turf and asphalt sleek
from the recent sprinkling. The streets at this hour were fresh
and shady and she walked along them happily. At the library she
stopped to look at the new books—gay, with red letters on their
white jackets—to touch them, skim the pages, feel a little shock
of pleasure at the implications discreetly revealed by some title. A
few casual words with the librarian and she was on the street
again, walking to the shops, to Smart's, to Harrod's, making her
indifferent, almost mechanical purchases.

After that, the soft shade of the plaza and the fountains—two
senile stone figures symbolizing Doubt, under the trees with their
fragile leaves. Finally, back to the house and luncheon with her
mother and father and Brenda. They peeled their fruit languidly,
they were impatient for the ices. Her mother talked and talked in
her dry persistent way, about a scandal, about the social activities
they must endure throughout the summer, about this and that,
until at last they were ready and could go up to their rooms to lie
down for a while, alone, with open windows and blinds drawn
against the glare. The telephone rang two or three times, there
were inquiries, invitations: "Thanks, I'll go; no, it isn't necessary;
all right, that will do," no enthusiasm manifest in either request
or response.

The afternoon was a new cycle, less easy to review. At four,
there was a consultation with the dressmaker, a thousand details
to be decided, fabrics to be examined: the cool texture of linen,
sheer voile, luxurious prints. Then, at half-past five, tea at the
confectioner's with Monsieur and Madame Barque, the French
couple who had brought such excellent introductions. He was a
wine merchant from Bordeaux, a stubbornly silent man, but his
wife made up for that; she worked hard for them both, voluble,
enthusiastic, asking questions, agreeing with everything, punc-
tuating the sentences with shrill little cries of surprise.

There had been time, before dark, for a visit to her old friend,
Jorge Voldraz, in his architect's studio on the top floor of the
skyscraper in the Plaza Britannica, that studio with its four great
windows opening on the river and on space. Time to drink a

highball, she had thought, to chat with the people who were accustomed to drop in at about that hour, foreigners often, tourists—among them, inevitably, some Yankees doing the round of the museums and urgently asking for information about what was most typical and "native" in the city.

What was lacking in Voldraz? Perhaps only a millimeter, a final hairbreadth of intelligence, no more than "that." But sometimes "that" is so much! It seems like nothing because beauty, for instance, is simply beauty, requiring no other attribute. Yet, it is intelligence which gives value to beauty, leading us along unexpected and harmonious ways to an understanding of that final excellence, a clear perception of its terms. Without intelligence, humanity would be an uncharted island, desolate and choked with weeds.

Voldraz had once made gallant claims upon her—those superb orchids appearing every third day!—but latterly he had given up hope, retreating silently into himself, making no protest, showing no resentment. He was a rare sort of bird, he seemed not to have any amatory pride at all, for he continued to accord her his dignified devotion. The flattery implicit in this attitude of his gave a pleasant warmth to the long winter conversations in the top-floor studio, in that isolated world of calculus and carpenter's squares, of slide rules and designs in perspective, so high above the level of the city.

Nothing seemed to trouble Voldraz; fair weather or foul was all the same to him; all he asked was to be able to work without interruption and follow the precise routine of his daily life, from the newspaper which he read upon awakening, at the same hour each morning, to the three pages, exactly, of some treatise which he allowed himself at night. It was curious that, in his home, one so often met unregulated persons, both men and women, persons whose dress and general appearance were unlike others'—a man with haunted eyes and long fair curling hair, a woman who disdained familiar ties and customary patterns of behavior.

But, on this particular afternoon, Voldraz had been alone, working. They sipped sherry and talked, sitting by the windows, watching night stalk in giant strides across the sky. What is he like inside, she kept wondering; what *are* people like who have found solutions for all their problems, answers to all their questions? Of these satisfied ones, Voldraz seemed to her the most representative and typical. Always, when she was with him, she felt a singular uneasiness and desolation, an icy sense of being alone with someone who lacked the essential human ferment, someone who was a kind of mortal divinity. . . . Brooding about this, and with the day's accumulated strains behind her, she had become increasingly inhibited. A great silence had sprung up between them, a silence not broken until at last she had got up and taken her leave. Later, walking through the dusky streets toward her home, she still had that strangled sensation in her throat.

Marta lifted her glass and drained it to the last drop. A tall man in a frock coat with faded receding hair asked to be presented to her. He stood before her stiff as a Prussian, smiled suddenly, then as suddenly became serious again. Taking out his cigarette case, he offered it around, lit a cigarette himself, and, without saying anything, looked at her fixedly, as though waiting for her to speak.

At this moment, Mr. Rague lifted his right hand and gestured in the general direction of the dining room. With the other, he still clutched tightly the bent thin arm of Ráices. The guests who were sitting down rose with almost automatic precision and joined in the march toward the table. The next act, thought Marta, feeling on her own cold arm the arm of the man whose name was beside hers on the place cards.

The penetrating odor of lavender, of perfumes and naphtha, seemed to grow stronger as they moved. Filing into the dining room, the serried rows of frock coats and light dresses had somewhat the air of a wedding procession, with the erect skeleton-like figure of Mrs. Rague in the first place. Her small steely eyes ranged quickly over the table, inspected the servants who were standing at attention. She was as pleased and exalted by this party of hers as the admiral, her revered and beloved Nelson, must have been before Trafalgar.

. . . He, whose dark face had the fierce vitality but the still almost childish lineaments of extreme youth, felt small and a little uneasy—not fearful, just oddly hemmed in and surprised—before

*these armed men who seemed to form a sort of patrol. Their
leader, at any rate the one who stood in the front rank with a certain emphatic authority about him—that strange man with his
cruel mouth and confused eyes, as though it were the mouth
which gave orders in that face and the eyes which obeyed—had
said to him: "We've come for you."*

*"But—what do you want of me?" he asked, showing no alarm,
only a profound perplexity. "What can you possibly want of
me? . . ."*

He practically burst into the house. Tossing his hat down in
the cloakroom, he rushed through the first gap of doors, questioned the servants, walked only a little less hurriedly through the
drawing room, and then, with a sensation of relief, shoved in
among the guests who were beginning to take their seats at the
table. He had no time to greet Mr. Rague, he was himself already
in the dining room, swept on by that confused tide of men and
women. He paused for a moment, nodding to this side and that in
courteous salutation. He had damp shining hair, irregularly
parted, and an extraordinarily mobile face. The veins of his forehead were rather swollen. ("Ah, we'll have to use the electric
needle on those," Dr. Islas had told him, and he had answered:
"Another kind of life would do the trick even better. Less worry,
less probing of the soul, not so many confusing questions and
answers.") He glanced quickly up and down the length of the
enormous table, hunting for his place; at last he found it and
breathed deeply, "Aah," noting with pleasure that his neighbors
were not yet in theirs.

Other people were sitting down, pulling out their chairs with
the monotonous sound of wood scraping against wood. It seemed
to him that the eyes of all these strangers were concentrated upon
his forehead, focusing on the very spot where he could feel the
pounding of his accelerated heartbeats. (How could that doctor
cure him who had no weapons except a little science and a curious Spinozistic twist to his mind? His science wouldn't work, nor
his way of saying, "Pleasure is obviously never bad, but good;
grief, on the other hand, is obviously bad.")

He was always late everywhere. Certain profound proclivities were simply not subject to modification. Nevertheless, in this case—the splendid-looking woman at his left; not so splendid the one at the right, stout and too ripe, she looked like the wife of a mayor—nevertheless, in this case, he should really have made a greater effort to be on time. With a smile curving her moist and charming lips, the young lady on the left offered him her hand. There were two rows of magnificent pearls around her powdered white throat. Julia Carves, read the place card. Yes, his effort should have been greater since the unexpected invitation from Mrs. Rague assumed, on her part, an attitude of good will toward him and his work.

Maybe it was just a capricious gesture; more probably, she had been impressed by what the English ambassador had said to him a week ago, in reference to that painting of his in the Exposition: "Such delicacy of design; your way of painting the crossed hands can be compared only to Giotto's. And that magnificent force of expression is very like van der Weyden." Mrs. Rague, to judge from her surprised and enchanted air, must have taken these comparisons literally. She had come up to him at once and looked at him with a certain almost insolent greed. "Do you admit a genuine kinship with the men of the Renaissance? What is your idea of the relation between painting and life? Should one be subordinate to the other—or is art completely independent?" She had kept on looking at him voraciously, like a district attorney who expects the poor fish at the bar to condemn himself out of his own mouth. He had laughed, good-naturedly, and replied with skillful and evasive urbanity: "Madame, all I see is the form and color of things, the form and color of creation. I won't deny, however, that the way I see forms and colors may sometimes be affected by my private contradictions and exaltations." It was, while tending to be didactic, a rather neat answer and it brought a friendly smile to Mrs. Rague's fleshless cheeks—a rare concession, indeed. The smile seemed to be compounded half and half of pride in her own question and approval of him. Such was the happy circumstance responsible for the invitation to this dinner at which he had arrived, as usual, late and out of breath.

The stout and mayoral lady favored him with an amiable smile. Miss Carves, at his left, was talking to her other neighbor. Quite serene now, he lifted the cup of consommé and studied the entire aspect of the table. This spectacle, in which he was not only an actor but of which he was at the moment the only, though still somewhat absent-minded witness, this show of sumptuous bosoms, of smiling eyes and laughing exclamations, of heads inclining now toward this side, now toward that, seemed to him full of reticence and mysterious ingenuity.

His wandering eyes were suddenly arrested, meeting in perfect coincidence with another pair of eyes, still and gray, cool in their transparency, singularly alone. They belonged to a woman sitting obliquely across the table from him, a woman with delicate high shoulders and a lovely coppery throat, superbly elegant, but with a touch of youthful solemnity about her, grave and silent as a child between the garrulous men who besieged her on either side. Not just for a second, but for perceptible moments they looked, they looked at each other, and it was his glance which was withdrawn first. The withdrawal was the result of an injunction from within; his lively pride did not permit him to deviate from his own reflective simplicity by seeming to ape the arrogant and falsely aristocratic manner affected by certain of the bourgeoisie. If he was here at all, it was out of politeness and perhaps because of the demands of an art which had to be passed around to achieve its purpose and sold like other merchandise.

This necessity had always infuriated him and he refused even to recognize it except in his darkest moments when everything seemed finished, anyway, and he was resigned to see himself as merely a single cell, without excessive importance in the collective organism.

He turned away his eyes and lifted the cup of consommé to his lips. It was glutinous, pleasantly chilled. He drank, taking no part in the conversation going on around him, no longer amused but inwardly bound—and aware of it—because of the influence, the near presence of that marvelous woman sitting almost across the table from him. She was laughing now, no longer abstracted in spirit but gay, the whole upper part of her body turned toward the animated fashion plate at her left. He had a lean dark sensual face; throwing back his head in convulsive rapture, he would shout, "Splendid! Quite splendid!" at some point she brought up, and then return to the monotonous tone of his ordinary speech.

Farther away, almost at the other end of the table, where the virtuosos seemed to have congregated, the art critic, Grovenoles, was analyzing the corporeal makeup of a camellia for the benefit of his neighbors, an old lady and a pretty young girl. He held the flower between his fingers, lightly, as though to emphasize its extreme fragility, and listened to himself with evident delight.

Lintas lifted his eyes from the consommé and suddenly fixed them again on the woman opposite. He saw the butler, abnormally pale, standing behind her chair and leaning over to whisper into her ear; he saw uneasiness mount in the coppery features, the eyes widening, the mouth half open; he saw, then, how the butler, in the very act of handing her a piece of paper, caught an urgent signal from Mrs. Rague and hurried to the head of the table. Though there were more than twenty guests between them, Lintas heard plainly the hoarse voice of his hostess. "Where is Miss Brenda?" she was asking. "Why hasn't Miss Brenda come?" Lintas looked around. Not a single chair was empty, and possible absence had been efficiently concealed by the servants. And yet there must be something wrong. He perceived with great clarity the intense uneasiness of the two women, the quick exchange of glances between them. The moment passed. Mrs. Rague's face remained drawn, she looked overcome by fatigue. The young woman, however, began to smile as before, a merry dazzling smile which brushed away any semblance of care.

Aware of some odd significance in the apparently insignificant episode, Lintas turned to his left-hand neighbor and asked her a question in a tone which he tried to make entirely casual. She replied with a name: "Marta. Marta Rague." Brenda? That was the younger sister. . . . He lifted his eyes again, this time without deliberate intention, merely as a natural reaction to the movement of the waiter who was setting a fresh plate before him. The young woman's guard was down; she seemed unconscious of her surroundings, staring ahead into space. For a moment, and it was like a kind of possession, he felt, full on his forehead, the impact of that gaze.

The orchestra had loosed a veritable torrent of sound, great

surging melodic waves which beat with insane clamor upon the
brain or died away in murmuring cadences, only to rise and crash
again. Worried and preoccupied as she was, Marta gave only the
smallest part of her attention to the music. Her mind repelled
that incessant assault; it was fixed in stony anxiety upon a single
image, the image of her sister, Brenda. Brenda, who needed her so
much! Brenda, who was waiting—while she herself wasted time
here—in that other place, at that street and number which had
been noted on the folded little piece of paper next to her glass.
But the agonizing interval must be endured; she could not leave
until her going would be unnoticed.

This problem of Brenda! These increasing and, it seemed to
her, ever more terrible surprises. It was to her, always, that
Brenda came, confidently, as to one who could not fail to rush
headlong to her aid. Once, in Lausanne, when they were children, Marta had jumped from a high rock, risked death to save
her from drowning. Brenda knew—though nobody had ever told
her so—that her first terrified scream would bring Marta plunging from any rock, at any time. Marta knew—though nobody
had ever told her so—that some day that old anguished nightmare
might come true: Brenda brought to her rigid and bloodless, the
fair hair streaming over her face.

The sisters never discussed these things, nor others, either; between them was a mutual silence, an invincible reserve. But the
prescience which they shared, which they communicated to each
other by means of small disregarded movements, special tones of
the voice, gave to that reserve an element of drama, something
mysterious, quite indefinable, and at the same time tormentingly
real, a burden which they carried in silence together. One day it
would happen, one day the vortex would seize the younger one
and she would be brought home with her fair hair streaming,
bloodless. Marta was never quite free from this premonition and
the impotent dread it aroused. It would make her turn to her
sister sometimes with a sudden wild tenderness, the emotion a
mother has when she wakes, weeping, from the tragic world of
nightmare, wakes into the real world and becomes aware that her
children are safe.

It was strange how this ominous silence had united them, this silence which had never been broken by a single relevant word. Their bond was fundamental; it lay beyond words, beyond the trivial judgments of daily life or its easy confessions. They were more strongly united by what they did not know of each other than by anything they might possibly have known. United by harrowing subterranean fears as heavy and thick as blood. There were certain nights—nights terrible, without egress—when one of them would ask herself: "Is it now? Is she going to plunge in after me now?" And the other, out of her secret foreboding: "Is it now? Are they going to bring her to me, is this the appointed time?" The next morning they would meet, full of health, greet each other casually—and yet, with a particular inflection, such an accumulated store of love and gratitude!

Marta thought of a train journey they had once taken together. Brenda had been sick with some obscure but harassing ailment and they were going to consult an eminent doctor somewhere. She remembered how Brenda had stared placidly out of the window, not in the least concerned, while she herself had suffered tortures of apprehension. . . . It had always been like that. One of them whirling in the vortex, the other watching with anguished heart. One abandoned to the pleasures of life, the other turned toward its potential pain, toward the specter waiting in the wings and ready at any moment to enter the farce. And now there was that bit of paper, twice folded, lying beside her glass, that paper which was like so many other papers bearing similar tidings, similar appeals for help. This time Marta had an idea of the nature of the business; she had been suspecting it for some months, observing Brenda's behavior, her excitement, her evasions.

How could she rid herself of these black thoughts? Or, rather, how thrust them into the background of her mind until the opportunity to slip away arrived? She made an effort to listen to the conversation around her. ". . . Oscar kept insisting that golf wasn't virile, but I told him that was nonsense. It's certainly much more virile than tennis." No escape there; what was her other neighbor saying? "No, no . . . ! Please don't speak to me about those indigestible films. What is the screen, what is the theater, essentially? Sheer spectacle, that's all. . . . Well, that's what I want, a good show, not a metaphysical disquisition. All those shots of men looking at clouds—perfectly ridiculous! As though there were anything spectacular about a cloud!

Marta turned away wearily. The man's words were like the heat which she could feel radiating from his body on that hot summer night, a vaporous exhalation, nothing more. Seeking a focus for her attention, she felt herself drawn again toward that other man across the table, the one whose eyes had so curiously held hers. Who was he? To what manner of being did that countenance belong, that face with its serene wisdom, its unforced air of superiority? It was a superiority almost unconscious of itself, profoundly natural, having no rigidity, no bias, no tendency to prejudge or oppose or quarrel with things. Who was he? The tie was—well, a little carelessly made; the coat badly pressed at the place where the tight sleeves fitted into the back. The hair grew beautifully, sweeping back from the broad and tranquil forehead. Oh, these questions! Questions which she could not help asking herself, everlasting hope that this time, this one time, it would not turn out a sham, that she would not suddenly be faced with the sour, the contradictory reality.

Had she ever seen those features before? Which of the three unfamiliar names mentioned by her mother in listing the guests belonged to him? She had heard them in passing, without the slightest curiosity or interest, and she was quite unable to remember them now. Yet it gave her a sharp, a thoroughly unexpected and unjustified pleasure merely to look at the clean resolute lines of that face, that unknown face obliquely opposite hers. She tried almost mechanically, so quick her instinct, to grasp what might lie beneath the serene exterior—a basic tendency toward what? He might be almost anything, a leather merchant, an obscure financier, maybe just somebody's rich husband, any imaginable thing. . . . Was it possible that the chestnut hair, so light at the roots, had been burned there, that the single large wave sweeping back from the forehead was artificially set? Oh, well. . . . But what was wrong with the fish? It seemed underdone; and why did the wine taste so harsh?

The Gershwin *Rhapsody* stopped suddenly, leaving the air still charged with a thousand metallic vibrations. The conversation,

which had been held back for a while by that symphonic flood-
gate, poured out again in overflowing measure, a melopoeia of
laughs and exclamations. Marta absorbed all at once into herself
the last clangorous vibration of the music, the gesture of the man
she had been watching, at this moment raising his napkin to his
lips, the expanse of heads and bare shoulders, and the fixed image
of Brenda.

After replying for the third time to his left-hand neighbor,
whose half-open lips besieged him with questions, Lintas bent
over his plate, which still held some fragments of fish—black ray
with a delicious caper sauce. He hoped to be allowed to eat
quietly for a few minutes. But he had hardly managed to get a
morsel into his mouth when he was asked whether or not he
believed in the survival of the novel and its triumph over the
theater. Having nodded affirmatively, he was immediately subjected to an enthusiastic barrage of arguments to the contrary.
His neighbor's lovely eyes sparkled, she was eager to persuade.
"Just think," she said. "We have no Balzac today. Not even a
Dickens."

Resignedly, and without conviction, he ventured a hypothesis:
perhaps the genius of the age was not conducive to formal perfection; perhaps it tended rather to some work of complex, of
quite gigantic imperfection, conforming to no classic norms, but
vitally expressive of its own terrible abnormality. . . . The young
lady was not convinced. In her elegant and distinguished way, she
seemed genuinely regretful over the current lack of a Balzac, a
George Meredith. "Have you read Meredith?" he asked. "Oh,
no!" she said. "But he *is* great." At that, he returned pointedly to
his fish, dissecting it slowly, with a surgeon's precision, separating
the flesh from the large bones which looked like the strings of a
harp.

But what difference did it make whether the lady had or had
not read anything at all? What difference could it possibly make?
His own question amused him enormously. She could have said
"Yes"; it would not have mattered. What is reading, anyway?
A drug, usually, at best a delightful stupefier. He knew so many
people who had read so much and every day they became more
stupefied, more irremediably blunted, more sleepy and docile

from the effects of their interminable reading. . . . Reading, indeed! He would have to ask the young woman another question,
one with more sense to it, at least a pittance of sense.

For instance, he might try this: Have you ever felt near you, in
your room, say, a sudden presence, George Meredith himself in a
grim or merry mood? All that faulty, persistent, humanly frus-
trate, tortuous accumulation of words, all that meditation, all that
exhausting labor of an artist, year upon year of difficult creation
till the man was ground down by it, ruined. . . . Tell me, have all
these things by some chance become incorporate for you? Have
they taken the form of a shy human being with inadequate yet
sometimes persuasive ways, hesitating yet sometimes positive
affirmations, daring yet sometimes correct hypotheses, and—yes,
with this, too—an endless chain of dreams? That vast aggregate
of letters, has it ever sounded to you like a living voice? I'm not
asking you if you've read, I'm asking you if you've *heard, seen*
Mr. George Meredith, Mr. Balzac, Mr. Dickens, Mr. Shakespeare.
. . .

Do you believe they were great and triumphant spirits? Ah,
they were men as irresolute as you yourself in your darkest
hours, as insecure, tormented, disillusioned and despairing, more
doubtful than you that the morning would ever come. What
good is it to read them, to accept them only in their triumph and
not in their perpetual anguish, their inefficiency? What good is
it to grant them your passive acquiescence? They want more
much more; they want you to answer them, they crave a human
response. All art is a great, a terrible demand for response. Give
them what you can—your irritation, your rebellion, your love;
but, in any case, give them yourself, your living, reacting self!

This idea, which it would have been stupid to reveal to the
woman—such magnificent arms she had!—now eating silently beside him, this idea did not amuse him at all. He was so dependent
upon his friendship with certain books, so dependent upon
the invisible presences which filled his room. Here, in this
other world, he felt a discomfort almost physical, ignorant of his
role in it, breathless, like a man going from a boiler room into the
frosty air. He was inhibited and he resented it, with a harsh and
bitter resentment which was directed against himself as much as

anybody else. One should become a hard-shelled animal in time!
And, after all, the moral world was as diminished, as lacking in
compensation and avenues of escape as the physical. (We get
used to seeing a cobweb and, when it isn't there any more, we
demand it, we need it.) As sad and stupid a universe as one could
well imagine!

It had cost him a real effort that afternoon to gather himself
together and get dressed. Every day he became more attached to
his room, more reluctant to leave it, more disposed to retire into
it completely. He had been reading Walter Pater earlier, *speaking*
with him, but not for long because he had not wanted to exhaust
too soon the intricate conversation between the author and himself on the subject of Pico della Mirandola. For years he had
heartily disliked the Pre-Raphaelites; they had seemed to him so
pleased about their pleasures, their delight in forms and essences
and balms and rhetoric, so unbearably sublimated. Then, a few
months ago he had become reconciled with some of them—like
Pater, like Ruskin—because of the rare dignity they displayed in
comparison with a world spoiled by an excess of the opposite
tendency, a world in which all sensibility was frozen. That
world, *that*, with its lumpish stupidity, its baseness, its compla-
cent acceptance of its own ignorant and conventional aridity,
made the romantics whom he had once despised appear like rare
creatures, indeed, invested with a quality which now seemed almost superhuman.

Mankind, you dismay me.

Mankind! Spewed forth, flowing in slow masses, like lava,
down the more populated slopes; so corrupted, so cautious and
mindless in its defensive animality, so stripped of natural good!
Naked, obscenely belligerent on its common bed, arguing, fighting, hands curved like claws over the little wealth it has, determined to retain it along with its disgusting system of hate and
hunger and hysterical tyranny!

Phui! It was better to look across at that woman with the
coppery face and the proud and lonely eyes. Or simply to eat this
very fine slice of meat seasoned in Madeira. While the night held,
to close one's doors against humanity, work for its improvement,
slowly, from inside, without illusion or greed or injury to anyone

and, also, without much hope. . . . Hope will come for those who
do not hope any more. Hope will come after time, long time has
passed for those who no longer hope.

Lintas raised his wineglass and drank with pleasure. His eyes
searched for those others, obliquely across the table, but they
would not be caught; their abstracted and wandering gaze was
turned now to this side, now to that, even straight ahead at the
ambassador, Portinori, Marco Portinori. The moist red lips were
half open, the teeth dazzling white against the dark face. . . .

His doors were closed, he kept closing them himself, each time
more determined to let nobody in. Cloistered, that's what he
was—in mind and spirit, at least. Not so much in body—he still
liked that sauce and that meat so much, he still reacted strongly
to the soft scent, the cedar, which came to him from his left-hand
neighbor's head. That head, with its hair combed upward in
spirals, had been turned for some time toward the gentleman
farther on, giving him its pleasing and very feminine attention.
. . . He was firmly resolved, nevertheless, to take things calmly,
like this, without drama, letting life come to him naturally and
avoiding involvement with others. And yet there was that secret
resentment, that charge which he preferred against himself for
being in this place at this moment. . . . Did one then, finally, have
to take such people into consideration?

The stout lady who looked like the wife of a mayor glanced at
him inquiringly over her swelling bosom which was barely contained within the tight décolleté. Having caught his attention, she
gave him a singularly beatific smile. "Do you know anything
about that new treatment for cancer?" she asked. "The one all
the papers are talking about, I mean." And then, as he stared at
her blankly: "I'm terribly afraid I'll get it, you know. They say
heredity is so important, and both my grandparents . . ." She
lowered her eyelids piously, she saluted the earth with sorrowful
comprehension. "Yes, both of them. . . . From the same disease.
Would you believe it? Both of them!" She looked again toward
the floor whose brilliant parquet showed not even the least symbolic trace of earth.

The lady had no reason to be alarmed, he said. Though he
knew nothing about the treatment, she had no reason to be

alarmed. . . . It would be many years, he thought, with amusement, before death touched that padded shoulder, that ripe and
powder-blanched bosom. Destiny, he felt sure, was not yet ready
to abolish the mysterious difference between the healthy flesh of
the lady at his right and the bit of cooked meat which she was
even now putting into her mouth.

The hot high-pitched moan of the violins rose again above the
clamoring brass. Waiters moved about swiftly and silently, taking
away plates, substituting fresh ones. In this interval between
courses, the diners turned to each other with renewed gaiety,
lifting the glasses of strong white wine to their lips in an almost
isochronous gesture. Talk grew louder, more incessant; waves of
laughter swept the table and broke with a sound like splintering
crystal. There was an air of superlative distinction about the
spectacle which played itself out under the pale frosty light of
the immense chandelier, the revelation of a genius which bubbled
as freely and carelessly and uselessly as a geyser.

In the midst of this luxury, this brilliant and aristocratic play, it
was idle to think about the tragic suddenness with which life
might intrude upon the comedy, paralyzing it with an admoni-
tion, a single fateful reminder, a *Mene, mene, tekel, upharsin*
boldly written on the wall. It was idle to think about it just as it
would have been idle to speculate about what was going on in the
inmost depths of Mr. Rague and Mr. Ráices, sitting near each
other at the head of the table, chatting and smiling with the
utmost cordiality, so of one mind, seemingly so happy, their heads
almost meeting across the intervening guest. Everything was idle
at this moment of music and laughter and liberation except to
become part of it, to share its gaiety and freedom from constraint.

The ambassadors studied their polished nails and conversed politely with the matrons in black silk; the young girls wondered
whether there might not be a coincidence of tastes and aspiration
between themselves and one of those lofty-browed young men;
an old English author yawned openly. Among the younger
women there was an effort to appear somewhat more advanced
and independent than was customary. They tossed their heads
ostentatiously or threw them back, shrieking with laughter, their

throats distended like a pouter pigeon's. The bachelors, on the other hand, maintained a discreet and solemn air, an almost cat-like composure, looking around without seeming to look, superbly indifferent.

"How animated everybody is, how charming!" said Senator Birlas, slipping a red carnation into his lapel. Another guest, sitting opposite, pointed his beard derisively at the woman beside him. She, for her part, gave the senator a distrustful glance and sipped with feverish avidity the claret which had just been served. Her cheeks, like those of several other women, were already deeply flushed.

Several times during the dinner, the ambassador, Portinori, had made desperate and futile efforts to get a hearing; finally, one of his neighbors silenced the entire table with a loud and categorical *pst*! All eyes were immediately turned toward the ambassador, scrutinizing with a not very cordial curiosity the adipose curves, the pendent chins, the nose almost lost in the rosy moon face, the small quick suspicious eyes, eyes which had kept many secrets and embraced many foibles. The ambassador abandoned the peach Melba on his plate and stood up while Mrs. Rague waited expectantly, without any attempt to hide her satisfaction.

He wanted only, the ambassador said, to express his thanks to the Ragues for their hospitality and to congratulate them for having reached their lofty position in life without any concession to the vulgarity with which the times literally crawled. . . . There was something abbatial about that broad clean-shaven face and the slow mellow sententious voice; over their ices and wine, the company listened in a sort of sleepy enchantment. "Cardinal Jiménez," he was saying, "wore sackcloth under his holy purple in order to belie the worldly glory in which he moved. Just so do we all, no matter how luxurious our visible garments, hide beneath them others riddled with holes, the painful reminder of many mistreatments, a moral coat of mail. But, when we enter this house, we know we are among friends and we leave our armor behind with joy."

His hand, raised in a peaceful idyllic gesture, remained poised in the air as though to prolong the music of his words. The company, however, had soon lost interest, most of them return-

ing indifferently to their own conversations. Among them, only
Mrs. Rague would have liked to preserve the diplomat's phrases
intact, to have them recorded, kept, and remembered by all. But
she knew very well that, where there are a dozen people, there
may be a dozen rebels, and she had no illusions about her guests.
Contemplating them with glacial politeness, she removed her
emaciated and deathly white arms from the table and gave the
signal to rise.

Before leaving the room, she went up to Marta, gripped her
violently by the arm. "Where's Brenda?" she whispered. "This is
another of her unconventionalities, I suppose. It's up to you to
put a stop to them." She joined a group of guests who were
drifting into the garden. The rigid smile was back on her lips.

Replete, their faces glowing, the guests scattered about the
garden and the drawing room. Time to dance! The orchestra was
ready, the violins nostalgically prepared to reconquer lost ground
as a Strauss waltz took the place of the syncopated symphonies.
Standing near the open door which led to the garden, the conductor lifted his baton and smiled, a smile enthusiastic, almost
triumphant, as though he were leading, not this small phalanx of
musicians with whose debts, miseries, and squabbles he was so
wearisomely familiar, but a brilliant and tightly packed ensemble,
the aristocracy of music, figures genuinely potent beneath their
apparent obsequiousness.

The garden was enormous and lit only along the borders of the
lawns by small delicately swaying lanterns. But, on the open platform where five or six couples were already dancing, a powerful
spotlight threw its spectral rays. . . . Lintas remained in the drawing room, sipping his coffee. His table companions had been
snatched away by their jealous husbands and he stood by himself,
solitary in all that luxurious stir, next to a tall column holding a
Greek statuette. He knew that Marta was dancing outside in the
garden, but he preferred to wait for her here, patiently, like a
contemplative stranger who hardly expects, amid so much gaiety,
a response to his own essential loneliness. What difference did it
make? His case, as far as it concerned the rest of the world, was
already lost. He asked for no concession from the benevolence of
others; he would have been content, indeed, if they had forgotten

him entirely. Was it not the way to reach that enjoyment known only by those who have nothing—or everything? He always remembered those lines of Thomas Hardy in which the author remarks that one may have the air of a monarch, though one has neither possessions nor hearts over which to rule, though one has apparently lost both the one and the other. Hardy was right. To have lost both the one and the other. To have been left behind by both the one and the other. Or, rather, to have taken another road, slower, less secure, less open, a secretly more ambitious road. . . .

People were clapping, enthusiastically. They wanted, and received, a repetition of the waltz. The conductor's delight was boundless; it seemed about to burst open his red and swollen face. He lifted his arms and, before beginning the music again, paused a moment as though he were making a promise, as though he wanted this promise to be felt: "You shall be as gods." It was true; the offer of the serpent had—so cheaply!—become reality. Now, after the good food and the wine, light-hearted and a little dizzy, turning and turning in the dance, they all felt like small triumphant gods. Like gods!

Lintas turned around quickly—but no, it was just the waiter with the tray. He put his cup down on the shining silver surface, thinking how, every day, one's last despairing hope in mankind was taken away, empty, like that little cup. Yes, and the next day there would be other men and other hopes. Human credulity was endless, it was never really crushed, never quite beaten down. Hope gone inevitably returned, a constant tide in an inconstant ocean. "Excuse me," muttered a timid little man, pushing past him to get to the waiter with the *fines*, ancient cognac in huge belled glasses. . . . Let him pass, one had to let everybody pass, no matter how trifling the reason for their haste!

And now, at last, there was Marta, coming in from the garden with her table companion, the man with the yellowish dissipated face. They looked at each other again, a strange look, at once challenging and reticent. Then Marta tore away her eyes, walking erect and dignified toward the sofa. Lintas's glance followed her. She seemed overcome by the heat, which was far more stifling outside than here in the great hall. And yet, even here, it was close; there were too many people, drinking, talking, laughing, bodies curved back in laughter or swaying toward each other in an uncompleted caress.

Lintas did not hesitate, his instinct did not hesitate. Perhaps it was not quite the right moment; the orchestra had stopped playing and people were migrating indoors. Moreover, he had no idea of what to say or what to do. But he did not hesitate, he walked straight over to her; in a moment he was standing before those eyes and their quick, light, questioning scrutiny. He spoke out of some extreme of violence and bitterness in himself; he said harshly: "I'm Lintas"—just his name, nothing more. She kept on looking at him without a change in her expression, without any apparent reaction, coldly almost, completely disinterested, like one who counters a gesture too vehement with the indifferent serenity of centuries, a proud and sovereign calm. "Yes," she said, "yes, yes," hardly acknowledging to herself the faint resonance with which the artist's name rang in her memory, not interested now in the fierce persuasiveness of this man whom she had stared at with such uneasy curiosity during the dinner and who was now offering her his hand. "Yes," she said. "I know your name." She presented her companion, who rose and bowed ungraciously.

Neither of them, not he nor she, was willing to give in. They were both shy natures, fundamentally reserved. He had come to her, hating himself for what seemed an abdication from his preferred and haughty loneliness, indeed for seeking her out at all. As for her, she would have hated herself if she had not opposed this stranger's overt claim upon her with an attitude corresponding to it, a glacial lack of response. They were the sort of persons whose loneliness becomes deeper in crowds, who find it almost impossible to overcome their own distrust. Salt of the earth though they are, they live silent, suspicious, withdrawn. What civilization will finally release these hermetically sealed beings, allow these clear but secret lives to flow freely into the great human sea? None, perhaps. . . .

The orchestra saved the situation, rescued them from the embarrassing silence into which they had plunged. The instruments crashed out in their tremendous delirium at the very moment when to speak at all began to seem to Lintas both foolish and inopportune. He asked her to dance and she rose. The gray eyes were only inches away; holding her close to him, he felt the softness of her dark skin, the firm delicacy of her breasts. And, as they danced, he realized with a sense of strangeness that that hard, healthy, sensitized, and vibrating flesh had no weight, that the whole shy and lovely body was utterly alive in his arms. He felt himself invaded by its fragrance, the touch of its skin, fenced in by a living wall; yes, the body which he was holding so closely held and embraced him.

They danced without speaking, seriously, listening to the deep monotonous murmur of the singer whose voice, carrying the melody, blended with the instruments.

Afterward, they went back to the same corner of the drawing room, to the sofa on which she had been sitting when he came up. The silence between them was comfortable now, an intimate silence charged with curiosity, with a grave and secret satisfaction. It was the feeling certain great exiles might have, meeting each other suddenly in a far country, walking the same road, still shy and silent but with full comprehension of their mutual reserve.

"I've seen one of your paintings at Steiner's," Marta said after a while. "I found it very somber but curiously attractive."

Lintas nodded. "I know the one you mean. It illustrates an old Russian poem, a terrible and desolate poem in which every human illusion seems finished with—forever."

"Did you paint it simply as an illustration? Or were you—well, linked to it in mood; did it express you, too?"

"In art one can't do anything without committing oneself wholly. Not, at least, in art which has any chance for survival . . ." He hesitated, then went on with some difficulty: "Yes, I was in rather a bad way at the time. Bucking my own illusions, running into all kinds of blind alleys. I'd just left the university, you see, and I was appalled by what seemed to me the falseness of life, its rigid conventionality. . . . Of course, I was too solemn, I was attaching far too much importance to myself." He met her eyes, smiled faintly. "I think I can say, quite honestly, that I'm not like that any more."

He gave an impression, Marta thought, of unforced sincerity. And yet there was something extinguished about him, a joyless passion which survived only in the haughty brilliance of his glance, the dark immobile flame of what must once have been an arrogant rage against life. . . . They were both too arrogant, they could not really speak fluently with each other. Their dialogue was full of pauses, of withholdings, of guarded words which did not in any way jeopardize or allow entry to the airtight caverns of their souls. Some obscure instinct warned Marta to double her resistance to this stranger, to show him only the harsh winds which swept around her private island, its stubborn and jagged coast.

She glanced away from him at the radiant throng around her. The dancers were moving to the slow rhythm of a waltz in loose fluctuating patterns, concentric ripples which overlapped each other only to drift apart again. Their glistening heads were close together; the sweet surrender of certain ladies was conveyed as it were in time with the music to the gluttonous observation of their partners. Tongues licked dry lips, a double chin quivered with emotion. . . . Among the young people things were somewhat different. To a greater or less degree, each of them seemed to feel in that transitory embrace a dream which might just possibly come true, ecstasy, drama. Life would decide and, meanwhile, one must assume an attitude suitable to that future dream, that ecstasy, that drama.

Marta sighed and turned her slow weighted gaze back to Lintas, who was at that moment taking a cigarette out of his case. And then, with a sudden sense of shock, a sort of wild impatience, she remembered Brenda's message. For a little instant of time she had been held, beyond thought of other things, by her curiosity about this man, by the interest so strangely mixed with misgivings which his character and the candid resolution of his features had inspired in her. It was as though an imperious voice had summoned her, making her step deeper and deeper into an unknown land. But now she had to leave, immediately; she must not waste any more time.

When she told him so, offering some vague excuses for her departure, his reserve slipped for the first time and his voice was warm with solicitude. "Has anything happened? Don't you feel well? You've become so pale, just in these few seconds."

"No," she said dryly, throwing back her head in disdain, as

though that sudden impulse to go required neither explanation nor comment, as though it had merely to be carried out.

Lintas stood still amid the crash of copper instruments, whose maddening explosion had followed without interval upon the final strains of the waltz. While couples parted and reunited, while they swayed, unresisting, to that furiously syncopated rhythm, he stood there like a statue, proscribed again and isolated, a stranger among all those people, that inexplicable tumult. An embarrassment, an inhibition which he was unable to define kept him rigid as he watched the bare coppery back move hurriedly through the throng, move farther and farther away, and finally disappear.

. . . He stood there motionless, the graceful statue of a very young man. One hand lay over the knob of the wooden door, the other held a piece of bread, white bread between white fingers. "Come on!" said one of the patrol, one of those in the rear. "This is no time for conversation."

In the darkness, in the heavy opaque nocturnal air—there was a storm off in the east, an occasional flicker, queer animal screams —it was hard to make out clearly the faces of these men who crowded around him in a confused and undifferentiated mass. All he could see, in his uneasiness, was the curve of a nose, broad-based and aquiline, disordered hair straggling darkly over a forehead, deep horizontal wrinkles, a fat, sweaty neck emerging from the open collar of a dirty gray shirt, and a neglected beard. But he could feel the general impatience, the fixed and threatening glare of all those eyes. . . .

The headlights of the car made bright dizzy patterns on the back asphalt of the street. At this hour, the theater district was at its luminous height, with strings of bulbs crackling dryly over the ancient marquees. One had to be careful not to run into the knots of human bodies which swarmed there nightly like moths around a flame. Torpid and bewildered, moving backward and forward, they filled the sidewalks in front of the brilliantly illuminated bars and restaurants and spilled over into the gutters. The vivid glare of the headlights picked out a face here and there, indiscriminately; it outlined the flat terraced branches of a plane tree and swept across the homogeneous façades of the mansions of the rich. Finally, as the car headed east and entered the poorer quarters of the city, it revealed in all their nakedness rotting balustrades and shabby peeling walls and people who shied away, as though stunned, from the lights.

Marta's eyes were wide open; she drove smoothly and expertly through the turbulent streets, but the eyes of her soul were fixed on a panorama that never moved, that was changeless and final: herself nailed as it were to a post, motionless in all that tumult. Brenda was a part of the tumult; she whirled around in the midst of it, frenziedly, like those figures in the drawing room at home, dancing among the expensive flowers, the Tchang vases, and the tapestries. But there was another face which remained unshaken, a man's face, thin, with honest eyes. She rejected this image, she wanted none of it. "I don't want to think," she kept repeating to herself obstinately. "I don't want to think." Inside, her eyes shut tight, they refused to see, those same eyes which were so alert to the risks of the traffic. And yet they would not remain sealed, they kept opening, they clung to that immobile image. She fought against it, against herself. "I don't want to think," she said. "I don't want to think. I don't want to think. . . ."

The woman who came to the door had a sour, flabby flesh, and extraordinarily thin fingers. At first, she kept the door partly closed, but, when she heard Marta's name, she opened it wide without a word, standing pressed back against the wall to give her a free passage. Marta went in and followed the woman along a badly lit corridor, sharply aware of the sound of her slippers flapping on the tiled floor. They came to a small reception room, much darker than the corridor, where the woman asked her to wait. "I'll tell her you're here," she said, and disappeared behind a pair of double doors whose glass panes were covered with thick brown curtains. Marta looked around her at the artificial plants, the small prints of the Côte d'Azur, the lace pillows, and the statues of imitation bronze. She heard the ticking of the clock. There was a pervasive smell of melted fat in the room.

After a few minutes the woman came back. "You can go in now," she said. Marta went through the glass doors and across a

room which was full of white-painted furniture and surgical
cabinets. She was not surprised; she had expected just this. Two
years ago the revolutions of Brenda's life had landed her in a
similar setting. . . . The fumes of formaldehyde pricked her
nostrils. She quickened her steps and pushed through into a small
curtained alcove.

Brenda was lying on the bed, exhausted, deathly pale. At sight
of her, a wave of terror and tenderness swept over Marta.
"Again?" she said, too distressed to consider her words. Her
sister's glance and the subdued voice answering "Again" struck at
her heart. She pressed the limp hand while the low voice went on,
anticipating her questions. She was perfectly all right, just a little
sore. The operation had lasted a quarter of an hour, without
anesthesia.

Marta sat down on the edge of the bed. "How did it happen?
Who's responsible?"

She didn't have to worry about that, Brenda said gently. Her
green eyes, hurt but uncomplaining, childishly soft, were full on
her sister's face. She had sent for her, she went on, only to ask
her to make up some excuse at home and to help out with the
expense. It had cost more than she'd expected it to, more than the
last time. . . . Of course, it was a nuisance, but she had tried to
make everything as simple as possible. The only danger was infection and she didn't think there was much chance of that. . . .
What hands the woman had! Marvelous, really—one felt the
pain, the sort of tearing inside later, but, during the operation
itself, nothing, not the slightest pang. . . . This time, though—
well, it was different; the pain had been there all the time, she
could hardly bear it right now. Not a physical pain, a moral one.
That extension of her own flesh, that bit of a creature beginning
to live, already alive inside her—she had destroyed it when she
would so much rather have let it live—have *had* it, nursed it,
saved it!

Marta let her talk on. She sensed in the prostrate body a profound excitement, an excitement which communicated itself to
her, which was canalized, intense. The whole body seemed to
have become a haven for this explicit sorrow. She could have no
idea, Brenda said, no idea whatever of what such a laceration

meant. A life torn from another life! (The green eyes hardly blinked, the skin was as pale as opal, the throat shockingly wasted.) Torn out by the roots, dragging with it obscure desires, protests as yet unformed, dragging them ruthlessly from the innermost depths of the being. Because this time, if so much hadn't been against it, she would have liked to forget everything—yes, even the criminal carelessness of the man involved!—if only she might have freed from the vortex of her own life this other budding life, this new thing which could have been different from herself. Different! To create out of oneself another being, out of the whirlwind a little quiet creature. . . .

Marta leaned over and squeezed the hands which lay so limply on the sheets. All she wanted to know, she said, was the man's name. The hands lifted impatiently. What did it matter? Why did she attach so much importance to that? The important thing was something else: this frustration, this failure, this betrayal of her flesh, this mutilation which she had deliberately brought upon herself—her conscious will set against the blind and laborious work of creation within. It was important to be so enmeshed in false values that one was unable to free oneself from them even for this supreme act. Ever since the operation early that afternoon, her mind had been painfully occupied with those words— she did not have to say them, they were there on her lips the whole time—the words: to give birth. To give something of herself to the light, give night to day, yield dark flesh to its dawn, to the sun. What she had yielded instead was a disgusting clotted chunk of dead flesh. The woman had shown it to her, the bloody mess held over a basin by a pair of pincers. Though she had been almost defiantly self-controlled while the woman had chopped around inside her, she had almost fainted then; she had wanted to scream, so great was her dread of that sour-smelling scrap of flesh. . . .

"This is my business," Brenda said. "Mine alone. No man has anything to do with it any more. All I want now is to fix things up at home."

"All right," Marta said. "I'll take care of that."

The younger girl's eyes clung to hers; they were telling her imperturbably: this will happen again, again and again and again.

It's useless to try to escape from the laws of our own being. If they were only imposed upon us from without. . . . But they're not, we carry them with us, in ourselves. What can one do if one's very nature is luckless? If joy clashes with misery and misery with joy till one cracks under the strain?

Would she be able to come home tomorrow? Oh, yes, certainly. The woman had assured her she could leave around midday, provided, of course, that nothing happened, no complications. And the night wouldn't be dull, she had plenty of things to think about.

Marta was hardly listening; she was remembering the different occasions on which, without being able to do anything about it, she had watched Brenda set off on dangerous paths. How ineffective we are when we try to influence others! Of what use is reason against an instinct which works in the dark, which can always open a way to its goal? Why shout arguments into an ear which does not hear them, which is waiting for a whisper from somebody else? Not since their childhood, as far as she could remember, had there been an unclouded period in her sister's life.

They had lived then, not in their present mansion, but in the small house in Florida, the house on the hill with its great circular sun room facing the green terrace and the river. In the winter they had had lessons in the drawing room, but the summers had been all laughter and air. Jorge Acevedo used to come and play with them, remaining until nightfall. On the tennis court where they spent most of their time they could hear, from below, the noise of trains going past; from above, the song of cicadas and crickets; later, as it began to grow dark, the croaking of frogs. Each plant in the garden had a separate language for them, each star a legend, each hour its special meaning. Jorge used to laugh at their stories.

They had learned, along with the names of the various trees, the names of the stocks issued by the Palmas Produce Company; they had reckoned the days by the company's advertising calendar. Sometimes, after dinner, they would come upon their parents in mysterious conversation; from these sessions their father, already elderly at the time, would emerge in preoccupied silence.

Meeting them in the garden, he might stroke their heads and murmur, "Your mother wants me to buy her all Argentina," and, if Mrs. Rague were near, she would immediately launch her counterattack: "A man who lacks ambition is a defeated man."

At sixteen or seventeen, Brenda was already fully developed, a woman. Marta saw her becoming daily more reserved, more secretive; the atmosphere of the room adjoining hers was thick with a series of incommunicable reveries. She never appealed to Marta now until after the situation became critical, and then, as the other realized with bitterness, it was only to make use of her. As far as Marta was concerned, the men in her sister's life did not come into focus; they remained shadowy shapes who succeeded each other rapidly and then disappeared into some queer other world. There had been a December not so long ago when she had been summoned, as now, for much the same reason. Otherwise, nothing. That reserve did not break; it did not even crack except in these brutal scenes.

"O God, give me strength!" Such, at first, had been Marta's cry, a cry repeated year after year. She received it, it was hers now, and now she might have cried—this lonely one, this woman of rather too dignified loveliness—"God, what am I going to do with this strength, what am I going to do with it?" (Ah, creature, human creature, it is hard to tell what in you is more oppressive: your great strength or your incurable fear. Ah, creature, you have learned it already, there is only one thing which you have, which is yours without alteration, and that thing is death. For the rest—how inconstant it is, even that which you have chosen for yourself!)

Marta smiled. She bent over and kissed her sister, she squeezed her hands again with a tenderness that had in it not the least shade of reproof. (Why add to the bitterness of one who already knows it in full, one for whom the world has but a single color out of so many colors?) Did she need anything, would she like her to stay? Yes, of course, it would be better if nobody noticed her disappearance from the party. And, if the danger of infection were really remote, there was no particular reason for her being here.

Brenda looked at her. "Anyway," she said, "I have to be deliv-

ered again. I have to get rid of this loathing that's in me, otherwise I can't go on. And I have to do it alone."

The Tchang clock on the first-floor landing struck eleven. Ráices smoked his Havana cigar—the costly aromatic fumes issued
slowly, they hung in the air—and maintained his ground firmly.
He had just finished explaining, for the fourth or fifth time, his
position in the affair. Now, sitting comfortably on a sofa in the
library, he leaned back and accompanied the melodic phrases of
the orchestra with a soft whistle and a rhythmic shaking of the
head. He was quite sure that in the end he would win his point.

But Rague was not an easy opponent; he was experienced and
wily and as obstinate as a jaguar. He would not, without a struggle, give up anything he had decided upon. He sat across from Ráices on another sofa, in the same attitude as the latter, his head
almost touching, on the bookshelf behind him, a copy of *Jeru-
salem Delivered* bound in white parchment. A small table beside
him held an emptied liqueur glass and a pile of cigarette butts.
"Look here," he said. "If you'll just use your head a little, you'll
see things my way. By buying up the entire issue of the Max
Issalor concern's serial A bonds and some of the Bahama-Santa
Fe's serial Z bonds and counting upon their immediate transfer,
you'd be operating under unsurpassable conditions in a market
without enemies."

Ráices said nothing. Mr. Rague settled more deeply into the
dark upholstery of the sofa, throwing out chest and belly and
opening his arms wide in a gesture of perplexity. "On the other
hand," he went on, "suppose we agree to the delay which you
suggest, you'd stand to lose much more than we should. There's
no doubt whatever that market fluctuations—consult your charts
for August, September, and October—are going to show a far
less favorable aspect. They may even become definitely perni-
cious. You'll lose a minimum of around thirty per cent; we—
nothing! Because to sell now, within the fortnight, is not the
same thing as selling within a month. You're not going to tell me,
I hope, that you're banking on surprises. In that case, I'd reply
that there have never been better reasons for expecting, not increased variations, but a steadying of the frequent ups and downs

of the past three months. Even you can't deny that. . . . Listen,
I'm not thinking of my own interests when I tell you: let's agree
without further ado to settle the business tomorrow. Really, I
keep wondering why you're so cautious about the whole affair,
why you're so uncertain about its possibilities, as though it were a
major enterprise to come to an obvious conclusion. Look here,
it's as easy as giving birth . . ."

Ráices smiled.

Decidedly, she would not have been Eugenia Rague if she had
been able to continue speaking, even for five more minutes, to
that young woman upon whom boredom rested like a traditional
weight. Dora Gervers was physically enchanting, but of an irremediable stupidity. She indulged in no mental activity whatever; there was literally nothing behind those beautiful teeth, that
fixed and unalterable smile, except a cautious and quite commonplace sensuality. There she sat, with her hands crossed in her lap
and the smile on her lips, while her hostess carried the entire
burden of the conversation, exhausting theme after theme in a
hopeless effort to extract from this statue a single sensible reaction. Her only response was an occasional luxurious "Certainly!"
—a surprised "How true that is!"—accompanied by a wide opening of the eyes and practically no opening of the mind. But there
was no doubt that her fashionably dressed hair reflected the lights
in an extraordinarily attractive way. She knows it, too, and far
too well, Mrs. Rague thought irritably. Good God, these girls are
capable of trying to compete even with one of Raeburn's portraits. Poor Sir Henry did not choose them for reasons beyond
the physical, but, at least, what a quality of tone he had and what
knowledge! Mrs. Rague decided she could not bear any more.

It took her hardly a moment to make her excuses, get up and
walk through the drawing room. Her lorgnette was held high as
though she were about to inspect a herd of stray cattle. There
was always something calculated in her manner of walking, a
certain deliberate majesty about her carriage. She went up the
first couple of steps of the grand staircase and stood there, watching with obvious delight the fairylike spectacle below. Everything pleased her—the sparkling joy of the younger people, the
giddy music, the prattle, the pompously elegant attitudes, the

whole magnificent show of lights and laughter and exquisite movement.

The servants came and went in their frock coats and black waistcoats, moving deftly between the gentlemen in frock coats and white waistcoats. They carried huge silver trays—guaranteed sterling—of delicious ices. (A chef had experimented four days to achieve them, using pineapple and strawberries as a base.) Many of the guests refused this delicacy, however, preferring to concentrate on the liqueur. In the great circle which had formed around the dancing couples, they were, naturally, the most effusive and obstreperous. Other guests showed a fatal propensity to gather on sofas and harass unsuspecting passers-by with a flood of confidential autobiography. All of them savored intimately the delight of living in a world of such extravagant opulence where the eye could shift from its contemplation of luxurious human beings and fall with surprise on some primitive or contemporary masterpiece.

Mrs. Rague looked around and saw Lintas sitting abstractedly on one of the carved walnut benches nearby, his virile head outlined against the black silk of an old Mongolian shawl. Ah, her prize! That was going to be the prize of her evening; from him would issue the word which she wanted spoken, the precise and categorical opinion on those precious canvases of whose presence in the house many people were unaware and whose real value was not known even to the man in the modest gallery at Antwerp who had sold them to her agent. She hoped for a great success from this transaction, a quite immeasurable yield. No expert appraisal was necessary—one had merely to use one's taste, the sensory delicacy of the true amateur—in order to see the quality of those three paintings, not much bigger, any of them, than an ordinary book. What she had bought for a few thousands she could sell for many more—and with renown, moreover. Not in vain does one discover—thanks to a sure instinct—behind the rather miserable mask of dirty crusted varnish the miracle of an authentic Titian!

But this Lintas, this man with the slow steady voice and the naturally elegant gestures—far too infrequent among the bourgeosie—this man to whom she had so recently and casually been

presented, did he know enough to make a discriminating verdict
in such a difficult and delicate matter? She was inclined to think
so. She had boasted more than once that she never made a mistake
about men; and, a week ago, when she met Lintas at the exhibition, she had decided that his culture and discernment in artistic
matters were beyond criticism. Now, having settled the question
in her own mind, she walked down the steps and approached him
with dignity.

Lintas was, at the moment, absorbed in minute scrutiny of a
dancer's foot, carved out of black diorite, which stood on an
otherwise bare wooden table. It was an oddly graceful piece, but
firm, with a certain refractory hardness in all its contours. To
pass from this hardness to another hardness, from the stone foot
to the stony determination behind Eugenia Rague's smile, was a
transition which could be made without difficulty or astonishment. Thinking these thoughts, he clasped ceremoniously the
freckled hand which was extended to him. A superb emerald
bracelet dangled from its bony wrist.

"I'm so glad you came," Mrs. Rague said. "Quite apart from
the personal pleasure it gives me, I have another, less disinterested, reason for welcoming you. I'd like very much to have your
opinion on my most recent acquisition, three small canvases. . . ."
Without really interrupting herself, merely by a backward motion of her arm, she stopped in their tracks Jílgoles and a lady to
whom he was talking. "I want you to meet Mr. Lintas," she
said.

She continued making introductions with the native efficiency
of a cowherd calling in his flock. In a short time she had gathered
around them a considerable number of people, whose presence in
the circle had all the air of being motivated by a purely spontaneous curiosity. As a matter of fact, there *was* a kind of vague
expectancy noticeable in these men and women so skillfully con-
scripted into the group. Among them, listening intently, with his
great nose in the air, his mouth half open and his eyes heavy with
lack of comprehension, was Senator Velarde, a man who had
displayed some capacity in the halls of Parliament, but was pretty
stupid outside it. There, too, was Miss Cisneros, the daughter of a
well-known buyer of paintings.

Mrs. Rague was enjoying herself. One of her greatest pleasures lay in displaying her dilettante's virtuosity to an attentive audience, and she reveled in the belief that that particular corner of the great room had something about it both more intimate and more distinguished than any of the others. . . . Watching her, Lintas wondered to himself: What is my social obligation at this point? Shall I express approval, corroboration, or surprise? He decided, for the moment, on simple acquiescence.

"One afternoon," Mrs. Rague launched into her speech, "I was sitting on the terrace of a café on the Cannebiére when a very well-dressed and rather ducal-looking gentleman came up to my table. 'Madame,' he said to me, 'I'd like to ask for a few minutes of your precious attention.' Before I had time to consent, he was already sitting down opposite me. I found out soon enough that he considered himself a sort of executor, not of material properties, but of a theory which had been entrusted to him by a professor of languages who had died some years before. The theory—which he expounded in quite tiresome detail—was that the greater part of all social evils resulted from an improper use of words. 'I'll give you a rough example,' he said. 'When we mean *squash* we say *watermelon* and when we mean *watermelon* we say *squash*. That's the way things go in the world.' "

Mrs. Rague looked around at her guests and smiled, as though inviting them to share her enjoyment. "I maintained a discreet composure," she said. "Of course, the theory was quite absurd; if there's injustice in the world today, it's due only to the bitter envy with which the poor regard the fortunes of the rich, and things will improve only when this failing of theirs is torn out by its roots, its moral roots."

Nobody ventured to challenge her statement and she went on serenely: "You know, in spite of his absurdity, I can't help thinking of that gentleman sometimes, whenever, for instance, I find the power to apply critical sanctions to myself weakening in me. Heaven knows, it may have been that casual conversation which taught me to prefer even the bare skeleton of truth to the richest combination of words. All my life I've been preoccupied with truth, truth before anything else. Perhaps I've had no other real passion. You know that, don't you, Berta Steligmann? You've traveled over two continents with me and you know how I am.

Everything I see, everything I hear, smell, or touch must be indisputable authentic; I won't permit even a shadow of doubt to exist."

She fastened her cold eyes on Lintas. "This is where you come in, Mr. Lintas," she said. "I haven't been speaking capriciously, I mean what I say. Will you, who are such an excellent artist, show yourself a generous spirit, too?"

He nodded in agreement and awaited developments. The circle of eyes took possession of him, surveyed him with a sort of animal-like distrust. Who was he, anyway?

"I need your unbiased judgment," Mrs. Rague declared, "a judgment as strict and uncompromising as the eye of a vulture. Yes, that's exactly what I mean—like the eye of a vulture. . . . I've got those three little things upstairs," she said. "I haven't wanted to bring them down until they'd been—well, shall we say 'christened'? I'm counting on you to tell me if they are what they seem. . . . Shall we go up?"

Lintas followed her and all the others followed him. Mrs. Rague had pronounced "Shall we go up?" in a tone loud enough to be heard in various parts of the drawing room. So it happened that a good-sized crowd started trooping up the wide carved staircase, a noisy and impertinent caravan, highly amused, curious people who did not even stop to wonder what they were curious about. The ladies' bracelets jangled metallically against hands which rested lightly on the broad baroque banisters; the gentlemen's shoes struck the rods holding down the thick carpet. At the head of this motley laughing throng, Mrs. Rague walked with her dignified air, serious and silent.

They reached the great covered gallery on the first floor. The lighting here was somber, almost shadowy. Three large easels, separated from each other but meticulously aligned, held Mrs. Rague's most recent acquisitions. She passed in front of the first, pointing at it wordlessly with her lorgnette, then came to a decided stance before the one in the middle. Lintas stepped forward. "It's impossible to see in this light," he said. With a brusque gesture, Mrs. Rague opened a path through the dense crowd and turned a switch on the wall. A strong white light flooded the gallery.

The canvas was a small detail from Titian's *Perseus and*

Andromeda, showing Andromeda's head and part of her mana-
cled arm. It evoked at once the entire painting, the clotted sky
and tempestuous ocean of the original painting. Lintas had seen it,
years ago, at Hertford House. The face, a little fleshy but dominated by the strength of the great black eyes, was turned toward
the left in an attitude of expectancy.

Lintas scrutinized the small painting for some time. Then, followed by the entire group, except for a few people whose independent curiosity had already led them to the same place, he
walked over to the one on the left, a little later to the one on the
right. He bent over all three to examine them more closely. Then
he stepped back, his brows lifted in a stare.

"Well . . . ?" Mrs. Rague was coyly inquistive.

Lintas looked at her without answering. He shoved his hands
into his trousers pockets and turned back to the canvases, as
though trying to include all three in a single act of judgment.
"What did they tell you about these pictures?" he asked.

"Well," said Mrs. Rague, like one unfortunately compelled to
explain what is already obvious, "the one you look at first is a
preliminary study of the *Perseus and Andromeda.* The others are
unknown primitives, dating from the fifteenth century or, possibly, the beginning of the sixteenth. It's of course superfluous
to tell you that I acquired with them a certificate of authenticity."

There was a long pause.

"I'm afraid you've been cheated," Lintas said at last. "I'm very
much afraid of it." He lapsed into silence again, glancing with
slight interest into his hostess's eyes. There was an angry glitter
in them, a lightning flash of furious opposition, and then they
became calm again, as composed as before.

"Why do you think so?" she asked suavely. "What makes you
believe such a thing?"

Lintas went up to the central painting. His index finger outlined partially the contours of the figure. "All one has to do is
look closely," he said. "The whole thing is stupidly deformed. . . .
These canvases are like certain objects which assume, from afar, a
form different from the one they actually have. Viewed from a
distance and with—you'll forgive me!—a degree of optical gross-

ness, the plastic masses seem to be perfectly handled. It's an impression which fails to survive a nearer inspection. . . . Look at this line, this rendering of the creases in the twisted neck—how uncertain it all is, and how hard."

Mrs. Rague did not move. Most of the others, meanwhile, were crowding around the painting and bending over to examine the discredited contours of the figure. Their genuine surprise at Lintas's verdict was expressed by shy gestures and little muffled exclamations. Their hostess, however, was not in the least disturbed. Emphasizing her words with an ironical, a very subtle and elegant smile, she said: "My dear sir, what a daring judgment! I don't want to mention the names of Mayer, Stavinowsky, Limnplatz, and Barolca, but the character of these experts and the fact that their opinion is contrary to yours leads me to ask you if you're not afraid that you're making a mistake."

"No," Lintas said briefly. "By no means. As for judgments supplied by art dealers, let me remind you that these are, quite naturally, influenced by their business dealings."

"Not when the transaction involves connoisseurs," Mrs. Rague remarked.

"Then I regret having to disagree with a connoisseur. There's no doubt in my mind that you're very knowledgeable about these matters, but you asked me for my candid opinion and I've said all I could."

Mrs. Rague drew herself up. She made a circular motion in the air with her lorgnette, indicating that the discussion was over. "It's not important," she said. "Let's go downstairs, shall we?"

At this moment, Ambassador Portinori, detained by who knows what senile idyl, came panting up the stairs. He had to turn on his heels and go down with the others, his head wobbling resignedly on his apoplectic neck. His lips just brushed the golden Florentine hair of young Miss Goves. "*Cara mia*, I'm always late," he murmured vaguely. "*Beata lei . . .*" Miss Goves, who was not at all stupid, flung back her head and laughed, as though the ambassador's remarks, to which she paid no further attention, had reminded her of some amusing and satisfactory experience.

Mrs. Rague preceded her guests. The ironic smile still edged

her lips; her eyes were hard, brilliant, and fixed. She was determined to have the last word in this little affair. As they reached
the bottom of the stairs, she turned, her milky, spotted hand
resting on the newel post. She looked drowsy now; in an effort to
conceal her fury, she had dropped her eyelids until only a slit of
shining orb remained. Her lips moved slowly, her tones were
honeyed. "I cherish the hope, Mr. Lintas," she said, "that, within
a few weeks, my little Titian will be vindicated in your judgment. It would be painful and—yes, unexpected, if this were not
the case. I am forced by circumstances to believe in these canvases which you have so casually dismissed." She opened her eyes
wide to let everybody see their ironic glint.

Lintas bowed. "If faith can move mountains, Madame," he said,
"I don't see why it shouldn't also transform a mere fake into an
authentic masterpiece."

She became harsh again. "Don't worry," she said.

Everybody was smiling, highly amused by the entire episode.
The group broke up, some of the people remaining to chat about
it, others joining the dancers on the floor. . . . Neither air nor heat
nor noise came through the open windows of the great gleaming
room. There was something about the heaviness of the night
which was like the sleep of reptiles who seem sunk in a sort of
leaden eternity from which nothing will ever rouse them again.
The flowers had the semblance of death; the more powerfully
scented among them—the magnolias, the jasmine—discharged as
though crushed their heavy fragrance. It mingled with the fainter
smell of old wooden chests, of ancient tapestries, and of the bare
flesh of the women moving ceaselessly through the room and in
and out of the shadowy garden.

"Yes, Miss Marta," said the gatekeeper, and she went in. Passing by a mirror in the hall, she paused and arranged her face.
Then she crossed the drawing room, walking in a direct line
toward the door leading to the garden, but, before she could
reach it, she was stopped time and again by greetings, questions,
importunities. "You're as nimble and decided as Cytherea," an
intellectual-looking man breathed in her ear. She laughed and
went on. When she got to the garden, she ran into Guezales,
who immediately asked her to dance. She had to put her hand on

his shoulder and whirl around rapidly, she had to submerge herself again in that unquiet sea.

Satisfied that her absence had been unnoticed, she drew back her head a little from the head of the man who held her so closely, whose breath and perfumed hair offended her nostrils. Herself again, serene, she needed only one last assurance. Her eyes searched anxiously among the revolving figures for that presence which had impressed itself upon her with such power, which still stood, unalterable, before the eyes of her mind. But she could not find him; there were too many people in the garden, the light from the hanging lanterns was too dim. She had the feeling suddenly—a feeling which had the force of instinct, too violent and painful to be ignored—that he was no longer there, that nothing of him remained except what was engraved in her mind; an extraordinary face, radiant with intelligence and candor and yet with something untouchable about it, too; a trace of some fundamental reserve, almost penuriousness, a spiritual dissatisfaction which had curiously become a virtue, which showed the secret stormy depths of an otherwise too disciplined life.

Meanwhile, she glided around in the arms of Guezales. Because her eyes did not find what they wanted to find, she clung nervously to this casual and unexciting companion, her hand tightening on his shoulder as they danced. She felt uneasy, apprehensive, profoundly dejected, as though some taut cord in her had loosened, as though the strength which had sustained her up to this moment were gone. Her eyes did not search any more, they simply stared at the darkness, at the dim faces, with that blind fixity, blasted by cold and wind, which the eyes of mountain climbers have. When she was asked a question, she replied in monosyllables, rapidly and mechanically, unable to conceal from the man who held her so tightly the blank inexorable loneliness in which she moved.

It was, for Marta, merely the intensification of a familiar mood, a sudden whipping-up of the same eternal despair; her life going on and on in its dreadful motiveless voyage through time, with never a haven for the spirit, never a place for it to rest. The old ache was in her flesh; she felt like a sleepwalker who wanders through an unreal, frightening world, who is jostled by throngs of people and yet cannot make contact, cannot speak or be intimate with any of them. She thought of her useless hands, of her whole being without fruit or the possibility of fruit, yet alive, having to live, having to go on, endlessly, knowing there is no port where it can drop its cargo, nor even a beacon to light its path, only the everlasting ocean, day and night, night and day. . . . It seemed to her that she had lost, along with that barely glimpsed presence, a direction unexpectedly offered, a clue, something like the light of dawn.

The music stopped. Guezales let her go and thanked her. Marta looked at his white tie, the bluish shadow on his chin, his meaningless eyes and nose. She said nothing; simply stood with her bare delicate back lightly touching the tall hedge behind her. From it came a thin bitter smell, an odor of wet leaves and new green stems. There was something of the same bitterness in the polite smile with which she listened to the elderly lawyer's easy phrases, his talk about "heat" and "old cities" and "much too charming to. . . ." but then she forgot to listen any more.

For, just as the orchestra broke into another moaning and delirious maxixe, she heard, from the far end of the line of hedges, the voice—tempered, cool, almost dry—of Lintas. She showed no surprise, not the least trace of it, but her ardent, serene face bloomed into incredible beauty. She walked slowly toward the house, up the shallow stone steps leading to the garden door. Then she turned around again, still unhurried, and walked back along the other side of the hedge. There were benches at the far end, in the darkness under the ivy, and quite a large group of people had congregated there. She heard her mother's voice, a little hoarse, reticent as always.

Something new came into her face, something very sorrowful and cold and tired. It informed her whole body, as the body of a primitive actress is informed, stiffening her breasts, hastening ever so slightly the long tranquil stride of her legs.

". . . as for your statement about the unauthenticity of the canvases, it just shows an itch to be contrary, to say 'no' when others say 'yes.' Please don't think I'm condemning you for it, it's the sort of thing one expects from youth. You may have what seem to you very good reasons for that 'no.' But youth is a phase, and those of us who've reached another phase judge things by quite different standards."

There was a prolonged pause behind the green hedge and then Eugenia Rague began again: "The spirit of revolt—what a lot one might say about it! You, Mr. Covenores, who've analyzed the processes of resentment—you could probably tell us a good many interesting things. The will, the need to revolt—to put oneself on top, on the upper side of the turning wheel . . ." Another voice interrupted. Marta recognized the blasé intonations of Javier Jarcelín, the bibliophile and former judge whose mind had long since been blunted by too much idleness and too much ease. "Of course! Of course!" he cried. "That's what I've always claimed. Behind every attempt at revolution, look for the motivating resentment. Exactly! We ought to shoot them all, those seditious revolutionaries! That was a very apt comparison, Eugenia. The wheel, I mean. Revolution is a complete turn of the wheel. Well, if the wheel is turning as it should, what do they mean by stirring up people the way they do? The whole thing's absurd, quite preposterous. . . ."

Marta could hear him draw a deep indignant breath, almost a snort.

"Never," he said, "never in the history of the world has the wheel turned better than it does today. My house is protected and so is my neighbor's house. He doesn't know what I do and I don't know what he does. Liberty is complete, equilibrium perfect. . . . They talk about unrest, about a new world, about the degeneracy of our time. Stuff and nonsense! Civilization has never before approached as closely the concept of an earthly paradise. Of course, one's got to earn it! Do they pretend to think that all can enter paradise? Absurd! If I hadn't stored in my memory the— how shall I put it?—the sap, the juice, the quintessence of the Pandects, the spirit of Magna Carta, the learning of Savigny, the Thomist interpretation of law . . . if I hadn't known how to integrate all those things, to lift them to the category of scientific principles, if I hadn't learned the art of interpretation, then obviously my paradise would have suffered a proportionate shrinkage. I should have had to give up my Turkish baths and been satisfied with the ordinary vulgar sort or even—who knows—the public ones. Instead of my princely editions, my firsts of Tasso and Aretino, I should have had to content myself with the undistinguished volumes to which the whole world has access. I should have had to substitute, for my wonderful meals at the Tour d'Argent in Paris, where I go twice yearly, the abominable food of some chain restaurant or obscure boardinghouse. . . . No, it's not enough to shout about the obligation of establishing a paradise on this planet. A paradise, after all, has its hierarchies too, and they're by no means gratuitous. One reaches them through merit, through a system, let us say, of progressive merit by which we impose our individual dignity on those who are inferior to us, who are born subordinate." The ex-judge's voice rose querulously. "What do they mean by wanting to change things? Absurd! Preposterous!"

"I don't know." Mrs. Rague assumed her most insinuating tone. "Perhaps you ought to ask Mr. Lintas. He's the innovator among us; he thinks there's a need for change."

Marta was afraid of what Lintas might say. But nobody spoke; only a burst of laughter broke the silence. Could *he* be smiling?

Mrs. Rague returned to the attack. "I insist that this itch for destruction can accomplish something positive. Why not? Certain assassinations can be positive, socially positive. Marat's death in the bathtub, for instance, and the beheading of Anne Boleyn. Isn't that true? I imagine it might benefit somebody if *my* head were secretly cut off . . ."

"God forbid!" exploded Jarcelín. "To deprive us of nights like this!"

Mrs. Rague ignored the interruption. "I can't understand the sort of people who like to be in opposition, who are systematically and obstinately negative. Now I'd hate to think that, because I admire Aubusson tapestries, I'd have to deny the value of—say, some primitive Peruvian fabric. But there are people who consider themselves too intelligent for such catholic appreciation. The verb 'affirm' has no meaning for them, they want only to destroy, to negate. I'd say they have a fatal tendency to see things in reverse. 'No' is their response to anything genuine. I believe this attitude is very characteristic of our age, an age in which the distorted sketch of a thigh is rated more highly than a perfect piece by Perugino . . ."

The silence was heavy. Marta came up and joined the group without being noticed. She looked over the shoulders of two women who sat arm in arm, listening.

Lintas felt the rebellious blood pounding in his head. A secret fury was in him; he could no longer withhold his protest against all this foolishness, this coarse indignity. "You asked me for the truth, Madame," he said, hardly bothering to restrain his cynical and insolent tone. "Now it annoys and irritates you. That seems to me far more indicative of a state of mind than what seems to you indicative of an age. Do you want me to believe that you prefer a comfortable falsehood to a harsh truth? What did you expect from me anyway? A polite willingness to play my role in the comedy, no doubt. But—forgive me—it's impossible to breathe in the air of such comedy, it's simply unbearable; one ends up hating oneself for putting up with it at all."

"What you do mean by 'such comedy?' "

"What can I mean—except precisely that? I've just heard that the world is a paradise because, by virtue of knowing the Pandects, certain people are permitted to enjoy the exquisite dishes served at the Tour d'Argent. I've just learned—or, rather, I'm learning it to my cost—that *you've* decided, at all costs, to believe that you've acquired some authentic examples of classical painting. At all costs. *Malgré n'importe qui, quoi.* I should, of course, have enrolled in the circle and said 'yes' to everything, added my confirmation in order not to interrupt the game. Instead, I'm guilty of a conflict, of having created a conflict. And there's no way to settle it. It's as though I'd opened the door and let in a draft which makes everybody uncomfortable. Somebody will have to get up and close the door, but it won't be me. I'm much more inclined to open it farther. If one had the courage to open more doors and windows, a great wind would sweep through the world. It might kill the frequenters of the Tour d'Argent, but so much the worse for them. Or so much the better, because only a few are lucky enough to die in full enjoyment of what they've coveted most."

"I consider that extremely impertinent!" Jarcelín said. Something innately cruel lurked in his eyes and around his peevish mouth.

"Nothing is impertinent. What *could* be now that we've heard your point of view." Lintas's sardonic smile became broader. "The proof that it's pertinent is your belief that it isn't. Of course, you're alarmed, you're one of those who fear the wind."

Jarcelín's lips moved, but he said nothing. He plucked angrily at the white camellia in his buttonhole.

Lintas surveyed him coolly. "Your gesture is not quite clear, my dear sir," he said. "I don't know whether it signifies 'yes' or 'no'. . . . As a matter of fact, gestures are most untrustworthy things. We indulge in them far too much, we'd be better off without them. It's no longer a question of 'words, words, words,' as Hamlet complained; on the contrary, nowadays people pick their words carefully in order not to betray their gestures. I don't mean simply external movements. The really terrible gestures are the ones which we make within our souls." He paused a moment, then went on thoughtfully: "You see, sir, you're one of the exceptions—you honestly like the food at the Tour d'Argent. Most people of your sort don't give a damn about the magnificent food served there. What pleases them is to be able to make the gesture of eating it. The same tendency is present in other and far more important fields. Even empires are gained by means of gestures today."

Mrs. Rague cut in smoothly. "All that sounds very well," she said. "But it doesn't seem to me particularly opportune." Her neck arched back. The low-hanging branch of a laurel bush almost touched her stately head.

"Quite possibly it's not," Lintas agreed. His features were relaxed. He had an air of great candor and serenity. "I didn't bring it up because I thought it was. The opportune is usually deadly. It kills off what is genuine. I don't want to be opportune; I want only to be honest with you, with everybody, including myself. I'm sorry that I have to speak harshly about your comedy —which, by the way, is mine, too, I'm thoroughly involved—but if I didn't, I'd go to bed uncomfortable. I might even suffer from insomnia. So I challenge your gestures with my gesture, which is impertinent and rude and perhaps rather savage. In this way, I can remain at peace with myself instead of adding my little lie to all the other little lies."

No one answered him; the whole elegant group appeared both shocked and irritated.

He smiled and went on: "We'll all go to bed more peacefully now—*you* believing that I'm hopelessly ill-bred, *I* who have made you see with me how disagreeable is this spectacle of wasted words and gestures. Such a lovely spring night deserves something better, something more real. Moreover, I'm deluded enough to believe, that when you wake up at dawn—each of you in his own bed, safely shut up in his own room—you'll still feel that unpleasant sensation, as of a draft, upon your skin. You'll get up to close the door and it won't do any good because the draft— that mortal wind!—is inside you, it blows upon you from within. . . . Yes, though you're afraid of that health-giving wind, though you feel it as a mortal danger, it's coming, it has to come.

"For more than four hundred years, the world has been shut up in a heated, stifling room. We've so perfected our system of mutual deceptions that we're oppressed by each other, unable to breathe, unable to escape from the prison of lies which we ourselves have made. I'm quite aware that this doesn't seem particularly atrocious to you. To me it does. I wish I knew where the door was so I could open it wide. But I don't know yet and I don't want to open the wrong door, one that might only lead into another suffocating room. The door I want to open leads to the fresh air, to the natural freedom of things . . ."

"A figure of speech!" said one of the men. He spoke with a sort of sluggish hatred. His white-cuffed hand flicked the ash from his cigar, a thick, dark, fragrant Danneman.

"A figure of speech!" Lintas repeated. He looked at the men deliberately. "When a horse is described to an ass, the latter says scornfully, 'Figure of speech!' "

Two of the others broke into spasmodic laughter. The man with the cigar said, slowly, without moving, "You'll have to explain that to me later."

"I'd never be able to explain it to you because you could never understand it. Every now and then the world divides into two factions, into what seems, because of irrelevant circumstances, a profoundly social bifurcation. Actually the division is eternal, and much simpler, and the tragedy of most people is, not that they suffer or lose in the battle, but that they've been fighting on the wrong side. There are just men who league themselves tactily on the side of the sinners and sinners who fight for the just. Men know little about themselves and, when they find out, it's usually too late, they're too thoroughly committed to change. . . .

"The eternal division is between those who are capable of governing their passions and appetites and those who are not. That alone is fundamental. We all come into the world the same dirty little creatures who have to be washed the first thing. But, once that outward cleanliness is achieved, our paths separate. Some of us have a basic tendency to injure anything alive and sensitive; others want only to keep it as it is, to warm and nourish it. The former are the impure, the latter the pure among humanity. What confounds these two real factions in life, what helps to divide them badly, putting them into the wrong category, is the derisive comedy of gestures, the artificial manners which obscure the truth. Because of it, humanity is three or four centuries in arrears. Only a few desperate passions have survived out of this prolonged lethargy of mankind, a few admirable outbursts—some cries of Rimbaud, some paintings by El Greco, a Ninth Symphony, some Masses by Bach. . . ."

Mrs. Rague lifted her hand to her hair, calmly smoothed its flat waves, and fixed him with her piercing glance. "Also," she said maliciously, "some rather lengthy sermons."

"Yes," Lintas agreed. "I'm a man of quite disgusting candor."

"Candor?" It was Jarcelín's high and sarcastic voice.

"And how!" laughed the man with the Danneman cigar.

Everybody began to laugh. White teeth and insolent red lips gleamed in the darkness. Lintas's eyes were somber, icy, contemptuous, his mouth bitterly awry. He reached for a cigarette with trembling hands. (But there was always a slight tremor in those thin, almost fleshless fingers; this nervousness was nothing new.) He lit the cigarette and looked again at the row of faces, glancing unhurriedly from one to the other.

"There's a third sort of fate," he said, stabbing the words home, "which I forgot to mention before. It belongs to those who've not yet succeeded in breaking through the fetal membrane."

The collective gasp was clearly audible. But Mrs. Rague still had a gesture in reserve, a gesture elegantly condescending and of the utmost refinement. Waving away the servant who was approaching with a trayful of glasses, she rose and clapped her hands, graciously, as though to say, "What *does* it all matter?" (The hands were long and white, with no other function than to smooth the dry blond hair every morning and slap cream into the flabby skin at night.) "We're spoiling our party!" she cried. "That's unpardonable. Come now—no more soliloquies!"

The group broke up, laughing and talking. Lintas, walking alone toward the terrace, found himself face to face with Marta.

She looked at him silently, shaken anew by his nearness, but fighting against the strange emotion he aroused in her as she so often fought against her own deepest inclinations. He said "Good night" to her harshly and stepped around her as though she were merely an obstacle in his path.

"Are you going already?" The voice with which she called after him had in it a rare and quite perceptible quiver.

He stopped and turned around. His eyes, still heavy with anger, looked at the woman who came up to him. And it seemed to him that she was worthy of regard. There was something so unquestionably magnificent about her!

Staring into those eyes, Marta knew he was wounded, and irremediably. "Come with me," she blurted out. "I'll drive you home."

Lintas protested. He preferred to walk, he said. He was accustomed to taking a long walk before going to bed.

"No," she said. "I'll drive you."

He felt, deep in himself, an indignation toward this whole family, this whole world, this whole conspiracy of lies. He protested again with all the rudeness of which he was capable. But that other honest glance did not waver; it met his staunchly, almost hard in its resolute courtesy. There was in it a fund of truth against which no subterfuge could prevail. . . .

The door of the car slammed shut. To Marta's interogative "Where?" he gave the name of a station. Yes, he lived outside the city, in one of its suburbs, about twenty-five-minutes ride on the train. "It's such a splendid night for driving," she said. "Suppose you let me take you all the way home. Then I can drive back slowly and get here after everybody else has left."

He asked himself what on earth he was going to do with this

woman. His thoughts, on this hot night, beneath that low and heavy sky, seemed to have an edge on them, they were at once rusty and sharp. He felt unbearably bad-tempered, wrathful rather than perplexed. . . . They swept into the dizzy center of the city, all lights and glaring white walls. Huge knifelike beams cut across the black lake of asphalt.

Lintas felt a need to wound, to say something hard and offensive, spattering with his contempt all that way of life in which he found himself still involved, from which he could not free himself. It was represented at this moment by the woman beside him, steering so skillfully through the hazards of traffic, her coppery throat revealing its strong full tendons as she twisted it from left to right.

"You know, it's very odd," she said. "Your character seems so strong, and—well, secure, and yet you attach so much importance to the idiotic whims of a frivolous world."

"Importance?" he said. "Not at all."

"Importance," she insisted, and repeated it monotonously: "Importance. Importance."

The sad unchangeable echo of the city came to them clearly, its mingled noises blending into the night like one sound, one continuous distant explosion. They had left behind them the theater district and the lordly streets of the wealthy, and now, at last, they were outside the city altogether, speeding down one of the broad suburban avenues.

. . . A few steps away down the street, the handsome game-cock which belonged to his neighbor, the harness-maker, was scrabbling in the dust. He observed it without any particular interest, remembering how, daily, he had seen its owner bend over his work in the same concentrated attitude, as of one who looks to the earth for nourishment and glory.

His hands, those still so childlike hands, were rigid, one over the doorknob, the other clutching the bit of bread. His whole body was rigid. Only his imagination—accustomed to the cruel pangs of thought and creation, hardened as is the flesh of an ascetic by the crude wounds, the dreadful crisscross marquetry of his own inmost being—only his imagination was free; it functioned and foretold. Now, in the moist night air, it was tragically lucid, that imagination which, morning, noon, and night, had alternately rejoiced and wept in its arduous pursuit of a song whose highest note was false, the rationalization of an arbitrary dream. Yes, it was tragically lucid now. . . .

That dark tree-lined road, washed as it was by the moonlight, seemed to her strange, like another world. She had probably used it before, but it must have been hurriedly and at a different hour. Now she saw it as something quite new, a magical region, all silver and shadow under the moon. The trees were old, thickly grown and fragrant—trees of heaven and giant jacarandas. The few houses were almost lost among their powerful trunks, showing only white patches of wall or the glimpse of a high red roof.

They had hardly spoken to each other in all this time and then merely of casual things. She did not want to chafe his susceptibilities unduly; he, for his part, did not want her to think that he took with excessive seriousness matters which essentially were not serious at all. As a result, their brief and conventional interchange was marked by long pauses. The pauses, indeed, became the most important factor in the conversation.

The moonlight splashed over scenes that might have been background for romantic tragedy, great parks and terraces that seemed plated with silver; it revealed here and there a small shining lake or a lonely bridge over a stream. Time and again a dry knotty branch would seem to clutch at the headlights of the car and then scrape raspingly along the hood. A persistent odor rose from the asphalted road, an odor as of marshlands, of darkness, and of death among the trees.

A bird screeched, frightened and sad. They seemed to be going deeper and deeper into the body of the night and, for a space of about ten minutes, neither of them said a word, leaving the silence inviolate. Another bird screeched and was still. A lunar trance lay over everything. Far away, they could hear water lapping against a shore and a muffled sound as of oars beating the surface of a pond.

Suddenly Marta began to speak. In a low, insistent voice, a hoarse voice which dragged out the syllables enchantingly, she protested against the sterility of the civilized universe. People couldn't really talk to each other any more, she said. The warm human exchange, the interweaving of question and answer that makes for a spiritual relationship, was gone, superseded by a single oracular voice, shouting loudly and emphatically about nothing.

He avoided replying. That perfumed and luxurious young body, that splendid head, the tall goddess-like dignity she had—who knows what subterranean distrust they inspired in him, what burning regret, what aversion? Mingled with these emotions was a shadow of respect which he refused to recognize, which he struggled against admitting to awareness, though he felt it inside him, felt it with a certain shame, like the unwilling reverence a slave gives to his master. What he was conscious of, however, what dominated the surface of his mind, was simply a relentless animosity.

Part of it, he admitted to himself, was a heritage from his lonely childhood in which women had played no part. The rest—he had good reason for the rest. Catching sight of his house, he smiled a little and touched her arm. She turned to him nervously, her face bathed in silvery radiance. "Your mission is over," he said. His deep voice had a satirical overtone.

She looked at the bright façade of the house, framed by two small pine trees; she saw the long narrow window which ran the entire height of its single story. It seemed to be the only building on the street, just beyond the circular causeway which led into the suburb. Beyond this asphalted circle, the road disappeared in a wooded darkness. . . . When she stopped the car, however, she noticed yellowish lights some three hundred feet away on the opposite sidewalk, the subdued gleam of an elegant lantern, a wide, open terrace. There were a number of houses built according to the most modern architectural style, and, though it was difficult to see clearly in the darkness, the whole place had the appearance of a small summer colony.

She accepted his invitation to come in and have a drink before leaving. They got out of the car. Lintas turned the key in the single paneled door and they went inside, into the hot darkness of the hall, which was paved with fine small tiles. Lintas went ahead to show her the way and led her into a large spacious room. He lit a couple of lamps and she looked around, suddenly overcome by that uneasiness with which an unfamiliar atmosphere afflicts the mind.

The lamps were carefully placed, one on a small table, the other near the window on the grand piano, whose black brilliance contrasted vividly with the prevailing whiteness of the room. It was evident that a strong virile taste had chosen every object and was responsible for its placement; calla lilies rising straight out of square white vases provided the only even remotely feminine touch. But none of this surprised Marta. What aroused her curiosity was the atmosphere itself, the sense of life it gave, as though some powerful invisible presence actually *existed* here, informing the air between these walls. She could feel it distinctly; it was the immaterial personification of a definite taste, a deliberate, highly conscious system of preferences and rejections. . . . A big canvas stood on an easel in one corner; except for a small Norman virgin and a delicate Negro mask, it was the only strictly artistic object in this artist's room.

Nevertheless, affected perhaps by the almost hostile reserve of the atmosphere, she had a desire to say something dry and disagreeable; she did it as one flicks a whip against one's skin to test its resiliency: "Do you spend much time in this house?"

"Yes," he said. "I hardly ever go out. I work here from morning till night, practically immured."

There was a plate of apples on the piano. They were fresh and had a strong smell. Marta sat down in one of the wide white armchairs. Lintas remained standing, looking at her.

"Years ago," he said, "the external world had no interest for me at all, no meaning except in the colors it contained. I saw everything as color; not objects alone, but temperaments, too. I didn't bother about people's natures, they were just this or that color to me. In a peculiar way, I was very happy, but I felt at the same time an instinctive longing for something more solid, a kind of dimension in things." He paused for a moment and then went on in his rich masculine voice: "With some slight differences, my life was very like what yours must be, absorbed in a kind of luxurious decadence, an expensive bias."

She looked at him without annoyance, as though his words

hardly touched her. "We all bear a false inscription," she said indolently. "Sometimes, instead of protecting us, it does us harm."

"Protect! There, you see! You speak of protection, of protecting yourself, as though it were natural, instead of a vice, to do so."

Marta shrugged her shoulders.

"I'll get the sherry," Lintas said abruptly, and went out, returning a few minutes later with the bottle and glasses. While he poured out the wine, Marta continued to look attentively at every object in the great quiet room. So close was her inspection that she might have been attempting to memorize the scene.

Suddenly a woman screamed in the street. Marta sat up, rigid with shock, feeling in every fiber of her tense body that terrible shrill lamentation which had a sort of gasping urgency about it, as though the woman who screamed were running, running away from fear. Then there was silence again, the solid leaden silence of before.

Lintas's face had lit up; he seemed to be smiling secretly to himself. "It's nothing," he said. "As a matter of fact, I'm glad you heard her. That odious scream isn't always inopportune. Sometimes, as now, it performs a necessary function."

"What *is* it?" Marta whispered.

"Reality, in its harshest and most appalling form." With the glass in his hand, he sat down on the arm of a chair, his own arm stretched along its back to steady himself. "It's good to have one's life divided in halves," he said. "It's as though one were master over two distinct domains, as though one could embrace, simultaneously, two totally different perspectives."

He brooded for a moment. A smile played over his face, a child's smile since it had no meaning, no relevance to his words. "Two distinct domains. In my case, both are rather sunless and dismal, but one of them is much less barren than the other. Much, much less barren. Just imagine, it's only about a year since this division occurred in me. Before *that*, I was one single and poverty-stricken land. That land is practically dead today. The other, the new one, is alive. The scream you heard played a fundamental part in this development."

As though something had put him on guard, he suddenly changed his tone. "Of course," he said scornfully, "for people of your breed, these are nothing but empty words."

She felt the lash behind his statement and hit out in her turn. "A breed without spite or petty resentments," she said. "I won't pretend not to know that we're hated for it. The vast majority is quite oppositely made."

"Not my breed," he said quickly.

"It looks to me as though it were."

He made a gesture which said clearly, "I don't care what you think," and then, almost at once: "Listen," he said. "I'm going to tell you a story. Have you any idea how I lived up to a short time ago? Like someone already dead. . . . I fed myself artificially on colors; I thought they were all I needed to nourish me—a flagrant self-deception. From early morning until late at night, I worked and worked and worked. Yes, it was a very effective opiate. I'd established a sort of relation between my art and me which seemed to me terrifically important. Anyway, nothing existed outside of it. I came to believe, absolutely, that an individual fulfilled his obligations to the community by the development of whatever personal talent was his. Really, you can't imagine how I deceived myself.

"Day and night, my art. I fed on nothing else. No love, no fun, no diversions of any kind. Just that one hobgoblin: my art. I hope you never know what it means to be so monstrously rapt, eyes, ears, nose, hands—all obsessed by a single pursuit. It's a kind of infatuation, but an infatuation with what?—since the point is, precisely, that one lives on the fringe of things. Perhaps with an illusion. Even in art nothing arises artificially; everything comes from the living sea."

He shifted his position, leaning back so that the upper part of his body supported his weight. "Everything comes from the living sea. And this sea was changing all the time, but too noiselessly for me to notice, abstracted as I was. I used to walk a bit in the morning, then lock myself up to work. The degree of my satisfaction was determined by the strength of the sunlight playing over the walls, the flowers, or the dish of fruit I was painting. In the afternoon I'd take a little nap, read a few pages, perhaps.

Then back to my colors again. There'd be occasional interruptions: the telephone, friends dropping in, friends as essentially cold to anything human as I. Every day the same thing. I thought I was happy."

"It sounds rather monotonous," Marta said.

"Worse than that: dead. . . . In 1934, I went to Europe, to Paris, Brussels, London. It wasn't really a change. The colors were a little different; instead of disorderly material, I saw material which had been formally organized by a Grünewald or a Piero della Francesca. Nothing unforeseen happened to me, except that I found myself rather hard up after a while. I had to go to cheaper hotels, then to boardinghouses, but I was never hungry. The original sin of moderation extended even to my finances. . . .

"In 1936, at home again, I fell in love with a woman, a rather intellectual foreigner. She bored me almost instantly and I suffered a moderate disillusionment. Nothing of any importance —the emotion was too slight. But things were happening inside me, something was stirring. I spent a rather critical summer, a season of dejection, doubts, fatigue. For long periods at a time, I couldn't work at all and I was in a chronic bad temper. That chair you've got—I'd sit in it all night sometimes, brooding and miserable. . . .

"Winter was the same, I couldn't seem to rouse myself. And then, late one evening—it was midnight, I think—I heard screams down below, an infernal hubbub. I opened the window and looked out. A green automobile, jammed to the brim with people, was just drawing away from the curb before the dance hall on the corner. On the sidewalk a woman stood alone and screamed, her arms lifted high, screaming and screaming. I ran downstairs. Face to face with that terrified woman, I recognized her as the wife of the bookseller who had his little shop on the ground floor of the dance hall. I often bought books from him; only a day or two before, he had offered me a very handsome Vasari, expatiating on its virtues in his laborious foreign accent. He was a very small man, rather sickly, with the face of a scared mouse. While the woman sobbed and gesticulated, I saw him before me, the red nose popping out of the yellowish sunken cheeks, the sparse hair and the high astonished brows. . . .

"The woman could hardly speak; she was like a dog in her agony, inarticulate but trying desperately to make itself understood. I got the story from her finally, dragged it out of her, bit by bit. A bunch of young men had come out of the dance hall and started banging at the door of the bookshop. There was an iron shutter in front of it and they pounded upon this with brutal insistence, yelling, 'Come out! Come out!' over and over again.

"Both she and her husband got out of bed, alarmed by the racket. When it didn't stop, he put an overcoat over his night-shirt and went downstairs, afraid they might break in the door otherwise. He opened it, trembling, no doubt, and was greeted by a tremendous roar from the gang. Somebody kicked through the plate-glass window. 'Eat your disgusting poisons! Eat your books!' they yelled at the little man. Still yelling, they shoved him into the showcase amongst the books and the splintering glass. His wife came down just in time to see him fall forward. When he got up again, there was blood on his forehead.

" 'Exemplary punishment!' somebody shouted. 'Let's take him to the woods!' They fell upon him all at once—there were about ten of them—and pushed him into the car, piling in behind. It was a luxurious convertible sports model with its top down and, once started, it went off like a bolt of lightning. Until it disappeared from view, the man kept calling desperately to his wife and she ran after it down the deserted street, screaming for help."

Lintas got up, a certain weariness evident in his movements. He took two or three steps toward the open window and stared out into the street. "I ran with her," he said. "If you could call it running. The woman was in such a state of terror that she could hardly hold herself upright. It was very late by this time and there was no light anywhere expect the feeble glimmer of an occasional streetlamp. Half running, half walking, we picked our way through the maze of darkness and unfamiliar streets and finally reached the woods. The ground was uneven there, covered with brambles. The woman stumbled along without seeming to notice them, stammering over and over again some of the phrases those young barbarians had used. 'Subversive literature!' she said wonderingly, as though she didn't understand what the words meant.

"We went on for about ten minutes, getting deeper into the woods. I remember that the scent of the trees was very strong. Suddenly there was a scratching noise, the glare of headlights. The car rushed by us at such speed that we hardly took in the jeers of its occupants and their contemptuous gestures. 'There they are!' the woman screamed and, almost immediately, we heard somebody moaning nearby. We pushed on and found the man lying on the gound in a little clearing. He had been horribly beaten and was almost unconscious, blood streaming down his face. His eyes pleaded with us like a beaten animal's. Under the old overcoat his whole body was shaking with fear."

Lintas turned around and looked at Marta somberly. The weariness had spread to his mouth, his eyes; it had grayed the clear skin. "A loose fragment of the universal fury had fallen upon that man and crushed him. . . . We helped him up, but he couldn't stand, so we put his arms around our shoulders and half carried him out of the woods. He flung back his head and wailed; he seemed to be addressing his lament to the sky; he grieved as though he were the last specimen, the symbol of a persecuted race. Meanwhile the woman cried, incessantly, monotonously. And I—I was awake at last, violently awake. The only thing I wanted was to find that gang of butchers. . . . That's another way in which the world is divided—into those who kill and those who want to kill the killers. An odd division . . ."

"What's so odd about it?" Marta asked steadily. "There's nothing older, more commonplace."

"It's odd because it's on this issue that a species, originally indivisible, cracks and breaks into two irreconcilable parts. Who knows what dark destiny will result from this fatal fracture? What will be its final outcome, what kind of civilization and culture, what methods of war—and of peace?

"But let's get back to the story. I left the bookseller at his house—he was in bad shape, his head and kidneys practically bashed in—and went to fetch the doctor who lives two or three houses away. I was so enraged by this time that I had to bite my lips to keep from shouting at him. My fury had changed from a dull and diffused hatred into something specific, methodical, a burning resolution to see justice done. And yet, there was that generalized indignation, too, an indignation directed as much against myself as against anyone else. That new consciousness of mine, that new being coming to birth in me, held me responsible. I had been deaf to humanity. I had not heard the murmur—so clearly distinguishable—coming from all the dark corners of the earth, the murmur made by those who are persecuted and humiliated and slain.

"For the first time in my life I felt *involved in mankind*. It frightened me a little to have been unaware of it so long. At the same time I was curiously excited. There's a secret delight in crises like this; one seems to come alive in the most unexpected places, like the dry stick of a branch pushing out shoots in spring. First, something begins to move deep inside one; it's the sap running free, the released emotion. One becomes transformed by that emotion, bigger and richer than before, part of something much greater than oneself. That's why a great faith is so profoundly satisfying to the man who has it. He passes a sort of frontier of the mind, he takes total possession of himself, his endless search has found a goal. There's no boundary more rigidly confining than doubt."

Lintas hesitated for a moment. He did not look at Marta now; his eyes were turned inward upon himself. When he spoke again, his voice was freighted with feeling. "The little bookseller died after a couple of months. One of his kidneys had been smashed to a pulp, but the doctor claimed that what really killed him was fear and a kind of unappeasable sorrow. Poor devil, he was so inoffensive and so weak, a predestined victim. Nothing came of the investigations, of course. . . .

"The woman has been queer ever since. Sometimes she's seriously deranged and runs around the streets here, screaming out in despair. You heard her tonight. I hear her often, occasionally for hours at a time. The scream affects me like a live coal on my skin, it burns me into wakefulness. . . . No one around here interferes with the woman; we know that the frantic running will be followed by exhaustion and collapse, but we don't go near her, we respect her despair. Maybe we're all waiting to be awakened fully. I don't know, but so it seems to me.

"Those who've been awakened in time are lucky. Some never wake at all; their whole lives pass without that illuminating moment. The moment when we suddenly *see*, when the relation between things is apparent to us, when our union with reality is achieved. And by reality I don't mean the material universe; I mean the realm of truth. It's possible to feel the truth so intensely that it seems to become corporeal, to inhabit a world like our world, to be as simple and solid and perceptible and real as you and I are."

Marta looked at him and, as though wishing to emphasize her disagreement, spoke slowly and distinctly: "So you see truth as a thing, something outside of us, weighing us down."

Lintas went up to the window and stared for a few moments at the high November sky. From where he stood, he saw neither clouds nor stars, only the pure black clarity of the overarching night. There was a faint but penetrating smell of ozone in the air, as after a storm. "No," he said at last. "I see it rather as immanent justice. When a thing is just, it's as tough as though it had form and a body in space. Is there anything more deeply moving than the toughness, the sheer will to survive, of a human being? The people I admire are the ones who resist, who, in the desert of life, do not permit themselves to be corroded. What I've been telling you shows the emotional process which results in the will to fight. I shan't abandon that fight nor forget it for a single moment; rather, I shall grow stronger with it."

They kept on looking at each other. His glance held a barely concealed challenge; hers was indifferent, distant. She had the proud calm self-possession which is the final glory of mighty fallen breeds.

"The will to fight," he repeated. "Do you know what's gnawing at me? Not to be able to express in action, in a definite and concrete way, my loathing for the class you come from. A class characterized more and more by its criminal exploitation of life, by its humbug, stupidity, and vice."

She smiled, but the expression on her face did not change. "I can't understand how anyone can be so—I won't say intelligent—so rational about means and so childish about ends. What *are* these classes you allude to when you pick out for special attention the one you consider most abominable? Do you call the social sector from which I come *my class?* Are you really so primitive still, so vulgarly childish as to believe in the caste system?"

"What else should I believe in?"

She shook her head in disgust. "Like a lot of other people, you're too close to what you're looking at. It distorts your vision. I've always refused to believe in social castes; I believe only in moral castes. Even a herd of buffalo or cattle will group itself according to certain mysterious sympathies. It's silly to believe anything else. . . . Of course, there are people who are drawn together by their common impulse to despoil others, whether in a material or a moral way. You might say that they then form a class, in your sense of the word. But beyond that, no."

She did not want to smile any more. It was better just to look around, to let her hurt glance take in everything in turn: the fruit so carefully arranged on the plate, the pictures, the piano, the great window opening on the night.

"I'm not speaking like this because I want to be nasty," Lintas said. "It would've been easier to maintain a sort of polite distance. But you deserve something better. You're worth fighting with."

"What do you know about me? As much as you know about some animal in the zoo."

"Maybe so. But I know this: if you leave here awake, I'll have achieved something."

Marta burst out laughing. "Awake! Did you say *awake?*" Her laughter stopped as abruptly as it had begun. For a moment, just a moment, she stared at him, her eyes brilliant and rebellious. Was there a shadow of perplexity in them as well? It was hard to say, because she was immediately cool and self-possessed again. It was he who was disturbed. He felt his brow clouding.

There was that compulsion to speak. He sipped his wine slowly and saw she was doing the same. "It's been funny in a way," he said. "For months I've walked around like a conspirator trying to set a fire. I was determined to communicate the blaze inside me, but I didn't quite know how to go about it. I'd start out early in the evening and not get back until dawn, still sleepless, having accomplished nothing whatever, needing to act and not being able to act. I think I've been in every public place in the neighborhood, every bar and restaurant. It was my idea to speak to the people there, to wean them from their trivial vices and show them what was going on. But, actually confronted by that appalling immaturity, I'd always give up and go out again without having said a single word to anybody. And I'd feel as though all my inspiration had died."

Lintas's brows drew together; he seemed in pain.

"That passivity we all have, that terrible inner dullness. I wonder how much in any of us is alive, whether the greater part isn't old and rigid, moribund. It makes me shiver sometimes." He turned to her squarely with a kind of appeal in his eyes. "Think of me as someone tormented, as one of those who cannot sleep, who must keep vigil, unreconciled in themselves, unable to make peace in their minds. We cannot sleep because of all those others who are keeping vigil, too—the hungry ones, the ones who have no peace."

The night air came in through the open window and stirred in the space between them, the space which they could not bridge. Everything he had said seemed to Marta excessively verbal, excessively intellectual.

"It's so easy," she said, "to give a heroic cast to vanity, to one's own hidden self-love. Don't you ever distrust yourself? Obviously not. And yet, looking just a little deeper into what you've said, I'm afraid for you."

"Yes?" Lintas said.

"There's one thing I can't tolerate—people who strike romantic poses. Evil isn't outside us, it's in us; it results from the fact that nobody is willing to be himself. You, for instance . . ."

"Basically," he said, "we're two different breeds. We haven't even a common language."

"Maybe it's language which separates us. Maybe, for us, it's a broken bridge."

"Possibly. Anyway, there's a barrier between us. You could overcome it. It's your job to overcome it. You see," he said, and paused for a moment, "the barrier is your mind, the frigidity of your mind." (Yes, she was cold, genuinely cold, but not in her mind; that wasn't the frozen area. The cold was all around her, all around her.) "And the mind," he was saying, "has the same shape as the soul."

She laughed and stood up. "Look," she said. "It's almost morning." She went over to the window, moving slowly and gracefully. "Just be careful of one thing," she murmured. "Don't let your vision of human fellowship begin with a break in yourself. You've painted a very vivid picture of a man who wants to get away from himself—at any cost. That explains your anxiety for action. . . . Be careful. A life is like a purse; there's no point in giving it away if it's empty."

Her voice became fuller, more urgent.

"We ought to fill our lives," she said, "fill them to the brim with all the variety of the world, with its sorrow and its hope and even its apparent uselessness. But we shouldn't try to change ourselves. Let's be like those creatures—scorpions or heroes— who don't seek a form because they already have it, because they are scorpion or hero from the inside out, entirely themselves. That is their virtue: to be themselves, to be powerfully whatever they are . . ."

"What is this—a warning?"

She laughed again, lightly. "Don't worry. We've had so many words tonight, I've just added my share. . . . And now I'm going home."

They went downstairs. From the doorway the mist seemed thicker, it had a body, it moved.

"If only . . ." he said slowly.

"If only what?"

"If only I'd been able to make you *feel* that reality I was talking about. If it made you uncomfortable, if you saw it as— well, as a not very agreeable guest who exists, nevertheless, and requires attention." And then, as she remained silent, "A guest whom it's impossible to forget, day or night . . ."

She looked around, at her car, at the trees, the streetlamp, the shining tar of the road. It seemed hardly worth while to answer that the only reality is the one we carry inside of us, from which we cannot escape. It was no use whatever telling him that she already lacked peace, that the torment he wished to inflict upon her was her habitual torment. And that there lived in her always a certain terror, a certain need. No, it was no use.

To the left, very nearby, were the woods. They rose like a dark wall, a strong and solid redoubt. A great restlessness came from them; they charged the air with their breath. She felt it in her nostrils, the cool harsh aroma of leaves and bark, the heavy emanation of earth. "What a wonderful smell!" she said.

He nodded. "Come on," he said. "Let's walk a bit."

There was a natural opening in the dense wall of trees and they entered through this. Above their heads the branches were thickly interlaced, shutting out the sky. The stillness was profound, but, as they penetrated deeper and the path took a sudden sharp turn, they heard for a moment a thin crystalline music, the distant tinkling of a waterfall. Then there was silence again, and alert vigilant silence as though, Marta thought fancifully, all the forces of the planet were standing guard in this secret deserted place.

"I can't rest," Lintas said. "Night and day I hear the sound of footsteps, overtaking me, leaving me behind. But what can I do? One can't force one's own ripening."

"No," she said. "One can't. And one has to watch it. Character may rot through want of action. It rots even more if the action stems from hatred, from a sort of perverted ambition."

They walked on through the woods. Around the base of the giant tree trunks lianas wove a tangled web, their weak, twisted tendrils reaching out with a sort of violence, grappling for a hold on the tough bark which was as thick and wrinkled as the hide of an elephant. They walked without speaking now, there was no longer any need for speech between them; they listened instead to the silence, the faint myriad-tongued voice of earth. The croaking of the frogs, persistent and melancholy, hardly seemed like a sound; it was part of the hot night, lying beneath it, a condition of its peace. And then, suddenly, that peace was shattered by a high, sharp animal scream, a scream which had something almost human about it, something in its frantic rising and falling which was like blasphemous laughter, like a curse.

They stopped and looked at each other. "It's very late," she said. They turned and retraced their steps. When they reached the house again, they clasped hands. It was better to say nothing except "Good-bye."

Parties, like people, go through a physical decadence, fade away gradually. By this time all the dancing couples had left the drawing room and it was deserted except at its outer edges, where some of the older people sat or stood around in desultory conversation, forming a sort of frieze along the wall.

Mrs. Rague was chatting with Ambassador Portinori. While she talked, she looked over his shoulder and stared at herself in the third-century mirror behind him. Clusters of grapes were carved into its frame; from that delicate cornucopia her face peered out white as plaster, with patches of color high on the cheeks and pouches of shriveled skin under the staring glassy eyes.

". . . I tell him so, Ambassador, I tell him every single day. But it's useless, he pays no attention to me. Yesterday we stopped at Hintermeyer's to order some flowers for those poor Álvarezes— too bad about their daughter, isn't it?—such a mediocre marriage. A French automobile salesman, imagine! Well, anyway, as we were going in, he said he had nothing in his pocket except a few cents in change. Really, he's disorder personified. He considers himself unfortunate, a prey to bad luck, but it's only his disorderliness.

"If he'd had more business sense, we'd have bought the old embassy building long ago. As it is, I suppose we'll go on stagnating in the same dreary economic pond all our lives, worn out finally by its monotony. I'd be very grateful to you if you gave him some advice. Perhaps you'll get some action out of this sluggard, though I doubt it. Disorder is second nature to him, he's simply incapable of system. Why, if it weren't for my stubbornness, we'd never have had this gallery of ours which, in spite of what anyone may say"—here her eyes flashed with fury—"in spite of that mediocre artist's opinion, is one of the finest and best arranged in the world."

The ambassador folded his hands over his belly like an abbot.

"It's certainly a handsome collection," he said.

Mr. Rague, who had been standing nearby, listening sheepishly, smiled a smile of infinite patience. His wife went on looking at herself in the mirror, her head waggling slightly to maintain a clear view. The orchestra broke into a popular fox-trot. Miss Goves, all white tulle and earrings, passed by slowly. She was talking with animation to a young attaché who, gossip said, had once lived shamelessly on some rich Englishwoman in Antibes. They greeted each other with the utmost amiability.

Mrs. Rague lowered her lorgnette and pressed shut her eyelids. The gesture was designed to convey distaste, impatience, and despair all at once.

"I've worn myself out," she said, "trying to breathe a spark of ambition into that man. You can see how little I've succeeded: he's as mild as a sheep. While I—I'm a fighter, Ambassador, a fighter!What haven't I battled for! It seems to me that the worst of all ills is to lack the will to fight. The will to fight? Everything in this house was acquired in that way; my obstinacy won out over every obstacle. Yes, my dear ambassador, it's I who am responsible. Because Rague, dear good soul that he is, is as guileless as a child! . . .

Marta drove back along the same dark tree-bordered road. But her world was not bounded by that whitish cement; it extended far beyond those iron railings covered with lush foliage, beyond the expanse of bare and uneven earth. She felt extremely light, as though her bones were hollow and the heavy blood had left her veins. Her vision did not take in the immediate scene; it was fixed on an enormous living frieze where men and animals suffered indescribably, where bodies were twisted and mouths stretched in a groan.

. . . *He said, not lowering his head, looking them full in the eyes, "I'm going to get my hat." It was an almost mechanical formula, words coming as it were unbidden to the lips while the imagination was busy about other matters, prefiguring what was to come. He used a hat seldom; at this moment there was certainly no need for it; what he really wanted was time. He wanted to be alone with his imagination, to take it back through that doorway, up the stairs, through the dimly lit dining room, and into the shadows of his own room—so that there, in the darkness, it might complete its work, the terrible prefiguration on which it was engaged, the picture. . . .*

Marta left the car in the public garage and started walking down the empty street. This was the hour for plunder, for great withdrawals, for nakedness and truth. Everything sentient seemed to have retired from the world; there were no lights, no noises, nothing. And she—she was wide awake, utterly wakeful, with a wakefulness that had no limits and no memory, that seemed always to have been. Like the air, she thought, like day or night, which have no limits either, and no memory, through which things simply pass unregarded. Her body had the lightness, the insubstantiality of air; she felt as though she were drifting down the street. But deep down, below the void, there was a bottom, there was anguish; she touched her own anguish as she drifted along.

She did not want to go home; the necessity of doing so filled her with aversion. While Brenda lay in troubled sleep, her mother was probably getting out of bed and stealing down to the kitchen for a last bite of turkey. Poor old Rague was undoubtedly snoring. . . . And, all the time, in a hidden part of the world, in its subterranean depths, other things were happening, vigils not painless like hers, but racked by atrocious torments. Far from this quiet street, desolation and cold and hunger ran wild like jungle beasts. She heard the screams of their victims—so many victims! —echoing from the farthest reaches of the night.

The mist lay lighter; the faint clarity which precedes dawn was already in the sky. More than ever before, she felt the need to become one with things, to mingle her blood with theirs. To live. But—to live! Live! What an obsession it was! Did *he* by chance have some understanding of it, that artist whose confusion seemed to become more accentuated precisely when he believed it was gone? When he thought he was beginning to understand humanity, he seemed not to understand anything at all. But yes, he was in pain, he was suffering. What luck to be like that, not half-hearted, not lukewarm any longer, but critically involved, willing to go to any extreme, to lose oneself or save oneself!

A touch of morning freshness was in the air. She took a deep breath, happy to be alone, isolated in her freedom. On this November night, the world did not end with her; it began. But in a shape so vast and indistinct, so nameless, that her realization of it was itself a pang.

She shook out the mackintosh she was carrying and, slipping it over her evening dress, walked on through the damp mist. Crossing a narrow dimly lit street, she came to the familiar plaza where the statue of López, seated and in civilian clothes, was solidly planted on a square plot of grass. If she turned left here, she would be in her own neighborhood, but she preferred to keep on going, so she cut diagonally across the plaza.

She lifted her head to the diffused spreading brightness up above. Mist filled her wide-open eyes and she was suddenly aware of anguish, the glad mood of a few moments ago changed into acute pain. There was nothing to direct her steps, no will or goal. She could go anywhere or nowhere, return to the eternally inert atmosphere of her home or delay a little longer. If she delayed, it was without purpose, out of a simple wish to wander, a need, perhaps, to feel the living world around her in these moments before dawn. Yet she preferred to delay, to live a while longer before going to sleep, to follow just a little while longer the rhythm of those who are awake.

There are times when, for lack of a single word, the nature of our desires remains undefined for us. To such an extent is the Word itself creative that, until we have given our joy or our sorrow its proper name, we waver in unbearable suspense. Until the right word, the *name*, ties us inevitably to the truth we pursue, we are unhappy. All cowardice is summed up in this alone: the fear of giving things their real names, so that their reality is dissembled in evasions. . . .

Walking along the street, through the paling mist, did she realize the cause of her uneasiness? The fixity of her gaze was like that of a somnambulist who marches on, unmindful of risks or obstructions, intent only upon the obsession, the merciless questioning in his own brain. It was enough to look at her, this Marta

Rague, to know that what was harassing her was a hatred of herself. She knew it, too. She was harassed because she yearned for something. Her whole being yearned, her brain, her skin, her very guts were clamoring. Not for anything from outside, but for something in herself that would go out, project itself.

Her glance lingered with mechanical circumspection on a stone gargoyle perched on a building nearby. It was the head of an esoteric female divinity, and, even after she had passed, it remained before her inner vision as though its function were to disturb another image there, to hide and conquer it. And then a word began to be discernible on the rigid gargoyle's head, shaped itself slowly in her brain. The word was: *Serve.*

She had a sensation of great relief. Without moving her lips, she repeated it over and over—*serve*—over and over again. To serve, yes—but how?

She went down to the highway and saw the word forming in the air, inscribed on the stones. Two workmen passed by and looked back at her, grinning broadly. She did not see them. There was a flower shop on the other side of the street; a woman was swabbing the window with a violet cloth and, behind the blurred glass, she caught a vague glimpse of rhododendrons, of long dark leaves and clustered bloom. *Serve!* The word was written on them, too.

She decided to walk just a little longer. Soon the streets would be filled with an army of employees, with women and children and others who got up early for the mere fun of it. . . . The mist took on a rosy tinge; later it would become bluish and then white again. . . . *Serve.* How different things were when one thought of them in this way. Was it possible to achieve direction suddenly, to channel that complex of flesh, blood, and nerves, of emotions and inhibitions, that complex which was oneself? She thought of the servants at home. They had always been there; it was *she* who was served. It was a topsy-turvy world.

Time was at her shoulder, touching her bare skin. She slipped easily into the day; her thoughts took quick possession of the life that was beginning to stir around her, the dawning life of a great city. She was by now unconscious of herself; she did not see her figure reflected in the plate-glass windows; all of her was turned

outward toward that mysterious and growing life. There were
three shrill whistles, then silence, then the roll of wagon wheels
along the pavement. The city was waking up.

It was probable, she thought, that she was walking like this
simply to tire herself, to wear herself out until that moment
when she could fall, utterly prostrate, on her bed. Certainly she
was seeking, in this already so familiar weariness, an outlet, relief.
There was really no need to wait until the people thronged into
the streets. She saw them as though they were actually present
before her eyes, a dense multitude, their lips moving to a dark and
secret melody, the eternal strophe and antistrophe of existence.
All of them were tragically involved in existence, their laughter
and their weeping made its music. The terrible swirling torrent
of it caught them up and swept them along together, and yet
each of them struggled painfully for his own salvation, for a spar
of personal meaning to which to cling.

There could be, she thought, no individual salvation. And with
the thought came the memory of a circus athlete whom she had
seen in her childhood. His muscles swelling and his whole body
in a state of unbelievable tension, he had lifted and held in the air
a huge iron bar from either end of which other men were dangling. . . . In just such a way does the weight of the human family
rest upon us all; and the more of it we bear, the more human do
we ourselves become, the more tired and lacerated, but also the
more invulnerable.

Whether one liked it or not, one was part of humanity, irrevocably bound up in its fate. One could be either an obstacle in
that slow upward progress or an instrument for unity, for
growth. Not to hinder but to serve—one should realize that,
learn it with one's very blood. Tragic is he who betrays his own,
with whatever motive, impedes the development of his kind.
Revolution itself was of no value unless it led to a more abundant
life. That man whom she had left in his lonely suburban house,
whose torment she had sensed—was he, perhaps, just another
hindrance, an indiscriminately destructive force?

She passed a small chapel. Its heavy black oaken doors stood
wide open, allowing the mist to pour through into the narrow
shadowy nave. She stopped and looked inside. A sacristan was

lighting tapers for early Mass and a woman with a lace mantilla over her head was kneeling on the floor. Marta stared at them for a moment, absently, not interrupting her own train of thought. Then she began to walk again, doubling back on her tracks, her hands plunged deep into the pockets of her mackintosh. The right one clutched a key.

The inside of the big old confectionery shop was brightly lit. A nickeled coffee machine gleamed on the clean marble counter and steaming cups of hot fresh coffee made little puffs of vapor all over the vast bare room. People whose faces showed a morning pallor sat around quietly, eating their breakfast. The scene gave Marta a feeling of contentment, an almost childish hope. She went in and sat down at one of the tables. Immediately, from all sides of the room, eyes turned upon her, curious apprais-ing eyes which had a latent hostility in their depths. They made her aware of how alien she must seem to these people, dressed as she was and with her bright painted lips. Keeping her own eyes averted, she asked for a cup of black coffee.

She felt herself thrust back, and yet what she wanted was to return to them, to let the tide of her emotion break like a wave over that human coast, flood it, sink into it. Not to break was to die. A phrase from Ecclesiastes, which she had loved years ago and repeated often, slipped into her mind: "Cast thy bread upon the waters, for thou shalt find it after many days." Sipping her coffee, she ventured to look over the rim of the cup at the hum-ble folk around her, observing with a sort of pang their gestures and the way they held their heads. A few tables away, a woman was carefully wrapping up what was left of her meal in a paper napkin. Watching her, Marta had a sudden sickening shock; some trick of light or nerves made her see in that serenely absorbed face the face of Brenda. But the illusion was momentary; the woman's face reassumed its proper lineaments.

Except for two old men who were sitting together, everyone in the room was as solitary as she herself. Separate destinies, each waging its own war, ambitious, vacillating, fearful or greatly dar-ing as the case might be. She would have liked to make common cause with them, to enter every one of those lonely hearts, but she had no way of reaching them, she could not project the force of her longing. . . . The waiter held a match to her cigarette and she inhaled the smoke slowly, feeling the first nausea of that long wakeful night. And yet she was reluctant to go. Leaning a little forward, her chin cupped in her hand, she continued her self-imposed vigil.

When she left the confectionery at last, her spirit was tense. What is tranquillity, human tranquillity, how achieve it when the ground burns under one's feet? Each in his own way must be heroic, must walk along that burning road with arms and soul outstretched, a spacious being unhindered by frontiers, content with no partial goal. In spirit she could possess herself of the man with whom she had talked that night, of the woman praying in the chapel, and of the people who ate their breakfast alone. What she bore within her now was not her private individual conflicts, but something more complex, a vast incorporation of everything she had seen and known. Her state of mind comprehended the man's uneasiness, the woman's prayerful mood, the bitter fatigue of those early workers; it comprehended, too, the man who had just passed her with his impulsive and conquering stride. She felt at one with all of them, a free citizen of all those contradictory moral climes.

She cut through a cross street into the broad avenue of her own home. She felt tired and happy. Using her key, she opened the great black door of the house and went inside.

She stood motionless at the window of her room and looked out over the roofs and treetops. Beyond them lay the land, her country, in all its abundance. She resembled this land; she was capable of as great a variety in climate, she could absorb it all, live with it, make of its very diversity her life.

It was dawn and she was alone in her room.

Her whole being felt painfully extended, but this cruel extension was itself abundance. She touched the entire enormous world, she understood everything, the far reaches of that world and the depths which she had plumbed in herself: they were one and the same. Yes, she understood it, she sensed it as one who puts his ear to the ground senses the approach of a galloping host.

Different moments of her life came suddenly and spontaneously to mind, but they were united with other incidents, near and far, which were utterly foreign to her.

Foreign and yet not foreign, chords in the infinite music of the universe. To live was to multiply relationships, to create link after link with the world. Her brain was flooded with reminiscences, they poured in from all sides: the taciturn stranger she had met ten years ago after an illness; but he was not alone; another image accosted her, somehow associated with his; no, not an image—a sound, the sound of falling water; it came from the waterfall next to the mine where she had seen them bring up the dying men, three men in dark workers' clothes, hauled out of the dark earth to die. And the sound of the water was mingled with the terrible gurgling sound of extreme thirst and delirium; and this in turn brought vividly to mind another image, the horde of suffering refugees on the train, refugees from Odessa and Frankfort, their heads bowed in despair after months of wandering and waiting and refuge denied. And the fair-haired children, wild as little wolves, who swarmed all over the train and played games in the corridors. . . .

They crowded her mind and, with them, were all the newly born and the dying, the cold, the hungry, the imperiled ones of the earth. The sowers and the reapers were there, those who were joyful and those whom disaster had overtaken. They clamored for understanding, they needed to be justified, explained, and accepted. And she gave of herself; she rejected only the men of ill will, the hateful mercenaries of the spirit, those who betrayed and persecuted and destroyed.

She stood by the window and stared at the misty reflections on the pane. Her lips moved silently, shaping themselves around a chance poetic phrase she had read in a newspaper. The writer had said that those who die in a just cause are still alive, they do not die altogether; and then had come that phrase which she remembered so vividly: "Reckon with us; we are the multitude; our faces are turned to the free wind, to the sea, to life."

Something deeply buried and sorrowful in her rose to the surface, pierced through into her consciousness like spears of living grain. She began to undress, painfully, unaware of what she was doing. Why did the world appear to her in the shape of a great slaughtered beast? A slaughtered beast. . . . With deep affliction, she thought about Brenda, about the corpse of a child. Her own heart was like that, exhausted, cold and inert. God, when would it come, when would the final punishment come?

It was dawn and she stood before the window, her eyes fixed, her arms rigid against her body. After a while, she finished undressing and went to bed. Her head lay heavy on the pillow.

The events of the night flashed before her in a single dizzy instant. . . . The music of the orchestra is a frantically whirling figure which clutches now one, now another couple, compelling them to its own mad rhythm until the whole room sways and gyrates under the brilliant lights. The ancient faded tapestries grow paler and paler, dissolving at last into pure mist, a gigantic featureless curtain of watery mist. Ambassador Portinori laughs, incessantly, convulsively, while, off in a corner, Mr. Gunter declaims the poetry of St. John Perse to a group of bored and elegant listeners:

> *"Je t'annonce les temps d'une grande chaleur et les veuves*
> *criardes sur la dissipation des morts. . . .*
> *'Un grand principe de violence commandait à nos moeurs."*

. . . A great principle of violence . . . a great principle of violence has dominion over us! How Mrs. Veres lifts her plaster-white arm and drops the white camellia so that Esegovio may pick it up and return it to her! With what histrionic ecstasy she then sniffs at it! The gesture—everybody knows it—will be followed, as always, by frenetic dalliance on silken cushions and then by the furious hysteria of the lady who can no longer endure her lover of two days. . . . A great principle of violence has dominion over us. . . . The tray is passed around. A dainty young man waits hopefully, his whole soul extended with his glass. For the moment he is nothing but an incarnate desire, the desire for wine. Laughter explodes here and there like firecrackers and there is the steady hum of talk, talk that goes on and on, endlessly, endlessly. . . .

Why was the image before her eyes an image of death? Dead night, dead mist, her own body suddenly stricken, the great dead silence of dawn? (What could one do? What gesture would serve against it, against the death men dealt to each other everywhere?) She shook her head; she tried to dispel the torturing hallucination. There was no clear cause for the pain she felt; it was an affliction mysterious but cruelly keen, boring like an auger into her very vitals. To lift the hand was to injure; one was culpable always. And tomorrow would be no better; awakening would bring no change.

It seemed to her that she could sense death uncoiling far away. That strange forlorn feeling she had, as though somebody had gone away from her, leaving her bereft. And those screams—were they screams that she heard?

The world was full of screams, of vague menacing shapes, of crimes, horrors, follies, manias, persecutions, and debaucheries. Ah, if only the tormented peoples might kindle to flame, the hands grasp a sword to lay them bare! But her hands were empty. Her eyes empty too.

When at last she fell into a heavy sleep, the servants were already up and about. The mist had yielded and light streamed into the great drawing room. Furniture was polished, a feather duster flicked over the face of Cardinal Wolsey. And, while he waited for a girl in a dotted red muslin dress, one of the menservants wielded his broom over the shining waxed floor and, whistling cheerily, swept out the freesias, the magnolias, the geraniums, the roses, and the first jasmines of the season.

It was eleven o'clock at night. There was a violent protracted pounding at the door, blows that sounded as though they were made by the butt end of a Mauser. Opening the door, he saw a patrol of armed men, filthily clad, with unkempt hair and beards, their rawhide belts smelling of sour cheese. One of them, the one in front, said, roughly but without conviction: "We've come for you."

He stared in horrified astonishment at that brown heavy face in which weariness clashed with a profound and nervous irritability; he saw the cruel mouth, the furious eyes, the powerful soldier's body. . . .

In his hand he still held a bit of white bread, homemade bread which he had picked up a few minutes ago from the carving table in the dining room. He remembered suddenly that he was alone in the house, that neither his mother nor his sister was at home. He remembered, too, the scrap of paper which he had left lying carelessly on the table. On it were the penciled beginnings of a poem.

He, whose dark face had the fierce vitality but the still almost childish lineaments of extreme youth, felt small and a little uneasy —not fearful, just oddly hemmed in and surprised—before these armed men who seemed to form a sort of patrol. Their leader, at any rate the one who stood in the front rank with a certain emphatic authority about him—that strange man with his cruel mouth and confused eyes, as though it were the mouth which gave orders in that face and the eyes which obeyed—had said to him: "We've come for you."

"But—what do you want of me?" he asked, showing no alarm, only a profound perplexity. "What can you possibly want of me?"

He stood there motionless, the graceful statue of a very young man. One hand lay over the knob of the wooden door, the other held a piece of bread, white bread, between white fingers.

"Come on!" said one of the patrol, a man at the rear. "This isn't the time for conversation."

In the darkness, in the heavy opaque nocturnal air—there was a storm somewhere off in the east, an occasional flicker, queer animal screams—it was hard to make out clearly the faces of these men who crowded around him in a confused and undifferentiated mass. All he could see, in his uneasiness, was the curve of a nose, broad-based and aquiline, disordered hair straggling darkly over a forehead, deep horizontal wrinkles, a fat sweaty neck emerging from the open collar of a dirty gray shirt, and a neglected beard. But he could feel the general impatience, the fixed and threatening glare of all those eyes.

A few steps away down the street, the handsome gamecock which belonged to his neighbor, the harness-maker, was scrabbling in the dust. He observed it without any particular interest, remembering how, daily, he had seen its owner bend over his work in the same concentrated attitude, as of one who looks to the earth for nourishment and glory.

His hands, those still so childlike hands, were rigid, one over the doorknob, the other clutching the bit of bread. His whole body was rigid. Only his imagination—accustomed to the cruel pangs of thought and creation, hardened as is the flesh of an ascetic by the crude wounds, the dreadful crisscross marquetry of his own inmost being—only his imagination was free; it functioned and foretold. Now, in the moist night air, it was tragically lucid, that imagination which, morning, noon, and night, had alternately rejoiced and wept in its arduous pursuit of a song whose highest note was false, the rationalization of an arbitrary dream. Yes, it was tragically lucid now.

He said, not lowering his head, looking them full in the eyes, "I'm going to get my hat." It was an almost mechanical formula, words coming as it were unbidden to the lips while the imagination was busy about other matters, prefiguring what was to come. He used a hat seldom; at this moment there was certainly no need for it; what he really wanted was time. He wanted to be alone with his imagination, to take it back through that doorway, up the stairs, through the dimly lit dining room and into the shadows of his own room—so that there, in the darkness, it might complete its work, the terrible prefiguration on which it was engaged, the picture. . . .

None of the men said anything. They let him go inside and he stepped into the dark narrow hallway, his soft soles light on the damp, sounding tiles, a certain urgency about his movements as though he had to arrange everything quickly and hurry back. Downstairs, the patrol was waiting for him, wrapped in a mist which could hardly be called mist at all, which was rather an emanation of the hot sticky darkness, of the night itself. Under the blurred moon, the men stood waiting, nervous and taciturn, in unmilitary attitudes expressive of boredom, of impatience and fatigue.

He, too, was in darkness, the deeper darkness of the shadowy house. Only the small gas lamp in the dining room was lit; its feeble rays fell on the table, on the shabby brown cloth cover and the piece of paper with its penciled, unfinished lines. He went upstairs, noiselessly, his five senses fused into one—a different sense, imaginative and prophetic. And inside, deep in his guts, was that dreadful anguish, that growing and already unbearable perplexity, that trembling. . . . But his body did not hesitate; his legs walked upstairs without a pause. He passed through the dining room into the bedroom, leaving behind him on the table those closely written, interrupted lines. He had eaten at that table every day, he would have liked to speak to it, to say good-bye. "Goodbye," he said to himself, feeling a sudden profound depression. He took his hat, an old black hat, from the rack at one side of the dark oak wardrobe. Next to it were the two plain wooden shelves which held his books. Bending his head, he saw without looking at it the title of the book which he had been poring over, night after night this past month, and the familiar title seemed to him strange and remote: Hymns to the Night. *Hymns to the night; he had not thought those would lead to this. He trembled. He was trembling inside. Again he went into the dining room, not looking at anything. They lead to this.*

He had known about his cousin several days ago: the wall, the shots, the body falling broken and heavy to the ground. Neither Estefanía nor Celsa had been given permission to bury him; the permission had been denied them. "His shirt was all bloody—like this," old Eleuterio had said that night, his hairy hand sweeping over the entire expanse of his own chest from one side to the other. . . . Days ago. . . . He walked through the dining room. They lead to this. He was, suddenly, rebellious, angry, beside himself, bitterly rebellious, his whole being a loud scream of rebellion. But it was only for a moment. He mastered himself instinctively, lowered the tone of his rage, became humble again, became calm. A line which he had written recently, which he had just finished writing, hammered in his head: "You will give your blood to the blood which takes it." He started down the stairs, tentatively, unsure of himself until his foot touched the fourth step.

At the end of the dark passage there was a brighter square, the door. One of the men was crouching on the threshold, bent back and cap in hand, his rifle pointing up the stairs. Now he got up quickly. From the darkness of the stairway and the hall he could

*see them, the men of the patrol, moving about, regrouping them-
selves. One of them bent down to pick up a match he had
dropped, struck it against the stone, and lit his pipe. His cold
eyes, protruding under a gorilla-like brow, met the eyes of the
others. . . . He had reached the last step. "I'm ready," he said.
"Let's go." He had the piece of white bread between his fingers.*

*They pushed him around without a word, organizing them-
selves clumsily for the march. When they had him in the middle,
they started off. . . . The gamecock spread his wings and ran,
almost howling, a peculiar outcry foreign to his species. From
behind the drawn shutters the neighbors peered out and he was
just able to see Justa's horrified face. She was the youngest daughter of a farming family which had come from far away and settled
in Europe. He had always said to her, seeing her stand in the doorway when he came home in the afternoon, "How silly you are,
Justa, your face is so blank." And she had always replied with the
same word: "Boy . . . boy . . ."*

The frightened face disappeared from the window.

You will give your blood to the blood which takes it. *No! He
felt that scream inside himself, that ferocious scream: No! No!
His throat was working. No! Why should he give it? But, within
him, another deeper voice was speaking, an ancient familiar voice
which seemed to issue from the source of everything, from the
primeval earth itself. It was slower, steadier; it spoke—oh, tortured and almost eternal!—from the very depths of his being:*
Yes. (You will give your blood to the blood which takes it.)
Yes. . . .

*They went through the darker parts of the town. The lime-
whitened walls of the houses made an icy glare on the stones of
the narrow road which lay between them. "Where are we
going?" he asked. The men were slouching along in disorderly
fashion and some of them began to laugh. "You'll have time to
ask later." One of those in the rear said something jokingly which
he could not make out, but he heard the reply: "You'll be surprised!" And, from another, nearby, with a broad coarse smile:
"Don't worry!" Routing two startled goats from their peaceful
pursuits, the patrol turned into a wider, better-paved street which*

*was bordered on both sides by neat ditches about a wagon's
breadth in dimension.*

*Just where the pavement came to an abrupt end, there was a
sort of small hill and, beyond it, a narrow lane. The houses here
were old, decrepit, bathed in the dull orange glow of the lanterns which hung from the rotting window frames and above the
doorways. The doors were open and armed sentries stood before
them. He had to make a real effort not to ask himself anything, to
bridle that icy taunting rage and keep on walking; without asking
anything, without asking himself anything at all, he saw the fear
and surprise fixed in a sort of stereotype on the faces of the few
civilians they passed.*

*They stopped suddenly in front of the largest of the buildings,
an old farmhouse transformed into a barracks, whose cracked and
peeling walls were covered with obscene posters. The leader of
the patrol—that corpulent man with the new red scar across his
face—left them and went inside. Two of the others walked over
to the window and sat down in its embrasure. With rifles
propped between their crossed legs, they rolled cigarettes and,
whistling cheerfully, began to smoke.*

*The leader came back with an officer of some kind, a pale
young man, very well-groomed, whose whole appearance was in
sharp contrast to that of the soldiers. His eyes gleamed; their
shrewd, suspicious, and concentrated glance seemed to pierce the
darkness.*

*The poet stepped forward. He spoke with a certain vehe-
mence, as though his spirit, too, had advanced a step. "I am . . ."
he began.*

*"Yes," the officer interrupted. "We already know who you
are."*

*The soldiers laughed and one of them yelled, "Sure we know
who he is. . . . Sure!"*

*He looked at them, disheartened, almost desperate. "This is an
outrage," he said. "It's an outrage," he repeated, but calmly,
without any exaggerated emphasis, as though he were merely
testifying for himself—before the night, before God.*

*"You and your ideas . . . !" The officer's voice, his bad breath,
were like a slap in the face.*

"What do you mean?" the poet asked. His eyes glued them-

selves upon those of the military man; he endured without flinch-
ing that superior air, that little mocking smile with the hatred and
suspicion behind it.

"Ideas, huh? Ideas . . ." The soldier laughed again. One of them
was chewing tobacco with the busy attentiveness of some
ruminant beast; the others smoked. The officer glanced toward
the leader of the patrol and lifted his shaved white chin in a
meaningful gesture. They went off a little to one side, speaking
together in low tones. A few steps away from them, the two men
sat in the embrasure of the window with their rifles between their
legs, smoking calmly and contentedly in the dim light cast by the
lantern which hung motionless over their heads.

He took in everything: those men, that low-toned conversa-
tion, the cracked walls of the old farmhouse, the puddles of water
on the ground, the infinite reaches of the night, and his heart felt
oppressed, heavy with doom. He thought about his mother and
his sister; he saw him in his mind's eye—who knows why?—
stitching at a black rag, pulling out the stitches again, tugging at
the black thread. His mother's hands showed the wrinkles of
seventy years of middle-class poverty. Seventy years, in the midst
of which he had come into the world to give her a brief pleasure,
a prolonged sorrow. The brief pleasure was over.

He looked at the endless night, the sparse stars, he smelled the
hot moist air. . . . He wore a hat, but no tie; the collar of his shirt
was open at the neck, showing a patch of skin of a shade between
bronze and copper, and the hair just beginning to sprout in the
hollow of the chest, in that bony part where, as a child, he had so
often endured blows and pain.

The officer looked at him from a distance and then went back
into the house. Meanwhile, the leader of the patrol clapped his
hands in a peremptory way, the men sitting by the window got
up lazily, and the group fell into their loose formation again.
"Let's go," said the leader. . . . He knew that everything was
moving toward an inexorable end and his body felt suddenly
empty, emptied as though the blood in it had run out. He was
very white, his stunned white face seemed to blaze against the
night. "I want to speak to somebody first," he said. "It's neces-
sary for me to speak . . ."

But they were already beginning to march again. "Might as well

save your words," the leader had answered, grinning crookedly
because of the red scar that pulled at his lip. They went up and
down another small hill. In the wavering and watery light of that
uncertain moon, their faces looked spent, worn out as by too
much use. The leader kept lifting his hand and scratching persist-
ently at his forehead. Then he would stop a moment and tug at
his cap, only to begin scratching again. Why were these actions
so important? They had, it seemed to him, an eternal validity,
and he watched carefully so as not to miss a single detail.

Where they descended, the hill was rugged, its bare grassless
slope sprinkled here and there with whitish fragments of rock.
The men of the patrol were quite silent now, their heads high and
their nostrils dilated as though sniffing the air, their eyes adjusted
to the abrupt changes of the countryside, the alternating light
and shadow. There was the sputtering sound of a motor in the
distance; a little later, at the point where the road twisted downward and flattened out, they saw it, an army truck with two
sleepy soldiers in the cab. "Hey," they called out, their right
hands raised in a friendly salute, their teeth bright. . . . It was
near midnight. . . . The truck jolted along over the uneven
ground, disappeared from view. Now that the road was clear,
they could see, not three hundred feet away, but almost hidden in
the folds of a ravine, a whitewashed deserted house.

"It's an outrage!" he said. "An outrage! An outrage!" His
teeth clicked against each other as though he had to chew the
words, as though their substance were hard. "There's no reason
for it, no reason whatever!" The words were ineffective; they
simply poured forth—stupidly, unhappily—and melted into the
air. The soldiers seemed determined to ignore that obstinate repetition, not to speak, not to answer, just to keep on going. Their
hobnailed military boots pounded on the stones.

He raised his head and drew in a difficult breath and went on
protesting, with absolutely no pause between the repeated
phrases, himself resolved not to listen, not to think or calculate or
imagine. But, in spite of him, some images transgressed, breaking
through that barrage of words, that concentrated defensive
hammering of meaningless syllables. They invaded his consciousness, took possession of it, filled him with fierce and desperate

anguish. He grasped for words; he hung on to them furiously, hardly blinking his eyelids, his whole face stiff with the terrible effort not to think, not to think. . . . "It's an outrage!" he said insistently. "No reason whatever!" he said. "It will be avenged, avenged!" he cried out to the unresponsive night.

One image, particularly, eluded his vigilance, slipping neatly through the verbal barrier into the cruel disorder of his spirit, the jungle of horror and indignation and rebellious perplexity which was his inmost self. It was the image—distant, rather indistinct, as though blurred over by frost—of the little boy who had been killed in A——, the doctor's child whom he had seen lying on its back in the rain-washed street, the small naked body white and motionless, without blood, without life. And now he himself seemed to be lying beside the child, though his body, his own body, had no shape; it was like a cloud that has fallen, a cloud with open eyes stretched out on the wet stones. "Outrage!" he screamed. "Outrage!" again and again and again. He felt the recoil of the rifle, the numbing blow. And the silence.

It was like a blow, that sudden clutch at his arm and the shove which sent him reeling against the wall of the house. He got up, his mouth bleeding and horribly twisted. The fingers of the man's hand were curved like a claw; they seized him again and knocked him to the ground, and again he got up with that tremendous rage in him and his mouth set in a rigid grimace, a terrible silent weeping. He moved forward to attack, but the man got out of his way. Then he saw the patrol, standing in formation before him.

He let out a scream—a savage scream, the scream of a child, absurd in its monstrous inefficacy—and ran off to one side, toward the spot above which the morning star shone bright and immobile, marking the limits of earth. He was running, his legs hardly touching the ground, when the shots rang out. Bits of plaster fell from the whitewashed walls. A rooster crowed in alarm.

The patrol stood without moving, stiffly, as though waiting for the last infinitesimal echo of the discharge to lose itself forever in space. Afterward they walked slowly over to the body, circling it, examining it intently, pushing it a little with the toes of their boots in order to see the face. It would not have been possible to see it except for the fact that the lime-whitened wall reflected the moonlight.

The blood flowed out slowly; it seemed to crawl out like an animal, making shining patterns on its way to the earth. From the limp, upturned hand it trickled along the rigid wrist and fell to the ground. It moved around, snakelike, until it touched the bit of white bread lying there. The bread became moist and red; the blood soaked into it and through it with the quick avidity of a living creature, like something that is guided, infallibly, by instinct.

The men of the patrol gave themselves up to their fatigue. They began to feel a loathing for each other; in their mouths was the bitter taste of tobacco and bad food, in their nostrils the odor of sweat, the rank sweat of unwashed bodies and dirty heads. They walked separately on the way back; they pulled off their caps and freed their matted hair. Their mouths were half open and they looked up imploringly. . . . But not a shred of comfort came down to them from that millennial sky, only the remembrance of time on its imperturbable march, only the promise of barren fields and sultry lunar weather.

ALL GREEN
SHALL PERISH

TO MY BROTHER
Dr. Enrique N. Mallea
Judge of the Court of Appeals of the Southern Coast

I DEDICATE, WITH AFFECTIONATE ADMIRATION,

THIS CAUSE, LOST

IN THE FIRST INSTANCE

For the waters of Nimrim shall be desolate; for the hay is withered away, the grass faileth, there is no green thing.

Isaiah, XV, 6

For man also knoweth not his time: as the fishes that are taken in an evil net, and as the birds that are caught in the snare, so are the sons of men snared in an evil time, when it falleth suddenly upon them.

Ecclesiastes, IX, 12

PART ONE

I

Forty-four successive days of drought and fire laid waste the hills, the valley, the wild scrub; the earth's sparse and bristly head of hair bared to the sun. In the daylight hours, boundless and distant from the sky, stretching as far as the eye could see, the countryside seemed an endless ashen surface, vast and white. White was the dry earth; white the pastures; white the pampas grass and the skeleton elm. White the *carob* and the *tala*, gnarled and knotted and rigid like dead nervous systems drawn from the earth into the burning air. The fields everywhere revealed the earth's spectral, hungry face and parched mouth, its squalid paw stretching limply for miles on end. Below, cleaving its way through the valley among the *yuyos* like a twisting fissure, the bed of the stream held only stones and a thin thread of clear water, as white as the land around it. From time to time, a lean stray animal approached to drink, then made its exhausted way through the thorny bushes. In all that region of desolation and drought hardly any cattle remained. Sometimes a solitary horseman would appear against the skyline above the deserted house, or a fleeting automobile covered with dust, or, on the slope, a lost calf. All else was barren: stony hills and ridges, to which nightfall alone brought the respite of shade.

Years before, though as sparsely settled as it is today, the region had been fertile. Suddenly the sky seemed to dry up. Now it was so high, so remote, so cloudless, that whoever lifted his eyes to it saw only the reflection of its mortal abdication. In prosperous years, on the other side of the hills, a good distance from the solitary house, a small village had sprung up. In spring, the hawthorn grew green and the treetops were lightly tipped with gold. Then hostile winds brought alien sand from the distant coast; a sand dune camped on the lowest and most exposed spot in the vicinity, and others soon gathered around it in sterile assembly. Great tracts of land on both sides of the hills were spoiled.

The pastures received the full weight of the invasion; the rains decreased; the blighted fields dried up, and the population gradually moved away in slow migrations. Up above, only the solitary house remained. It was like the last refuge of Job in that barren panorama of sterility and death. Near the top of the slope, a four-sided conversation in dumb show was carried on by the white house with its dry-stone wall, the hilltop, the hollow of the valley, and the ever-present hawks.

Carcasses rotted beside the trickle of water where the stream had been. And they were the bones of animals already old, long accustomed to privation and the scorched grass. The few surviving cattle lived by Providence alone. Every now and then, after many weeks of waiting, a large storm cloud would take shape and kindle a choleric hope in the heart of Nicanor Cruz. But he was now so used to disaster that he had come at last to defy his hopes. For by now they were all he had to fight against. The clouds would pass, having brought nothing more than a brief darkening of the pallor of that fearful sterility. Nicanor would laugh—his way of crying. And his laugh, like everything else, had ended by becoming a part of its surroundings. It was as burned-out as he was, barren, brittle. The famous laugh of Nicanor Cruz.

His laugh was like the baked branches of the *tala*, like that great expanse of parched earth and dry grass, as coarse and futile as a curse. It seemed foreign to a creature of God. As they said in those parts, that laugh was not the laugh of a Christian.

The drought was like a conflagration; it burned out the vegetation from underneath, sought it out, killed it in the womb. Some grasses put up a terrible defense, prevailed, bore sap, nurtured themselves from within, grimly held on; others gave in without a murmur; still others seemed to be born to live in that desolate region. Like the moneylender in his lean years, these were sinister from birth. Stealthily, carefully, the sand worked together with the fire of the sun to bring about the destruction of all remaining life. It enveloped the stalks, flew from sprout to sprout, cut away and carried off the small tops of plants, stifled species after species. And when the rain came, brief and volatile, its fleeting and ephemeral visit had no effect on the agents of despair.

This time the drought lasted forty-four days. On the seventeenth of January the last rain streamed down the windows of the house on the hill for an entire day and night. The wet stone glistened in the dark. It was cold that night, and Nicanor Cruz galloped over his land, his leather cape stiff with mud. He galloped along gravely, his right hand hanging loosely by his side, his wet left hand holding the reins. His hands were as dark as an Indian's, covered with dirt, unlikely, mythical, of the color and consistency of a very old piece of leather. Nicanor Cruz galloped over his land. When he returned at dawn to the house, the woman's eyes were still at the window. They withdrew. The next day the sun came out again. The cattle fed, and some of them appeared, dark and lean upon the hill.

Some distance away, on the estancia La Oración, everyone seemed always to live in the best of worlds. There, from the high white tower, the viewer could take in great distances. One could see the town, the bay, the commercial city stretched out along the Atlantic.

Forty-four successive days of drought and fire laid waste the hills, the valley, the wild scrub.

. . .

In the large room, Ágata Cruz looked at the clock. It was twelve. Nicanor was about to arrive. Her heart hardened. She drew the two rush-buttomed chairs up to the table and went out to the porch. An endless file of ants moved steadily toward the terrace. Twenty yards from there the *agapantos* and the privet hedge had been eaten away. Ágata Cruz looked at the hillside, the skinned white slope, the calcinated valley. She breathed in the hot air. The white house stood on an elevation, perched in even repose on the simple columns of the Argentine colonial style. Up the columns streamed the ants, fine streaks against the white-washed stone. A little lower down, in the stable, Estaurófilo was giving water to the lean horses in a large tin bucket. A broad-brimmed black hat protected him from the sun. He was tall and bent, his enormous legs thrust into trousers which hung from his shoulders by coarse cloth suspenders. Apathetic, Estaurófilo held the bucket. The horse drank slowly, like a spent creature. Ágata Cruz went into the house.

The half-open doors and the heavy screen left the room in shadow . . . a hot sticky shadow. Ágata confronted her image in the mirror, lips parted, large vacant eyes, soft dark hair. She ran her hand slowly through her hair, over the firm flesh of her cheeks. Dissatisfied, she moved away from the mirror, went to the kitchen and reluctantly took the lid off the stew cooking on the stove. Steam veiled a young face of extraordinary beauty in which pallor, strain, and depression had enhanced with the incandescence of twilight.

The kitchen window framed the ridge of the hill, naked and scrawny like the spine of a hungry greyhound. The hillside was dotted with stones and shrubs. Near the top, one of the rocks, caught by the glare of the sun, glittered, as if paralyzed in mid-gesture. From there, Ágata could not see the remnants of the orchard, the last line of defense of the garden: vegetables, apple trees, orange trees, peach trees. The privet hedge marked the boundary of the home area.

She heard the noise of the screen door closing. Nicanor hung his hat on the back of the shutters. He was a thin, nervous man with the peevish eyes of people who cannot sleep. They resembled the eyes of a frisky, nervous horse, eyes of impatience and alarm. His dirty shirt, open at the collar, hinted at the beginning of a coppery chest; his neck was stained and black. He sat down immediately on one of the rush-bottomed chairs by the table and started cutting grooves in a little piece of wood. Ágata brought in the steaming dish. The homemade bread, the wine, the lukewarm water were already on the table. When had that silence first grown up between them? Ágata sat down. They helped themselves. For the thousandth time she looked at his hands, bony and olive, cutting the white bread. Living together for fifteen years had estranged them more and more.

While peeling the fruit, she said: "Soon there'll be no *agapantos* left. Everything is eaten up."

He raised his eyes and looked at her. "What can be done till winter? When the hydraulic ram gives us more water, things will straighten out."

But in fifteen years, things had not straightened out. Ágata stood up, brought the hot water, prepared the coffee. He started cutting grooves in the wood again.

"The main part is already done," he said. "This afternoon Estaurófilo will have to help me put in the stakes." Estaurófilo came to the door and stared uncertainly toward the table, waiting. His arms reached down to his knees; from one arm hung a mouse-colored greasy hat, the only one he had known in his thirty years of life. Then he came forward and took the pot that Ágata Cruz handed him and went out, slamming the door. He left a smell of stable and barley in the room.

"He will have to be told," Ágata said. "Otherwise he leaves and doesn't come back until after dark."

They spoke impersonally so as to avoid using the familiar form. They hadn't addressed each other directly for a long time.

Nicanor said he would speak to Estaurófilo during the siesta. She lay down on the sofa, fixing her eyes on the ceiling. He picked up his hat, put it on, and went out. "So long," he said.

"So long," she answered.

Nicanor always worked straight through the siesta. Ágata watched him go down the valley, every day, at siesta time, to the bottom of the hollow, where he was building the new ram. They would get more water in order to save the farm. A wretched, miserable profit, a starvation wage, but absolutely necessary. Since it was bread, it provided them with food if nothing else. She saw him working through the siesta, under the blazing sun. She would have liked to be proud of him, would have liked to be able to care. But she could not. Her heart, all of her, was closed to him. Days and nights had enveloped them in a veil of silence. Nicanor would look at her with rage and hope, and once she had seen tears in his eyes. She would have liked at least to respect him, but rancor was devouring her whole being, just as the *higuerón* was destroying the fine tree near the house.

Estaurófilo returned at night, driving the three horses on foot. Two were sorrels, the other a gray. He spent his life driving horses; he lived with them. He spoke to them. He would feel strange resentments, bear grudges against them, and then make it up. He was gruff and suspicious, and the sound of human speech made him wince. Some said that he was the son of sister and brother; others, of father and daughter. His irrational moroseness was known everywhere, but no one knew his secret. Suspicious people watched him turn sullenly to his horses as if he confided in them his disdain of everything human.

He came back that night, driving the three horses on foot. From five to seven he helped Nicanor mechanically, lending him the service of his hands without understanding what he was doing. After that, he hurried off to see to the horses and brought them back from the pasture to the stable. His hands wet, Nicanor stood up and watched him go. What stroke of fate had bound this poor idiot to his misfortune, to his wretchedness? Nicanor saw him run up the gentle slope. Stooping down again, he worked away laboriously at the gigantic bolt. It was beginning to get dark. He went on working a little longer, then, picking up his tool kit, climbed the hill in the direction of the house. His powerful shoulders barely moved. Motionless, Ágata stood watching him from the porch.

When he arrived, they stood silently side by side, watching the ants. The insects streamed from the ground to the privet by the hundreds, right to the porch floor, then on up the whitewashed pillars. Without admitting it, they both were remembering vaguely the mythical invasions they had been told about in school: Nineveh and Babylon. Nicanor intercepted the progress of the ants up one of the columns with a piece of paper; the black thread turned patiently aside and then went relentlessly on to invade the roof.

"If they find a way to get down inside . . ."

Ágata looked up at the roof, and then looked down again. The blue hills were already changing their skin in the darkness. Estaurófilo, scarcely visible in the gloom, was on his way home to his hut with a bucket of oats in each hand, his light-colored shirt swaying to and fro in the night air, his sleeves hanging straight down, pointing to the invisible buckets. Ágata went to have a look at the geraniums, while Nicanor remained seated in the deck chair with his head thrown back and his feet crossed. Close at hand, the wanton magpies were screaming. Like silent messengers, an *hornero* alighted on the roof and a bat flew over.

Ágata set out along the usual path. At least three hundred times a year she started out on that evening stroll before supper. As she passed, Estaurófilo interrupted his conversation with the horses, stood up, and remained motionless until she had slowly crossed the neighboring field. Then he went on talking. Ágata plucked a sprig and a leaf of thyme, and crushed them between her fingers. Many a time, on going to bed, she could still smell the herb's aroma on her hands; and she would lie face down on her palms. Like Estaurófilo, she knew well the sad substitutes for human conversation. The stardust sky, the hilltops, the forbidden trees, the very darkness, held for her a distinct presence. Here she had taken her questions, complaints, and disappointments during the last five years! She was able to recognize even the shape of the darkness in each place. And of the young trees, she knew even the slightest hue of laughing green and the old ones' way of dying. She knew the nearby message of the water and the signs of coming rain. And of the atmosphere, she knew the song that the last solitaries, the favored ones alone, could recognize.

She crossed the trickle of water, where in the daytime, small lizards scurried among old leaves stiffened by the adverse air. She listened with pleasure to the noise of the water, which was like the voice of a girl who, even though exhausted, gabbles merrily on. She went slowly across the stones and then walked along the hard grassless path. A toad leapt to one side, and a nimble *cuis* scuttled across the fringe of light. A thousand images of her life rose to the surface of her consciousness on these walks. Past and present were one. Only in this way was her life related to her surroundings. On this particular night she was anxious to get back early. She always went as far as one of the first large rocks; now she started back from the stream.

A century-old willow, the only one of its kind in the vicinity, stood desolate, its branches trailing. Ágata thought of the man up there. He had announced that the ram would soon be working, that there would be fresh water for the orchard. She thought with indifference of this possibility. So much had already been lost that to recover a small portion of quiet seemed to her almost irrisory and sarcastic, like a candy brought to the deathbed. All nourishment is wasted on dead souls. But he would renew his promise from time to time, with a sort of blind obsession; and she would listen as she listened to the autumn rains, waiting for them to pass. With sullen, resentful shame, he sought a remedy for his broken soul. Blind to his failure, he summoned up a final hardening of his obstinate will for a last-ditch fight with nature itself. And she, in the face of this hardening, this tenacity, this rough deliberate blindness, could only feel herself taking refuge behind her own compact coldness. She had not always been this way, but had reached it by stages. Years before, Nicanor Cruz's obstinacy, his bitter resolve not to admit defeat, had aroused compassion in her. Later, as time confirmed her worst suspicion, she allowed the poison to reach her nostrils, breathing in the infinite futility and emptiness which he bestowed upon her. Compassion disappeared. She no longer suffered with him. She opened an account of her own in suffering. From then on, his bitterness and hers went each its separate way.

The two were different. His was the bitterness of the defeated male, thrashing about in apocalyptic helplessness, overwhelmed by a reality which resisted all human endeavor and then mocked and laughed at him for good measure. She was hurt; she carried a desert in her womb and a desert in her soul and a desert in her heart and a desert in her mind: she had been dragged by that man against her will to his own recesses of darkness and taciturnity. He was resentful; she was hurt. And both were launched upon life like lepers of time, mutually stripped of charity.

That morning he had said once more, monosyllabically, that the ram would soon be ready. After her walk, she climbed the embankment into the night. There stood the house, surrounded in darkness by the sleeping fields, white, solid, earthy, stretching for miles of wild and living species. The warm atmosphere was like a weight upon her. Nicanor, seated, smoked and rested, a light patch in the darkness of the porch. He must be looking at the mountain sky, so full of stars, whitish dots, and constellations that it seemed a single cloud, placed high up there, deceptively, to hide the real background. Ágata stood there and gazed down below at the black gorge of the valley. It seemed a void, and yet it was filled to the brim with life, plants and insects. Suddenly a firefly flickered like a momentary star in the depth of the night. Then the song of a bird; now a swift bat took flight. It was nine o'clock, but time seemed to have stopped. Neither of them broke the silence. They were at opposite ends of the world there, together, staring at all that which did not stare back, and for which their two lives were of less importance than the life of any flying body which plows and rends the night with its wing, only to discover it in its entrails. Ágata stood there for a long while, her body parallel to the column of the house, her arms crossed, erect. Then with scarcely any inflection in her slow voice, she broke the silence: "It must be time to eat." Unwillingly Nicanor got up from his chair.

II

In the morning, Ágata opened the cupboard and put away the freshly ironed shirts, breathing in the scent of lavender. That whiff of freshness belonged to the circle of her friends. Then, in the passageway, she started to squeeze the oranges and looked out over the valley. The heat was suffocating, and her skin seemed to redden around the white triangle exposed by the open collar of her dress. She thought of the animal's thirst, of Estaurófilo. Did the poor half-wit really feel this scorching heat, or was his skin dulled like his mind? In the evening, she had seen him in the window, standing motionless facing the horses. He had been with them since the day they had settled there one wintry July. And that tall scarecrow of a boy, with dangling arms and vacant stare, had been a silent premonition for Ágata of what was to come. Where would it all end?

Can it be that only physical misfortunes put an end to life? Can it be that all we bear within us the tumultuous sum of our divergent impulses, which can find only one outlet, one conclusion, and not the myriad paths we seek? Can it be that all the directions of the soul end in one single failure? If we contain such a multitude within us, why so few solutions?

She looked at her work and then lifted her head. Fate had endowed her features with beauty fifteen years ago; but nothing that is given to us survives intact. Our original appearance does not determine future growth. It is the inner suffering of the soul which shapes our features. That beauty which had once been praised in so many places had become defensive and withdrawn within itself. As the mimetic crustacean comes to resemble the rock to which it clings in its innermost desert, so Ágata had taken on a certain bitter hardness and the color and consistency of one who has been exposed to bad weather.

Once indoors, she rinsed her sunburned hands of juice and sweet pulp. By twelve o'clock the house was clean and tidy. The pans of fresh water were placed on the floor of the dark shuttered living room in the hope of mitigating the scorching heat. The small kitchen window let in a blaze of light, and it was a nuisance to have to shut the door to the passageway. From the luncheon table one could see the narrow shaft of sunlight on the tiles of the adjoining room.

Nicanor came in and sat down opposite her, his strong masculine face covered with perspiration, his black disheveled hair sticking to his forehead in two limp waves. His mouth was heavily lined by two dark furrows running down from his nose to his chin, and his eyebrows seemed set in a permanent expression of suspicion. Once again, they exchanged a few cryptic remarks about the geraniums, the farm, and the insects that had been feeding on the fruit trees since October. She watched him eat with unchanging appetite, masticating slowly and monotonously. Ágata went back in her mind to her wedding day, to the first knot binding them in their mutual barrenness, and reflected that, actually, neither had betrayed the other. Nobody is bound to become different from himself. She ought to have known in advance that peace was never likely to blossom in this somber man of slow speech. She saw him again as he was in the days of their courtship, standing facing the blinds of the window looking into her room, in the suburb of the city. Was that taciturn fellow so very different from the embittered man who sat before her? Each of us nourishes his own moral offspring in his own likeness. Don't the "facts" of each life really take their tone and form from the soul within? The miser's fortune is never more than abundant poverty. Are not defeats or victories only meaningful in terms of the character of the person who experiences them?

Ágata saw herself behind the window of her wooden house in Ingeniero White. She was then twenty years old, and had the will and eagerness for life of those who have grown up in secluded isolation. Her father, Dr. Reba, compensated for his widower's loneliness with alcohol. The old doctor had originally come from the Swiss canton of Vaud and was a Protestant. After two weeks' courtship, he had married a sickly adolescent. Her mother died when she gave birth to this first daughter, this Ágata who was named after the stone on her husband's desk the sick woman used to stare at in the solitary afternoons. Perhaps she felt gratitude toward that stone which had kept her company during the long afternoons of discomfort.

The doctor did not change his way of living after his wife's death. His life consisted of endless drives in the sulky around the almost deserted village. There were few patients near the wooden house in the port, and as he was usually called in too late, his jolting drives along bad roads at night seemed a mockery, a futile search for death. . . . Ágata grew up with the sand and the tamarisk trees. The headquarters of the dock police—the largest building among the gray-green houses of Ingeniero White—stood about two hundred yards away down the unpaved street, among the hedgerows a few steps from the dock. Ágata's first childhood memories were always tinged with the hazy picture of her father weeping over her cradle in the lonely house. The foreigner, so suddenly mutilated, felt keenly the loss of that young creature into whom he had poured his exile's desolation and who had left him just as a ship on weighing anchor leaves behind the man waving it farewell. Ágata sat on the laps of the many foreigners who came to call on her father, and she played games. She learned early how to mend her own dresses when she tore them running races and playing tag. The house consisted of a bedroom, a dining room, a bathroom, and a consulting room. Of these, the first and the last looked onto the street. For hours on end Ágata would sit watching through the blinds the traffic on its way to the port. With her first friends came the first confidences, the first reticences, and the first bits of worldly wisdom. She learned many things she would think over at night in the dark, unable entirely to overcome her surprise and dismay. These natural revelations brought on little ripples of malice which penetrated down to the soles of her feet. The adolescent began to catch glimpses of the other side of her father, as children do one day. The tender protector of indefinite character began to be succeeded by a very clear picture of an old doctor, half drunkard, half philosopher, really ignorant of the art of healing, who "treated" his patients with the frothy and predictable comfort of his proverbs, observations, and experiences. He was a discredited doctor, a gratuitous distributor of soothing conversation. Sitting with Ágata at the table, in the brief intervals during his twelve hours or more of visits to and from patients, he would talk to her as he talked to them, almost impersonally, like a clergyman who, because he is deaf to the true needs of his flock, talks to himself without being listened to.

The port of Ingeniero White was only seven and a half miles away from the city of Bahía Blanca. The doctor used to go into town, enter his club, have an aperitif there, and talk about the war—the one called "great" at the time. The end of World War One was drawing near when Ágata was thirteen. Like a number of skeptics, being an optimist in the human sense of the term, a Dionysiac demolisher of windmills, institutions, and giants, he was indulgent toward "the common people of God," perhaps on account of the mild contempt he professed for himself. Even to have despised himself more would have seemed to him inhuman and useless. "We are children of one and the same cause," he would say, "and always end up in sin, albeit by different paths." This clumsy professional, in his worn gray coat, who despised philosophy, never read any book but the Bible. But far from being a stimulus to his religious sense, the Scriptures were a drug to him. On reciting chapter and verse, he would sometimes half close his eyes, just as he did when telling his daughter about the founding of the Bahía Blanca, his attention absorbed by the sound of his own voice. His gray and passive existence found ample room for escape in the proverbs of Solomon and the complaints of Ezekiel. From her early childhood, Ágata had listened to those prophetic assertions, which to her ear were like the distant echo of totally removed and unintelligible poetry. The old doctor would often stay up late playing cards with his cronies in Bahía Blanca. On those nights he would return to the port in his other vehicle, the small dogcart, whose iron wheels soon announced the end of the paved road of the city. Ágata was left alone in the solitary house at the port. She fought down her fears to the extent of becoming almost cold within to all imagined dangers, real and legendary. She would fill in her time with thought, asking herself questions about the reasons for life and answering them as best she could in her child's heart. When her father returned, he would find her fast asleep, like one dead, and he would approach her bed filled with forebodings, abashed as if he had known for years that that nascent life would never be confided to him in spirit, as if he were already a stranger to what this tender dream cherished. His hands had not touched any woman but his wife; when she was gone, what could he know about that prolongation of his blood belonging to the other sex? He exercised no parental authority or restraint and talked to her as if she were a grownup. Somehow the girl built up within her the defenses for her helplessness.

After the games in the sand and among the tamarisk trees, the doctor would take her on Sundays to the Ateneo, the nearest movie in the city, where human hearts were joined in fictitious passions. On returning one night from one of these special occasions, she saw in the hall of her house a mixed group of people standing around a dying man who lay on a stretcher. His body had been shattered in a railway accident. She was shocked for many days afterward, unable to explain to her own satisfaction the exact reason for her anguish. "We are all frail animals," said the doctor; "our most terrible illusion is to believe ourselves immortal. Suddenly an artery bursts and we are no more than a mass of protoplasm." She watched him talking, smiling and slightly obese in his gray morning coat stained with the years. This old man never seemed to ask any questions. When he brought her a book, a handkerchief, or the length of a dress, it was never the one she longed for. Being daughter to this strange, evangelizing atheist, Ágata grew up without any belief, hard, hermetic, and shy as a young animal in the wilds.

When she approached her twentieth birthday, her character began to change. She met other girls and learned for the first time—her first welcome thought—that she was beautiful. A gap opened in her confinement. She began to let herself be seen at the parties in the city. Dressed in silks or organdy, the wild flower seemed suddenly tamed. Shyly, she let the men crowd around her, as they exchanged the conceited and distrustful smiles of those who fight for gallant preferences.

As she opened up, the city, Bahía Blanca, also like a flower, but of stone, closed in about her. The founding of South American cities is like a chapter in vegetable biology. One afternoon, on a piece of land in the south of Argentina, a general and a French engineer planned the site of a fort, the development of the future settlement. How many human civilizations had evolved and perished when this bit of desert emerged from its stupor in 1828? Around the fort which acted as a rampart against predatory Indians, the military population started to grow. Four years later, Juan Manuel de Rosas and Charles Darwin stood before those salt marshes stretching out toward the bay. The army brought the stores, the stores brought the traders, the traders brought the professional men, and with the professional men came the tide of transients. At the club, the doctor spoke about the frequent Indian raids, as if he had seen them, the revolt, the lifting of two thousand nine hundred heads of cattle by the army chaplain Bigio, the burning of houses, and the rape of the inhabitants.

Who was going to raise cattle in the face of that danger? The only animals raised were slow-moving ones: sheep. A few bold settlers, some intrepid Italians, dared to settle down; wheat fields started to multiply rapidly; the state thought of founding an agricultural-military colony there. And finally, after a hundred burnings and attacks, after the last raid by three thousand Indians, the city was free of danger. The stone flower began to blossom into a thousand streets. The doctor loved to tell how that remote salt marsh, which in 1868 was scarcely worth seven thousand bushels of wheat, was to become in less than fifty years a metropolis of a hundred thousand, one of the most important industrial cities in the state, and, in the corn trade, the first shipping port of Souh America. . . . "Seven million eight hundred thousand tons of produce from the region in a twenty-year period." The mild atavism linking him to an ancient Swiss canton repeated these numbers with amazement. The doctor had seen the gigantic flower open, expand, spread in the neighboring districts: Colonel Dorrego, Colonel Pringles, Colonel Suárez, Saavedra, Tornquist, Puan, Villarino . . . And he would repeat these figures and these names, thinking them over and going back in his mind to the time of his arrival in the country, when the powerful city was still a small town; reflecting how his name was, by chance, bound to this silent civic conquest much more gloriously than the names of men in the country of his origin to some obscure plot of ground. But, after it had come to full blossom, the city—the flower—started to close up. First, its inhabitants carried it inland; afterward, settlers came from outside to trade by day and then go back. They brought their children with them; they withdrew. In school these settlers' children were Ágata's companions; these fair silent children named Nordenskold, Ricciardi, Vidder, Soren, Senisgaldi; and she would look at them with inexplicable pride. The city had closed up; the prodigality of the country sent them there to study, after which they would go away; after which, in the neighboring districts of the South or on the pampas, they would erect their personal scaffolding on the horizontal cathedral of the tilled land.

The doctor would go jolting into the city every morning, calling on some patient of his at the Los Vascos Inn or the

Lopetegui Hotel. He was an inveterate and opinionated conversationalist, and he liked, above all, to visit these places where, after the temperature had been taken, or the liniment prescribed, he would be invited into the bars for a drink, and in the courtyards overhung with vines he would exchange unending conjectures with the travelers and salesmen. These chats gave free rein to his evangelical propensities. Only when he found himself alone in one of those sordid settings, with a solitary coughing patient, he would assume an air of severity and repeat from memory, whenever the occasion arose—in the shape of a complaint, an oath, or a gesture of impatience—the parable from St. Luke:

> A certain man had a fig tree planted in his vineyard; and he came seeking fruit on it, and found none. And he said to the dresser of the vineyard: Behold, for these three years I come seeking fruit on this fig tree, and I find none. Cut it down, therefore: why cumbereth it the ground? But he, answering, said to him: Lord, let it alone this year also, until I dig about it and dung it, and if it bear fruit, well; but if not, then after that, thou shall cut it down.

This familiar medication did not, as a rule, bring any benefits in the shape of hard cash but more frequently a brace of fowl, freshly killed partridges, or a plucked turkey. Nevertheless Ágata never had any need to deprive herself of the expensive clothes made for her by Medina the tailor, nor the Bordeaux shawls from La Nueva del Plata so well suited to her pale complexion. When the doctor did not accompany her, she would go in the tilbury with one of the stable boys and do her shopping, passing swiftly from store to store. On the way home she would discuss the prices and materials with the boy. He would listen to her with amazement, making clucking noises with his tongue to hurry on the horse. Once, on arriving back from one of these outings, she found the doctor sitting bent over his old writing desk, crushed, lost in his thoughts. When Ágata, at once so intimately related to his life and so distant from him, asked, "What's wrong?" he first kept silence and then complained of his bad luck. Between the old man sunk in the armchair and the young woman seated on the edge of the chair opposite him, any mutual confession would have been impossible at that moment. We are, at times, mere wild mutes. Without looking at her, the doctor told her how a patient of his, suffering from typhus, whom he ought to have saved, had died suddenly through his inefficiency. Another, younger doctor who had been called in had brutally thrown it in his face: "You'll be killing half the population with your medicine of wait-and-see!" His only answer to this youthful insolence had been a look free of anger. Where life rushes in, age has no rights. He raised his head and fixed his tired eyes on Ágata. "It's time for me to retire," he said gloomily. But her instinct discovered another cause for his sadness. What was preying on his mind was not the advance of old age but his everlasting inefficiency. In three years, he had saved none but those whom God had saved, and, in the long run, who knows if his uncertain hand had not been, by some ironic twist of fate, on the side of death. Helpless, Ágata watched him suffer like an ox that night, in the poorly lit study. From one of the walls, the venerable head of Louis Pasteur looked down. She looked at her father's hands covered with light hair and freckles, swollen, ineffectual. A great pity swept over her, an infinite compassion. But how could she find words to ease a pain whose cause belonged to the dominion of things? Ágata rose and placed on the old man's head a hand even more unskilled than his own. She tried to mumble something, and her voice broke in her throat, as if she knew it was useless, before speaking. Although it was an effort to go out—they were comfortable and warm inside, thanks to the gasoline stove—the cold August night surprised them walking in the open air.

III

At that time, this man still young, now chewing his fruit in front of her, had not yet entered her life. It seemed incredible to her that there was a time when she hadn't felt the hatred, the rancor toward him that now completely pervaded and sickened her. There had been a time when she had considered bearable the caress of those hands, the touch of those selfish and coarse claws which at that moment looked so dark against the skin of the apple.

Life delights in cruel games and at times seems to practice its sarcasm on a single person. When, passionately curious for intelligible proofs, for reasons above all, Ágata was twenty, her closest friends were Delia Novo and her brother Matías, a young man with a stammer, a long nose, prominent eyes, and a thin neck. Her other friends lived in the city and she rarely saw them except when there was a party. Delia Novo had an incredibly limited mind. She and her brother were two almost vegetable creatures, swayed only by foolish fancies. The world in its magic phase—how Ágata longed to transform it into intelligible signs! Her lonely childhood, her lack of childhood, had nourished in her a boreal prudishness; she was afraid to confide her questions uselessly and consequently was forced to live in the world within her, in terms of dreams and unfathomable mysteries. But at that age, who can resign himself to the unknowable? One wants to know at any cost the limits of the unexplainable, the true nature of certain mysteries, the exact boundary between spiritual and carnal love. How misguided is he who believes that those who have renounced the flesh are the great metaphysicians! There is no greater torment than the fever of rich—that is to say—divided natures when they try to see beyond and concentrate their gaze upon the prospect of the desert. With no religion, no vocation for reading, this young girl born by the Atlantic, spent long afternoons questioning the unanswering waters. As the force and volume of her thwarted instincts increased, and fever, sleeplessness, and loneliness grew within her, she came to feel a hatred for the wooden house which had never given her companionship and where her mother had died. She soon found herself seeking desperately for outlets. She knew that in each being, marriage releases and evokes life, and she asked herself what her other possible existence might be like after this first lonely one. With what kind of soul would her own be blended? The chatter of Delia and Matías during those nightly walks along the docks of the small village past the tamarisks did not accompany her as closely as her own restless speculation. She pretended to listen to them, but in her heart she wondered when her virgin life as an abandoned orphan would come to an end. She developed within her a fearful impatience, and for three months, the doctor, on his return home,

found only the muteness of an imprisoned animal. He knew only
too well what the young animal required, but he didn't dare
broach the subject; on the contrary, dissembling and evasive, he
shirked it with a certain guilty cowardice. He refused to imagine
what his own frustration might become if he were forced to live
alone. And Ágata instinctively understood his attitude, his passive
willingness to condemn her to the same lot. She understood it
instinctively and rebelled against it by means of her harsh silence.
Sometimes, on returning from her distant calls, the doctor would
tell her stories about her mother, whose total fame had consisted
in having once given a piano recital. Her teacher, then in her
seventies, a Miss MacGregor, had been one of Liszt's pupils at the
Pest Conservatory.

At the dances at the club, the city hall, or the Sud-Americano
Hotel, once or twice a month, Ágata's spirits changed, and of that
inner shadow, only a nostalgic hint remained hidden in her
laughter. Like the moss that covers the stone, this well of sadness
attracted men all the more. She sought among all those coarse
heads, heavy shoulders, massive jaws, determined brows, brutal
laughter, drinking mouths, hands used only to working the soil,
that secret rhythm which would suddenly dominate the body we
have before us and make it desirable, different, beloved, necessary. She found nothing but petulant superiority in manners and
attitudes, blank, indifferent faces. She would agree to drink a
glass of port or an orangeade with someone, and as they drew
together to dance, would place her hand on shoulders to which
she was completely indifferent. She would look with shining eyes
and parted lips at the reflection of the lights in the salons, in the
rooms which always seemed to be somewhat bare with the bleak
austerity of aulic sheds. Here, all the money of the district managed to make its presence felt. In the women's dresses and the
men's rings, there was a timid attempt to show off. Once diffidence and suspicion had been overcome, *la compadrada* came to
the surface. This was precisely what Ágata found most repugnant
about these simple people, these strugglers—the possibility of the
braggart hiding under the cloak of docility.

After these experiences, she would return as one returns from
the hunt, tired and empty-handed. More days of muteness, cold-

ness, boredom. Her boredom! What constant occupaton and careful labor that slow, dull, perverse boredom entailed! It was indispensable to attend to it, care for it, live with it, quiet it, advise it, shelter it, calm it, feed it. It was as if she bore within her a tyrannical invalid. An uncontrollable intruder, now vociferous, suddenly drowsy, then torpid. She awoke with it, carried it about with her while she did the house; she took it to the window with her to look out at the casual passing cyclists, at the merchant sailors, at the girls returning from their errands, at the Turkish peddlers crying out their cheap wares. She took it out for a short walk before midday under the shady tamarisk trees lining a nearby land. She took it to the table and mixed it with a dry, merciless rudeness directed at the doctor, who had become garrulous. She amused it in the afternoons when she sewed clothes, and in the evenings, with long walks along the paths across the grass where the fields began. Finally, she smothered it at nighttime as she turned over the pages of the magazines, looked once more through the yellowing pages of a collection of the fashion magazine *La Moda*, discontinued since her mother's death. Many a time, during the night, no longer able to bear the loneliness of her room, she would dash to the window, open the shutters, put her head out into the cold air, gasping, like a dying bird. The wind lashed her eyes. It was as if it blew her own ice upon her, something sharp and bracing which was good for her. If only she had had a sister, a brother; but she had no relations except the wind and the ocean, the great cold that came at night. At other times, she would wake up just before sunrise, when the outline of things still assumed in the dawn a vague blue wakefulness. She would go to the street door and watch the fishermen pass by, then she would return to her room and begin to darn a pair of socks, the doctor's shirt, garments that smelled of an old man. She would then go to the door of his room and watch him sleeping. The small, stout body under the blankets let out two different kinds of snores. His forehead was covered by a disheveled lock of whitish hair. Ágata once more felt a terrible pity for that poor old man, who was as lonely as herself, and wept to herself, at dawn, for him. Why, her conscience asked itself, are our feelings so different from themselves, so contradictory and tremendously versatile? We have not yet ceased being cruel, when repentance already gnaws at us, and just as we are about to humiliate ourselves, dark pride once more takes possession of us. At that moment, she would have given her whole life, she would have renounced all other happiness without complaint, had she only been able to attend to him; but she knew that when he awoke, when that shadow started moving again, when that mouth framed one of the Christian proverbs, she would feel the same hopeless desolation, the same aggressive confusion. . . . Many a night, as she watched the rise and fall of the tides from the end of the dock, she had compared her own condition with the mass of indomitable water. Those waters rocked the shipwrecked bodies on their merciful surface, airing and consuming them by moon and sun, but it was enough for the waters to feel their weight a little to awaken their animus, for them to rise in wrath and swallow the guilty object.

Pulled in two directions, Ágata felt rage and pity for herself. She detested herself for loving herself. She hated herself because of that. She would rather have been deaf to her anguish, as Delia Novo was deaf to all the shades of hunger. She envied the honest, the sober, all who replied to the world's offer with self-restraint and acceptance. She was of a different race. She suffered hunger and looked it in the face, admitted its presence within her inmost self, told herself, There it is; and her look took on an exacting brightness. It would have seemed to her an act of hypocrisy to turn her eyes away from her thirst, to lull herself with deceiving songs, to drown in the noise of the outside world. No; she knew that sometime or other she would have to offer her soul to somebody; that sometime or other she would have to offer it in exchange for another strange one, for love; so, the only loyalty was not to mutilate her demands, not to reduce or impoverish or falsify them. Exterior falsification was enough; there was enough pretending to the outside world; what was within her should be untouchable.

Suddenly, at one of the many parties she went to, in September, she met Nicanor Cruz. He passed in front of her unnoticed on the evening he was introduced to her. She preferred to dance with the friend who was with him. Later, as the evening drew to

an end, she began to notice the obstinate insistence with which
the eyes of this well-built man with his lemon-colored, almost
greenish complexion, sought her out in the throng of people.
(Years afterward, he would remind her of the questions he had
asked her at that dance; she had completely forgotten them.) It
was at the Sud-Americano Hotel, and the room was full of Englishmen from the railways—engineers, businessmen, farmers,
dealers in cereals. A bank clerk followed her about the whole
evening, trying insistently to lead her toward a promissory conversation. She made no attempt to disguise her annoyance, and
the bank clerk, his pride touched, made a fresh advance in which
he did not hide the venom of masculine punctiliousness, nourish-
ing his tenacity. "You're wasting your time," she told him, and
he bit his lip with rage. Then she danced with the traffic manager, an old railway man; next, with the two friends who were so
alike. On the way back to Ingeniero White, while her father,
who was considerably the worse for drink, drove the creaking
dogcart, Ágata thought of the dance as an anonymous show, and
could not retain clearly in her mind any of the faces she had
seen there. She remembered standing at the refreshment table, a
glass of dry sherry in her hand, listening to the stout assistant
traffic manager as he described his native village of Carnarvon,
the capital of Wales, in picturesque Spanish interspersed with
bits of English words.

About that time, the doctor took to drinking as never before.
He felt suffocated at night. He dreamed aloud and was bad-
tempered and grumpy from morning to night. He was rough
with his patients and every now and then, from her room, Ágata
heard an angry retort. One evening when she had gone out for a
walk along the waterfront, she saw him emerge from one of the
local bars built of corrugated iron, a thing she had never seen him
do before. She caught up with him and saw him home. He was
half-delirious, his tie all stained and the legs of his trousers rolled
up. He had rolled them up in a rainstorm three days earlier. That
night Ágata sat at his bedside until he fell asleep.

When she no longer felt any resentment toward him, she experienced a sense of rest, but at the same time her loneliness was
redoubled.

A nearly constant wind beat down on the bay. The calm days were few and the sand from the dunes was carried in by strong gusts of wind. The sand penetrated every corner of the house, piled up at the entrance of every door, won its way into the bedrooms, opened the yards, blinded people in the street. Each house was turned into an island. From the backs of the innermost rooms could be heard the constant whine of the raging wind. The windows had to be closed, the lights had to be turned on in broad daylight. The inhabitants were obliged to live buried inside their rooms, which smelled of stew and stale bread. Lips became parched. On looking into the mirror one discovered nearly invisible grains of sand in both corners of the mouth. The dust would sometimes last for days. Ágata came to hate the climate more and more. She already regarded it as an influential protagonist in her life. Sitting in the dining room, she would remain huddled up under a blanket for hours, doing nothing, listening to the fury outside. The house was gloomy; the neighborhood almost unpopulated; only the tamarisk trees were there, enduring the ferocity of the weather as she herself had done from infancy. With each passing moment, it seemed more impossible to her to come to terms with such hostility. She was an animal at bay. For her, the world of men was something wild and wooded, where it was difficult to penetrate the web of deceit. She began going to town with the stable boy to pay calls. Dressed in her simple clothes, quiet, correctly courteous, she talked, during these calls at the country houses and in town, of a thousand different topics which didn't touch her spirit. She listened politely to the particulars which she was told, and answered amiably. Conversations that might have been instructive to her, or that referred to books or art, left her as indifferent as those that referred to the changes of weather. She slowly and carefully explained her father's ailments and was reserved as regards his future health. But every now and then, someone would recount a dramatic incident involving a personal passion. Then Ágata's eyes would light up with a sudden flash. Her whole body would lean forward, hanging on words which seemed to come from a kindred spirit.

It was strange, as she was so completely removed from any spiritual vocation, that she should be naturally so refined and alert. She spoke with slow assurance and her instinct saved her from any lapses into bad taste. Ágata was conscious of this instinct and found her bearings quickly. Like a fox in a cage, she looked upon the movements of the outside world from a remote distance. By one of those paradoxical tricks life plays on us, her need to escape from her solitude, far from opening up new channels, seemed to erect inaccessible barriers around her. Those who approached her mild outer flame didn't know what deserts they would have to cross to reach the depths of her being. Only this incorrigible Nicanor Cruz, who would not open his eyes to anything, was actually going to stand in her way and stay there, obsessed by her fascination and prepared to enjoy her to the full.

One night, her father brought him into the dining room to give him an aperitif after having attended him in his consulting room, and Ágata recognized the man she had danced with weeks before. He was sparing of speech, heavy in his movements, crafty in appearance like the country people. "Just imagine, Mr. Cruz has asked me to go out shooting with him next month at his place, several leagues from here where there are still red partridges!" Mr. Cruz was standing there, with the dining-room door behind him, his eyes fixed on the woman he desired. She knew instinctively why this stranger had come, what his idea was when he sought the protection of the doctor. For the first time, laughter burst forth from the depths within her, convulsive laughter that she locked away, turning the key on it four times, in order to greet the newcomer. What irony! The laugh was strangled in the bleakness within her. She poured out two glasses of vermouth, and almost immediately, without any transition, experienced a strange sensation, a painful relief. She could compel steps, direct them toward her, create in them obscure ponderings, mobilize controversial instinct. Could it really be so easy to leave this gloomy house and emerge into life? If this man had come, others would too; the flock, the sheepfold in the center of which is the one who cannot be resisted, who demands recognition, whose form one knows beforehand. The conversation was full. Nicanor Cruz spoke slowly. His words became monochords as they ascended the mountain of a phrase. Although he was not provincial, this rhythmic slowness gave a peculiar cadence to his speech. The doctor had taken a fancy to this stranger who had come to him bearing a valuable letter of introduction, and immediately offered him a splendid opportunity for cynegetic glory. When, having exhausted the usual topics, Nicanor rose to go, the conversation had reached a dead end. The doctor offered to drive him back to town. He accepted the invitation, and together they got into the dogcart. Ágata did not miss the obstinate covetousness of his eyes, although the hand which held hers was evasive. He looked at her from the dogcart, and the doctor with his whip signaled good-bye. What was going away in that carriage, the black hood of which she saw ascending the slope, diminishing and disappearing? How can the proximity of a stranger who is indifferent to us nevertheless encourage vague questionings, open the door to obscure possibilities?

Ágata went indoors laughing—she remembered it now—willing to forget it or jokingly to talk it over with Delia. But as she went to her room, she sensed the physical presence of a door leading out of that closed house. It was as if, in a dream, scarcely a yard away, she could see a doorway opening out onto space. She went to her bed and lay down. The palm of her hand touched her old coverlet without feeling it. (Many times before she had squeezed it in anguish and then smoothed it out.) Her eyes turned obliquely to the window; she wasn't thinking of the man who had just left, but of her own life. The wind was silent, the night calm. About ten, the doctor arrived; his eyes were bright and Ágata guessed the stages into which he had divided his journey. She felt the dry smell of sherry saturating his light morning coat. But, as usual, she never asked him a word about that. Halfway through the meal, she questioned him about Cruz. The doctor told her that he was the son, the only son, of an old speculator in grains and that his father had started him in business with a small estancia. They were silent again for the rest of the meal. The dining-room lamp gave out a milky-white light; by the table shone the black leather of the two spare empty chairs, almost never occupied by guests. Months before, a distant relative of the doctor's had arrived for lunch, dressed in the uniform of the Salvation Army; another time, an Italian priest. That night, as on other nights, Ágata slept without dreams, and dawn brought no special joy. But the days that followed were not the same. Nicanor Cruz paid recurrent visits to the doctor and by his tenacity succeeded in making her dance only with him at a party at the club. Perceiving how things were progressing, she told herself in all honesty: "I don't like this man." But he was always before her, solid, silent, unavoidable as a stone.

Ágata had to know exactly who he was, how he lived, what kind of nature there was within him. He tried to tell her in a thousand ways, either through the doctor or through some friend who reached Ingeniero White with indirect messages. Ágata looked away, did everything she could to overcome that obstacle so as to look beyond it. But life compels us to accept its challenge. Whichever way she turned, she always found the same thing. And on the other side were the wind, the gloomy house, the fine sand, and the unchanging tamarisk trees. People looked upon Nicanor Cruz as an excellent match. He was well-to-do and sound in soul and mind. Though the father was an impossible old miser, the son was a good sort of person. Not extravagant, to be sure, but methodical, and moderation is the virtue of the middle class. Settled in the country, at a short distance from Bahía Blanca, Nicanor Cruz spent whole weeks in town. He went to the clubs, played an occasional game of cards in one of the cafés, and watched the hard-fought ball games in the fives-court of the La Marina Bar. He was well reputed to be virile, and disdained the weak inclinations of those outcasts to whom fools sometimes refer as "learned" or "cultured." He knew only the hard and straightforward language of life. All the rest was effeminate, useless. Nicanor admired physical courage and enjoyed tales of manliness, those narratives in which a moan never comes from the lips of the mutilated hero, in which the male defies life when it harasses or tries to dominate him. He liked rough words, dry wine, the challenge of a card game, dark clothes, unsugared maté, the docile female, but all this, passively, without boasting, as if it were a secret creed which suffices if it is within one. For he never swore nor drank, nor sought pleasure in women, and he gambled in moderation. Those were his standards of heroism; he didn't need to practice them, nor did it matter. He was content to lead a life of sober virility, without striking poses. He did what he thought he ought to do and nothing more. By nature a "loner," he detested politics. The inflexibility which never left him made some people in town wink at one another as he went by. They called him *el amargado* (the embittered fellow).

There was no reason why he should be. He wasn't really embittered, merely taciturn. He was the son of who knows what cruel, mysterious moment in the life of his parents. And his misfortune was the means by which Nicanor Cruz first touched Ágata's spirit. What dominated her then, was a great appetite for passion. That was the peak. But below, at the foot, slept the feminine lake. One day, one of the stones flung by that sad and tenacious being touched the surface of that lake. Ágata raised her eyes. It was one afternoon when they were talking, while waiting for the doctor at the door of her house. She raised her eyes and saw, in that body she didn't like, the shadow of a misfortune. It was the first time she had really looked at him. No woman needs more than this. To look just once. The seed is in the earth. That afternoon, when she opened the window of her room and gazed at the port and the tamarisk trees, something fundamental had changed, the flight of her soul was suddenly held in abeyance. Rather than wait for the expected one, was it not perhaps her destiny to create, to build, out of two griefs, peace?

She immediately rejected the idea. No, love is not that; and one has a right to love, to love itself, not to what differs from it or resembles it. During the days that followed, she avoided Cruz. It bothered her to see him one afternoon through the shutters, standing at the corner, patient, calm, expectant. Whenever the doctor referred to him, she eluded the subject, and said to a Miss Aguirre, who had come on a subtle errand, that she could not give that man any hope of courting her. Some weeks went by; nothing happened in her life. The doctor was still a prey to his unfortunate weakness; the August wind beat itself against the docks with more fury than ever. Cruz settled in town and nearly every evening managed to pass by the gloomy house in Ingeniero White. He killed the rest of his time at the Confitería Jockey Club, listening to a group of friends or watching the endless ball games at La Marina. At night, his friends dragged him to the stalls of the Coliseo Theater—whose name was an insult to the right-thinking people of the town—a nest of scandalous French-women; and later he would automatically go along with them to drink half-liters of beer at the Kayserhof Hotel. Ágata found out afterward that he never spoke a word about her to these frivolous acquaintances. They only noticed his increased silence, his air of caring nothing about anything. The women at the Kayserhof Hotel laughed at the contrite giant. . . .

Meanwhile, what desolation and silence in the house of the port! As the cold of winter increased, Ágata's outings became less frequent and she experienced the weariness of women's conversation. With the eyes of an animal that has received its death wound, she heard only that insipid, monotonous chatter. If only she had been able to incorporate a germ of variety into her life. But when we are made for waiting, how can we manufacture within us the disposition to attack? On cold days, she walked to and fro about the house, glanced once more through the old magazines. In the solitary dining room she turned over in her mind her usual obsession, as she watched the coming and going of the patients at the consulting hour. They were rough men of the merchant navy, sailors of coastal traders, Englishmen employed in growing enterprises, men suffering from secret diseases. Frosts fell, it was terribly cold; the weather kept her incessantly at the back of the house. Was she going to sink back once more into that incredible destiny? To be entirely confined behind those panes, dulled by damp cold, to bury herself deeper and deeper? In the insomnia of dawn there came to her mind the image of that sad man. . . . She would get up, move about, perform house-hold chores, to forget the intrusion. People who appear ferocious and dry on the outside are often vulnerable within. She wondered what her life would be if one day the doctor were gone. Would she have to wait till then, and with what luck? Why should all hope be necessarily triumphant? Supposing that instead of glory, time brought her only boredom? If, instead of something better it brought only misery and more misery? Lying on her bed, she struggled with these questions. Why is a woman a being reduced to waiting? Why couldn't she go out and find out for herself the quantity of illusion she might allow herself? Why is a woman of twenty inferior to a she-wolf, a heron, the roaming animals, who freely chose their way for themselves in God's open country? Why is the female of the "highest" species the least free, the most guarded prisoner?

One afternoon, the doctor told her that Nicanor Cruz was going to call for him. When he was there, she heard them talking in the dining room, and unlike other times, entered the room before they left. Simply dressed, Nicanor gazed at her with gratitude in his heavy, serious eyes. She behaved politely and Cruz would have preferred to stay, but the doctor dragged him off, assuring him in snuffling tones that the political situation of the province was hopeless. "A pity, the elections," the doctor said. "If the radicals had been less confident in their attitude . . . but everyone wants to win, and it will all end in failure." It was exactly one week later when Nicanor Cruz, who was standing guard at the corner, approached her one afternoon.

"I want to marry you, Ágata."

He said that one winter afternoon in August, firmly and yet diffidently. Many years later Ágata was to see how decisive determination in him was often stifled by some strange inhibition. It was as if this timidity were a superficial flowering, an anguish sallying forth and putting decision to rout. She smilingly dissuaded him. They walked together along the quays. He told her of his solitary life at the estancia, the need he felt for a companion. She was looking at him; she had already given her answer. "I'm not a gay animal," she said. But that night, during her last vigil, her decision was taken.

It is strange, very strange, how life intervenes with its voice in our life. When we want to move we have often already been caught, and the step we take no longer belongs to us. Even the strongest wills obey only the orders of a rhythm that is alien to them, in which they are compromised. What power impelled her from her home forced her out, and delivered her to that man whom she didn't love at all, of whom she knew so little? When she said, "I'm not a gay animal," she was already surrendering the animal within her. But when we feel that it is life that impels us, we no longer resist, not even to survive. Those who shut their eyes and hang themselves, or throw themselves over a cliff, life no longer loves; and what prompts them to kill themselves is not death, but life. What is most mysterious about the suicide is not his courage, but his resignation.

Ágata accepted that agreement with all her will. She shut her ears to the deep song that dwells within us, like a river, sometimes heard and sometimes voiceless. She let the strange river flow within her, but didn't hear it. She didn't hear the siren of illusive probabilities, but rushed into immediate action. The doctor did not intervene; he bowed his head and approved. He thought that perhaps he would one day be welcome to the luxurious calm of a prosperous estancia, with tall casuarina trees and a lake and a park in which to wander and meditate. The wedding was fixed for December; the doctor's birthday was on the eighteenth. Cruz went to Ingeniero White three times a week, and after having tea at the doctor's house, walked with Ágata along the docks until well after nightfall. Theirs was the halting conversation of the silent, full of wariness, of incipient allusions. They were seeking motives for diversion. A remark, a grotesque passer-by, a funny-looking ship would cause them to burst into short laughter. She had not interrupted her nocturnal worries; on the contrary, sleep would overtake her much later than formerly, while she was grappling with incessant questionings; but this time, they didn't concern herself, but him; what he was like, what mutual aid they might lend each other in their new life. She also thought of the purchases she had begun to make—white morning dresses, hats, household goods—during mornings spent at El Siglo or at the Bazar Colón. The wet floors smelled of new lye. The gradual building up of the new scene she was going to live in awakened a strange sensation in her; it was like gradually acquiring the coins with which she would buy her separation from these winds, this solitude. What new people would cross her path? "The first years, the two of us will make an island of ourselves," Nicanor had said to her. She thought of the sunlight, the calm, the green of the sown fields, the rustic beatitude that surrounds the thistle, and pictured the serenity of their future island in communion with that sea. Everything is better than the bitterness that awaits the melancholy one.

What a commotion there was for three days, caused by the

wedding in the house at the port! Now that she had finished her meal in the house in the hills, with this man who seemed a stranger and who was then the hero of those festivities, she remembered it. He silently chewed the cooked beef. She saw once more the house on her wedding day and said to herself, "The walls which had considered me their property since birth were spying on me." While preparing her trousseau with her friends, she could feel the eyes of those bare walls fixed on her movements. She felt their harshness, their ruthlessness. There is no greater ruthlessness than that of things. That look devoid of clemency oppressed her until the last minute. For two days before the eighteenth, the doctor kept arriving with numerous parcels and a fragrant basil flower in his buttonhole. (When he visited some wealthy patient, he always used to pick a sprig of thyme or basil from the gardens.) The nails, the wire for the garlands were ordered from Morel and Lamaison. Delia Novo went to and fro about the house, from the kitchen to the dining room, excited and irritated as if the event were all for her. Nicanor Cruz did not hide his pride, an arrogance so great that it turned his features into a mask of rigid pallor. He went in and out of the house, supervised the preparations, bought this or that, undertook the payment of whatever was overlooked by the doctor during his absences. The delivery man from Bahía Blanca brought the purchases from the confectioner's, a freezing apparatus for making ice cream had been hired, benches they had borrowed for the long tables. The Italian priest who was a friend of the doctor's visited the house more than once, on the pretext of tendering fortuitous advice, and in passing the row of cakes, would pick off a sugar ornament or a cherry. Ravenous children gathered, openmouthed, by the door: "*Via, via,*" the priest would say in passing. They parted like the ears in a cornfield and returned to the door. The children made her smile, she liked them so. On the last morning she saw herself all dressed in white, her lips so bloodless that it seemed to her when she looked at herself in the mirror that they belonged to a ghost. Cruz contemplated her without saying anything; it was only later that he asked her: "Are you happy?" She smiled. With the doctor, they both entered the dining room full of people; the priest stepped forward, happy and beatific in his sacramental robes and ornaments. How many strange and unknown people! So many people, people who went to few parties, their eyes shining because they were there, having a good time, enjoying the port and the spongecake. And, when she smiled, why didn't she feel as if she were smiling inwardly as well? Oh, the abyss, the inner abyss, and its inhabitant, the tyrant of the soul that never rests, the somber lunatic who scratches at us from within! It was hot, and the murmured words seemed to rebound from the closed shutters. The three railway engineers were dressed in black. One of them had presented her with an inscription burned into a board: "Holy and pure are the drops that fall when the young bride goes from her father's hall."* Nervously, since dawn, the doctor had squandered his proverbs, looking at Nicanor Cruz, or whoever was near; ". . . the path of the righteous, like a shining light, goes before, and increases until the perfect day." He would repeat meaningly, "and increases until the perfect day." When he did not speak, his lips seemed to continue murmuring inwardly. The old man kept on changing from laughter to seriousness. If anyone had gotten near enough to him, he would have heard in those murmurings the tone of a prayer for his own approaching solitude. But, on being taken inward, he would have repeated aloud a saying he had invented and which was his favorite: "I am a moral centaur; I have within my body a man, accompanied by his antagonist." At eleven, he went to the street door and welcomed a lady in her seventies, dressed in black and covered with rings and cameos of the nineties, who descended from a tilbury with difficulty, as befits ancient immovables. The two Misses Caronti arrived a little before noon, just at the hour announced for the blessed sacrament. What was the meaning of this sudden devoutness in a house of unbelievers? The friendship with the Italian priest had committed them to this modern liturgy. Satisfied, he kept vigil by the great table, wearing his stole like a representative of the Lord, standing on the surface of the turbulent waters, triumphantly bearing witness to the faith. And all the guests there seemed strange and unknown to one another, barely united by circum-

---

* In English in the original. [Trans.]

stantial curiosity. The words of the priest resounded as if from a hollow. His voice was hoarse, slow: *"Ego conjungo vos in matrimonium."* The doctor waited, his head bowed on his chest.

Contrary to custom, they stayed on until late afternoon. Ágata benevolently listened to the advice tendered by the elderly maiden ladies. In the dining room there was a smell of green magnolias, cheap powder, orange-flower water. For a moment, Ágata thought she was going to faint—many months later it would still make her sick to think of the acrid, last scent of orange-blossoms. They were going to slip away unseen. Only the doctor sought her out, approached her in the hallway, looked into her eyes, his forearms on hers. Neither one or the other, exiles from the realm of speech, would have known what to say to each other. Ágata noticed those bloodshot eyes, that colorless mouth, that forehead as yellow as the skin of the dead, that body whose life would leave it before long. "Take care of yourself," she said.

Through the back window of the carriage that was taking them to the city, she looked back when she reached the rise. Behind her she left the port; there behind her, she left solitude, there behind her she left her childhood. Soon they would reach Chiclana and O'Higgins streets, the Central Hotel. As the December evening died away, the solitary hamlet she was leaving behind seemed to her a vanquished specter, a dead moan paralyzed in the throat of time. Many times she had thought that at that moment she would feel joyful. But what weighed her down now was a strange affliction. It was like leaving prostrate and helpless the being whose inert immobility has held us in bondage, but from whom we cannot part without ties, which, while we flee, still bind and hold us in a sort of abstract stupor. Each one of the parts of the world was overwhelmed by its immense desolation. Rigid was the steely sky, rigid the gray air, rigid the dark-green hedges, rigid the wooden dwellings; rigid the circular space where the coast ended. That land could bear nothing but malice. Agata gazed long at the sky. She felt deeply afflicted—bereft. Her childhood was a province of that inhospitable, rigid, gloomy territory. Those dead limbs had left her mutilated, but perhaps she could be saved. In response to a gesture from Nicanor Cruz, she ceased to look through the back window and turned toward him. It seemed to her that, within that provincial coach, another world was beginning.

IV

They finished their meal. In spite of their various precautions, the heat was intense in the whitewashed dining room. On the table, a finger of clear water remained at the bottom of the jug.

"Everything they sold me was of the worst quality," he said, "and I paid top price for it. This year they had very poor grain. But they only think of themselves. Collect your money and let the next fellow take care of himself. . . ."

"There's nothing to be surprised at," said she. "Over at La Oración they've always been like that. The old man died in a bed whose sheets hadn't been changed for four months."

"Yes," he answered, "but when some important person comes from the ministry, they serve him a feast. They give him fat turkeys and over dessert they plead poverty."

She wiped off the table, and he watched her as he stood, his face covered with sweat. For a moment, during that long silence, he was forced to think how much less unpleasant it would have been to sit there and talk in harmony, without reticence or bitterness. How often but one step, a thing of no importance, separates us from happiness; yet, to take that step which is so easy, is more difficult by far than crossing the sea of life itself. Nicanor Cruz slowly crossed the room and from the window contemplated the valley strangled by the sun. On the borders of the scarcely visible line of water the ground reverberated.

"To think," he said, "that to bury the old man at La Oración they wrapped him up in one of those filthy sheets . . ."

Ágata did not lift her eyes. She continued wiping the table, then she went to the kitchen and returned. What did one more cause for horror matter to them? The whole world was rotten and the ulcer might appear anywhere. If the word charity had not been invented . . . But to what sarcastic end did it exist? Why make life more brutal with illusory palliatives? Hell would

be bearable if the word paradise did not exist. Why grant ourselves stations beyond those of which we have knowledge and
experience? There was only one station in the world: the gutter.
But what we wanted, it seemed, was a refuge to run away to. She
remembered the corpse of that old man devoured by flies. In the
light of the tallow candles, ten relatives at La Oración anticipated
pecuniary reward, the material juice of the dead man. But did
this voracity differ essentially from the solicitude with which a
husband takes from his wife the part he considers his own? Don't
we all feel like ignominious rulers over the rights of those we
love? Nothing satisfies us in the lives of others, except what they
cannot give us, except the inalienable part.

That afternoon the intense heat raged even more. Exhausted by
the vile weather, Estaurófilo seemed to stagger between the
horses trickling lukewarm water from the two buckets hanging
from his hands. When she went for her evening walk, Ágata saw
him, his dry lips, wet skin, and wandering eyes. He looked so
forlorn that it seemed to her that she was seeing that half-living
man for the first time! She said something to him, but without
being able to attract his attention. He had been with them for
twelve years, and during all that time they had never noticed any
change in him! He was a crushed and distant specter, a feeble
sparrow, indifferent to the hawk as it swooped down on him.
They had just settled on the little farm at Los Cardos, near Bahía
Blanca, when they found him one autumn morning sitting by
the fence on the open road. He didn't answer when they spoke to
him, and seemed so exhausted that they carried him into the
house. Where had this will-less shadow come from? Where was
he going? They let him sit in the pantry. And after some days a
laborer got him used to sleeping in the shed. Only the horses
attracted him—the tame grays—and he found himself the humble
job he would never leave: to serve them. Long afterward, Ágata
considered that his arrival had been like a substitute sent by the
hope which had disappeared two years after their marriage. Time
is measured only by those in agony. In such a short span as two
years so many things can die. Now, as she looked at the night sky
in the first days of March, her throat as dry as the air, she
thought of the summer when they arrived at Cruz's estancia for

the first time. Some cattle were grazing on its thousand hectares, two hundred of which showed, on the other hand, that they had been sown with corn. It was wonderful to see the fertile landscape, so green and luxuriant in its homogeneous expanse. The grimness of Ingeniero White was here fruition, a future. Ágata's laughter came to know a little more of her mouth.

"In a few years," said Nicanor, "we'll be able to leave this place, live in the city and return on visits. . . ."

A lover's promise. He loved the soil too well for that proposal to have been made with any other intention than to wheedle her. "I'm going to love this," said she, caressing with her gaze the beautiful, fertile summer, and the farmhouse with its lookout. It was a small house built by the first settler in those parts, a rich and sedentary old Frenchman, after the model of some European villas: a white square with a gallery of blue panes of glass and a lookout. The windmill made the pleasantest of sounds at nightfall and the mornings were so fresh that one bathed in the air. A garrulous and flippant man called Caligosa, who lived in the vicinity, jokingly claimed that he had invented multiplication because, each time he thought he had lost all his money, the best of buyers suddenly appeared. Caligosa had lost a son as the result of typhoid, and he wanted to build a school so as to give it his name; but when he had collected enough money the devil tempted him, and in three nights of playing monte the cards robbed him of it. Sometimes he would come to tea. When Nicanor told him that he was changing the name of the farm and that instead of Las Flores he would call it simply Ágata, the neighbor became alarmed. Was he going to tempt fate that way? The name of an establishment or a ship should never be changed. "Bah!" Nicanor said, mockingly. What was the use of believing in such things? All the farms called Shamrock had ended up as dry grass. . . . Who could believe in good luck! "Those things are just not done, my friend," repeated the other, denying him. "They are not done." Friendship with a third party is what newlyweds need. They wish to seem united before others. When Caligosa left, they remained alone once more in the countryside, exchanging their knowledge of nature's variety when they met with the unrecognizable song of a new bird, or a flower whose name they had only just learned. What a joy those mornings were! It amused her to make that silent man laugh. She and Nicanor would ride along the sunlit tracks between high grasses, passing wire fences and owls, stopping among the walnut trees to talk for a long while about the countryside. Sometimes a laborer would accompany them. Nicanor superintended pensively; they were building their cathedral, not vertical but extended in time, which in rural language is called the future. Some books came to the house by chance, but this young married couple only understood life. A copy of *Martín Fierro* slept forgotten in the corner table, together with a collection of *The Mosquito* and a *Geneviève de Brabant*. One afternoon Caligosa left a copy of *Facundo* behind; the book aged on a table in the bedroom without being opened.

When his strong back was turned to her, Ágata looked at this big man, making him out; the stuff he was made of was ambition, reserve, mistrust. And he never gave of himself. On Sundays they amused themselves for a while watching the girls dressed in red muslin and their air of offended dignity at the compliments of the tipsy workers standing in the doorway of the store where there was a bowling alley. In the evenings they would enter the bar in darkness, where early films were shown to an audience of customers seated at the tables. But the wave of silence was lying in wait, was about to fall upon them. Cruz's optimism soon came to an end. Taciturn, Nicanor thought only of the buyer of his grain; his mornings and evenings consisted of the same caviling brooding. He soon returned from laughter to his air of silence. How Ágata wished that through an expressive torrent of words, the life of this elemental being would completely drown the somber fire which still remained in her heart! But his attitude, far from helping to put it out, seemed to add fuel to the fire. She had to fight alone to kill herself, so as to give Nicanor a docile body and a spirit without reticences. He took them while scarcely returning from his abyss. How could she attract that deeply gloomy man? Full of hope at first, it was not long before Ágata became demoralized. It was the monster of incalculable silence which was to devour them in the end.

Everything in life is commerce, a great or small barter; gambling is commerce, a vocation is commerce, loyalty is commerce,

affection is commerce, love is commerce. Woe to him who per-
sists in not paying what is required. A capital in passion is not
increased with the coinage of moderation. Living in common has
only one fortune, and it is that which develops compensatory
coins in two beings. Ágata remembered with a sensation of sickness that slow, profound defining of the two capitals which she
managed with her husband. Maybe the great fault lay with providence for having endowed her with an intelligent sensibility
when she should have been obtuse. She was uncultured and rude,
but inwardly sharp as a knife, and each new ranging thirst she had
within her, overwhelmed, exalted, and fatigued her. Happy are
those who have but a single object; winners or losers, their desperation is exhausted in unity. But to live each day externally,
stifling through disuse our inactive wealth, our inner thoughts . . .
She saw that man bent over his accounts, stupid about them,
without solving or understanding them. He was blind to what
was not shown, not palpable and evident, like a burrowing animal. "Come here," she would say, and help him. He would smile
pessimistically. "What do women know of these things?" She had
the intuition of a recluse; but how put an end to the arguments of
an obstinate man? The first year, Nicanor miscalculated what he
should sow, and had to sell at a loss. He would half-close his eyes,
he could not explain it. Yet, with an immediate foreboding she
had warned him of precisely that possibility. How can those who
are only related to the most immediate reality distrust women,
related as they are to the moon in their premonitory and prophetic aspect? At the beginning she had a tender kindliness for
Cruz's confusion. She saw him become hardened in the fight, give
up his calculations, and go stubbornly into the fields to fight hand
to hand with the soil.

There is nothing more like a dune than the sands of the spirit:
the slightest breeze lifts them, whirls them around, and casts them
in the eyes of the man who does not protect himself. To put
down what she felt rising in her, the sands of a certain new
defeat, the fear of becoming more sterile than ever, Ágata needed
a solid element, just one resistant and concrete thing; and as her
husband, with his spirit dried up before maturity, could not give
it to her, she thought of producing it from her womb. But that
desired stability—a son—did not come either. Nothing came but

silence and more silence. Worry. Losses and more losses. While she proposed imaginary trips from her hunger for wandering, seeing things, leaving her own environment, the man who had brought her into his company was confining himself all the more clumsily within himself, clinging to his defenses, becoming one single being with himself, not out of self-love, but because of a foreseeable error: that of wishing to be more consistent, more himself before the woman he loved. The most precarious thing contained in certain undeveloped masculine types is the belief that the more a thing controls and confines itself, the stronger it is. In this manner, when it most wishes to love, to save, it only kills. Those who live only with iron, kill and die by iron.

As he fiercely shut himself up within the narrow confines of his manhood, in his certainty of the future, in his contempt for little weaknesses and despairs, she began to lose herself at times along those compensatory paths which the imaginative person knows too well. From the corner of his worries, keeping manfully to himself, Nicanor began to look askance at those escapades, the counterpoint of his gloominess. He was suspicious; suspicious of himself, of what she thought of him, of what was working within her. Human eyes are fatally partial; he would have been amazed to the depth of his soul could they have shown him that it was he himself who had first placed that coin of incommunication and reserve in circulation.

Occasionally on Sundays a distant relative of Cruz's would come from Dorrego to visit her, and in that aged and enfeebled flesh, suspicious and dressed in mourning, in that tapir-like profile, Ágata saw with horror the conjugal destiny which awaited her. Willfully closing her eyes, she threw herself toward that man. She would dash against his terrible silence and break it, dig in the dry earth of Nicanor Cruz until she found the source of water. For months she outdid herself in motherly care; the woman in her wanted to tenderly undo that hard knot of atavistic defenses; and she despaired. What was the use? Why deceive herself as well as Nicanor? What was the true value of her company, her smiling confidence, and continual encouragement through all the monotony of his farm work, when she knew in her heart the brutal fact that beyond him everything in her was death and that he would let himself die in his rigid defenses so that she could be born once more for him, for them both? Of what use to her was her desire to make a human being out of that stony entity as solid and sure of himself as a rock? Could she forget that rainy night when she went out to receive him holding the lantern high? How could she forget those resentful eyes which were sullenly raised to her? For the first time, she was certain that a feeling of inferiority gnawed and tore at his entrails, slowly, inevitably turning him into a desert of bitterness and resentment. "You think I'm a primitive," he had said to her one night, "a rudimentary type; you can't get enough mental oil out of me." Standing before her, he stared at her, with that suspiciousness and sour remorse which time would only increase and intensify. In vain she had tried to show him the uselessness and injustice of such thoughts. From what tormented progenitors had this suspicious and distrustful man come? He felt that his mind was dull, his words insignificant and hard to utter. Day and night this deficiency turned him against her with obstinate and systematic blows. She talked all the more, insisting on filling bitter silence with animation, loquacity. She laughed, she jeered at him, she exhausted all her means. By way of reply, he merely gave up his morose rejoinders and took on that smile which now never left him—a slow, bitter, false smile. It was the attitude of the male who knows full well what the female thinks of him, and who when he sees her coming, feels only contempt, disdaining the margin of superiority with which, to his cost, the other is clothed.

This was the cancer from which sprang the degenerate cells, the new, growing tissue, making a way for itself and destroying the healthy parts. Of that dry, gentle man she had known, in the afternoons on the quay at distant Ingeniero White, all that remained was this castaway, immersed in his hard resentment. Her morale gradually slipped away from her leaving no more than a wayward body which was lent, never given. In the mornings, when she served him his coffee, she saw him doing his best to dissemble the malice of the growing story; Ágata was aware of all he would have done to wrest her from herself, to save her, but the organism on which he lived lacked that joy, that possibility of hope without which any battle is lost before it begins. Once a month, the doctor would come to lunch. After the first effusions, after having accompanied him on his outings with a Winchester slung on his back, mealtime for the three of them seemed to be a kind of waiting for something absent. They were three strangers, with few words to exchange, met together to eat the roast sprinkled with salt and water. Faced with that picture of which she was a part, Ágata painfully asked herself if she didn't carry this compulsory dryness everywhere. "Am I the one who imparts this desolation, the poisoner of the air, the one who makes it arid and unbreathable like this?" No. Only too clear-mindedly she understood that for her husband their first days of married life had been the perfect gift; neither in the deepest night nor at dawn had there been any gratification which she had refused for the consummation of pleasure. If the retreat of that virile tide originated anywhere, it was not in the flesh, nor elsewhere in their marriage, but in some troubled zone of that primitive psyche. He had discovered that a woman's heart is a house with many concealed rooms not easily entered; but instead of waiting for time to open her doors to him, he somehow felt like an unwanted and inadequate guest, a pariah in the house of the other soul. Instead of wishing to enter, instead of trying to live in and fill those rooms gradually, he drew back, became sullen, and with an almost congenital solitude shrank away into his own quarters.

The doctor saw none of this on his two- or three-day visits. He was very old, and his mind was becoming feeble. The sight of a red partridge put a single theme in his mind, just as a bat might on entering a prisoner's cell. Ágata saw him dying by degrees. Sometimes she sent him white quince jam and in return would receive fat letters in which more than one sentence was out of joint. During the cold of August he would arrive at the station in a summer suit and heavy overcoat. "Poor Father," she would say to him, "poor Father!" She would have liked to know how to remonstrate with him, but their language together had always lacked that knowledge.

Ágata looked thoughtfully at the stream whose current was so weak that a willow branch had fallen in its midst without moving the water around it. The breezeless night had encompassed the surroundings and occupied the whole countryside. It was March, but the autumn still had a long time to go before it would take over the watch from that unfortunate summer. To think that she hadn't felt her father's death! She was so inured to adversity that she had had no reaction to that sudden blow when it came. It was during the fifth year of their marriage, and they made a hasty journey to Ingeniero White to gather up what remained of what had once been Dr. Reba. The neighbors hesitatingly told her how he had looked one morning when the servant girl opened the door of his study. He was fully dressed, with his body half fallen across his old desk, the pale-red reflection of the lamp shining on his back. His stiff cuffs showed the large and anachronistic cufflinks. He seemed to be in a tired sleep, surrounded by dusty books, with his bottle of cough medicine standing beside his already cold skull. Ágata thought: if he had at least had time to repeat once more "This is the rest; give rest to the weary." But it is the most usual thing for the visitation not to give the spirit time and to fall on its victim as swiftly as the guillotine. Nicanor accompanied that corpse as though it were just one more of his many problems. His rigid face showed only reserve. After consulting Ágata, he solemnly gave some of the dead man's belongings to the neighbors—old silver objects, mildewed pencils, medals—and ordered that the consulting-room effects should be auctioned off quickly. Nicanor kept the old Bible for himself without enthusiasm, a large Spanish edition translated by Scío in archaic language with innumerable personal commentaries scribbled in the margins in pencil. On the trip back, the afternoon sky was the same as upon the day when they had set out: gray, leaden, somber. In the train, she told him some stories about the old doctor and the question she used to ask him in her childhood; Nicanor listened, making no comment. Then he asked a few things about the life of the doctor's family in Switzerland. She answered him as one answers a child, trying to make the dialogue seem like a very important, very deep conversation. She added details, went out of her way so as to tell him about simple characteristics of her father. She attracted Nicanor through the interest of her voice, which embraced the most insignificant words. He listened, staring out the window at emptiness.

From that time on they began to live like animals. God! Is it possible that men cannot rise when they have fallen to the bottom of their own abyss? There is no journey more remote, more of no return. No journey more ominous throughout its long hours. Deeper and deeper within, ever more within. Fleeing first through bearable regions, then desert after desert. And this journey of Man toward his abyss, toward the almost inhuman source of his being, that return journey to the original solitude from which we all spring, that most cruel of journeys, where we are forever finding the worst emptiness of all, the void of bitterness, the vacancy of silence. The vacancy of those who bear the "accidioso fummo" within them and pay their vital pittance of hellfire with the dreary melancholy of their lives. If Ágata had read Dante she could have identified their breathing in the lonely house! "Tristi fummo nell'aer dolce que dal sol s'allegra, portando dentro accidioso fummo." Where morality is concerned, we are susceptible to all diseases. The one who lives with us must pay for our faults. Great is he who kills himself in his wound and restrains himself so as not to waste the body of another; but the law of the species compels the darkest surrenders and abdications. One day she had fallen into extreme despair. "What is this? How can we live together killing each other this way, without even becoming angry, without hatred, and always this passive dragging of sordid mud?" . . . He looked at her as though saying, look at yourself. Could she expect a child from those physical struggles in the darkness of the night? What kind of monster could have been produced by those violent rendings, those muffled screams? Both still wanted to keep that last point of contact, the compliance of their flesh as a refuge of hope, but when they gave themselves, they came together destroyed. The open window cast a gloomy light on the naked bodies and a voice seemed to say: "Why persist? After that mad effort you will return with me to agony. . . ." (How intensely he now harbored his resentment against her! How impotently she enclosed herself in her slow bitterness!)

More and more they lived like dumb, rudimentary animals. The affairs of the farm went slowly, without improvement, without change, and Ágata no longer joined with her warnings in the making of the plans. Nicanor and the foreman decided everything. When the latter came to the dining room once a week to share the table as a guest, he looked inhibitedly at the woman who

ate with downcast eyes, indifferent to masculine calculations. The
Basque cook served the meal. Only when Caligosa came, she
would talk slowly with him over their small glasses of port wine.
As he was a man of some reading, he would write out ingenuous
passages for her and she would take them up, multiplying them,
with her intuition alone. She would listen to him until it was late,
staring at some invisible spot. On returning from the worker's
shed, after tiring out his horse, Nicanor could not hide his impatience with these conversations. Roaring with laughter, Caligosa
would say: "There's certainly no philosophy in this fellow!"—
unaware of the boiling oil he was pouring on the wound. Nicanor
would go into the house to wash his hands.

"Philosophy is a good crop," he would growl between his teeth.
Caligosa continued to be very jovial. He would turn to Ágata,
winking in Cruz's direction, saying: "I've never seen anything
wilder." Ágata added something to the story which Caligosa had
told. The interpretation of a legend seemed so absurd to her!
Caligosa defended it stammeringly; anyway, they were only
things out of books. His tone accentuated that relative condition.

Temporarily reduced to inaction by impotence, by delibera-
tion, Ágata didn't dream of the city, nor of the worlds of fiction
or travel. Something deeper called her spirit, where the secret current ran untouched. During the day, the continuous tension did
not let her think of anything but their cruel situation, the ruin of a
companionship which could have been clean, translucent; but in
her sleep below the level of conscious thoughts the human forest
appeared in all its infinite variety, the plethora of possible coun-
tenances, attitudes, gestures, physiognomies, the most different
forms of spirit, the most dissimilar features that the earthly traveler can perceive in a human face. In the lucidity of nocturnal
insomnia she saw herself fused with her illusions. In those encounters she opened up like a flower to zones of feeling seemingly dead. She saw herself projected in a thousand rebirths before
those faces which came unexpectedly into her mind. When
Nicanor's decrepit aunt, a murmuring ruin in mourning, came
to live with them for three months, she acted as a temporary
catalyst for Ágata. The tension lifted a little. Ágata entered more
deeply into her dream. She saw herself leaving the world of the

taciturn and entering into the rhythm of love. A young visage
was bent obliquely over her, bringing with it a fresh breeze. In
that unknown mouth there was an insistence on taking her out of
her bitter confinement—she heard her own inner "Yes, yes,"
listened in the shadows to that whispering insistence. Her rap-
tures received the aid of climate. She remembered now that
sunny days had extinguished those internal constructions, while
thunderstorms revived the poetic state of mind. How many times
the storms on the feast of Santa Rosa had passed over that trance
which lifted her for a while from her monotonous vegetation!
And wrapped up in the rains which battered the wheat in the
four corners of the district, seated in the doorway of the house,
watching the play of lightning, the unceasing mobile curtain and
the falling of the water, she soon felt close to many human lands.
Ah, probable accidents, possible meetings! One had to wait years
for them, and then perhaps they came in a single moment. The
important thing is that they should find the soil of the spirit fertile. Welcome all external frustrations so long as frustrations
from within do not come!

Ágata tortured herself in that way. The world, the world
which she did not know, began not in this spot, not in this little
lost farm, but farther off, in the realm of her imagination. When
she thought in this fashion, her almost expressionless face would
light up from within and she was even ready to go out with
Nicanor to a rodeo. Her communication was open to all that
invisible world. She would even forget herself, ride behind him,
and look only at the immense horizon in the March landscape,
thinking that one had only to pass beyond the next curve to find
something else. In the moments when she escaped into her dreams
and hope temporarily dominated her, she seemed a fortunate
being. Her eyes lost their hardness and the evening breeze welcomed their brilliance. Above, a walnut tree survived in the middle of the countryside. The cattle gathered around it in a large
circle. The Shorthorn and the Aberdeen Angus were now reduced
to mixed breeds. But, like the spectral hardness of the windy port
of her childhood, what could these animals, this landscape, this
large clump of alfalfa, the low clump of wheat define, except their
island, in that vast tract of unbroken plain? Her non-world, her

non-life, her denial of human commerce. At her side rode the man on horseback—rough, pensive; he did not lift his eyes from his immediate task. He detested any liberation from that yoke and did not wish to free his soul, but rather to bind it more and more to the soil. Such was his law: soil, soil, soil. And what the free wind swept from that self-enclosed being was everything except the knots, the stern partnership, the embrace with the dusty roads hundreds of miles in length, along which the thistle crawls.

When she thought of her other ruin, the economic one, she would think back to the tenth year of their marriage. Sales went from bad to worse and the stored grain was rotting; in the end it had to be sold for nothing. And yet the sun did not rise black; it rose as usual, shining and magnificent. The biblical disaster gnawed slowly at the wheat, at the linseed, when it did not smother them at a single blow. At one time it was ashes, at another, hail. A clouding over, then nothing: the dead body of the grain, the great sowings of lifeless grain. She wept the first time she saw it; after that she was hardened. Then she became like the others: lips that uttered no complaint, hands that were ready to start all over again. At the end of ten years of mean combat, Nicanor decided to sow all the farmland. The wheat ears grew bravely in August. Each day the eye confirmed that liberation of grain, that irruption toward God. The laborers' horses wended their way along the edge of the immense enclosure, of the ears of wheat raised en masse, suddenly bent like one head, by the north wind. There were days when Ágata felt confident: her husband returned with silent fatigue, he would repeat some casual saying. One of the workers had made it up? Nicanor would assent, pointing out the man from Catamarca, Vélez, or the immigrant, as the author of the witticism. Then he would become silent again; but in the nightly sleep of the house, bitterness slept during those weeks. They went to Dorrego more often, and Ágata laughed in the shadows of the bar where they showed films starring the handsome Raymond Griffith. She remembered an afternoon when they talked with amazement about the unusual loss of color. They were returning from Dorrego to the farm, the reds and blues were real sunrise tones and not crepuscular, over where

the plain seemed to rise; soon the colors were gone, the air remained black; a narrow gray track between posts appeared on the
road; they drove through as though they would never arrive. The
old Ford looked like a poor dark insect on the rough plains. They
seemed so small, so mean, so inadequate, sitting in the front seat
of the car in the desolate magnitude of the landscape! Now and
again they would see an owl perched on a post, an unexpected
hare would jump, a sluice gate jutting obliquely in front of the
car as though intending to attack them. Only in those moments
did Ágata feel the nearness of God. The immense, flat countryside showed her the great disproportion of Man, his limitations,
his insignificance. In that unbounded expanse one seemed abandoned and far from everything; and yet, like a single shout, it
seemed possible from there to reach eternity, the universal sky.
No limits between one and infinity. At the same time, what a
miserable sensation it is to be traveling side by side through the
desert without a spoken word! Sometimes there is a person, a
sentiment, a date toward which we can divert our thoughts,
toward which we can jump over the metaphysical pursuer. But
neither he nor she could do anything other than measure their
separation.

That was the year when Nicanor played his trump card. Each
day he examined what he had sown, the same way in which a
doctor tenderly observes the health of his beloved. On going
once to meet him, Caligosa found him laughing to himself. This
single harvest would make up for many years of economic insta-
bility. "If we can pull through this . . . ," Cruz would say, his
eyes anchored in space. In the evenings he would look through
the catalogues from Buenos Aires. With a blunt pencil he marked
a cross alongside the radio set, the chosen object. Ágata also had
to mark out on that list of wares what she wished to buy. "It will
be revenge at last," he said angrily. "One doesn't rot away at
work in vain!" Soon he included a journey up to the capital in his
plans, but the idea of Buenos Aires, that other desert, left her
cold. Worse than the desert, the multitude. This made her wonder if in reality she knew or didn't know what she wanted. The
world or her bit of peace? Restlessness or repose? Who knows?
She was only conscious of her thirst, of her insatiable thirst. The

more we expect from life, the less we know what we want. What limitations could she dream of, to her demands for another life? What she did know was that she was not *that*. She knew that her womb had not given her her bread. Deep within, she knew her body had taken on the form of a great omission, just as the form of darkness is its omission of light.

Winter passed without bad frosts. Though his crop was not yet out of danger, Nicanor felt secure. He exulted. His hope had an inexplicable bitterness, an inexplicable impossibility about it. On the night of the tenth of November, Ágata played her usual game of solitaire after dinner. In the afternoon a very cold breeze came up from the south. Now, on this very hot day, after five years, she could remember the details clearly. Nicanor opened a window; slightly worried, he went out into the fields. He was there for a long time. He returned silent. She was surprised at his refusing the usual tea. When she asked him if he was not feeling well, she tried to put into the question a solicitude that she did not feel. When she awoke the next day, he was already up. She saw the untidy bed in the room, the cast-off sheets. Ágata was preparing breakfast when she saw him come in, his face pale, like a man struck by a thunderbolt, struck dumb. He went to his room, refusing to show his face. He turned down the sleeves of his shirt mended at the collar. "This had to be," he said dryly, and then, "I am the one that brings disaster. Out there all the wheat is frozen." He motioned with his head toward where, for so many years, the sound of wheat ears had covered the fields. He was cold, frozen like his wheat. They went out together and saw the ruin, the glumes containing the dead flower, the great burned tract, the frost's crude jest on the feast of San Martín de Tours.

She felt compassion for that poor beaten man. She had to lift her solitude by the roots before that specter which from then on sat opposite her at the table, more abrupt than ever, which never spoke its thoughts or feelings. As she had never felt love toward him, Ágata had to make a superhuman effort to build up an attitude which would not contain the shadow of herself, but the reflection of an invented tenderness. But how was she to reach the wounded man, if behind him was the other one, that resentful monster, more alive than ever? The more she fought to win the necessary battle, the more she was aware of how much bitterness and wrath were about to explode in that other body. There were moments when it seemed to her that she could see him physically blow up, that she would see that bronze-colored human box break into pieces from impotent grief and rage.

What lonely silent nights in the gloomy house!

They could not continue on the farm. Nicanor was mortgaged down to his bones. It was necessary to look for something else, to make a fresh start, but on a humbler basis. The old usurer was tired of this unproductive son. Cruz made short journeys to Bahía Blanca, to Dorrego. Through pride, he would not go to his father. He! He was going to beg? At last, with the details of some nearby farms, they set out in the Ford on a number of journeys of reconnaisance. He got along with monosyllables. From then on, they began to avoid addressing one another directly, to speak with systematic evasion. In the evenings, when the Ford ate up the miles, only the sound of the engine would be heard. She wore a gray tailor-made, and he never discarded that dark suit with worn lapels and sleeves. They saw farms as squalid as the dogs that came out barking to meet the car. Betrayed once more in her efforts, Ágata patiently bore those excursions through the benighted countryside, those departures at dawn, that endless search for a rural hole in which to thrust themselves. By then there was nothing left in her heart, nothing as they returned each night, but the mark left by the sight of the dry grass, the solitary carob trees, the bent posts, the unending wire fences. Desert, desert, within and without; and despair and weariness. She thought that the worst had come when her great inner fatigue gave its form to everything outside; when each tree, each animal became to her eyes the symbol of a defeat.

v

On the first of March, they came at last to this ridged countryside where they had lived for the past five years. For the first time in his life, Estaurófilo had gotten into the Ford, bounced on the back seat among the bundles of clothes, all through the trip, his frightened eyes sought in the summer sky the road they were following. But the muteness of the sky had also been made for the just. Only Ágata heard him utter an unintelligible sound every time they passed a new mill. After a drive of five hours, with still a long way to go, the three of them were almost suffocated by the vibrating and the dust.

At last they reached the high land, spreading itself in the solitude of the hills, and they stopped the car at the threshold of the house. The sunset gave the ridge a bluish somber color; having played their part, some shades of red were just departing on the other slope of the hill. The combination of those fading shades of color gave the place an air of abandonment, desertion, and exile. The house seemed to have been forsaken a century ago. The paint on the walls had peeled off. "They say it is all right on the inside," murmured Nicanor.

Ágata got out, while in the back of the car, Estaurófilo, fearfully, seemed to have reached his last hour. As she saw those deserted rooms, saddened by the sunset, Ágata felt a weight on her heart, and at the same time a great bitterness; and drowned in the inmost recesses of her soul, a grotesque sense of injustice. Through a window that was too small she saw the dry stone fence, which ran below like a meek herd of rocks. Far away, the whitish and bristly pasture carpeted the plain. That would be her horizon. And then Nicanor was saying: "We shall have to work pretty hard on this . . . Molas had told me it was better, I don't know!" And the insipid exclamation bore a curse against so many inaccurate reports.

This was how this stage of their lives had begun. Nicanor hired some temporary laborers. With great pains, they had to recultivate a land which was already so tired, that it seemed to complain at each shovelful. Nicanor worked sullenly, trying to hide his humiliation and confusion. What could this desert produce? At best, poverty. In his innermost self, this beaten man, his aspirations exhausted, nursed from then on a still more muffled rage against that other being with whom he lived, and to whom he would no longer be able to offer the slightest hint of his manly efficiency; to that being who had already discerned in him, in each look, the defeated and definitively obscure man.

He looked at her as if saying: In your heart you have buried me, I am dead. And she stared at things, tired, mute; she stared at the fields and at the sky.

Summers came; winters came. The great loneliness came. The now permanent silence came. And the hatred.

Many times she wept, in the still night, pressed against the pillow! Many times he went outside to smoke! . . . The house seemed to be a station of sorrow.

Months and years went by like a nightmare.

Now, forty-four successive days of drought and fire laid waste the hills, the valley, the wild scrub. And Nicanor believed he had solved the irrigation problem, thanks to his ram. If Caligosa had been there, how he would have laughed at that obsessed man! How much better it would have been to wander once more in search of another land, or to say good-bye to his last ambition and accept a job as a salesman in town!

But who could tell this son of a despot that his fate lay in rotting on a regular salary and dice games on a café counter? Far from being disheartened, the thoroughbred prize fighter is blinded by blood.

Every afternoon, Ágata went for her walk. Conversations with the shrubs, long dialogues with trees and clouds, brief interludes with the song of a blackbird! She always went up to one of the first big stones. Here she sat down and sometimes discovered to her surprise that she was talking to herself. Life, what a joke! We are hardly out of one hole before we find ourselves in another. Who can be proud of having abandoned oneself like a cut ear of corn. We give no one the keys to ourselves, and the lonelier we are, the more we shut ourselves up between walls. Solitary beings, immured in life!

Sometimes, in the kitchen, she was overwhelmed with disgust. She spent days without eating, and after preparing the spaghetti, the meat, the lettuce, she would lie down without tasting the food while Nicanor Cruz slowly ate. He said nothing. He made the usual noises as he poured the wine, as he set down the bottle, as he cut the bread, as he chewed the mouthfuls. . . . Deep inside, he despised that incurable woman, that madly obsessed being lying on the bed. If only her soul had been less proud, not so cold, imaginative and presumptuous, everything could have been different. There would not have been that silence, that abyss which lay between two inhabitants of the same house, at the same stage of life. But we chain ourselves to something unknown, and afterward, all is anguish, difficulty, despair, daily bitterness. Life cannot be made over.

Quite frequently, though without such regularity, Ágata managed to get hold of a newspaper from Bahía Blanca. She devoured it slowly, from the advertisements on the first page, to the news on rural affairs, national politics, and European dispatches. To her, they sounded like echoes, not only from faraway countries, but also of a world which no longer existed in time; remote, unfamiliar, congruent but definitively dead. Ágata looked with curiosity for the central page, filled with family social events, weddings, births, deaths. The eyes of that prisoner devoured each letter impassively, unblinking before so many worldly changes and events.

But, in the bottom of her heart, each item was related to all the others, and sometimes she would remain looking at the newspaper without reading. Her mind wandered while she invented endless stories. Different as they might be, all bristled with sharp contrasts with her own life. Even the fate of the woman sold as merchandise to a bourgeois husband seemed more fortunate to her than this constant living with bitterness. Some Sundays, a day on which a few cars filled with veiled women were seen to pass by the outer road in the early morning, she seemed to doze into a reverie, as if charmed by that sudden movement which assured her of the existence of the world, of another world. From her still lips flowed memories of nursery rhymes full of pleasant images.

"What an infernal heat!" she exclaimed involuntarily.

And Nicanor, mute as he stood beside the chest of drawers, slowly drying his hands with the small turkish towel with the brownish fringe, answered, "Yes."

They even shared time in such an individual way that they seemed not to share it at all.

Sometimes, through the window, they would see a loose-jointed car as it passed by, climbing the hill.

Every once in a while, they would both hum at their work. But they kept their voices down so as not to grant them to each other.

Obsessed, Estaurófilo wandered to and fro, around the house, searching the ground for unknown invisible objects.

At sunset, two day laborers squatting on the ground saw him come and go, and laughed at him on the sly.

VI

After those days of intense heat. Nicanor's efforts to increase their water supply failed, and his look became even more bitter. The despair which overwhelms the thinking man enrages the unimaginative one. He was like a madman who had swallowed his wrath. But she seemed resigned. As winter approached, she slowly mended piles of clothes. She said good-bye to the linen garments which she still kept from former summers, and without nostalgia folded in the wardrobe, beside the soap, those clothes of loose and discolored texture. Who knew when she would wear them again? The first cold reached the house, borne on the back of turbulent days laden with threatening storms.

Ágata nourished her afternoon walks, her short excursions, with that constant problem. It's all right for the contemplative to feed on the object of their contemplation; for the religious to live by their prayers; for the great doers to gather satisfaction from their acts; but the spirits destined to ask the motive of their daily sufferings, what can they do by themselves? There are souls who answer and souls who ask, minds that affirm and minds that question, decided and slow, perplexed temperaments. . . . Some turn everything into an answer; others turn everything into a question. How can the latter manage without an audience? As there are lives which do not blossom but in solitude, others die away without their mate. More than anyone else, Ágata was in terrible need of confession and comfort. Nothing in her life was of any use if she could not confide it to someone. Without sharing them, all the events of her life held somehow the musty scent of the useless and dusty articles stored in the attics of old family mansions.

She plucked a sprig as she passed by, and lifted it to her nose, so small and short (a learned friend of her father's always used to say that it was the nose of the Callipygian Venus, and the old doctor applauded the statement with a curt cough). Everything she carried inside was rotting away, like the aromatic sprig. Even at the cost of mutilation, she needed to expose the fresh sap, the juice of life, instead, there she was, uncut, unsmelled, alive and hardly living. The vein which does not give up its blood, poisons its surroundings. If only she could have been like that sprig, broken, torn off!

The blue that pressed down the ridges in December now gave way to a great unvarying pallor. Everything vegetable was clawlike; on the ground, all was bleached. The features of the countryside looked strangely out of joint, and it seemed to those disheartened souls that the nearby stream had completely dried up. Even so, the picture was less cruel than during the summer. Ágata asked herself if the old desolation of the house in Ingeniero White was going to keep her company forever. And on that fading July evening the flight of the scaly lizards did not convey an answer.

By that time she had had her first clear and definite quarrel with Nicanor. Estaurófilo had come into their bedroom at sunset, confused and hesitant, with the pail for feeding the horses in his hand. She and Nicanor were outside, and by chance they entered the house together. The idiot was staring stupidly at a picture of the doctor hanging on the wall over one of the beds. "Get out of here!" shouted Nicanor, and kicked him brutally. The idiot ran away with a moan, leaving the pail on the floor in a puddle. She lifted it and carried it outside. "I have already said I don't want him inside!" cried the husband once more. And she answered bitterly, without raising her eyes, that his rage was stupid. As stupid as that poor defenseless idiot. And it was useless cowardice. And then, beside himself with fury, he shouted that he was already sick of her and of everything else. "Good and sick!"

She started to answer violently, but then got up and went into the kitchen. The terrible trembling of mutual frustration and rage remained tense between them. She felt like shouting or running away. How terrible to be so impotent!

She brought the plates for the roast to the table, muttering between her teeth, "Sinister man!"—and he heard her. "Sinister man!" Then he rebuked her, asking what it was she was muttering, and she burst out and shouted at him all in tears, full of hatred, despair, and rage. "Yes, you brute, you mule, you sinister man!"

Soon they were both shouting. And just as suddenly they were silent, trembling from the violence they had unleashed, unable to find new insults, as if their reason had dried up.

After that episode, they entered a new state of merciless incommunicability. The thought of separation was too modern for them. They were primitive and had some basic notion of Christian principles. Besides, they were united, fiercely united by their mutual frustration, barrenness, and that sad, lonely rancor. They had neither family nor any other horizon. Nothing was left but to bear the rain, the rain of sinister days. There was no other possible way out, no other possibility, no other idea. They clung like beasts to the menial tasks they had to fulfill.

There was no other quarrel. She went on preparing the evening maté, attending to her household duties; because, in truth, she would not have been able to raise any conclusive cause as an excuse for her hatred before the court of God. In a world of concrete things, are we, by any chance, guilty for what we kill without weapons? Provided we act without visible tools, we may strike the most atrocious blows with impunity. But they remained, after that ominous evening, more depressed than ever, knowing that the torn places would never heal in life. From obscure and chronic habit, she used to count the hours of the day. She had been waiting for time. Suddenly, she stopped waiting. They were in a pit and had to close their eyes, imitating the unconscious passiveness of sleep. From the kitchen window, Ágata saw the sky, pale on approaching winter. Sometimes her hands would grab the earthen water bottle or the maté itself as if they bore something extremely valuable. As she caught herself doing this, she smiled in a way which, if she could have seen herself, would have horrified her.

With a violet dress and black shoes. Ágata received one evening a strange sour gift. Nicanor brought some tangerines and placed them on the table as he said: "This time they are not sour." She cut the first one with her usual lack of appetite, saying nothing. Everything was as sour as her life; sour the time and sour the fruit.

The sweet and mysterious elements of life seemed to her far away, in a different continent from the one in which she was confined.

Nicanor began to make more frequent visits to the village. Finally, he took the Ford every evening and returned after nine o'clock. He muttered some news. Words were difficult for both of them. The wombs of these words, like tyrannical mothers, did not give up their offspring easily. Around the twentieth of July or so, just as he began to eat his dinner, Nicanor said that on the following evening, at sunset, some guitar players from Puan would stop at the house. Ágata looked at him while she drank her broom tea. Her husband's hands were still young; the blackening of sun and soil lent them an even more visible vigor. Whereas she, in her inner and outer pallor, seemed like an overripe lemon covered with white mold.

The guitar players from Puan came the day after, at sunset. There was a tall widower with a prominent Adam's-apple on his parchment-like neck, elegiac and mournful, and a tall boy with a soft voice. She and Nicanor sat outside to listen to them, and Estaurófilo approached with the other two laborers. The tall, thin singer, all in black, looked austere and funereal beside the young boy. On their two chairs, straight, erect, they looked like two liturgical assistants. The song burst out dull and weary in the twilight solitude of the immense countryside awaiting the imminent winter. The two players sang in a monotone songs from different regions of Argentina. "Vidalitas" from La Rioja, songs from Tucuman, and although their themes were different and sometimes rather dissolute, they had a barrenness in which there was a religious and sadly solemn feeling:

Debajo de un limón verde,
donde el agua no corría,
entregué mi corazón,
*a quien no lo merecía.**

It grew darker, and a great sadness was communicated to the space by that human duet.

Suddenly, the tall one in black started on a single twang; and it sounded as if desolation itself had come to scratch them all. Then, the boy resolutely attacked a humorous phrasing.

"Juy! Atanasia, hierba de Santa María! . . ."

Nicanor burst out in a peal of laughter, and Ágata shuddered; and she understood that all her hatred was directed against that laughter. *". . . Hierba de Santa María! . . ."* It was a sour and inhuman sound—like the shriek of some lonely animals which live in the woods; a sharp, dry laugh.

The guitar players left at nine o'clock in their old basket carriage. The air held a slight scent of mint and Ágata sat for awhile in the corridor, after supper, to breathe in something of the soft, cold night. She had hardly touched a piece of homemade bread, a few spoonfuls of milk pudding.

She was pursued by the sound of that laughter. The figure of her husband had disappeared, the only thing that remained was the echo of that almost guttural shriek, that way of releasing God knows what pent-up and resentful dogs of the soul. She had only one idea, the simplest one, the most rudimentary, but one that held all the tenacity of an obsession: "I can't stand it any more."

Ágata raised her head toward the great clear stars in the milky sky. She was forsaken, like a beast. Imprisoned by her own existence. Her own life was her cage.

In that house you could breed nothing but hatred, you could eat nothing but hatred.

My God, she thought, her mouth dry, make an end of this. I can't stand it any more.

---

* Underneath a green lemon tree,
where the water did not run,
I gave up my heart
to someone who did not deserve it.

And, as she pictured herself soliloquizing with God, she felt a strange merriment inside. A laughter as strange and false as his.

VII

Winter, the great walker, dressed in its own raiment, pushed forward.

A gnarled tree pointed to the paleness of the hills. Was La Oración a desert, a few miles away? Not one of its laborers ever came down this side of the hill. At most, some commercial traveler from the east crossed the lower road.

As she got up, Ágata noticed the frost on the water in the tub, under the tap. She liked to wet her hands, to feel them burning under the freezing water and become numb, like the cedron tree or the glacial hawthorn. These insignificant and sometimes absurd pleasures had become the only parentheses in her long obsession.

Oh, God! How cold those last days of July were!

By chance, one evening, Ágata looked for the first time at the edge of the tiles on the roof over the veranda at the useless hook of rusty iron which hung there. It must have been used in days gone by as a means of hanging the game to dry. Now it was just a blackened hook, a fixture up there. With the brilliance of a spreading fire, a dark thought went all through her. She saw herself free at last, hanging from that hook . . . She thought of it not with horror, but with a great sense of release. To stare at that hook became a relief. If she was not to reach another shore in this world, she could instead cross to this one, where everything was rest, or perhaps, only God knows what music, what images, what passive sounds . . .

In the end, the entire obsession of fifteen horrible years was transferred onto the hook. On coming out the side door onto the porch, she would stand ecstatic before the little fixture of bent iron. And she would think with an odd sense of secret well-being that there was a way out!

Those who mean to kill themselves have only one great compensation, and it is that while our destiny is an eternal obscure conjecture, a crossroads and an uncertainty, they know, all of a sudden, that they are the masters of their futures. They know it and govern it—since they are going to stop it. This lucidity, this power of the suicide is their tragic joy.

For many days she was lulled, swept off her feet by this certainty of escape.

On one occasion, because of a badly roasted chicken, they treated each other harshly. After that, silence again. And the winter.

Nicanor would sit and smoke in the dark, rocking back and forth in the rush-bottomed chair. In the eternal dry calm of the night the recurrent creaking noise was the only thing to be heard. Indoors, by the lamp light, Ágata turned the pages of the copies of *La Moda* for the hundredth time.

On the third of August it began to rain unceasingly. The icy rain blotted from sight the nearest trees except for two *talas*. The house looked smaller among the four planes of the water scenery. Under the downpour, the closest *tala* seemed to be weeping with the eyes of an old, ailing dog.

Nicanor went out with the last mouthful of breakfast, and in spite of the rain walked over the fields throughout the day, with a single break at lunchtime. They ate in the almost dark dining room. And had she not felt that great weariness, she would have said:

"Those soaking clothes are dangerous."

She didn't say it; her eyes went slowly over her husband's drenched brown flannel shirt and over the angle of wet chest. One more swagger. Why couldn't he relent before the elements? He showed that he enjoyed the rain and the cold and that if those were to be counteracted by anything, the few mouthfuls of soup were enough.

But man is one thing and God is another. The defier of storms came back that night with a chill. It was eight o'clock. She saw him take a pull at a bottle of *caña* to conceal his shivering. And as if he were talking to himself he let the news of the state of the fields and the prospects for the month fall from his lips. But he couldn't even master his voice. A high fever was overpowering him. In the bedroom, he changed his clothes to come to the table, but on getting up from where he was sitting, he had to lie down on the coverlet, his eyes wide open, his hair drenched and disheveled, already giving in to intense trembling. Ágata mechanically prepared the aspirin and the warm wine. And, as if he were joking, he let slip, "It looks as if I've caught pneumonia."

Ágata felt that within herself she was as hard and indifferent as a petrified tree. She came and went from the kitchen to the bedroom, preparing medicines like a kind of sleepwalker. Listening to the rain outside, she only felt cold within, an atrocious cold which filtered into the house through the chinks. She threw a woolen coat over her shoulders.

That night, Nicanor Cruz, drenched in sweat, became delirious, and she spent the whole night sleepless in the other bed, lying face upward, her eyes open and fixed. She thought relentlessly, dryly, of her father the doctor and of her friends in the port of Ingeniero White, and of the faces and the things she had seen in those fifteen years. She was there, her face upward, listening to the ravings of that being who did not utter a single human name, only fragments of phrases or names of grains and fruit trees, all mingled with low-toned complaints and moans.

The following morning he was still delirious. The two laborers offered to drive the Ford and fetch the doctor in the village. The rain had become faint, but the roads were impassable. The worker left at a quarter to ten. With indifference, Estaurófilo closed the gates behind him while he held the gray mare by the reins.

Ágata looked out from the porch, standing there like a statue beside the agapanthus.

During the morning, she wandered around the house like a mechanical toy triggered by inert springs, taking care of the sick man, urged on in all her actions by a profound instinct for detail. Such tugging caused in her a kind of sleepwalking. Sitting up in bed, perspiring, with his eyes bulging from their sockets, from midday on, Nicanor kept shouting for his Mauser. There was no such weapon in the house, and in his fever he was surely remembering the casual hunting parties of his twenties, with the Mauser given him during his military service. Motionless, a few steps from the bed, cold, her arms crossed in a gesture of patient fatigue, Ágata waited for the calm that would follow the delirium. In the humble white-walled room, the day seemed grayer. Outside, the rain had stopped and it grew colder and colder. In the evening, the sick man came alive all of a sudden and his cries and alarms subsided into the humming of a half-wit. Ágata sat down by the bed with a number of *La Nueva Provincia*. She did not think about the doctor, or the weather, or the urgency of the cause. She thought that she would have wished that illness for herself. To get lost in unconsciousness, to sink, to disappear . . . ah!

It was nearly six o'clock when she heard the vibration of the Ford. She received the long-nosed doctor at the threshold. He was dressed in black and was as dry and wrinkled as a raisin. Was she old Dr. Reba's daughter? Of course he knew him! With her father he had once prescribed those Stollz pills which were once passed off as a cure for hay fever. They were good for nothing! "Ah, if we doctors had to return the money we've charged for a wrong diagnosis . . ." He talked as he stood there in his shirt sleeves, washing his hands. Ágata held the towel for him. And then she had to give him another clean one to examine that man covered with sweat who stared at him without recognition. The doctor cleared his throat as usual, and straightened up with the towel in his hands, looking at her, to warn her: "This room must be warmed, to a constant temperature of sixty-eight degrees. You must give him pyramidon and digitalin. I think I've got some in my bag. And if he has a convulsion tonight, we'll have to give him an antispasmodic; I also brought some potassium bromide. Pshaw! He's got an ordinary case of pneumonia—but a weak heart."

Garrulously, the doctor drank some of the cheap brandy they kept at home; he said that he had to get back at once. Such cases are quite straightforward; you just had to be careful. Within an hour of the doctor's arrival Ágata went out to call the workman so that he could get the Ford ready to take the doctor back. Going out to the porch, the doctor was lighting a cigarette, when he saw Estaurófilo standing there. "Who's this goose?" he asked Ágata, who had already come back. But he immediately realized the truth. "Oh, you are an idiot!" Ágata felt reproved. "Go away, Estaurófilo." But the half-wit remained there, impassive, looking on.

Ágata went in to fetch some money to pay the doctor.

"Clouds," said Estaurófilo, and looked at the doctor with amazed eyes. "Aha!" the other calmly exclaimed. "Clouds." "You seem to like them," said the doctor. Estaurófilo assented. "Hum," he said. Ágata reappeared. "He means the horses," she explained to the doctor. "What? But he said clouds . . ." "He calls his horses clouds," she replied. The doctor burst out laughing. "Clouds," said Estaurófilo. "He is offering you his horses, so that you may ride one of them," Ágata added. But the doctor was already getting into the Ford and left immediately.

She was filled with the fear of remaining once more alone in the house, with that strange man whose sickness made him stranger than ever. A dismal idea passed through her and she busied herself in the preparation of her dinner in order not to think at all. Some boiled rice and a tomato was all she required. For over a year—along with the sensation of pressure inside her head—she had lacked all appetite. She could stand only cold meals, meals one can swallow without much chewing. She put her meager dinner on the table. The light of the lamp with its blackish wick filled the room with shadows, and from the next room came the snores, the moans, the babblings.

The workman knocked at the door to ask if something was needed. With her hand on the knob, she looked at him, her eyes frozen, expressionless. "No," she said, "thank you."

When she shut the door, Ágata heard a horse neighing; then silence, and then, again, the delirium in the next room. She could taste the bitterness in her mouth. She hardly touched a few mouthfuls, left the fork and the bread crust on the plate, got up and started washing the dishes. The moonlight cast a dim radiance through the small window. Outside, on the porch, was the iron hook enveloped in the scent of mint. If in that instant she had had a reason for smiling! Suddenly she was struck by the thought that it was ages since she had last laughed, that now she would not even know how to make the gesture. When she entered the bathroom she looked at herself in the mirror and was surprised at not finding any wrinkles in her face, but only great pallor and an incredibly lifeless expression on her lips. . . . Her mouth was not quite horizontal and one of its angles went up her cheek more perceptibly than the other. She didn't know she was very beautiful and that her expression of defeat and suffering gave her features a singular spirituality.

She took a stove to his room and put some eucalyptus leaves in the kettle to boil.

She could never have given an account of that awful night. In the bedroom, which was badly lit by the table lamp, saturated with the smell of eucalyptus, she waged an unequal battle until midnight, from her own bed, to oppose the patient's restlessness, that feverish proximity, with her own great passivity, hardened by fifteen years of endurance. She remained motionless in her bed, face upward as usual. It was useless to try to persuade herself that, within her, anything still remained intact. The patient's moans were interrupted now and then by a snore which was broken by sudden cries. Then, in desperation, because she was at the end of her tether, Ágata began to cry without being conscious of it. Her mouth was contracted, her eyes wet with tears, her mind a festering wound. She was like an orphaned fawn in the forest, reduced to extreme desolation and hunger.

She had not cried for a long time, and this suddenly helped her to recover. She was afraid of even her most human gestures. They seemed only to lead to despair. She came to. In a minute she was as hardened as before. She turned on her right side and fixed her eyes on the feverish man. This strong man breathed with difficulty, as if he had to fight to maintain his breath: Ágata's eyes were still fixed on Nicanor, but she did not see him. What she saw was this infinite misery, this ignominious and useless life, the futility of it and of the world. Only at dawn a kind of drowsiness fell upon her.

The day in store for her was still worse. Nicanor woke up, no longer delirious. His soul compressed, he neither spoke of the preceding day nor of his illness. He was there, in his bed, like an irritable dog. He learned about the doctor's visit and refused the digitalin. What for? Only weak flesh needs help. He breathed with difficulty but he looked hardened by that feminine treatment. One must not prescribe ointments for the oak unless it is rotten, and then, no ointment is of any use. Ágata heard him addressing her directly, as he had not done for a long time:

"You can't take it any longer. Confess that you are fed up."

Ágata looked up.

"With what?"

"With this. With taking care of me."

And he laughed, with his bitter laugh.

On the bed, over the sheets, his veined arms were the color of burned bread crust, so black that they almost looked dirty.

Ágata lunched alone again. If she could only live like this for a few days. She could take her bread, look at the things in her room, lift her glass of water without that poison facing her. When she finished her lunch, she felt giddy and sat down at the table. She felt a strange pain in her eyes, something like neuralgia. Then it wore off and she went out onto the porch and breathed in the dry, intense cold. She had to throw a coat over her shoulders. The hills looked more pitiful than ever. The agapanthuses were dry. Down below, the fields were the color of straw.

What was this calm that terrified her? She was not looking at all that, at the straw-colored grass, at the arid hills. She was empty, void of herself, of heart, and of thought. She saw nothing. What came to her eyes was the most terrible and cold of griefs. Her womb, her throat, her skin, her hands, were desolation made flesh. The shape of her hands was the shape of terror, of a special brutal affliction.

She crossed her arms, and by instinct pressed them with her hands. What she looked at was ending before her very eyes; life seemed to rush in, in a strange surge, and she remembered the days when, as a child, she had listened to Mozart's Requiem in church. The choruses sounded now in her ears.

Why did she remember that?

The rest of the afternoon was unbearable. She went from one room to the next without being able to rid herself of her obsession. There was no future. Life was a river that ended, died, in her. She was opaque. Beyond, there was nothing. And the obscure echo of the choruses droned on in her ears.

Nicanor spent the afternoon sitting up in bed, in order to breathe better. Because when he lay down he breathed with difficulty, he tied a towel to the bar of the foot of his bed and clung to this taut rag to avoid choking. He had decided to get well by himself and say nothing.

Ágata suddenly felt that she had to be in the bedroom, near a living creature, however much she hated it, if she were not to go mad, to start running or shouting or throwing herself on the floor or lose her mind. She went in and sat down in the rocking chair, trembling. And in this way, the two of them spent three long, silent hours.

At dusk, Nicanor began to moan in a low tone and to curse his illness. But, within himself, it was obvious that he feared it.

Ágata rose and went mechanically out onto the porch.

Neither Estaurófilo nor the workers were to be seen, down below, in the deserted fields.

She shuddered at the night without crickets, frightened at thinking what she was thinking. Could eternity be worse? And this thought evoked the terror of the following day, of a day exactly like the others. Those stars were fixed up there. . . . What silence, what glory perhaps, that eternal immobility. . . .

She ate nothing. The cold in the rooms was scarcely bearable. By Nicanor's bedside, the water with eucalyptus leaves boiled in the stove.

Oh God! she thought with a sob within her, oh God! I can't stand it any longer . . . I can't . . . I can't . . ." She thought it without emphasis, gravely, as if it were a confession or a release for her forsaken soul; as if she wanted to put the blame for the act she foresaw on somebody else. She could not bear more days like these. Enough. It is better to turn life in, to give it back.

What great exhaustion and what indecision! It is so hard to act.

She shook her head and went into the bedroom. Nicanor was exhausted again and delirious. He was muttering incoherently. Outside, the wind began to blow, and as the shutter of the kitchen window began to bang, she went to shut it. The wind hit her full in the face. Ah, that cold!

She began going from one place to another like a sleepwalker. From a chair in the dining room she rose to go to the bedroom; it would have been useless to try to keep her mind on *La Moda* or *La Nueva Provincia*. It was as if within herself she carried a swelling sob that could find no outlet. As if she could not give it birth.

She undressed. Was she going to bed once more, to get up once more? She looked around: The usual things were there, always the same—the things!—and that being, her husband, who soon would return to his normal self. She felt a swelling protest rising within her.

Suddenly she got up and opened the dining-room windows, rushed to the door and opened it, let in the ice-cold wind. She went back and brought a chair, a rocking chair, and placed it on the porch in the open. She collapsed in the chair, her arms lifeless. Let everything end. Let the wind sweep all it wanted in that human habitation. She heard the noise of the wind lashing the house, possessing it, taking it by storm. She felt the icy cold, with such a relief! . . .

The vast sky was up there, faintly milk-white. The stars could barely be made out amid the silvery powder. The hills and the countryside were one vast darkness. The wind brought with it the smell of mint, the keen scent of the *suico*. Yonder, the walnut trees and the Carolina poplars were bearing, as she was, the full brunt of the frozen wind. The rustling of their leaves, hissing and crackling, came up to her. Oh God, to give herself up to life at last. To the perfumed life of the open, without chains! She seemed to see the doctor in his gray morning coat, taking a walk in the streets of Ingeniero White, drunk and solemn. The old man entered and drew near her bed, mumbling a verse from the Bible, and there was Delia Novo, astonished, her eyes wide open. . . . Everything was numb with cold. A great crowd of people laughed in the dying Sunday afternoon, by the wooden houses. (The cold wind froze her to the bone. The windows banged and the loosened creepers flew about like black hair in the night.) She was dancing among the railway men in the Sud-Americano Hotel, with that tall gloomy man. The only thing she knew about him was his name: Nicanor Cruz. Why was there not a single child near her? In no time the wind had left her bloodless. She was frozen, exhausted. Everything comes to an end, everything in this house . . . everything. . . .

On the following day the workers found Nicanor Cruz dead, frozen, and Ágata alive and unconscious on the porch of the house.

PART TWO

VIII

Behold Bahía Blanca, city of the south, lashed by Atlantic sands.

Like the cautious paw of the cat with the trusting kitten, summer plays with the city by the sea. Swiftly, a sunbeam moves down from the dome of City Hall and fiercely nullifies the square. All at once the still leaves of the sycamores are host to the joyous chirping of the siesta. Weary lawyers' assistants and their employers exchange glances of mutual, blunted envy. Tied to their old victorias, in four sparse rows around the municipal square, thirteen rachitic horses, heads drooping, stand forever at ease. Throughout the square, young clerks from the offices of Notary Pontevín heatedly nourish their hatred of old clerks from the offices of Notary Balaguer. Idle shoeshine boys, café waiters, lottery brokers, ambitious schoolteachers, sedentary, dyspeptic accountants, on their own responsibility dare to defy the December sun and walk the streets. And in the Italian restaurant, among the odors of sawdust and pickled fish, provincial deputies—Asiatic and prophetic—enjoy a sumptuous lunch.

Here all is prosperity, all is commerce. Into the city—stony oasis on barren land—flow and are shipped out tons and tons of grain. International grain dealers, *criollo* concessionaires on commission, Hebrew experts, speculators, salesmen engage in their second-hand machinations for the home office. The controlling octopus is Buenos Aires. But in the midst of its rural moderation and monotony, this city swept by sandy winds is the promised land. What effort and energy, how many barren years of sacrifice and monotony have gone into the making of this shining prosperity! The intense summer heats, the winds, the dust swirling up Avenida Colón. The gray city, the oasis of the *quintas* of the well-to-do, the houses of the farmers who came to live in the city, the doctors who came to sacrifice themselves and make money, the cunning lawyers, the stores of agricultural implements, the consulates. The square, like a Sahara at siesta time, and proud O'Higgins Street, full of foreigners and *elegantes* . . . In the evening the young cashiers show off the splendor of their silken shirts, while girls in red, cherry, blue, and bright-green dresses walk in the opposite direction in order to exchange meaning glances. At the door of the lighted shops, members of the Rotary Club and politicians, conspicuously aloof, exchange antagonistic greetings. The owners of shoe stores and of shops selling optical instruments discuss misgovernment and the harvest with prominent customers, contemptuous of the sheep farmer who has come to town to bargain. "Seitz lenses are very expensive, the price of calfskin shoes has gone up." But the owner of the consignment house loses four thousand pesos every week playing monte at the Casino. And afterward, people say . . . ! Every evening at eight o'clock the city pours the cream of its society—young men and young women on a spree—into the Copacabana. Some officers from the naval base come in, manly and nonchalant, giving a touch of style to the "social gathering" with their spotless white uniforms. . . .

One can take long, gray Avenida Colón right up to the muddy seashore. Few people come during the week; whole caravans on Sundays. The Buicks, the Chevrolets, the Mercedes-Benzes, the Oldsmobiles, spattered with mud up to the windshields, have come from miles away, from Santa Rosa, Dorrego, Tandil, Tres Arroyos. One after another, the automobiles turn onto the steel-gray asphalt of the avenue.

Ágata withdrew from the window. The mirror of the ancient wardrobe reflected an almost perfect likeness. Indifferently, she drew near and looked closely at her face. There was still an hour before it would be time to go down to dinner. She closed her eyes and for a moment kept her eyelids shut tight in front of the mirror, her head slightly thrown back. Her eyes were weak; and two weeks spent in devouring a book, however slight the attention paid, had left its traces, not only in the whites of her eyes but also on the eyelids, which were redder than usual. She opened her eyes again and looked at herself with little satisfaction. Deliberately she rubbed lipstick back and forth on her lips. Then she quickly put on her simple black-felt hat. Her emaciated face in the glass looked paler than ever.

The hotel stairs led her to the avenue. She entered O'Higgins Street through Drago Street. Clinging to some obscure, circular fate, she went the same way every day. And every day she found a world full of novelty, a new world. At each moment she awoke anew to glory, again and again savored unknown wonders. Every shopwindow was a landscape. No sooner did she stop, astonished and attentive, before a display of astrakhans at a furrier's, than she was struck by the potpourri in the window of an antique dealer, where a map of the Indies presided over the infinitely heterogeneous stock. With a curiosity and a suspense that only a few months ago would have amazed her, she listened, as she walked by, to fragments of vulgar conversation in which she felt the crackling rhythm of life.

She had been reborn from a stupor. Timidly, with an indescribable fear, apprehensively, like a cripple who has begun to walk without his crutches, she had come back to life from those days in which, by right, she ought to have died. She had believed that night that the frost, like a mythical force, would tear her to pieces, leaving her destroyed in the chair on the porch of her house, facing the desolate countryside. But when she opened her eyes she was in a bed at La Oración, with two strangers standing beside her, staring at her as if they could see this absent and feverish creature returning from death. They told her she had been delirious for three days—and she recalled the olive-colored body also delirious in bed . . . her last memory. Before she spoke, the two men in gray shirt sleeves looked meaningfully away, lowering their eyes. Then . . . they started to tell her, as to a stranger, and not without certain misgivings, the part played by the people of La Oración in the "misfortune." She heard them tell her without any perceptible distress how she had been carried, unconscious, to the estancia; about Nicanor's wake in the solitary house where she would have to return to settle everything. What had happened? Had God set her free? Or was this, in some mysterious way, her damnation? One of the men was weak-looking, ill-shaven, with short trousers that did not reach his ankles; the other, short and squat. As soon as they saw she was better, both men left the room. Summing it all up in her mind, she thought that these two must have buried Nicanor Cruz after robbing him. And it must have been in this very bed where she was sleeping now—she thought with disgust—where the old man, Nicanor's father, had lain, years back, with his sheets dirty after four months' use. She felt repelled, stunned. Only afterward did she begin to think that she was free, and that the fateful motive force of her life lay buried under the ground, made one at last with the earth he resembled.

She wanted to get up at once—to leave. But she was still weak, and it wasn't until the next day that she was able to walk to the kitchen. By the fire, as he took his maté, the elder of the owners of La Oración told her about the wake and the burial. Breathing in the pungent smell of the smoke, she listened to the sordid description. The laborers and Estaurófilo, with the two brothers, had stayed till midnight with the body. The room was almost in darkness with a single candle burning. At midnight, the two men had returned to La Oración and the laborers had stayed behind with Estaurófilo. "That fellow's eyes were so big," said the man with the maté, "that it seemed as if he had sent them out to pray by themselves. . . ." But at that moment, neither joke nor tragedy lessened her astonishment. Everything had happened as if heaven had intervened. Will and action were completely alien to her the night Nicanor died in that house on the hill. Was she now to feel sorrow, pain, demoralization because of the dead man? And since she did not, how many people must think her a monster! Neither sorrow nor pain nor discouragement. A strange and somewhat sickly depression, yes, a sort of indifference; it was the cause of the languor in her, while she sat in the kitchen, talking with this garrulous *estanciero,* half gentleman, half laborer. He avoided telling her that Nicanor had been buried without a coffin. She wanted to know if he had a cross, an inscription; she protested that she must go as soon as possible to see to that. She thought that what she had wanted was to die.

And she went back to their house and dismissed the laborers, and was told of Estaurófilo's disappearance. She sold everything in the house at a poor price, in order to avoid having to spend a single night there. (All her personal money lay untouched in the wardrobe of the bedroom.) The deal was settled with the elder brother of La Oración; the deed would be signed later on. "It isn't worth much," said the buyer, half closing his eyes to gaze into the distance. "If I didn't buy it, it would bring even less." She was taken to the station. She went by the night train, a dusty carriage full of noisy, bearded people, separated families, and gypsies.

She arrived at Bahía Blanca half dead, and spent two whole days sleeping in the room assigned to her. Only afterward did she really notice the big cream-colored anteroom with mirrors of the most important hotel in the district. And she opened her eyes to the city.

The same streets, the same places, that twenty years before had seemed to her a magic world. Except that now everyhing was much bigger, and that not even one familiar face was left. And some places, like the big store, La Marina, which in the old days used to delight her with its two huge staircases gracefully converging in the back, no longer existed. She still kept in her nostrils that peculiar smell of oilcloth and muslin which had hovered about the old shop. Now she couldn't place it. She walked slowly along the streets, stopping now and then before the shopwindows with a queer sensation at her total lack of urgency. There was nothing that was not translated into novelty. She smiled, unaware, her lips slightly parted. Her large eyes were fixed on the brilliant and varied objects on display. Her past life seemed remote to her then, utterly remote, sunk in time as if it had been a prenatal existence, prior to her coming to life. And that sensation, she thought, had been the work of a few days, only a few days of being able to sleep, of waking up, of being mistress of herself, without human or material coercion. But within herself, she nurtured a strange and secret creature; there was something untouched in her, a song that had not yet begun, whose first note quivered there inside, waiting for deliverance.

Every time this idea came into her head, she became depressed, hesitated a few minutes, overwhelmed by a mixed sensation of bitterness and hope. Every thought which seemed to go against her solitude immediately awakened suspicion in her. Then unexpectedly her soul reacted, surrendered, and there was nothing left but hope. Why not? It was the voice of God that had begun to speak in her life. After such a long time!

She walked along the main streets until she was exhausted. Everywhere she was followed by curious glances which her looks aroused. She was worried; this curiosity pursued her. Suddenly, she emerged from her absorbed delight to meet those insistent, inquiring stares. But then, how foolish, trying to pass unnoticed, incognito, among these people. Myths were growing up about her, little by little. . . . This pale woman with large eyes, so pale, so distraught, at once terribly attractive and terribly silent, had already thrown a stone into the pond and rippled the quiet surface. Only in the hotel did she feel completely free from observation. She could go up and come down from her room—her peaceful island—with no other witnesses than the hotel employees whose curiosity had long since been exhausted. Her table stood in a corner of the almost empty dining room. And while, during her first days in the hotel, she had shyly avoided talking with the waiters, now she exchanged a few words with them.

"How strange," she said to herself during one of her solitary meals, "I don't feel like going to Ingeniero White. I haven't the slightest wish to go. What a strange feeling! I won't go. Yet, all this implies a certain premonition, a certain hope . . ." Only a person seated directly in front of her at that tiny round table would have noticed the almost imperceptible movement of her lips. In the end, truly lonely people come to speak to themselves as if they were talking to someone else. But those active tradespeople from La Pampa, or obese salesmen from Toay, who devoured the larded rumpsteaks in the dining room, hardly perceived anything more than a distant and severe modesty in that lonely woman in deep mourning.

Ágata, tall and slender, walked with the gentle, dignified movements imminent maternity bestows upon expectant mothers. Actually, her womb was nurturing a new creature inside her, but it was not precisely a child. She knew well the inner restlessness, born close to our hearts, which does not affect our sense of external peace, and although she was unable or unwilling to classify it, to give it a name, to look it in the face, she knew her uneasiness was the same she had felt when she first became acquainted with Nicanor Cruz. She remembered having asked a Swedish girl married to an Argentine, "Does love change you, carry you away? Does your whole being merge with his, do you find yourself only when you think of him, or do you keep something in reserve, some part of your own personality?" She was conscious of embarrassment, of the garden sand under her feet. The other woman had frowned, bewildered. "To tell the truth," she stammered . . . , "to tell the truth . . . I only think of him." But Ágata wanted to know exactly to what extent love meant a loss of self. The sheeplike abandonment with which most people accepted whatever course life placed in their path irritated her. And yet, she was not by nature a thinker. Her longing for knowledge came from her emotions, not her reason.

During that first day, and every day thereafter, she bore within her a being which was not her child. But her nights were different. At night, almost without fail, her sleep was interrupted by the ghost of the years buried in the hills, by the ghost of that sullen, bronze-colored man. She would never rid herself entirely of his laughter, his hard resentment. . . . Sometimes she would get out of bed, put on her dressing gown, and press her face against the cold window pane. And somehow the blackness of the night would take on the terrible shapeless form of Nicanor. She had to control herself so as not to open the door and shout for help, to convince herself that she was really alive, that he was not there beside her. And when, after a while, she finally fell asleep, she would suddenly be awakened by the sound of her own anxious breathing. But how could anything take away from her now what had become ingrained in her soul? Ágata got up refreshed and heated her first cup of morning coffee by the light of the first rays of the sun. She couldn't get enough coffee after so many years of broom tea and other medicinal infusions! Her copy of *El Atlántico* lay abandoned on the floor of her room. The news she had devoured in the isolation of the hills could scarcely attract her now. The petty heroes of Bahía Blanca society were no longer remote poetic figures, merely those dull faces she came across every day in the street. When she went out for a walk after a lukewarm bath and a brief retouching of eyes and lips, the newspaper lay unopened on the bed. Her first stop was the bookstore across the square. Here, as a little girl, she had savored the smells of imported tobacco. She wasn't looking for books now, but trying to recapture the flavor, the feeling she remembered. She wandered indifferently past stacks of books, sometimes opening a volume at random without bothering to lift it from the table. She read: ". . . Orthodox liberals blush when they read that Cervantes called himself the *servant* of the Count of Lemos." And in another book: ". . . the war announced to the peoples of the world as the promise of a universal regeneration, both in its course and in its end, betrayed that promise. . . ." She noticed the name of the author on the cover. Benedetto Croce. Who was he? An Italian. What would Italy be like? She remembered Caligosa's stories. What was the use of all those rows of books? She left the bookstore with a bad taste in her mouth. Although she wouldn't admit it to herself, every particle of her being was drawn only by the "thing" she bore in her womb. That inner "illusion," that contained fire beneath a mask of frozen composure, was all that propelled her on her aimless daily walks through the streets and shops of Bahía Blanca.

Ah, the sierra . . . the sierra, the distant sierra!

One afternoon in the darkness of a movie, watching a stupid comedy, she felt as if her heart was about to stop: a sudden dizziness and then a rush of hard, staccato beats. Years ago, she had had similar sensations, with sleepless nights, lasting over a period of months; then it had stopped. When she went to bed that night, it happened again. Each day thereafter, her walks were interrupted by the same violent pounding in her chest. She scarcely hesitated, and continued on her way. Ágata had never believed in science or in doctors. But one day, during the siesta hour, just to fill in the time, she walked into a doctor's office. The nickel fixtures, the lithographs, the books in hard covers, the piles of faded, waxen copies of *Le Monde Medical*, how familiar they were to her! And the doctor, bent over his tottering legs, was as ancient as his books. For twenty minutes he had tried to convince her that she was suffering from a cardiac anxiety. . . . Ágata left the consultation room smiling, determined never to order the drops of liqueur and the valerian he had prescribed.

A long time went by before she made the acquaintance of Ema de Volpe in the hotel. Ema was always overdressed, with a predictable garish splendor about her, and she was as lonely as Ágata. There was something foreign and exotic about Ema de Volpe. She seemed to have been born to shrug her shoulders and take nothing seriously. "I am what the French call a courtesan. Nothing ever gets me down. I'm happy and take life as it comes. Luckily, I don't have a brain in my head, and I'm glad of it." One night, when they were leaving the dining room, she asked Ágata for a light. While breathing in the smoke through cyclamen-colored lips, she eyed Ágata from head to foot. Then, in the cream-colored lobby, she attached herself to her "new friend" and subjected her to an interminable series of direct questions about her personal life. Ágata, distrustful and aloof, withdrew into her shell, and gave only evasive answers. But Ema belonged to the stubborn breed. She chose to "open up" to her reserved companion and showered her with "confidences" in order to oblige her to respond in kind. For the moment, Ágata was unable to go to her bedroom. They sat down in deep armchairs. "Imagine, what a life!" Ema was from Rosario, had married twice but had separated from both husbands. "What's to be done? I wasn't born to maintain common idle men. I like to go as the wind does, wherever I please and whenever I please. But—don't get me wrong. I know what the score is. I've laid aside a couple of tidy little nest eggs. You never know what may come up." Compared to her frivolous, worldly companion, Ágata, intense and self-contained, seemed like a primitive. After the autobiographical outpouring of that woman, her monosyllabic sentences seemed unfriendly and inadequate. But when, after a while, at that first meeting, she cut short Ema's confidences with a sudden "good night," it was evident that she was made of much sterner stuff and of a more violent disposition than her shrewd fly-by-night companion.

Yet, they were already acquainted. We often meet people stickier than pitch. And that woman from Rosario was condemned to verbosity as is the sting ray to the chance hook. After meals, she waited for Ágata in the hall, ready to acknowledge, with a special glance, the superiority of her bright-colored dresses—all of them in contrast of course—to the other's simplicity. Grief and solitude had rid Ágata of that conventional aftertaste: human beings are always human; a person is always a person—full of horror or poetry, beauty or ugliness, openness or mystery. People cannot be pigeonholed. That is why, having met this frivolous woman, once the first moment of apprehension had disappeared, she kept no mutual reserve; she listened to her with indifference and curiosity; she *witnessed* her.

But she succeeded in protecting her troubled conscience from the contamination of her flamboyant friend. At first she found listening to light conversation restful. After that came dialogues on casual subjects; she laughed, and only came back to her reserve when the other carried her curiosity too far. Once again, it was as if she were saving, as if she were hiding, as if she were taking special pains to conceal from the casual glance of any other human being that "thing" she bore in her womb, the "hope of love" she kept in her inner self. If this unread woman had known theology, she would have been able to explain her sensation as faith, although faith is nothing more in the end than the substance of the things we hope for. The substance of the things we hope for! With sorrow, that dreadful sorrow which she tried

to avoid and which deceived her with the make-believe of tranquillity and rest, she felt the body growing, moving about, and
she came to live more and more in her inner self. And Ema de
Volpe, prattling away, looked in vain for confidences from that
Indian-like woman, who sometimes smiled at her with a soft, sad
smile and at other times withdrew suddenly into a stubborn,
jealous reserve. "Bah! She is crazy," she murmured to herself, and
then said to her: "You must try to renew your life as soon as
possible. . . ." Ágata cast her distrustful eyes upon her. Then,
Ema de Volpe smiled.

They never went out together. Their friendship was carried on
inside the hotel only. If the other had suggested a walk, Ágata
would have refused bluntly. She protected her isolation desperately, and her hope. Here, she needed to be alone. Being sullen,
she clung to her sullenness. Occasionally they went for a short
stroll after dinner, along the broad pavement of the unfrequented
avenue on which the hotel entrance fronted. They did not go any
farther than a few steps from the porch. One night, while walking their ten steps, Ema de Volpe asked suddenly:

"Why are you so reserved. Why don't you ever tell me anything?"

"Anything about what?"

"About yourself, about your own life."

"I am always hearing people talk about their own life!"
While saying this, Ágata threw her head back in a resolute gesture. "I have always considered life as something foreign, as something which has nothing to do with me. My life; what is it? Our
own life! . . . Is it really our own?"

Her voice seemed heavy for such a delicate body. She had
broad shoulders and a thin waist. The two women were dressed
in dark clothes. The December sky had few stars. Their faces
shone unsteadily in the darkness. No one passed. They were quite
alone with the night. Ema de Volpe persisted, but was interrupted:

"Please don't insist on that any longer. There are so many subjects to talk about!"

Ágata raised her eyes and looked at the life in the dark-blue
space. The Avenida Colón lost itself in its monotonous barren-

ness. In front of them, the night communicated with the infinite. It came from eternity, and that elusive pause where it stopped to pass from one instant to the other caught the two women on the pavement illuminated by the thin light of a streetlamp. Life belonged to the night, full of human fates, like a womb of night-mares. The night protected people's health but destroyed them as well. In different worlds, it started fortuitous relations, favored scenes of entreaty, brutally destroyed the dawns of love. God's night! If, while walking along that avenue one could reach the intimate center of darkness, the very center of life . . . Ágata did not listen to the babbling of that poor, conceited adventuress. She fancied, with trembling surprise and relief, the store of gifts hoarded by the night. It touched upon so many windows! Some-where at that very moment some young people were kissing each other; at that moment, sweet disputes for two; at that moment, couples married and followed their diverse fates. At that mo-ment, men and women, tired of wandering through life without a definite goal, met for the first time; at that moment, in the best of possible worlds, splendid events, longed-for happenings took place; humanity justified itself. Houses were filled with joyful returns, with tremblings, with care; people prayed—great hope was mixed with great sadness. . . . When Ema de Volpe suggested amid yawns and laughter going back into the hotel, Ágata, soli-tary and expectant, said nothing.

IX

The dark night of the soul! What other name could one give to the everyday awakening of the reluctant heart, alone, without its prey? What did that intense, deluded creature expect to find in the cave of each hour, in the abyss of each day? Everything harassed her. Only time had at first been an escape for her, and now this door was beginning to close in on her as well. Sitting in her room in the hotel, she no longer found pleasure in anything. With every morning, with every evening, with every night of sleep, she consumed her life; and if, several weeks before, she had completely or almost forgotten that dark-skinned ghost, those eyes, and that laughter which shattered her, tenacious and hateful, time itself seemed now to take pleasure in evoking the crude remembrance before her. What was there to do but to put on her hat and go for a walk, exactly at the same time and along exactly the same street? .... She didn't know that Aeschylus had written hundreds of years before, in *Choephoroi*, that the dead killed the living. She couldn't start walking without hearing people whispering. Worse still, as she turned onto one of the central streets, she saw someone following her close behind and off to one side. She didn't even raise her eyes to see the stranger, as if all favorable or ominous facts about people must emerge from within her, not from without. In her room, she had to wash her fingers with a nail brush again and again to get rid of the soot of the street. Ema de Volpe had left a book of poems in her room and she perused the remote stanzas slowly and reluctantly: "You cast a veil of darkness—over the beautiful world, and you believe you see things because you measure—darkness with a pair of compasses." It was utterly impossible for her to keep her attention concentrated on anything for long. For her attention wasn't alien to her being. Her attention was herself, and Ágata within herself couldn't stop any longer. If she did she would die. No; she could not stop. Although she remained sitting for hours waiting for the time to go and meet the evening in the town, the waiting inside her moved ahead on as the visible works of the clock on the old marble mantelpiece ticked off the minutes. And that idiot Ema de Volpe had given her a book for her to sit and read!

When she could bear the boredom no longer, she approached the balcony and, from behind the windowpanes, her hand clutching the mauve curtains, watched the fauna of the city. She was a huntress in wait. If only the human form of her future were to pass at that same minute! But she saw, as they passed by, only drinkers of aperitifs, big-bellied gentlemen, dissipated youngsters, leaden-eyed salesmen, and many others, visibly crushed. Her mouth and her eyes full of disgust, she went on looking eagerly for wonder and joy. . . .

If she had been able to cry or smile or laugh at herself, this would have been a relief. More than once, as Ema de Volpe entered her room, Ágata received her with a start. It would have been childish to confess that what filled her silence in the half-dark room was peering through the windowpane. When she was unable to see any longer, she looked into the room, and an unreal movement took the place of her immobility.

She was laughing, in her imagination, with a man in a garden; his face was dear to her; she was suckling a dark-haired baby—why did children attract her in such a dense and dark way?—she came to life again, hand in hand with a man whose face she couldn't make out; she walked along the seashore, the wind lashing her face, accompanied by a man who slowed his steps to keep pace with hers, those of a tired woman. . . . She hastily muttered something to Ema de Volpe. She would rather have died than confess such weaknesses. The other woman thought: How strange! and looked at her as if she were looking at a woman who slits children's throats.

Tired of watching through the window, Ágata turned one evening toward her room, picked up an old mirror of dull silver, a remnant of her wedding presents, and bit her lips to revive the blood a little, to make that impassive mask say something. Her face seemed to give substance to everything adverse. Would she ever tell herself anything? Alas, never! She felt an aversion toward herself and would have liked to surrender as soon as possible, in order to get rid of herself. But, at bottom, our blood is always faithful to itself, takes offense when it is not taken, is always seeking to mingle, and strives to engage itself in that conversation, after its own manner, in that mysterious relationship which is born of intercourse. She put away the mirror with disgust. "Lord," she said, "Lord," and threw herself fully dressed on the bed. The whiteness of the ceiling matched her complexion exactly. In the end, we finish up by resembling what we hate. Those sudden rancors against herself, were they not the same feelings that had tortured Nicanor? The very exhalation of failure! What was the use of all our defenses and contrary wishes if it was to be the same old thing all over again. . . .

In the hall of the hotel she had exchanged a few remarks, in passing, with gentlemen staying at the hotel. Once introduced with due respect by the manager, she listened without curiosity to comments that were always alike, and which seemed to make all souls, in contrast with their conjectural diversity, a single unleavened attitude. Some of them told her about their trips to the south, others about their visits to the highlands which in the neighboring districts face the Atlantic; others, while laughing, spoke about a frustrated holdup on the road between Bahía Blanca and Tres Arroyos. These gentlemen seemed the masters of the world, but when they opened their mouths, they came to an end. Speech showed them up as dull and empty. If only it had been possible to recognize among them at least one different from the others. It was only then that Ágata interrupted herself for a few minutes. "But what do I mean by different?" Maybe he had to be somebody quite out of this world, the type of person we call "ideal." Or, at least, somebody who proved to be definite in his fatal energy, obsessed or arbitrary, irrational or prudent, but who would proclaim at least his species, his true soul. . . . He could be a transgressor, an anarchist, a vain, ambitious man, provided he was capable of revealing his true self to the outside world. Who knows!

While in bed, her slender body at rest, her face white against a bedspread a thousand years old, her eyes devoid of inner scenery, her limp fingers relaxed over the material they rested on, everything in her suggested a corpse, with the exception of that knot which, from the depth of her being, still insisted on having hidden rights.

January passed by, like a dismantled vessel, without bringing any enticement on deck. Although she didn't give up her reserve, Ágata drew closer to Ema de Volpe. But the latter did not give gold in return for nothing. If one persisted in being reserved, she said to herself decidedly, I shall not be prodigal with my gifts either. They talked much more than was their wont; but of that vixen's comings and goings, Ágata only knew that she returned. She once spoke vaguely about some friends she had in the city, "a very amusing group," she said; but the worldly woman did not trust the lonely one.

Ágata came to know the neighborhood around the station, where you saw the workers of the zone coming and going around the old horse trough. The fine rustic fountain of greenish iron which stood in the middle of the crossroads had an old-fashioned charm. She liked to look at that fountain, no longer in use. It reminded her of Estaurófilo and of her strolls in the evening, her only diversions during that terrible time. Patience is the great test of life. Things burst out when you least expect them to. What was that child doing on the edge of the pavement close to the railings of the station; what was he playing with? Ágata walked slowly, then stopped for a while to look at him as he continued putting on the ground an amazing variety of objects he kept in his trouser pockets: tops, marbles, small balls of yarn, erasers, bits of pencils. In front of the station, bars and secondhand shops opened at the approach of night. Striped trousers hung close to quilted work baskets, bristling on the outside, the inside covered with fine satin. Some coarse leather shoes seemed to her the ideal thing for walking on the grass. The owner of the shop looked at her, half inviting, half smiling. No, she was not going to buy any of those things. She amused herself awhile, watching a Turk and a native who were arguing about the price of some weapons. The Turk raised a Winchester, complaining to heaven over the injustice of the stubborn buyer; the native looked at him sardonically. The two separated to let her pass, while they cast one of those glances at her that make people feel naked. Before reaching the central part of town, the streets were monotonous, all alike, without any claim to originality. As she passed by, she heard in more than one place the stentorian voice of a radio vociferating without rhyme or reason. After walking for a long while, she got to Chiclana and O'Higgins, an oasis of light. Here the lights vaunted the ostentation of big capitals. Every pedestrian was assaulted by luxury. Every time she went there Ágata discovered new signs, new advertisements and propaganda.

In this manner the moment came which fate had reserved for her to meet the chosen one.

When Ágata came in, Ema de Volpe was in the middle of the group in the lobby of the hotel. They were all standing up, talking. In the center of that rude chorus of laugher and jests, Ema looked like a Corybant in her violet dress, her liturgical hairdo shining with brilliantine, her angular and studied fingers befitting a woman who has done nothing in her life beyond tasting the cigarette she holds in her hand. In less than three minutes, Ágata knew that the thin man, who was leaning on the manager's counter, was the lawyer Sotero, that the other one was his partner, and that the three young ladies, three open-minded sisters, were called Berlín. ("You know," Ema de Volpe told her on coming back later that night, "people who have surnames after cities' names are of Jewish descent. Didn't you notice that all three of them have a Jewish air about them? The eldest one looked like Ruth returned to life.") To tell the truth, the three had a foreign appearance and a certain ritual-like manner of moving about and reacting in unison.

"Ágata Cruz," Ema de Volpe introduced her.

It would have been impossible to cross the hall without running into the group, which opened up to greet her.

"These are the Misses Berlín, and this gentleman is Dr. Romo, and this is Dr. Sotero . . ."

The group closed in, enveloping her. Hands were stretched toward Ágata from different directions, then withdrew mechanically. Dr. Sotero held a glass in his left hand; so did the others. Ema de Volpe resumed the interrupted conversation and burst out laughing, bending her body backward. Ágata felt ashamed of her vulgarity. She was shy, and in her presence, the others showed less enthusiasm for Ema de Volpe's witticisms. A cigarette which he had just lit hung from a corner of the lawyer's mouth. While arching his eyes, half closed because of the smoke, Sotero hid behind his mask of irony and scorn. In the hall—flooded by cream-colored reflections—one of the Berlín sisters burst into a loud and incoherent account of personal misfortune. She was alluding to a fortune lost in three nights gambling at Puente del Inca. Ágata felt an unbearable uneasiness rising in her throat. She would much rather have passed without stopping, so that she could enter her room and be in the dark, her face pressed against the window, looking out into the street till dinnertime. The man introduced as Romo addressed her in an insinuating tone: "I hope you will accompany us tonight." "No," Ágata said in her dry and rather snuffling voice, a voice which contained violence and remoteness. "I'm very tired. I'm going to have dinner and go right to bed."

Ema de Volpe looked at her reproachfully and not without

anger. This foolish woman spoiled everything with her rigid system. She felt like making her behave herself.

"Stay awhile, Ágata . . ."

Instinctively, Ágata did not look to her right at the man who was leaning against the counter, the smoking cigarette between his lips. She felt his presence without looking. Before he looked at her, he made her feel shy. She listened, annoyed, to the giddy cackling. ". . . and when he lost a hundred thousand pesos, that's not all he lost." The girl who resembled Ruth deliberately batted her freckled eyelid of reddish lashes. "The proof was that Etelvina gave him his walking papers, without any ado, just to show him that she wasn't attached to him for any other reason . . ." Ágata felt that she must look emaciated and unpleasant. She said goodbye with a barely polite gesture, but she had not taken Ema's insistence into account. In spite of herself she was forced to postpone her farewell to that group of strangers.

"Sycophant!" shouted Dr. Romo. "Look here, sycophant."

For the first time Dr. Sotero's voice fell upon her. She felt it suddenly all through her body. The tone of his extremely deep and warm voice reached her entrails:

"I have already told you not to give me nicknames in the presence of people who don't know me."

The other laughed sardonically without closing his eyes, white and oval-shaped like eggs stripped of their shells.

"All right, all right . . ."

Those two understood each other.

Sotero turned to Ágata:

"This man tries his imagination by giving me the oddest names he can think of." And he pointed to the sardonic man with his shoulder.

What an unusual voice! She thought she could rest while hearing it.

Like the choir which suddenly enters the stage, the women were whispering aside—and Ágata, for the first time, looked that man in the face. His large forehead and temples gave his features, from the eyebrows to chin, a very fine appearance, delicate, thin; and his lively, shining eyes were not entirely lost under the eyelids, enlivened by a perpetual tendency to laugh. The forehead

and smile were strongly marked in that face. But nothing could
be compared to his voice; she noticed that it paralyzed in an
unexpected, strange way.

Was she born to feel it? Confused, ready to withdraw, Ágata
answered with a clumsy assent. She didn't know what he had just
said to her. At that moment, suddenly, she was merely a body,
sensitive to that presence and to his voice. Why was she so receptive to emotions? They reduced her until they made her blood
stop flowing; her veins seemed suddenly empty and she remained
somehow annulled. Extremely abashed, she cast a quick glance
about her, fearing they would notice her unusual vulnerability.
But with the exception of the man called Romo, who was looking
at her and Sotero sardonically, the rest of the party were all
talking their heads off.

Ágata took off her hat and tossed her hair to lighten her forehead. She was dressed in a black silk jacket and skirt. She could
hardly stand the heat, and at the moment, when she felt it most,
an isolated gust of wind fluttered the floating curtains of one of
the windows near the inside of the hall.

". . . with you," said the man who talked to her without blinking, in an assertive and masculine tone.

Then, before she could think about it any more, she was
pushed, dragged, and cajoled; and amid the hysterical cries of
those enjoyers of life, she climbed into one of the cars just as a
boisterous summer squall began to fall upon the city. The storm
helped that mad outing, amid cries, malice and laughter, before
which she was coy, lost, ridiculous. She had the distinct sensation
of looking like a strange, dry bird, stubborn in her misgivings,
next to these rough companions, who quieted her, exclaiming
that they would take her back after dinner. The greatest chatter-
box of the Berlín sisters hummed, in the back of Dr. Sotero's car,
the first bars of a song then in vogue. She had a contralto voice,
and Ema de Volpe criticized her dissonance with a sudden spurt
of laughter. "Envy, pure envy," replied Miss Berlín in improvised
semi-song. And Ágata, stiff, was saying to herself: "Where are
you going, mute wild beast . . . ?" Before reacting, she was
again suffering the mystery of that voice, the voice of a man of
the world. As he took the wheel, he was telling her what had

happened to some inexperienced tourists from Pucón who were passing through Bariloche, and he seemed to drag his voice, at once ardent and relaxed, his intonation naturally oscillating between maximum liveliness and headlessness, between impulsiveness and reluctance. . . . It was as if, at every moment, he was awakening and fainting with an unrevealed, very sensitive intimation of confidence, of affection.

Ágata, seated in front, between him and Ema de Volpe, fought to get rid of those three simultaneous urges: her mistrust, her indecision to come back, her visible weakness before this indomitable, obscure force emanating from a newcomer. She preferred to obliterate herself at once and to stick to the sentences, hearing them without feeling them. But her feeling of being at once inhibited, trapped, and moved did not disappear so easily. She answered a trivial question mechanically, feeling as if she were in mid-air. Her sensation of something weighing upon her, of carrying a burden in her womb, had disappeared. She felt light, almost happy.

It was strange, the way they all felt confined in the car by the furious pelting of the water on the hard leather top. The water accumulated on the windshield, dripping thick tears. Sotero turned on the windshield wiper. "*Voilà*," he said. And it was as if that common word had been somehow charged with intimacy.

Ágata reacted. If she had always hated the weak, wasn't she now playing the fool? Where was this ridiculous rapture taking her? Poor devil! The hatred she so often felt toward herself emerged again to break her. Again she answered, "Yes, no," under the deluge, resuming her role of miserable, unsocial, wild female. She lowered her eyes and looked at the watch on her darkened wrist. It was a quarter to ten. The car lurched forward as it crossed the ditch.

They were swallowed in confusion by the dim light of the restaurant in Punta Alta—a sailors' bar. The mere jump to the sidewalk was enough for them to be soaked. The heads of the women were like wet hens. For these special customers, the owner had prepared the typical rice with squid. Before the insistent and mocking stare of the sailors, Ágata felt, for a second, distant, as if she could have left her empty body there, allowing her conscience to roam through remote, unknown places. But at her silences, her rudeness, the lawyer Sotero smiled easily. In fact, he smiled at everything with a widely understanding air, like a man who has lived and knows beforehand that everything comes in due time. The attitude of long experience. "What do you want?" he once said, meaningfully, to a friend upon his return from the South Atlantic capital. "We are professionals of life. . . ." And that was his true vocation and his worship; the profession of life; life subdued by an easy, mechanical technique. "Is there any difference between a living body and a file of papers?" he had said on that same occasion while smoking his cigar in the comfortable coach. "No, life is the same thing: you have to oper- ate on it or treat it with the same expertise with which the doctor handles his patient or the lawyer his case. Every circumstance, every development, every fact is a process; you either save them or lose them. Success depends on the skill of the professional. . . ." And then he half closed his eyes, as he half closed them now, waiting until the ladies were seated before he sat down.

A woman suddenly thrust toward destiny, how was Ágata to know whether what was happening was a nightmare or a dream? Anesthetized, she drank down the white wine; she celebrated the others' cheerfulness in her own way. She shook her head when the charming speaker insisted on making her drink too much. It had already made her a little tipsy. How defenseless and vulnera- ble she was! Suddenly, a stab of anguish hurt her from within; then she made one more effort to abandon herself to the pleasant sensations coming from outside. And into the sea of that unex- pected meal, at last she plunged quite free, as free as someone like Ágata could be: the dose of bitterness and melancholy was in her blood. Nothing would ever take its own taste from her mouth. . . .

Dr. Sotero laughed, above the fray, above the world. He natu- rally felt himself the owner of everything—like a god, who would have thrown adolescence away in order to move into fields more suitable for a still greater experience.

In a whirlwind, Sotero spoke of literature and music; he had a taste for reciting maxims, verses, fragments of poems. Invariably, his ego came inevitably to the fore. He seemed to have learned everything he considered fit to attribute to himself; but he did it very gracefully and with that special voice, at once manly and soft, full of mysterious tenderness. He liked to be heard, to hear himself, and no doubt he had never asked himself if he was liked or not. His whole person proclaimed aloud one profound conviction; life belongs to those who take it. His lips were full of Milton betrayed and true Góngora. . . . The fine features around his mouth were like those of a greyhound. As he grew excited by conversation and hurry; a thick vein in his forehead swelled, which couldn't be anything but subtle to the touch, still young. How old was he? Perhaps forty, perhaps somewhat more. Ágata was asking herself those questions—the simplest ones—while, all around her, unlimited enthusiasm was expressed for the rice with squid, the fish filet, the wine from Río Negro. Ah, the questions! She would never stop questioning and questioning herself. Her tenacity in self-interrogation made her seem, with other people, still more absorbed, still more elusive, still more irremissibly distant.

Sotero half whispered in her ear:

"I like diffident women . . ."

And she felt that voice within her and looked at the swollen vein in the lawyer's forehead, and seemed impassive and somewhat absentminded even before the phrase had died in the air.

Dominant, he insisted softly.

"And you are such a woman."

"I, diffident?" She seemed to look at the bottom of the room, at emptiness. "Anything can be said about one, according to the appearance of the moment. Diffident? . . ."

Ágata shrugged; and the lawyer Sotero felt inwardly that though his words "I like diffident women" had not been noticed, it had somehow been taken, accepted, assimilated. He laughed then, expert, without loading the conversation toward that side, the gallant side, and purposely leaving Ágata to ask the questions, he shot a joke at Ema de Volpe, raising his glass of white wine in a toast. His thoughts were far from following the moment's gesture and joke, naturally insincere. His mind, his invisible attention was directed toward Ágata. "I must make this woman believe that I am not too interested; the arrogant ones fall that way. The classic techniques are the ones which pay off." And he started a malicious, equivocal, triumphant, ironic game with Ema de Volpe.

On returning to her hotel room, Ágata experienced a night of liberation, of pleasure, of fear. How could she sleep? Face upward, in the darkness, she was seeing with more light than ever, though without knowing what. She was drunk and confused, not because of the wine, but because of a sudden transformation, a racking through her body, and there she was, made pure pleasure and fear. Ah, what a withdrawal of the body, what a liberation of all weight! She felt herself in a trance; and at the same time, who knows, maybe alive! Anyone watching her would have seen her lips lightly smiling. And, at the same time, a fear . . . But was not this fear the background of a glory, of a strange, delicious mirth that she could have touched, it was so alive? No, it was not a nightmare; it was a dream, still present. Ágata smiled happily, looking at the ceiling. Even to the strange sound of a distant train—drawn remarkably near by the silence of the night—she seemed to listen not with her ears but with her soul. Everything came to her soul. And the very noise of the hotel elevator was not a dissident hissing, but another sound in the ecstatic symphony. She had suddenly forgotten her attitude of perplexed huntress at the window. The hunt was inside herself, hunted, made herself, had become her instant of liberation. And afraid of thinking totally about the circumstance, of counting too much on that man as yet, she hardly touched in its immobility the idea of being freed to emerge, of being released from her lair, of moving toward an air incredibly more breathable. . . . Everything is light to the dark beast that advances and goes beyond the mouth of its cave. (The constant images of animals and wild, harassed beasts must be a reminiscence of childhood in her.)

This man . . . she turned her body a little in the bed, again in suspense. This man . . . behind his boastful talk there was something light, fragile, childish. Ah, to discover traces of childhood in men of forty, how laughable! But in some ostentatious, vain ones—like this one—there exists a remote, hidden flame of helplessness and need. And then, that voice, that tone which got into one's soul, so human, so alive . . . Ágata resumed her former position; she remained stretched out, motionless, on her back.

Was he really impressed by her? His way of insinuating himself seemed to contain something true, a warm force ready for use. Ágata freed her arms from the sheets, and in the darkness they were two long shapes of clear light. In the end, if things are not thought possible, they will always pass us by! When she had come back to the hotel with Ema de Volpe at one o'clock in the morning, Ema had insisted on talking, and before leaving the elevator had dropped guesses with an obvious air of complicity. Leaning on the glass table with her cigarette smoking in her hand, she had said, ". . . I know him and I know when things are real. My dear, get ready for the siege. . . ." And Ágata, who could not stand this vixen, heard her out that night with care, with relish. The other had spoken later, leaning against the wall of her room with her showy, strident gown, like a kind of infallible prophet who foretells what is going to happen without bewildering herself too much with her prediction. Ironic and knowing, she let each word fall like a fatal drop. . . . "He is a magnificent man and I wouldn't miss the opportunity. I have seen women half dead for him, and he didn't even look at them. Both brains and looks. And besides, such a great soul, such a great soul!" Ágata would not have attributed this superlative to him. She would have said that he was obviously a sensitive man . . . had he not told her, who cared little about these things, his emotions on listening to Tchaikovsky's Pathetic Symphony at a recent concert, his preference for young poets, the hours he would spend reciting a classical songbook, by himself? . . . but not that he was what Ema was saying. Could this man of great refinement be hiding within him an exploiter, an inferior? No; she rather thought him gently persuasive, delicately eloquent, for all his vigor and stature. Suddenly, Ágata thought of Nicanor. What a tremendous difference between that silent, resentful man and this charming talker. But if, at last, a door was now opening, if now a light was truly appearing, all those sinister years had not been lived in vain. Ágata raised herself and took a sip of milk from the glass she kept beside her every night. Miserable being! As if, on raising her body, something had changed its place in her mind, she harshly stuck to the distrust which had accompanied her life so tenaciously. What did it mean, really, this abandoning herself to an almost irrational optimism? She was surprised to find herself so weak, so docile in the face of hope. Why fall again into the danger of loading things with immense possibilities? Why this haste in devouring destiny? How naïve! What great inexperience! There she was again, the wretched woman, late in the night, building dreams. As if life were not solid, material. As if life were made of the stuff of dreams. But . . .

Like a flash she remembered a few scenes of the evening. That sarcastic Romo—why should he, again and again, with special meaning, have called his friend "sycophant"? And over the table, the two men had toasted each other, with hardly perceptible winks of understanding, as if they needed to relish in common every minute of bustle. In his refined voice, Sotero called the waiter three times because the famous wine seemed a little sour. The owner, approaching, protested in confusion. Nobody had ever made such complaints. "The importer, needless to say guarantees . . ." Romo smiled with amused sarcasm at the merchant's confusion. And there, calmly, Sotero, for a few moments, was deep in those brief silences which seemed to serve him as background—for they did not interrupt the masculine siege—the constant vivacity of his eyes, that inner mobility, that glow. . . . When he started talking, the world seemed to stop. His voice went on. . . .

That other strange and morose Nicanor Cruz. . . .

Ágata, crouched in her bed, glancing with dismay toward the balcony where the drawn curtains left an open door to the pale glare of the receding night. Better consider things as lost, before they are so. But if it were so, if it were necessary, this time too, to be pessimistic, would she have to resign herself to let the voice of this awaited man pass by? She turned on her side again. Suffering, she tossed her sheet away. Let this man pass by? She felt the image of those refined features, of his glances, engraved on hers, that mysterious force. . . . God, why is it that one can never be certain! Everything in life is problematical. Is everything fair game, everything danger? But this man, who was so near, why had fate brought him? Were there not also certain laws? . . .

Finally, to that fervid questioning, dawn at last brought its heavy sleep.

X

Five days later, just before going out, she noticed that she had used too much makeup. Did a pale face need that much coloring? With a swift movement of her hand, she wiped her cheek; but, overcome, by fear, did not do it completely. Her slightly tilted hat was not at all attractive, and her face, without a little color, made too dull a picture. Why, if she was burning within, didn't that wretched heat rise to the surface? She was deathly pale.

On recalling those days, she was to think obstinately somewhat later that they were perfectly happy. If happiness is the highest state of fulfillment, why—she would wonder in her most lucid moments—is it also the state which most resembles a delirium? Or was happiness not that, but what was to come, what would come later? She pondered. All that frenzy, could it be more than a beginning? Could happiness eventually smother one as misfortune does? Could it? Every time she dressed carefully to go out, she looked at herself once again in the mirror, undecided between one or the other of her two only dresses, and said: "I must have some clothes made. It's high time I thought about it." Ema de Volpe would always reply parsimoniously: "Have done with your mourning; no one deserves it for more than twenty-five days." These questions would fill her mind. But what can one who has always lived underground know of noon? Did the drunkard ever think about the taste of wine? Her breakfast remained almost untouched. The newspapers were left unopened on the table in the room. The street formerly scrutinized was still there, but no longer seen. Ágata was incapable of any sensations but those of her present emotion.

From the seventh to the thirteenth of February, her life, in truth, changed its course. In some way that seemed mysterious to her, all her being which had risen to the surface had begun to blossom; and a flower, when it is born, is overcome by joy. All of her turned fully toward the wondrous splendor of a newly discovered world. Ágata carried this question on her lips: What was this frenzy that carried her away? Of what kind was it? And her lips, still trembling from her questions, would close, suddenly lifeless, leaving her amazed, her questions unanswered. Thus life gathered her up and flung her aside. This man, who had suddenly besieged her, lay in wait for her in the end. In utter astonishment, Ágata surrendered her dead lips. And when she trembled it was as if the deepest and most moribund regions of her nature had been shaken into birth, her last resources, her closed flesh. She laughed and cried as if that birth brought with it another destruction, a painful one. Indeed, one being had been destroyed and another was beginning. But how difficult it was to walk in a new world!

What a revenge upon her former life! The night she surrendered was a night of silence and tears. The young summer played with the city. And Sotero, before whom she felt entirely annulled, was somehow a summer, creative in the heat of his secret persuasive force. First, he attacked with that laughing insistence, almost jovial, apparently quiet; then came the storm: that rapid, insistent endeavor, those rude, cutting arguments—all enveloped in the flow of his voice itself, delicate and assailing. She suddenly found herself unresisting. It was not merely a pleasant voice that was speaking, it was life—that which was always beyond her, and which she ardently desired to incorporate unto herself. What was speaking was the very feeling she lacked. She closed her eyes, she listened. And it was, to her ears, like a song. It was, within her entire being, something she could not leave outside, something she must accept, receive, shelter.

What a revenge, after Nicanor Cruz!

"Why do you let life pass you by?" he had said on the eighth day, after a dinner at a German restaurant, where they were the only customers that evening, in the deserted garden. "Why let life pass, without gathering it up while it throbs, the way the hunter picks up a partridge while it is still alive?" From her great loneliness, she looked at him intensely. Why did he use her own language, her very own? She, within herself, would not have told herself anything else, would not have chosen other words. And the face of the skillful defender of cases must have felt the gaze of those huge, motionless eyes.

The torrent was released. Meeting at every hour, a continuous rushing out to restaurants first, in a rowdy group—harsh shouts

from Ema de Volpe and cynical jokes from Romo—then, solitude, the two together, the flowering. Those two rooms of the
lawyer's in the old hotel, with their brown velvet curtains and
the small Neopolitan pictures at the side of the cold bed. (". . . A
bachelor, always on the run, how could he live, except like this,
in lodgings . . .") The emotion that choked her, the gratitude, the
joy which was yet sorrowful, the surprise, the need to melt into
each thing as if she were a liquid being . . . and what was strang-
est of all was that everything seemed to acquire a voice, speech.
What before had meant nothing to her, now vibrated with many
different messages. The summer resort, its business streets empty
at the siesta hours, the central square, a last small Ford facing the
sun! Avenida Alem, which had seemed so desolate before, now
became gaily vocal. Sotero declaimed. Sotero talked. Sotero
smiled, protecting her. It was worthwhile to feel things this way.
By dint of reviving through her senses, Ágata's body seemed—by
a strange paradox—to be defeated. She didn't feel it, she sank
into an incorporeal state of pleasure. This woman who was now
walking along a side street beside this man, whose walk was confident and dominating like that of a god—how alien she was from
the one that only a fortnight before had lain in wait for life,
behind the closed windows of the balcony! She still eluded his
body a little. This bashfulness made Sotero impatient. Then Ágata
a would smile at that impatience, as if the impatient one were a
child and she did not wish to hurt him. "You don't know what I
know," he said, so close to her that Ágata could almost touch that
hair which was almost too fine, and which would soon disappear
altogether over that brow which was both powerful and delicate.
"Life, what do you think it is? A promised event? You silly one!
Life is each single minute." But she wanted nothing else. What
happened was that she wanted to stop at each minute, and he
wanted to gulp it down. Ágata's hand slid slowly along that con-
strained brow, crossed by a vein so wide that it seemed about to
burst. And when he said that, she wanted to stop every minute,
make it wide and deep, he still protested vehemently. "How easy
it is," he said in that voice whose deep tones acquired that delightful modulation, "to make that mistake!" All the people who
tried in any way to do beautiful things, to make them still more

perfect, thought only of stopping to calculate, to refine, to prepare. And they didn't know that the real richness comes precisely and only from that intensity. It is the same with the rich: the really rich man is not he who amasses and lays up wealth, but he who intensifies pleasure and enjoys it to the utmost. There is nothing more hateful than continued stagnation. Life must be lived as a dagger is thrust: swiftly and to the hilt . . . and Ágata laughed sadly at this spendthrift.

After the seventeenth day, she began to think that in truth they had never been quite alone. Something gave their meetings a secret air. Perhaps it was from trying to keep up the appearances of being people who meet in the ordinary, colorless manner. He himself advised her to leave him each morning at dawn and go back to her own hotel. "Tales are made up immediately, and it's so annoying!" Indeed, small towns are permanent courts of indictment.

And when they made up a party in the dining room at another, more modest, hotel, with Ema de Volpe, the Berlín girls, and the unpleasant Romo, she felt painfully happy at witnessing Sotero's brilliance, the indecisive display of a constant state of intelligence. Amazed, she felt in her very blood that penetrating delight of suspending one's own life to attend to another human river that flows onward and to which one is united, the restfulness of following it, of allowing oneself to be carried along by it.

She looked at herself as one who discovers in herself a sudden change of aspect, and she felt dissolved into an incredible joy. Whom should she thank? The friendly room, the friendly mirror, the great hotel, the street? She limited herself, without saying so, to thanking that savior who awoke her with a telephone call, burst energetically into her day, picked her up for lunch, before entering fully into the day of love. What did anything matter to them? Lovers reinvent leisure. Ágata no longer asked herself questions. She answered herself without them. He feeds me, she would muse on each return to the hotel, tired, but agreeably so; he gives me what I, miserable creature, didn't know about. And my need of him, my happiness in having him, grows, grows, grows. . . .

Her face, attractive in its asperity, pale and tired, would acquire a look of timid joy. Alone, with a cup of black tea before
her, Ágata would say to herself: "It's strange that I, who have
always been so strong, should be continually turning faint." She,
who was so weak, thought herself strong because she had
suffered. It is the mirage of the solitary ones: they all take desolation for roughness. And the sad, passive heart experiences the
rapture of its own greatness. Rapture! That's what she was living.
What could she call the fever with which she awaited, already
dressed, the moment when she would go to meet Sotero, the
restlessness which overcame her when the appointed hour of
their meeting passed without his having appeared; the anxiety,
her absolute inability to fix her attention on something else, to
deceive or amuse herself. If, before this, her life was one long
waiting, now it was a succession of short waits, far less painful,
but far more disquieting.

Not even for a day, did she fail to observe that man, to caress
him with her thoughts and guesses. She liked to hear him talk of
everything. She liked to love things, discover them, get to know
them through what he said to her. One afternoon, they went to
watch the horses' drinking trough, near the station. Sotero spoke
to her during the length of two blocks about the door of a
famous baptistery. He explained to her the high quality of the
copper used for the door, the meaning of the sculptured figures.
He cited a decadent poem in connection with it. Really, he spoke
so quickly that he seemed every moment to be putting into practice his theory of urgent living. And Ágata, without hearing him,
would respond with the opposite attitude, watching him in slow
ecstatic rapture, always serious, brooding, thoughtful.

In the gray silence of a Bahía Blanca afternoon, in the interval
between two meetings, in the refuge of her room, Ágata saw on
the table the white stationery with the name of the hotel, and on
which she had never written anything. If she could only write
down what he was like . . . She tried with great effort to scribble
a few sentences. How did people manage to write when that
white paper seemed only to strike her dumb, to terrify her? Yet,
she had begun a sentence: "Cold to one who doesn't know him,
he is all . . ." She threw the pen down. How could she be sure

of her inspiration when he was not there, when he was far away? She took down the receiver, hurriedly dialed his number, the only one she knew in the entire telephone system of the city. For an instant, she was breathless. Ah! Was he there? She only wanted to tell him that she was waiting for him. Another hour? Yes, of course, she could wait for him forever. And that single moment of expectation, of fear, tired her like a walk. . . .

We are all like that, incomplete! Although he was so near, she could not help being in suspense. And the day she received his letter, those lines written in pencil by the nervous hand whose haste she knew only too well, she wept for joy, lying on the bed, crushing that white paper with her body . . . *"Yesterday I seemed to be caressing a sad body. It worried me. But when I felt you react, quiver like a reed in my embrace, it was I who felt weaker, by dint of feeling that you were so much more sensitive and so much younger and nervous. If you were almost frozen a moment before, afterward you were ardor itself; and yet, that sad look, that desolate expression did not once leave your eyes. It never does."*

Didn't he know that within those depths, his image dwelt permanently? Didn't he know that her desolation was nothing but amazement? Didn't he know that, from being unable to say anything to him, from keeping back so much without being able to communicate it or give it, all her need to confide her thoughts was expressed through her eyes? Sometimes, what comes into a look is all our unconfessed life, the great substance of living dreams, hopes, hunger. No look is more intense than that of animals who look at us voicelessly. And didn't he know—yet! —that she was nothing more than an errant animal, that felt cold and sad? She had mistakenly thought that he had discovered her in her essence, when he said to her with a virile smile: "Not even a woman; only an obstinate puppy that doesn't want to come in out of the rain!"

Yes, yes, she wanted to come out of it; she longed for nothing else but to come out of it. But to abandon herself altogether, and not to be such a taciturn animal, to let herself go and reconstitute herself, but all the help would have to come from him, and he would need infinite patience. It was impossible to imagine a man

more open, more honest, more sincere. It was precisely this truth
—incarnate in a living being—that she sought.

From three to six in the afternoon, Sotero was submerged in
his work. Ágata never needed to ask herself what kind of cases
were defended by that lawyer, who stayed at hotels and described himself as having no roots. At a quarter after six, they
would go out in a car or on foot, for a breath of fresh air in the
long February afternoon. Sometimes they were swallowed up by
the darkness of a motion-picture theater; other times they went
with Ema and the others for a short swim in Maldonado. On their
way back, the Berlín girls would sing softly in the car. Romo
seemed to be courting the three of them indiscriminately, but the
eldest, the one like Ruth, was the spokesman for the others. She
patted him and continually whispered off-color jokes in his ear.
Romo roared with laughter. "Look here, Sycophant," he would
say scoffingly, "I'll have to tell you this later. It's not fit for every
ear. . . ." Sotero always reacted crossly to that joke, to being
called Sycophant. Once, the youngest of the Berlín girls loudly
announced a fact: ". . . and they say that you two make such a
lot, out of this secret business. . . . What! That business in . . ."
(and she mentioned a neighboring country). Sotero winked as
one who savors a tasty morsel, a real sinecure. "We sell small
plans, eh . . ." Throwing himself back in his chair, Romo laughed
in amusement. Ágata smiled, seeing the smile on Sotero's face.
Ah! How plastic she was to his slightest whims! What a splendid
follower! Perhaps because of that docility Romo always regarded
her with visible scorn. She detested that teasing dwarf. Ágata
gazed at the landscape. When she lost herself for a minute, it
seemed impossible to her to be racing in a car, filled with all those
people whom a benign sea of chance had brought up and left on
its shore. What had Providence brought her under her cloak? She
thoughtfully saw how they left behind them the eucalyptus trees,
the plantain trees, the Atlantic. Suddenly, the pressure of that
man's warm hand on her frozen fingers would bring the blood
back to her body and return her to reality.

When they were left alone, from the depths of her delight, she
was greatly moved. Although she did not care much about following the reasonings of the heart, there came a moment in

which she found herself parted, by goodness knows what magic, from the woman who had surrendered herself, and she was amazed to notice in her partiality for the man (from whom she had just parted, almost at dawn, to meet again a few hours later) a shade of maternal anxiety. Is that the tribute of all tenderness? No, it was more than that; more purely a desire to protect, an unutterable fear for him. But what fear? A fear. Wasn't the feeling sufficient to justify itself, although its causes remained unknown? Yes, it was so true that it flooded her. She, who had never protected anybody, who inwardly had done nothing but complain and hate—hating?—she had within her a secret fear for that being who was so affirmative and gay, who did not seem to need protection. As they came down Chiclana Street one evening, without stopping she called his attention to some children playing at building a neat bridge at the edge of the pavement, just after a shower. Ágata watched them curiously and, at the same time, lovingly. The presence of children, absorbed and solitary, always filled her with a feeling of anguish, as if she felt painfully within her how exposed and vulnerable those fragile, living beings were. And was she not bound to him—already—by that same painful feeling, that same sense of something irremediably fragile?

Mornings of exultation; gay afternoons and evenings; nights of cruel delight. Days when the circular, onward movement of the sun carried a glorious burden. Nights in which the cave of the soul, after the expectant darkness, slowly began to fill with pleasures. The pleasure of following in unison, deciphering and pitying the tragedies on the screen of a movie theater. The pain of dressing at dawn and leaving him half asleep in bed, daylight increasing in the room as one who awakens in another world. The delight of walking those blocks in the gray shadows of dawn, the strange sensation of entering the hotel, just as the menservants, in their striped waistcoats were sweeping away the flowers of the day before. Everywhere she found reasons for exultation. Life had opened; she had entered. She had been called to this new landscape. The landscape seemed an unction, a consecration, for it received her and allowed her to advance, almost in a dream—within it. The gay laugh and that incredible voice were always present. The world used them, now that it had decided to receive her into its luxurious halls. And she felt herself shiver with pure joy, remembering what Sotero had said in the other room when they had begun the night that was now ending in her own room at dawn. Earnestly moving those thin lips that were scarcely distinguishable in his sharp, emaciated features, with the dry skin of a strong man, he said: "You keep me in suspense, alternately contented, furious, quiet, restless, calm, nervous, silent, loquacious, dauntless, impatient, happy, unhappy . . ." And it was she who had kindled that flame.

How surprised that cynical Ema de Volpe would have been if, on suddenly entering the room, she had found this somber woman lying face downward and silently laughing to herself like a lunatic!

XI

Time changes, and with it laughter and tears. The shopkeeper becomes a gentleman. And after anger, joy disappears. The day after the cyclone, the leaves go to sleep; life comes back, life returns. Life does not stop.

Around the seventeenth of March at dawn, in Sotero's hotel, Ágata warmly refused to get up. Her demand that they be found together at the wakening of broad daylight was almost an entreaty. The lawyer smiled, but with male force dissuaded her from the idea. Rules, he seemed to imply, with his soft and graceful gesture of authority, must be followed. Convention is a code. Beware, beware of shocking the dragon. She was mortified by his refusal, because on this occasion she longed to stay more than ever before. Who knows what source of weariness, at bottom, still had to be killed? Without even sitting up in bed, like a great yawning dragon, he asked her to do as she had always done. Only then, Ágata resignedly started to dress, in the room filled with dawn, almost in darkness. She said nothing: the structure of her pride was not yet destroyed. She heard the noises of the city while she unhurriedly put on her things, beside the chestnut table where, just and legislating, stood the *Civil Code* and Locke's *Two Treatises on Government*.

It had been one of those mysteriously endless and heavy nights in which the northern wind distributes in each soul its allotted portion of boredom. In the German alehouse where they went after supper, Sotero had been very angry with Romo, and in front of the talkative women, the two men had carried on an argument started that afternoon and which they discussed uncomfortably with a certain reserve. Romo tried to change the subject, and his partner shot a curse at him. Ágata left her tankard on the table, and she herself felt hurt by his impatience. Why did that coarse sound appear in the voice of this highly refined man? Saying, "This must be settled tomorrow morning without fail," Sotero threw himself backward in his chair, his fingers touching the table, and breathed upward his load of discontent. With a shrug of his shoulders, Romo turned his attention to the one who looked like Ruth. And only after a while, peace descended to the table, brought back by a chance happy phrase.

When they walked by themselves along Brown Street, Ágata listened to his complaints: "I can't stand incompetent people. This one has ruined a deal which cost me four months to prepare." It was the first time that the professional bird had fluttered its wings between them. Ágata tried to change his curtness into kindness. To calm him, she sought an argument. And in the nocturnal street, by the side of that absentminded man, all of a sudden it seemed to her that she was talking alone. For the rest of the evening, each of his gestures was mechanical, even his caresses, and though his constantly polite smile did not change, he couldn't help being elusive, forced, really attentive to something else. A calm like the end of the world weighed on the hotel. They drank tea that the sleepy waiter served almost cold, from the bar on the ground floor. All night, Sotero paced the room from one end to the other. The windows were open, and on the second floor across the street the sign of a jeweler's shop shone with a deathly pale light. Ágata suffered that night. Like a damaged soul, didn't she have to fear the most insignificant enemy? The slightest distraction on Sotero's part was enough to cause her pain. Pity the somber consciences: the slightest wind from outside shakes them, scrapes them!

In the dark, to amuse him, she, who hated to talk about herself, told him once more, without fanciful changes—since she was incapable of feigning them—of her adolescence at the port, her father's gloomy old age, the sly observations of casual patients, her marriage that seemed to have been brought on by her own fearful temperament. She told her story badly, as do all those who have made a voice of silence. She laughed. "I thought myself a heroine. I thought the world was an enormous flight of birds, and that I had only to stretch my hand to stop the one I wanted. Then one sees that the bird is oneself, and that the world is the hand that claims one." She laughed at herself, and if he had looked at her in the light that entered by the window, instead of floating in his own thoughts, he would have seen how much of hopelessness and death there was in her laughter. "It's hard never to know a mother, and to be the daughter of a weak father. Winds come to one from every corner. I'd like to know what your childhood was like. . . ." Raising the cigarette to his lips, Sotero mastered his reluctance. "I—what's the use of saying it?— have always been a completely normal man. I had a happy child- hood, a childhood without strange happenings, without history, without interest. The things I could tell are the things any man could tell. And even now, am I in any way different from any- body else? I am a common type of man. And thank heaven!" And she, without paying attention, only offered her ears to that voice.

Often, during the time she was telling him about, she had listened at Ingeniero White to the deep call of the sea, a key below all others, audible only to those who know it, low-pitched and continuous. And that natural voice resembled this other human one. They had, under the surface, both of them, some- thing that did not come from the sea or from the individual speaking, but from much farther away.

That night left its mark. Nothing was the same afterward. Ága- ta's fear increased. The obstinate, dry, hard person of yesterday, how weak she was now! "You're really something to see," Sotero said as he looked at her. "Everything frightens you. How ab- surd!" But did he not know, as he said those things, that he was already administering the poison? Didn't his statement give an indication, only an indication, of a coming intolerance?

If she could only have followed his thesis and waited, before becoming alarmed, for the intolerance to come out! But she knew life too well, she heard it coming. Hadn't life always been alien to her? What she possessed, represented, encouraged what she carried inside, was a strange growth, a strange aging, a meandering: not life itself. That is why she saw it moving dangerously around her, and why she shuddered at each unexpected development.

The next morning, she received a visit from Ema de Volpe, who had brought a newspaper in her hand and who walked shamelessly about looking like an Italian actress. Ágata heard her talking about the two lawyers with deliberate malice.

"They're operators! They're up to something, the two of them. They only think about themselves. Do you believe in their quarrels? Bah! They're accomplices! Misunderstandings . . . lovers' quarrels . . ." Ema's remarks had a depressing effect on Ágata, and she was silent as she went to prepare her coffee.

The other woman shook her foot, her slipper loose at the heel, and assumed the same old gesture, that kind of disappointed contempt, a posture which hardly justified her bouffant hairdo and the luxury of bracelets in the morning. Ágata had a headache. Ema recommended an aspirin. Ágata preferred to take a pyramidon, because—she laughed—a woman with a bad heart must be cautious. But Ema, once installed in the armchair like a prima donna in her dressing room, seemed reluctant to leave before getting something out of the reserved woman opposite her. When she left, in time to dress for lunch, she oscillated between boredom and weariness. Now, she thought, alluding to the other one, we have her in a bad mood again. And, as if she did not belong to the sex: Women are disgusting!

As soon as the unbearable woman had left, Ágata telephoned Sotero again and asked to be alone with him for a while. Sotero agreed laughingly, to stop those joint outings and to be alone with her for a few days. "Though his work was demanding, well, they still would have enough hours to be together." Enough hours; Ágata took a shower and thought about the afternoon.

When she arrived that day at the Copacabana, half an hour before the appointed time, she already knew what was going to happen. Her great instinct for lost harvests. She already knew she was going to meet a man absorbed with the business of the "Or-

ganization." He had spoken vaguely to her about the "Organization" at one time or other, and she knew that that entity in
Buenos Aires was the one to blame for the sudden casual gloom in
his jovial character, weakened by sudden upsets, as a soldier is
weakened by discipline. And in fact, that afternoon, when he
arrived, he went again and again to the telephone and sent for the
newspaper; and the war news—which would affect the "Organization" indirectly—absorbed him and estranged him. Ágata
waited. What could she do against this confabulation of things?
She waited. The tide returned at last to the shore. She still had to
endure another annoyance: Romo, in great excitement, came to
the bar waving a telegram: "Here is the answer, Sycophant."
And this time, Sotero didn't complain about the nickname, because he was interested in the communication above all else.
After reading it, he was once again the same optimist as ever, but
he asked to be excused in order to exchange a few words with his
partner, and Sotero accompanied Romo to the door. In the meantime, she drank an aperitif at the table. She looked at them and
thought how tall Sotero was in comparison with that undersized
man. He was dressed in blue and smoked constantly. And when
he sat down once more, he apologized again and looked around
him in a satisfied way. Ágata didn't need to watch him long to
notice that his polite affability was there, but that his mind was
on something else.

Why should she bother to listen to him? While he lighted the
Virginia cigarette and smiled at her commenting upon the postur-
ing of the two dancers, who were giving a ridiculous interpretation of a sentimental tango, she thought with horror that in the
human species each person was really not himself, but his invaria-
ble propensities. Circumstances themselves take us to a more concrete understanding of the absolute. What she was thinking was
only an idea, but nevertheless, at that moment, she embodied it,
felt it, penetrated it. Each being is not, like the water or the wind,
subject to influences and change. Each being is a single, unmodifi-
able tendency. Each being *is* its tendency. To cowardice, to
courage, to worry, to happiness, to disaster . . . could she, by
changing anything, alter this fugitive, prevent the birth of the
distraction which she already saw in him. Or if, maybe, she was

mistaken . . . She was interrupted by laughter: "By God, why do you look like that! One would think you were the ghost of fear! God forbid . . ." She smiled and drank without answering, and covered his hand with hers. "Let's go and have something to eat," he proposed without transition. "What I have to do later would fill four days of hard work. We won't be able to be together tonight. . . ."

And his expression carried within it a tender, persuasive force. She was full of protests. But what was she going to tell him? Where would she start?

And what for?

What for?

The enemy was already attacking. The enemy. Her life. The one which had always been alien to her. A stranger.

She didn't hear the affable words he was saying as they walked along the street. What happened tonight certainly had no importance whatever. What was important was what was at the bottom of all that, the child already formed by time: estrangement.

In a minute, Sotero spoke of the "Organization," his need to establish a more direct means of communication as soon as possible with the chiefs. Otherwise, "nothing could be done well." The world changes. Things become more urgent each day. And each minute that is lost is a minute that the cause does not recover. Romo will have to leave any moment for Salta—"He's an excellent contact man"—and, who knows, no one can remain quiet these days. . . . Why did he use such mysterious language? She spoke at last. They passed in front of a shop of electrical gadgets and were about to reach the square. By the light of a streetlamp, persistent summer insects attacked again and again. The dark street hardly assimilated the pale reflection. Ágata's face was like a mask.

"Then there are no personal moments left?"

"Personal moments?" he asked.

"Moments in which life may enter people and fill them. One's own moments."

"What is this moment, then?"

Ágata made a gesture of inexpressible disgust.

"I don't know. It has already passed."

He looked astonished.

"But we're living it!"

"Living! . . . Are we living it? Before yesterday, yesterday still, but today . . ."

Sotero laughed. He said to her:

"You're not living in reality! Why that insistence to stop every moment to analyze things? It's better to kill time, by extracting every instant of its contents, instead of losing it in useless conjecture." He took her arm, squeezing it. "The night is ours . . ."

And he spoke to her protectingly, alluding to the hard years she had spent:

"Ágata of the hills. Ágata of the hills . . . Impossible!"

And that "impossible" had a hint of laughter in it.

That night she saw her unlucky bird fly near her. Her only joy seemed spattered with the blood of the dead guest; and the dead guest was a passion, whose beheaded body weighed heavily in that hotel room with windows open to the final summer breezes.

How could she explain it? Sotero was more cheerful than ever. Nervously he waited for every minute to displace the former and mount the new one at once. Time: "Pegasus." Was it possible for that devourer of minutes to sleep for two hours at a stretch? He suddenly insisted on talking about his affairs, on bringing them, by means of sudden allusions, to her immediate notice.

Ágata felt subdued. How she would have liked to drop anchor so that all would not pass, would not change! That time would not swallow itself. That night she took pains—alas! all she could —to turn her body into a magnet. She turned her inexperience into wisdom; her thin arms into tentacular embraces. But since when was the inevitable stayed by pleasant valleys! Unfortunate of unfortunates, he whose madness impels him to stop the clouds. Whatever wants to leave, leaves.

Between the walls of her room, a scene for her alone, that night she was obsessively aware of that voice, endowed with an almost magical attraction, so sensitive to certain external urgencies. Sotero seemed to wait for a special event. Bits and phrases of his conversation proved it: ". . . things will change from one moment to the next . . ." "If these messages are true,"—he had shown her with his forefinger, that afternoon a bold announcement on the

front page of the newspaper—"everything will change, quickly
. . . Should things change, I would be in charge of a good many
operations! A lot of people would be out in the cold. . . ." And
his eyes followed the inner movement of the idea, active, viva-
cious, while his hands caressed unethusiastically the arm of the
woman beside him. Ágata let him talk, let him take flight and
glide happily away.

Oh God, how monotonous she was! How montonous she felt!
She laughed, as if saying, "Ah, hopeless!" And during the days
that followed she forced herself to wait without tormenting herself. Let it be God's will, she thought. By instinct, she forced
herself to retrace some of the steps of her former existence. With
the morning sun she went into a few shops; and she entered again
the nearby bookshop to breathe the smell of paper and tobacco.
She walked up to the park to sit on a bench and dissolve the
moral poisons in the sun. For two consecutive days, Sotero came
quickly and optimistically to pick her up and return to the center. A few well-off beings rolled by in their showy cars on Alem
Avenue, going toward the park. And Sotero's joyfulness, his half-
mysterious expression, bestowed indirect reflections upon her.

She tried to resume her former life; but it wasn't the same any
more. She was brutally committed to this man. Everything she
did was tinged with him. And something still more serious:
tinged with the real danger she felt approaching. "I must
change," she said to him, and to herself. "Miserable, lost creature,
who cannot give variety out of herself."

And what an effort it was! The embittered woman was forever
laughing. Who would have recognized her in that happiness, in
that constant talk? It was true that she was helped a little by
drink, when before she would hardly drain the first glassful; but
even so, what a change. Ema de Volpe said to herself: "Well, this
works." And that week, the joint outings in a merry group were
resumed; the excursions, the nightly meals in Monte Hermoso, in
Punta Alta. ("If I am always alone with him, he'll always be
turning his eyes all the time to see what is happening outside.")
Romo had fallen completely into the arms of Miss Berlín. The
dwarf did not even talk; he was a single suspended fervor; the
laugh he still had was to celebrate her.

She was unskilled in deriving strength out of weakness; but she showered laughs upon the frivolous company. Sotero was greatly amused at the witticisms of this almost drunken woman. He would still recommend abstinence to her! He used to think she was obstinate, but now he saw her docile. Well, at last, she was endurable; before this she had been so full of fear, of absurd remorses. . . .

Absurd remorses.

For the first time Ágata asked herself what was going to happen, what was to become of her if this sorcery were broken. Solitude is good enough for us when we have not experienced what there is of better things. But the mystic, the lover, how can they return from grace to the desert and aridity without bringing death inside them? She trembled. The mere thought of this possibility annihilated her. And thus, the night when Romo gave a party—an "orgy"—to his Ruth, loquacious and generous in his pouring bottles of Rhine wine, she soberly refused for once to drink, and considered seriously the man beside her. She analyzed him, waited for his every word. And she knew she was not deceiving herself when she told herself: "He doesn't care for me any more. He doesn't care for anything for more than a minute. He is made for perpetual motion." And she felt, in her soul, on telling herself that, the ice which is felt by the one who, after giving up all hope, tells himself: "There is no cure for me now. Nothing can save me. I am on the verge of going."

However, days of fruition came. Does not the fruit which is about to fall reach its most succulent flavor in that crisis? At the beginning of the night they walked hurriedly down the central street, unattached, like two friends. They sometimes entered a movie theater, indifferent to what was being shown. They laughed about this or that. When they remained alone in the middle of the night, the windows already closed to the first cold of March, the shadow of imminent grief melted in Ágata's heart with a feeling of extreme joy. Forcing herself, she tried to blossom in unexpected laughs, while Sotero, like a grown-up child, seemed to relax his own happy forces, leaning on the laughter of that woman, so hard and reluctant toward the outside world. But at the exact hour, when his time for sleep arrived, to prepare for his work the following day, this selfish man seemed to indicate: enough. He shut up, he began to show reticence, he drank some water, and that marked the end of his night of companionship.

Afterward, at the moment when pleasure ended, Ágata did not count upon that man any more. Of her own volition, she stopped feigning exaltation. Her thin left eyebrow rose in that expression of perplexity and fixed pain which, in the end, always returned to her. Sotero withdrew, mounted on his own words. Defeated from the start, she told herself once more: "I have still something left—to wait." And each time she came near him, she arrived like someone already dead who would burn again for the last time.

And how far away was Nicanor Cruz! . . .

After an impossible night, that second of July, she got up terrified. At the end of a single hour of sleep, she awoke with one single idea: to pray. She immediately got in her own way and asked herself: "What does this absurdity mean?"—and answered herself: "It is necessary." But her "It is necessary" had no voice; it was an answer made with all her body—without ever having been clearly articulated. It was a cloudy day. She dressed and went out into the street. They were sweeping the entrance of the hotel. In two minutes she was in the square. "What am I going to do? I have never done this before." But she was urged from within. She marched toward it. In her great confusion, she felt in this dawn as if she carried them all in her mind and that they were at the same time far away, all those frantic creatures—the Berlín sisters, Romo, Ema de Volpe—and in the midst of all of them was Sotero, standing, domineering, his smiling eyes turned toward nothingness. . . . What a relief to enter the lukewarm darkness of the temple, to break the massive smell of incense, of candles, with her body. The dark aisle, and there, at the end, the sacred quiver of the minute gradual flames. . . . She remained standing for an instant. What were her lips going to say? She had no business there. She was an intruder. Her presence seemed to lessen the virtue of that house. She inhaled the dense, liturgical smell. And as if that station were not her road, as if she had been mistaken, she went out, returning to the ashen cold of the morning.

That day during lunch, beside the closed windows in the

crowded restaurant, Sotero was in the best of moods. He tenderly tried to persuade her—with what insistence!—that everything that is sown without inner conflict blossoms successfully in life. The worst mistake: to look back. Whereas if one is in the mood to keep things going naturally, instead of stopping to break them into bits with the acid of the spirit, the game is won. They sipped a dissolute white wine. Ágata felt herself floating, almost happily, in an alcoholic fog. She smiled, listening to him. He had to leave at two o'clock. So many important things awaited him. . . . At the door, he looked at her for a long while; he said: "So long."

But what she received that evening as she entered the hotel lobby to meet him, was the letter. He was wanted at the capital, perhaps forever, by the new fields absorbed by the Organization. He was leaving with Romo. It was useless to explain. All explanations are bad. That is why he had refused to hint verbally at separation. ". . . such is life. I'm not the man to be kept tied by anything. Good-bye, forget." The train left at eight. Ágata mechanically looked at her watch. It was ten past eight.

She went up to her room by the great staircase. There she stood for three hours, in the dark, all dressed up to go out, with her stare fixed upon the passers-by, through the windowpanes.

XII

She was not even aware that she couldn't cry; her only rational feeling was that she had lost her soul, and that her body, mere residue, moved with a mechanical indifference, deprived of external calls and inner feelings. She was not aware that her mute, mechanical behavior attracted an obstinate and annoying attention toward her. She was indifferent to everything.

In the morning, Ema de Volpe, full of indignation and commotion, was, of course, the first to burst into the bedroom. It was obvious that she exaggerated her condemnation and that these extremes of emphasis gave her life the necessary support to enable her to forget her own monotonous mediocrity. For a whole hour she spoke angrily of those "cynical and shameless birds."

To get away from her, Ágata had to dress herself slowly from head to toe, hardly looking at her or answering her, to go out into the corridor and leave her, still annoyed, in her swan-feathered wrapper.

Ágata walked toward O'Higgins Street. Her sleepless night had completely penetrated her spirit. She seemed to have lost consistency and to have gotten up from an incredibly long illness. A little remaining energy brought to her mind the fact that it was now some days since she had gone to the bank to collect a payment on the sale of the farm, and she entered the building, which was located on the same street. An employee questioned her insistently about a detail concerning the date. Ágata could not answer him exactly. She did not wish to make any effort, nor did getting out of that state of slight confusion matter to her.

A dirty sun intermittently bathed the pavements; then, the morning turned gray, enveloped in a single cloudy tone. The only mobility of her spirit consisted in hesitating between the extremes of one small thought: "He has gone. I am alone"— repeated monotonously into infinity, without so much as moving her parted lips.

She sat for a while at a table in one of the cafés near the square, from which she could see men hurrying across the street at the approach of midday. She took only one cup of coffee, nor did she notice, on leaving at eleven o'clock, that the obstinate proximity of the waiter was a hint flung at her niggardliness that she should order something more.

She walked unhurriedly and aimlessly along the main street— or what appeared to her to be the main street, owing to the large number of people walking in the morning shade—indifferent amid the best shopwindows of Bahía Blanca. A gentleman and a young countrified-looking girl entered a music conservatory. As she passed a shop, she saw a list of articles for auction chalked upon a board: "One Rönisch piano, a dozen cloaks, one fox fur cape, and a number of other articles . . ." The auctioneer, a gentleman in gray, vociferated at the end of the room, a sordid actor of melodrama in that scene of faded tapestries, Byzantine clocks, pier glasses. Oh, an auction! She caught at the word and revolved it around in her mind as though she had not considered it before. An auction . . . that's what she was!—a leftover from the process of liquidation.

With a great effort, she rallied and resisted weakness. Did she not yet know that behind every disaster there is always, even for an instant, something that turns it around and changes it? She shook her head as though say no to her central affliction, and continued along the street in the opposite direction, toward that disorderly but dense civilian army which was coming toward the square. She went against the tide. There was no one in the Italian restaurant as yet. Lithographs of Cavour and Mussolini hung on opposite walls of the desolate solon; the one of Cavour was old and dirty, while that of Il Duce was brand-new. At the entrance was the blackened recess of a revolving spit, the grate red with coals. And edging the upper part of the white walls, in monotonous lines, were bottles of wine, half-enclosed in straw, all around the room. The waiter approached and stood there. Ágata asked for a bit of chicken, and chose a bottle of wine at random. She started drinking before her meal, as soon as they brought the "fiaschetto." Suddenly she realized that she was sitting motionless, her eyes fixed on the door of the restaurant, her glass poised halfway to her lips, being watched by the owner behind the counter and the three idle waiters. She then gulped down the rest of the glass of wine and began to cut the wing of the chicken, without appetite.

In the end, how could one pretend to be more than oneself? We came out of ourselves; but only for a few hours. After the holiday, the amusement—we returned again to melancholy unity. Either one accepted oneself or one went away. One went away. . . . She thought that phrase over for a while. One went away. She took another sip and smiled, slightly animated. There was always time for that. Until one could go on no longer. There was always time for that. There was always time to be able to go on no longer.

Ágata finished the little bottle of white wine. A kindly unsteadiness raised her body from within, making her float without weight as though she were of the same substance as the atmosphere. She did not want to think about Sotero. Something would turn up, something would happen. Who knows what? Her life still had a long way to go before reaching the point of not being able to go on.

People began to enter the restaurant. Ágata took the new banknotes from her bag, paid, and watched herself leave, reflected in a large horizontal mirror on the left. She wore her hat cocked on one side, and was much thinner than when she had lived in the hills.

The exhilarating action of the wine soothed the surface of her consciousness a little. She thought of going to the railroad station and walking a few blocks through that neighborhood, which seemed to her to preserve a certain curious, almost appealing desolation, while at the same time she could walk along the platforms, watching the arrival of the expresses. Then she walked in that direction and received almost unheedingly in her ear a malicious endearment murmured with cold indecency. She didn't think of Sotero, nor of herself, nor of what was coming. She moved as though lifted on a gentle breeze, all thought suspended, aware only of the sensation of being dissolved in the gentle, grayish humidity of the early afternoon. She entered the station through the wide door—this time there was no child playing outside—and smelled the strong odor of insecticide. The platform was deserted, and it was obviously not the hour for train traffic. She examined the different-colored books, the detective stories with their sensational titles and flashy covers.

Then, like an object that falls suddenly to the ground, unintentionally, unexpectedly, the thought of her disaster fell upon her consciousness, the thought of that absent man and of her monstrous new loneliness. She paled before a bookseller who was watching her expectantly from inside a kiosk, and she felt split, as though slashed with a knife, by the thought that she was now a specter, completely without reason for coming or going. She left the book she had been glancing at on the edge of the counter and hurried back to the hotel, intending to shut herself up in her room before having to bear Ema de Volpe's questions.

She then remembered a Swiss boardinghouse where she once

had a meal with Sotero in the garden. She took a taxi and got out at the hotel, feeling strangely liberated by the idea of not having to see anyone she knew, nor being forced to make conversation. She packed hurriedly, counted her remaining money, and paid her bill. However, she did not take her bags with her, and indicated in the manager's office that she would send for them. A slight drizzle was beginning to fall as she left.

For two days, it was absolutely impossible for her to think, from early morning, when she went out walking as though stunned in imagination, until night, when she fell on her bed in that enormous room. The walls of the room were covered with flowered paper. She was unable to sleep except for short intervals, and with hardly any transition between dozing and wakefulness. She sat at the table during mealtimes with the same indeterminate fixity, answering the questions of the landlady and staff with reluctant monosyllables. It was heavy food, thick with jam and cream, which remained almost untouched on her plate. The mere taste of it made her ill.

A disagreeable couple, frustrated in marriage, dragged themselves around the house. She was rigid and meanly aloof to any greeting; he was small, thrust into a coat buttoned very high on his chest, and had the air of a minister of God, offended upon earth. Their very presence seemed to impose a moral rigidity upon the atmosphere of the house. The man looked at everyone with unrestrained disapproval. On finishing her meal—if it could be called a meal—Ágata found herself face to face with those censorious eyes. Seated in the garden the night after her arrival, she could hear them without being seen. Feeling like an unintentional spy, she heard the man as he dryly accused the woman:

"Existence is given us in custody. It's the duty of each of us to return it unsoiled. Through tying ourselves too much to others, we allow ourselves to become enveloped in confusion. We must guard our custody from contacts which draw it from its severity and solitude."

"Egomaniac," replied the woman, monotonously, like a hoarse crow. "Egomaniac."

She seemed to have limited her speech to that one charge.

Ágata lifted her eyes above the treetops. Was it possible that

everything in the world should be discord, forebodings of disaster, weariness of love? War there, and war here. The human
heart never became acclimated to union. . . . And the experience
of thousands of years, the history of human things, rich with the
infinite wisdom of the mind, had not taught the heart anything.

Her body rose like a shadow and passed by the seated couple.
The woman with the voice of a crow seemed infinitely hardened,
thin, ossified in innumerable grievances. She looked suspiciously
at the young woman who had just come out of the darkness, who
was now leaving.

Ágata found a detective story on the night table, left by a
previous guest, perhaps as lonely as herself in that bedroom
where a heavy smell of dampness rose from the floor and came
out of the walls. Ágata tried to enter into the atmosphere of the
crabbed, yellow characters of the novel, into their simple criminal psychology. But each time she opened the book she found,
after having walked for a minute under the vertical cloth signs in
the exotic streets, that her eyes were off the book and that she
had not been reading for a long while. She would pass in the
daytime from that permanent abstraction into the dark motion-
picture theater. There she would stay for hours. The events she
saw reflected on the screen seemed to her to belong to life on
another planet.

The landlady, an old woman dressed in lilac, with a circle of
golden braids surrounding the top of her head, approached her
officiously one night to point out that she left the table after each
meal without having eaten anything.

"Aren't you well? Can we prepare something else for you?
Something extra, perhaps? It's a pity to let yourself get weak like
this, miss."

Ágata fixed impassive eyes upon the woman. No, she was not
well those days; she did not wish to eat more.

"More?" asked the landlady. "More? . . ." And in her surprise
and confusion she let Ágata pass.

And in a short time, this woman made of dark adversity, upright, disdainful and apparently strong, let herself go completely.
Her spirit seemed only to contain inertia and dread. Why raise
walls against the flood? For the flooding is very slow, and almost

sweet, by dint of being the same as its coloration of sadness. When she passed near people, in the center of the city, in the tea shops, when she eventually entered to sit down after walking for hours, she heard no more than one theme discussed: war. And nothing nearby; a war far away. A few paces away from her, men's charged voices commented on victories and defeats. Nearly shouting, they defended their cause or attacked the adversary. Everything about these men seemed emphasis and passion. Sneers, fury, vehemence, negation, affirmation, theories. They exploded and broke, in all places, beside her, in the Swiss boardinghouse in the street—everywhere.

But, what had she to do with all that? Was the war, by any chance, never going to end? What did that external disaster have to do with her? Deaths, yes, but so alien. If it were at least a dear one, someone near, someone to feel for. But all discussions alluded to something remote, incredibly distant, which nevertheless had fallen into all conversation here, to explode clamorously into pieces. . . . Did nothing exist now but hatred?

What would she not give to be able to stand up and scream when she heard those bellicose conversations in the London Teashop. What was this? Were we not to go on living? Why was everyone rushing to destruction? What would remain of the way in which things were felt before? But she didn't scream. She was herself. She remained there, silent, listening. Ah . . . *la sierra!*

She felt sickened, diffident, distrustful. She had nothing to do, either, with those conversations or those people. She felt that she still bore some seed compressed within her, and that she could not let it fall to this ground at this time. Thus, with what remained to her of strength in her deception, she had enough impetus to abandon those places, leaving the strangers at the tables looking at her in the middle of their conversations. . . . There's the mad woman again!

The mad woman had blood stirring in her, but so sad. Was that horrible uneasiness which was swamping her by any chance sanity?

In the middle of the road, she stopped to think of that. If it were not sanity . . . sanity! What value had words for her? The whitish light from one of the streetlamps shone on her face, shaded on one side by her hat. A passer-by looked at her, waiting for her to lift her eyes. "Words aren't made to be understood." She walked on. "They are made for us to comment on each other, not for us to understand one another." That is why some understood poetry: because it was not said for anyone. Poetry was words in a state of resignation. If they are saved, it was primarily and to the extent that they had renounced all personal communication.

Why should she, who knew nothing about it, think of poetry? Hadn't she thought of everything during those days? She thought about everything to see whether anything was of use to her. What had she found? Only that one cannot depart from oneself for anywhere else. And if one did depart, it was always with return passage paid.

The night was damp and fresh, and the sky was starry despite the rain two hours before. On getting back to the boardinghouse, Ágata sat down on one of the benches in the little square to breathe the air. There was a vacant plot of ground opposite her, so that open space could be seen without obstacles. The dim electric lights scarcely illuminated the surrounding street corners.

She was so tired and so torn within that things themselves hurt her. The night air and the lonely benches and the spectacle of those low houses, visited by a fading light . . . Time hurt her. In that moment of extreme desolation she felt like crying. Her hands resting in her lap, she said to herself: "God, when will I find someone who speaks my language?" And this was hardly a question, because it was said without hope.

As the days passed, she lost even the desire to dress herself. She would ask eagerly at the hotel where she had stayed before whether there was any mail for her. Once they said yes, and she went hurriedly to get it. It was the notification of a further payment on the farm.

(What revenge for Nicanor Cruz! Standing up there on the porch of the house, near the agapanthus flowers, pale on the high hill . . .)

She took to thinking obstinately of Ingeniero White, of the familiar scene of her childhood, where all this that was happening to her seemed to be recorded. But she didn't wish to return. She thought of that spot and refused to go there. She continued to cling to material habits, mechanically entering and leaving the motion-picture theaters and cafés of Bahía Blanca. She no longer got up and left when she heard people talking about the war, or about this or that catastrophe. She watched them morosely, insistently, for long periods. They were smiling and happy men, dressed according to bourgeois usage, with showy, striped silk ties and good suits of English cloth; women and girls whose gold fillings added a metallic luster to their smiles. And the ten thousand dead of Agadir were commented upon for a moment by those enthusiastic talkers, and then easily put aside by the pleasing shine of the gold in their mouths.

Then Ágata felt a great estrangement from that world, which seemed brutally impenetrable and distant, as though in it she had already experienced the death people spoke about. And instead of continuing to go every afternoon to the center of town, where that showy and cosmopolitan world consumed its hours of conversation and spirited sociability, she started going to other places, in the opposite direction, walking alone for hours every afternoon, from sundown till nightfall, toward the region where, like the distant brightness of a tract of land on fire, lay Ingeniero White. She had to do no more than let herself be carried along the empty green-margined streets, between the two lines of solitary trees. She walked. She bit her lips for long periods to keep from crying. Who was there to cry for? Herself? How useless! God, but God, what a life, how all things go on, what sameness in all time! And to think that this interval of agony between the two nothingnesses of birth and death is called existence. Existence! During the first days of those walks into the open country she did not even notice the sides of the road, nor look at the few houses. Only afterward did she lift her eyes, devoid of curiosity, but mild, before those sheds, so terribly desolate in the provincial dusk, to those lost stores, to the monotonous, perennial rows of telegraph poles. Since nothing is going to turn up now, she thought, the best thing would be to go. It tore her to the point of destroying her heart to think how lacking in happiness her life had been, lacking sheltering harbors, variety, change. All her days seemed like one long, cold day! . . .

On returning from those dreadful rambles, during which she almost allowed the night to overtake her on the road, during which she faded darkly like the evening, she returned exhausted, to sit down in the boardinghouse garden. On one of those nights the Swiss proprietor—a kind of insinuating gnome dressed in black corduroy with a long gold chain hanging to his waistcoat pocket—approached her with pretended official curiosity, as if it were a chance meeting.

"Pardon me, miss . . ."

She corrected him mechanically, with intolerant acerbity.

"Pardon me, madam. It's—for my register, because of my wife's carelessness; I must put down your age." He assumed a half-courteous, half-servile tone. "Duty's indiscretion."

"I'm thirty-five," said Ágata.

The Swiss brought his ten fingers to his mouth in the ridiculous mimicry of sucking them with delight: "The very flower of life."

Her mouth remained rigid. The Swiss lingered there, next to the bench on which she was sitting, pretending to be taking in the fresh night air. He was inwardly restrained, but wished to continue the conversation. He took advantage of the opportune moment to cast his hook into the sea:

"I'm not only a hotelkeeper, madam. I have painted some pictures—oh, merely some Swiss landscapes!—which I would like to show if you have a little time to spare. . . ."

A few moments later, Ágata, suddenly incapable of saying no, followed him up to the garret. The destiny of those blotches— anodyne views of Mont Blanc, greasy impressions of Lake Geneva—did not include admiration by Ágata Cruz. In the little room smelling of fresh paint, the Swiss, holding the small un- framed canvases, was addressing one already dead. And it was he, abashed and perplexed, who had to insist on leaving his pigsty of a study, where this pensive woman seemed to wish to remain forever.

Ágata no longer turned her eyes on outward things: they re- mained fixed on her inward ruin. Anchored. If only something could have called her from without! Three days later she eagerly got on one of those buses which gloomily and heavily buffeted the afternoon air, bound for Patagonia. Nothing remained for her now but a fever to reach that spot whose boundaries filled her, pursued her: the port. To see the old house, to breathe the sea air, to recognize the familiar neighborhood . . . At least this remained hers, in perpetuity. In the old bus, she breathed uneasily amidst workmen in shirt sleeves, returning from Bahía Blanca, and passengers who would continue on to Bariloche. She didn't even examine those miserable faces, the remarkable openness of the poor, her fellow creatures and relatives. A very narrow, unending road lined with eucalyptus trees, like cypresses, connected Bahía Blanca with the port, passing through Villa Rosas. Trembling, it seemed to her that, suddenly finding herself in one of the streets of the town after this brief exposure to the elements, she would meet the figure of the old doctor, her father, with his stained morning coat and that ultra-human smile with which he prepared to repeat sententiously a phrase from Isaiah.

She controlled a great sob. Was she going to cry, at last? She was alone on one of the front seats of the bus; she thrust her head forward; and so as to contain her tears, she tried to fix her attention on the worn gray uniform which covered the driver's back. Her head at once became motionless and she gazed through the left-hand window at the trees, sheds, silos, the distant buildings. She could already smell the port.

Port, she thought numbly. I bring you your almost dead one. How many years had it been since she had been there? Fifteen. . . . Abandoned things do not receive us like the others. They have their way of complaining, of wounding.

She stepped off the bus with the group of workmen and, deeply moved, saw the green fence of the police headquarters, the houses so humble and small, which now seemed smaller; the wooden balustrades, the bars, the Union Café, made of wood painted green, with its balustrade and windows along the low second floor; the beginning of the main dock . . . She walked along the main street and came to the gloomy old house. On the walls were still the marks (little rectangles of a slightly lighter shade than the rest of the painted wood) of the doctor's plates. She saw her window, the little balustrade, the closed doors.

A good quarter of an hour had passed, when the front door opened and an elderly man in shirt sleeves came indolently onto the porch, smoking his Italian pipe. His manner changed immediately, and he fixed astonished and suspicious eyes on Ágata. What was this pale woman looking at, so fixedly, with that absent, mad look? Ágata started walking toward the bar, which was on the corner, a few steps away. She would not have recognized anyone. A few men were drinking at the tables inside and discussing the war.

Stretching quietly at the foot of the elevators, the port looked like an island filled with humble wooden houses, pale blue, pink, green. The road by which it was reached from the city formed the wide street, the Avenida Guillermo Torres, on which the balustrades and old wooden house fronts fronted. In the background on the left, last bastion against the sea at that end of the port, like an embattled castle, a distant feudal eminence disdainful of the fishing town, rose the electrical plant of wide German Gothic architecture, with a white, life-size St. George killing the dragon embossed in the center of one of the towers. And because of an optical illusion, viewed from the beginning of the wide street, the plant seemed to be united with the gigantic, progressively ascending cylinders of the silos, the elevators, whose mass ended in a tower a three hundred feet high. The tall building rose with terraced roofs; only at the top of the vertical warehouse did windows appear. Ágata looked with astonishment at those enormous buildings, still too new to be taken in. In her childhood, she had seen only the old grain warehouses, now destroyed and replaced by these enormous new silos. They looked like great lordly castles, cold and silent, erected on the shore of the Atlantic. Ágata crossed the black iron bridge in amazement. Only on close observation did these immense masses of brick permit a view of the huddle of fishing boats far below, their decks accidentally hidden by the displaced nets. Ágata went down by the bridge, walked between the wagons of produce, saw old Sicilians occupied with repairing their tangled brown nets. Grain, fishing, the railway—the whole population was dedicated exclusively to these three activities. Ágata turned and walked slowly up the bridge, stopping in the middle for a closer view of the life-size St. George mounted on a charger with its hoofs in the air, in the middle of the pink tower with false battlements. She stayed a long while, looking absentmindedly at the carved figure, the motionless arm with the lance on high, the marble growing against the background of brick. Then she turned her gaze ecstatically to the elevators on the right. Could anything in the world be larger? Caligosa had once described the elevators of Necochea to her. . . . From here and there the native wheat set out on long voyages to other worlds.

Ágata turned around and went back toward the bridge. She had to pass the police headquarters again. How often as a child had she played by the side of its dwarflike tamarisk trees? She inhaled the scent of the afternoon, slowly, because of her sense of oppression. . . . And she walked to the end of the quay, past the peaceful anchored ships, merchant vessels, cargo boats. There was the Atlantic. (She felt its air upon her tired face.) There, the world ended. . . .

Then, for the first time since she could remember, in that lonely spot, before the green, still water of the impassive sea, she cried as she had cried as a child of seven.

For a month, Ágata returned to the port every afternoon. By this daily process she returned to her childhood. The rest of the day was almost an illness. Terrible headaches awoke her at dawn. She had to get out of bed to apply a cold cloth to her forehead and lie on her back, awake, until she heard the first sounds of the servants in the boardinghouse. From that moment on, she thought of only one thing: her mind was fixed on the port. To go there and sit on some bench or other. She had even gone into a bar for a drink on cold days. Here, people were often disrespectful—though at a distance—with their looks and smiles.

At the end of that interminable month the weight of a strange, uncontrollable immobility fell upon her. It was difficult for her to walk, get on the bus or get off. To walk was her sacrifice. She reached the point of taking some liquid, the remains of some cold food left for her in her room. She had begun to live as if in a daze, a kind of total abstraction. Time hardly counted for her now. She had given up wearing a hat, and the wind of the recent winter lifted her hair and blew it back in two floating wings. She continued to wear a long black, close-fitting, double-breasted coat, and walked, hands in her pockets, eyes wide and fixed, her hair flying.

But each day it became more difficult for her to walk. She was extremely weary. Anxiety, palpitations, the vague pain in her chest had returned. Sometimes she would sit on the edge of the quay and stare at the water for hours and hours. When night had already fallen, she would take the return bus, which was usually empty, and which, before taking the Villa Rosas road, would pass by the sordid Guanaco Café. Now and then a couple of men animatedly discussing the war would get on the bus. Ágata got off at the corner of the boardinghouse, and sometimes she would find the Swiss at the door, smoking a cigar that filled the house with a sour smell.

How is it possible to become completely disinterested in the world! In the end, memory and attention became a state of death for Ágata. Only mechanical movements seemed to propel that figure which the little town of Ingeniero White saw arriving taciturnly, walking as if she could not stop, toward a definite spot she could never reach. And in her extreme weakness, she had recollection and eyes for that region only, for those few hundred yards of town by the ocean. No eyes . . . Did she really see anything? Did those anchored ships, the calm down-sweep of birds onto the green surface, the old police building, those houses of old wood, really impress themselves on eyes which seemed to look at them without ever losing their inner abstraction? The work of the port ended early. In the evening the bars were full and a placid shade descended upon the trees surrounding the police headquarters.

She had completely given up thinking, worrying, or making any kind of calculation. Submerged as she was in deep abstraction, just being in that little town, was enough to put her in touch with certain elements which, like a drug, lulled her faculty for suffering. Those elements were the sea, the sky, the wooden houses, all the things which had provided moral nourishment for her childhood. However, the time arrived when her weariness and affliction were such that she found the nights in the boardinghouse, the journey to the house and garden, unbearable. More and more, she was pursued by the malicious curiosity of the other boarders. They had reached the point of asking her the stupidest questions with crass dissimulation. After a particularly galling episode, she began to stay for a bite of something at the big corner café in the center of Ingeniero White, on the main street. It was strange how far away she felt from the world. She discovered that the nights were incredibly peaceful at the port, that one could remain for hours looking at the dim, starry sky in the mild winter of that year. If anyone had watched her leaving the café, bareheaded, her body firmly wrapped in the black kerseymere coat, he would have seen her smile vacantly on returning to the wharf to sit down once more, as she had done in the afternoon, with her face turned to the sea, her eyes fixed, her hands in her pockets.

And at other times her features took on a grave, obsessed rigidity, as if nothing now remained for her but the unsettled world of sea and sky.

She still saw herself—but as a ghost. If there had never been life in her, what was to be said of what was happening now? Talkative, strong men, workingwomen, children playing would pass close by her. The sick woman on the fringe of life observed them.

But if she had always been outside life, why not think that she would go on like this until she ceased to exist? Life belonged to others. Life was these poor people of the port, that work, that war everyone was talking about.

She was all a lie compared with the movement of people in the town. Only what is capable of communion is real.

Communion? Who ever thought of calling her to communion? God, the earth? Nobody, nothing. Was it possible that even in eternity she wouldn't have a place next to other souls? Those who have been loved, those who had loved on earth. They would take something with them. But those who take nothing from the earth, those who take only the seed of eternal solitude . . .

The afternoon on which she began to think of this, she was overcome by fear. From six o'clock until eleven that night she wandered about the district, unaware of the intense cold, without; anguished within. She remained obsessed with that single idea, her back somewhat bent, her hands clutching the railing of the bridge since nightfall, seeing only dark water in the distance, a light, not yet extinguished, of a ship anchored at the next dock. A police launch suddenly broke the silence with a deafening noise.

When she wished to return, the last bus had gone. She walked to the house which had belonged to her father, and which Nicanor Cruz had sold along with the rest. The door and the windows were closed. Almost all Ingeniero White was in darkness. She let herself drop to a sitting position on the steps and rested her head against a side of the pillar where the balustrade ended. A few meters away, she saw the tamarisk hedges, darker than the rest of the night. Now she suffered from constant palpitations. She felt them much stronger in her chest, quick hammerings which seemed to empty her of blood.

What terror! What terror in that idea! Even after death, after everything, the same solitude. If only she had done her best to love Cruz. . . . Was it not all the work of a terrible pride? What guilt! What a horrifying destiny for the one who doesn't love, who does not build anything in common by dint of tenderness and forgiveness. . . .

Ágata stood up, filled with dread. She had to walk, to find someone, speak a word to a living being! God—she thought to herself—God. And she had no other idea than that prayer. To find . . .

But the whole town slept. There was not even a watchman about. The big café on the corner was closed and in darkness. Only the silent night inhabited the town.

She walked along the wide street in the direction of Bahía Blanca. Mist and cold descended upon her from all sides, as heavily as bodies. And that cold and mist were also solitude.

She hurried, ran a little, and felt a violent fluttering in her chest which made her stop. She stood for a moment, holding back a suppressed sob, a sob too solid to let go. Filled with fear and anguish, she made an effort to continue. The big sheds, the trees, the paved road—she had to leave them all behind her. She forced herself to hurry, but when she had walked two hundred yards farther, she realized that it was impossible. She could not reach the city that night. She sat down for a moment on the curb, looked at the night, those enormous bulks, the stacks of grain set out in the open.

Then, overcome by an uncontrollable haste, she hurriedly turned back toward Ingeniero White. She might still find someone, a night worker on his way to the port. But what hammered at her from within was the thought that now she could never leave her solitude, neither in this world nor the next.

This obscure fear was not only within her. It departed from her like a guest, stood before her, was everywhere, in every house, every shadow, every stretch of road that came into view. It was horrible, inescapable, like a childhood fright. Like a body that begins to fall in a dream, Ágata dissolved into an abandoned sobbing, trembling spasmodically as she walked, crying, half-running. Tears ran down her cheeks. Once again she was completely the seven-year-old child who had grown up in this same air.

At last, she reached the old house and sat down, breathless and weeping. Her body was shaken by spasms of a seemingly inconsolable pain. There was a newspaper on the sidewalk near the steps, and during a pause in her weeping, drying her smarting face with the back of her frozen hand, she made out: "A tragic incident took place yesterday in the San Martín district. A man, obviously insane, stabbed a number of people, two of whom have since died. The murderer was later killed by the police." She read it again without knowing what she was reading or understanding anything, unable to feel anything but her own overwhelming misfortune, terrified by the image of her eternal destiny. Then she thought that perhaps beyond time she might find her mother and father. She latched on to this idea, and for the moment her sobs were stilled. But thinking, being what she was, she no longer had anything to do here, except to await the moment when she had ceased to feel that throbbing within. She let her head fall, embraced her knees with her hands, and fell asleep for a moment. It was not the same cold she had felt at night in the sierra. This was much milder, bearable. She dozed off, and woke up frightened. Her inner darkness was full of faces, of confused images. Only at the approach of dawn did she collapse upon the steps, and the weight of sleep drowned her completely.

Real madness surprises no one. That's why the people who had seen this woman completely without bearings, with long, disheveled hair, walking for the past three days around the dock or sitting on the steps of the front door of the wooden house for hours, took her in with hardly a comment. Only the owner of the house, an apoplectic day laborer, directed glances of hostile distrust at the intruder. But even this did not bring her out of her indifference. Only a prophet could have found a remnant of emotion in the look which that immobile woman, nailed to the wooden steps, gave the insistent children who gathered to look at her, keeping a prudent distance, wary and curious, like calves around a strange body.

XIII

For three long days she clung to that landscape. She could not stop walking any longer, and spent Friday night and Saturday night at the edge of the water, leaning against the small hedges, away from all human intercourse. She dozed, sitting in the square, a few steps from the sea, and a sudden start brought Ágata, once awakened, the fear of nightmares.

Oh God, how efface the shadow of time, of what is to come! How remove pain, the sum of loneliness, of endless loneliness, for years and years of endless loneliness? At every hour, day and night, suspected by watchmen, Ágata walked up to the docks. She saw in the enormous bulks, in the local trade boats, or in the *Fieling* that crossed oceans, the silence of the night and the great indifference of time, which does not look at us, but sees us, awaits us. . . . In the darkness rose the bitter face of Nicanor Cruz, Sotero's obstinate laughter; the great emptiness, the abyss.

By Saturday night, Ágata was exhausted. After tasting a mouthful at the table in the bar, she went over to the sidewalks of the Avenida Guillermo Torres. The darkness was suddenly interrupted by the lighted reflection of a café window. Small movie houses poured upon the street their boisterous advertisements. The clamor of masculine carousing kept her company until midnight. Seated in the square, she tried to fight off her obsession and salve her conscience by drawing on her childhood, in the recall of those distant and familiar memories.

Once more she rose and walked on. Memory sometimes refuses

to help: there was the horrible present. Anything else was better! She crossed the street. The town had been asleep for more than three hours. The infinite calm of the port weighed upon the cold. She was soon in front of the black structure of the bridge. The moonlight silhouetted the great mass of the electric plant. Here she stopped. If someone had called her at that moment, this ecstatic woman would not have turned; her rigid and desperate stare was fixed in the desert air. She could count those stars as so many unfortunate dates.

After a while, she grew tired of standing and sat down, leaning her head on an iron railing, her face raised, looking upward, as if that meant rest. Wasn't there, by any chance in the world, a soul similar to her own, someone to wake up, to call? If the universe, which indifferently contains night, could be seen in terms of human features! With sudden pain she thought of that stole-wearing priest who used to say, "*Ego conjugo vos in matrimonium.*" Delia Novo, the image of virginity, was there, pale, and some old gluttons in black waited for the moment to cut the cake, while that silent man who held her arm stood, a head taller than she was . . . One is always to blame. Have we, by any chance, come to enjoy ourselves, did we come to be an isle of complacency and whim?

Those suffering eyes, fixed on the night, did not close for four hours, except to be startled and to open once again. In the heart of that dark world which surrounded her was the ocean. Everything is booty; and the ocean, the tree, the earth, the blood and the flesh all are captured. Maybe joy does not start until the dam breaks.

In the forsaken night, what she suddenly recalled, what took shape before her, was Nicanor Cruz. She imagined that that resentful man was there, present in the nocturnal atmosphere, inviting her to suppose what their two lives could have been like if, by any chance, he had changed. If after another ten years of bitterness and resentment he had come to her one afternoon to tell her, not "Everything is lost," but, "You can come out. Look at the wheat. We have won all this splendor, all this wealth, with sacrifice and pain. This is the payment of life. Look at the battle with the soil, won at last." And perhaps then, rest and peace

would have shone at last in the face of that grim being. In the
night, this thought made her shudder, struck her for a second.

They lived, killing life! Instead of having killed within them
the bitterness, the tumor. The doctor always used to repeat:
"What endures of ourselves is what we are capable of surpassing
with the heart: Miserable the flower that longs only to be always
a flower! What endures of the flower is its perfume, the memory
of its shape. Thus, of us will remain the sacrifice that we have
made for something. Not ourselves. We are illness, short transit.
We don't cling to the part of us which dies, but to the part that
does not die. . . ." She let her head fall to one side and for a few
minutes seemed sound asleep. Her hands were in the pockets of
her black coat. Anyone seeing her might have said that she was
sitting there in the middle of the bridge, waiting for something.
But the indecision of her life, the dread of the day which was to
come, the new emptiness, the material fear which shook the dregs
of her conscience, awoke her with a start. And then she would
have cried, as she had one night—such a long time ago—in the
house on the hill . . . With a violent movement she grabbed her
head with her hands and sobbed for a few seconds, convulsively,
and then she lowered her hands and touched the cold floor at both
sides of her body.

She saw him. She could not stop seeing him, standing there. He
was covered with his brown tattered shirt. Nicanor Cruz. Dark,
jaundiced, sour, crushed by life like a victim escaped from the
Scriptures. His whole being seemed made of dry soil, looking at
her, telling her that what she thinks is true. If she had lingered
beside him, if he had not gone, in the long run life would have
defeated all rancor. Being enemies, they would have needed each
other at last, as people joined by adversity need each other, mute
between them, mutually insulted, hurt, but united by loneliness
in a single block of misfortune, years, resistance. Yes, they could
have looked at the fields together; without talking to each other,
like two wrestlers of God, tragic, tired, and whole in the cold,
grayish sunset.

Once more she was haunted by the obsession that if she should
suddenly stop living, her loneliness would be eternal, that all
companionship starts in this world, only in this world, and that if

one did not carry the seed from down here, everything would
be eternal horror. Filled with inexpressible anguish, she rose
without knowing what to do, and stood for a moment motionless,
destroyed, with her hands in the pockets of the close-fitting coat.
She came quickly down the bridge toward the town, away from
the marshes. Everything was silent, enveloped in dim light,
asleep, alien and distant. With a muffled sob she walked toward
the gray wharf. But on that side there was nothing but night and
ocean. She was afraid. All light was dead within her. She didn't
know what to do. She stopped and went back. Shuddering in her
nervousness, she crossed the little square and sat down. The moon
lighted a portion of the shrubbery, shaped in the form of chess
bishops. Motionless, Ágata waited for dawn. She shivered with a
light touch of the autumn cold. A bus, full of sleeping passengers
coming from the south, passed on the road without stopping.

Ágata made out the step of a sailor who was walking slowly
back and forth near the vast warehouses of the quay. She rose
and went directly toward him, leaving the square. What would
she say to him, what was she going to ask him? She didn't know.
She knew nothing except that force which pushed her toward
any living creature: fear, and the need of human warmth. The
watchman saw her approach. A few feet from him, Ágata
stopped and looked into that Asiatic face—and hesitated. Yes, it
was enough to have approached a living presence, warm inside.
Behind the sailor and by the light of a distant steetlamp, Ágata
saw the bulk of the liner *Fieling*, enormous, half immersed in
the night, a black centaur. What was she going to tell him, that
stranger with Asiatic features? She went on walking, her eyes
aching terribly in their sockets, unable to stand her fear. She
walked completely around the customhouse and returned to the
square.

This ice was eternity. Eternity wanted her to be alone; waited
for her alone. All the constellations were blurred, indistinct. Ágata
lowered her head. The breeze of dawn fell, hours later, on that
white face without the aid of sleep.

On opening her eyes, the first thing she saw were those
children of the port, toward whom she felt the last remnants of

available hope and charity which her soul possessed. She saw them, shouting and running, disappearing tumultuously beside the bridge.

Why had her fear changed into that fixed rigidity of mind? She stared. She was a beast with a look of fear. Within, all was broken, and if someone were to come close to those eyes he would shudder before their inhuman emptiness, as before an abyss. . . . Was this seizure of misfortune, this white jail, what Dr. Reba had sententiously predicted? "For man also knows not his end! But as fish are caught . . ."? Everything was prey. Not even man belonged to himself, neither the son to his mother, nor the plant to the earth, nor the bird to the air, nor the lover to love, nor the human being to life. Everything is prey. Everything belongs to another world. And in her fatigue, Ágata had within her no other idea. And fear, fear . . .

But it was a splendid Sunday morning. The sun was dazzling. The port and the village foregathered in their round bowl, the play of the light bathing in the hollow. Ágata looked at the morning. "Everything was prey. . . ." And all thought dried up behind that look. Everything was prey. . . . She was cold and stiff on the bench in the square, under the strong Sunday sun.

From the first prayers to the "*Ite missa est*," the strong women and the men who rested that day went to mass. In the street, the mass was but a pause between two movements of the faithful.

Ten or more children were playing in an empty lot. Suddenly they invaded the broad street.

Full of foreign sailors, the biggest bar in town was doing good business. Some English sailors had invited the chaplain, and they sat drinking cherry brandy until eleven o'clock.

Without following their comings and goings, in amazement, Ágata saw the parade of people returning from mass, and the men on their happy way to enjoy Sunday at the pool tables and with drink. She did not think about them, nor did she recognize their clothes as the Sunday display of finery. She was stupefied, exhausted. And on her face, which the night before had been frozen with the cold, her pale skin now burned with the rays of the morning sun.

Passers-by looked at her; questioned her silently, insistently, aggressively, without stopping: Sunday is a pleasant day, and lunch awaited all of them in their homes, the tastiness of the weekly dessert.

How strange and remote not to think any more! Why eat? Why live? Life provides for itself, thought Ágata. Thought? She stared. A young couple, luxuriously dressed, crossed the square without looking at her. Do some people forget that they are prey? Any deceit is valid for a few moments: days, months! But the final cry is behind all the laughs. The cry; the fear.

Two policemen in blue stared at her from the corner. But no one came up to ask her anything. She rose, however, walked a few steps and, for the first time, had to half-close her eyes to receive the sun fully. When the policeman left, Ágata returned to the bench; in front, a few Sunday workers appeared, coming from the quay. In the evening they would join in the idleness, the enjoyment.

Though her mind was a blank, a desert of sleeplessness and despair, Ágata suddenly thought about the city. When would she return? What for? If she could only stay in one of those wooden hotels crowded with traveling salesmen, adventurers. But it was an effort to live. When they picked her up from there she would be an inanimate body, without memory or future: a thing. When they picked up the prey.

She noticed, in front of her, a child watching her curiously, dumbly. On being discovered, the child ran away, and she looked at him, moved, impotent and grieved. Who could tell them, at that age, that everything is possible, even this! They have pure eyes and no notion of pain: they are innocent.

Coming and going, the people from the port passed by the broad street till noon. The women at the thresholds paid mutual calls. At the corners, in groups, some workmen talked, dressed in their Sunday best, diverted and assured. From time to time a voice rose, arbitrary, imperative above the others.

The sun burned its highest fire at one o'clock. Little by little, fishermen, women, workmen took shelter in their homes. The main street was empty and the hedges of the headquarters of the dock police received the full blast of the heat. Ágata was left alone in the middle of the day. When would the afternoon, the night, end! Ágata was all pain. She had run, laughing, through that deserted street more than twenty years before. And each trodden bit of that earth seemed to revive now that she no longer existed.

The swarm of children were the first to invade the street at siesta time. From ten hallways emerged as many savages. Those who carried slingshots, the soldiers, broke out in groups. Ágata, surprised, saw them separate, yelling to each other. Then, running across the main street, they disappeared, scattering.

After that exodus, the village remained calm once more. In the great silence the screams of the distant voices were heard. A lonely kite marked the hand of a poet in the sky.

They returned, a suffocated and dirty pack of hounds, around five o'clock, and this absent and motionless woman raised her empty, fixed, directionless eyes to that invasion. She saw them enter the town, disperse, red with agitation, and suddenly bored. For a second, the presence of the crowd of children cheered Ágata somewhat. Fights started here and there.

What had the approaching children come to do? There were three of them. They observed her, they stared at her. And when she tried, God only knows how, to smile, they were already gone.

But they returned with some others. Now there were nine. And from a few feet away, curious, reserved, they fixed their inspecting eyes upon her. The oldest had an adult's head with a dwarf's body. A colorless shirt fell in rags about him.

The one with a stick over his shoulder murmured disrespectfully, before the statue in a black coat: "She's an idiot." He turned disinterestedly to look at the other side of the docks.

What was going to happen? Ágata withdrew in an instinctive, dark fear. What could she say to these strangers? What were words for? With them, by human laws, one could explain nothing, everything became more and more confused. Poor creature, the one who couldn't bring a language into her silence!

The ten- and twelve-year-old savages started laughing and grinning, without moving from their post, in a half circle. One of them shouted "Eeeeh! . . ." The nine of them searched their minds for some way to terrify her.

Then another fear came to her.

There was no one near except two women talking on the next corner, a hundred yards away, at the door of a house. One of them, the elder, held a blackish broom in her hand. She was talking to the other, the younger one, with the matriarchal authority of all village women.

An exclamation split the air. Ágata trembled. "Let the chief ride on her!" The boy with this notion was already seeing the other one mounted upon the shoulders of the woman. . . . A chorus of laughter burst out, malignant. The group advanced toward Ágata, fanlike, with the hint of a charge. Three of those savages put six hands, six paws upon her arms. She rose, agitated, alarmed, without a single word. Then she took a step backward. In her eyes were fear and alarm. A wave of cold had fallen over the afternoon. Ágata started to walk toward the docks, and suddenly they stopped her with cries and curses. The angriest one took the stick out of his bag and waved it, scolding her. What was she to do, what was she to do! She could say nothing. Then Ágata turned and went in the direction of the main street, walking hurriedly.

The old woman, who was watching a hundred yards away with the broom in her hand, called to the boys angrily:

"Get out of there, get out of there! Scoundrels!"

The pack of hounds jumped across, like a single body. Once again they blocked Ágata's way. A blond boy with straight hair laughed at the top of his voice; two others took their anger seriously.

Ágata stretched her arms, opened her way, her eyes fixed before her, and ran up the main street toward the town.

The old woman, coming a few steps forward, approached the group; she wrinkled her face like a sour grape, and admonished the boys. Ágata heard her:

"Villains!"

The nine broke out in a single shout. They rushed her.

Then Ágata ran toward the road to Bahía Blanca.

"Let's make her run," suggested a tall, thin boy in a blue shirt.

The group knew what that meant; tactically they kept their

distance, they let her gain time. Ágata ran up the center of the street, her hair flung back, her bosom forward, her eyes immense, as if facing death. A lonely bird sang by the side of the road. She passed the first sheds. On Sunday afternoon the road was empty.

She looked askance at the sides of the street, the sadness of the enormous piles of wheat, as indifferent as eternal pyramids behind the wire fences, the abundant reserves of grain and coal—of the wealthy Dreyfus, Hardcastle, Massey-Harris, Cory Brothers ... At the sides—with what silence!—piles and sheds. The street was a narrow, never-ending gallery. Never. It was an enormous distance to Villa Rosas.

Feeling the first fatigue, Ágata stopped. She thought she heard cries in the distance. They were about twenty yards away from her. They stopped. With a unanimous gesture, with a pounding of their feet, they meant to continue the race. Ágata ran a little farther; then she stopped by the roadside, breathless. She had palpitations, the old palpitations, and she was out of breath.

The nine rascals were before her at once. They placed themselves at the same distance as when she had sat in the square, just a few yards away. They made grimaces at her, having enormous fun. A small fellow with black eyes whooped frantically, like a creature touched by God. His chest went up and down excitedly, but he was happy. Ágata fixed her eyes on one of the others. He was the most silent one of all, a small cur with a blond head, half hidden behind the others, expectant.

They wanted to rush at her once more, and she got up. She looked as if she were dead, standing in the midst of them, pale, horribly afflicted. She felt herself being grabbed; a hand shot at her head, almost clung to her hair. She saw that two sticks were raised. . . . Then, for the first time, she cried out and tore herself loose, dragging one of them, and started to run in terror. Perhaps she thought only, God, God!—and perhaps she thought something else. The sky was completely clear and cloudless. Below, it was growing cold. The childish cry was heard once more:

"Let the chief ride on her!"

One of them howled a vile insult at her. He sprang toward her. With a violent movement, she made him draw back, staggering.

Then all of them rushed in savagely. And Ágata ran much faster, getting out of the road, making a shortcut across country, which made them lose some time.

"Wait," said the one in the blue shirt.

They waited, furious.

"Leave me alone," she pleaded, "leave me alone . . ."

It was the first time she had spoken. They didn't answer.

They went in to grab her. Three of them went first; the others to keep her covered, remained on the road. The tallest of the bunch lit a cigarette and waited, commandingly, his arms akimbo.

"You try to look important," laughed one of the boys. Four others also laughed, a short, liquid laugh, and the tall one looked at them scornfully.

"Maybe he'll fall in love," said the one who had spoken before. And they roared with laughter, all except the tall one.

The other three approached her from the road. One of them carried a raised stick. "Out!" they cried. "Out!" She tried to tear herself away. The one with the stick still threatened her, without daring to bring it down. Then six others came running and Ágata had to return to the road to elude them, and she could not run toward the city any more. They went back diagonally and blocked her way. Then she ran toward Ingeniero White again, and it was the same way she had gone and returned one night, desperate.

Once again, with the purpose of prolonging the chase, of making it more complicated and amusing, they let her go forward. The town would enclose her like a bag; she wouldn't be able to get out of there. Tactically, they had to close her in. They didn't have to tell each other: it was the rule; this was how they acted in all their fights.

With sticks raised, they howled, screeched, mad with amusement. The woman in the black coat ran, her hair flying in the wind, and the gang pursued her, with a great movement of hands. They were doing what they had read about so many times. . . . War was like that.

They howled at the top of their voices, behind the woman who ran, and who was their prey. In that persecution they owned the victim. They were the owners of that battle, of that grown person. What compensatory wrath!

Ágata ran, and then sat down again for a moment, without knowing what to do, breathing with difficulty, and started running again. In that moment, if Nicanor Cruz could have seen those horribly forsaken eyes and those lips half open, panting slightly, he would have recognized with surprise the same eyes and the same lips which so long ago had laughed beside him, animated, at the public fairs in Dorrego.

By the road, not even a single truck or passer-by. The sheds on each side, solitary; the flight of a bird crossing them. Far away, alone, sarcastic, frozen, the picture of a guanaco crowned the shed in which the southbound travelers stopped to drink.

They caught her. They arrived, brutal, to strike her, to humiliate her. And once again, they let her escape, go on. Long before reaching the village, they saw the old woman who came hurriedly, short and blackish, a Fury with a broom in her hand. For more than an hour the scoundrels had not reappeared, and the old woman had decided to go out. Ágata, hesitating, stopped running, and without turning her head, walked on. She crossed the old woman's path. The old woman let her pass, looking at her askance. She stopped, vindictively, in order to admonish the boys once again. They ran on, filtering through the wire fences at one side of the road, and the old woman stayed there, muttering curses, the broom raised in her brawny arm.

Ágata passed the main bar and sat down, breathless, at the door of the small movie house on the central street. She was almost bent in two, ill. Her hair had fallen over her shoulders, covering her face down to her chin. She did not see the boys turn behind the dock police headquarters, dirty and angry, nor the old woman standing threateningly at the front door of her own house, a hundred yards from the one that had belonged to the doctor. Still full of indignation, she muttered insults.

"Scoundrels! Damned hoodlums!"

Everything remained calm for a moment. The old woman disappeared into her house. The pack of hounds erupted from behind the hedges, screaming; and this time they came ready for anything, waving their sticks, the one in the blue shirt giving the signal: "Let's go!"

Ágata let herself be struck. With a moan she rose, absently, and ran toward the docks. Some men came out on their doorsteps in their shirt sleeves. But the noisy crowd was already far away. She walked all around the quay and approached the headquarters of the dock police. But to avoid the eyes of the watchman, the howling swarm made her turn to the back of the houses. The old woman had come out again and was shouting at the top of her voice, impotently and madly:

"Scoundrels! Damned brats, damned brats!"

It was the time of day when the air is saturated with a strong smell of the harbor. Soon, the bells would toll. Before the rejoicing of the imminent Sunday sunset, the twenty-year-old girls started to laugh. There was no sun any more, only the cold and the smell of the port.

With her remaining strength, breathless, Ágata turned her back on the wharves. Once again some men appeared nearby. The savage crowd stopped.

Then, she went on running, and reached the dock itself, her eyes like those of a beaten lunatic. Impulsively, blindly, she sought refuge behind the last shed, a few steps from the anchored side of the *Fieling*. She fell beside the wall and leaned back upon it, her palpitating heart almost bursting. She could still hear the shouts of the boys in the distance, the mocking, the screams. And once again she thought of the face of Nicanor Cruz. Once again she saw him, arid and indifferent. She was still afraid, and she would have liked to die. She remained as if in a faint, there in the already nocturnal darkness.

The village seemed to be agonizing. Slowly, slowly, the radios of Ingeniero White started hurling familiar melodies into the space of the night. The lighted bars were filling with consumers of idleness, and the girls, ready for emotion, were saying their good-byes at that late hour of the holiday. The air of the village was full of band tunes and vague orchestras, and sweet refrains sung by a voice whose resonance held an ascending glory. Then, all was silence once more.

Ágata stood up and looked in terror at the high, clear sky. She screamed and ran toward the street where her house stood. Sobbing, she crossed the wharf, the little square, haunted by the specter of open eternity. With whom would she enter that valley?

Choked with tears and madness, she crossed the street, running. Her feet touched the wood of the familiar steps and she fell into a sitting position, shivering, completely without hope or reason. Her eyes searched the ground. Then she saw something. Her father's imprint on the wooden step. The worn trace of all the times the doctor had returned, half-drunk, from visits to his patients, overwhelmed by his sorrow and his failure, sad and sententious, with his bad heart. It was as if she had reached a sanctuary, found companionship at last. Sitting there, Ágata let loose all her tears. Sobbing, she placed her head, from which at last all light had been extinguished, over her father's footstep.

She had no notion or sense whatever of what was around her, of the town, of the enormous Sunday calm, or of the image only a few steps away, the bulk of wood which stood in front of the chapel and at the foot of which was faintly written: *Ego sum via, veritas et vita:* "I am the way, the Truth and the Life."

It was very late when she got up suddenly, as if called by a scream, and, without direction or discernment, started running against the darkness.

CHAVES

The saws had been buzzing since seven in the morning and their incessant racket was heard for several miles around, across the boundless wilderness beyond the woods, beyond the larch trees as far as the smooth-flowing waters of the river.

Scattered around the large angular and swarthy sheds of the sawmill, a few white houses, huddled together like a flock among the cedar trees, lay slumbering on the plain, as if mesmerized in their everlasting stillness.

From the back of one of the yards, a grouse scuttled at great speed. Autumn chilled the bushes. At nightfall, the tops of the trees turned bluish like the mountain peaks. The workers returned home. The night swarmed. The taverns opened their doors. But the world seemed very far away, beyond the beech trees and the cypresses, beyond the wide river, whose indigo surface reflected an endless progression of wealthy villas.

Sunday was the only day when no one worked. Every other day, about two hundred gray men came out of their whitewashed houses at dawn and trudged across the graveled square facing the wooden chapel, toward the gates of the sheds, which were perpetually resting like monstrous birds in the shadow of the ancient woods. The strident hum so well known to the villagers was heard all day long, and every sunburned, haggard face seemed to be sawn through, not by the saws themselves, but by the infernal din of the sharp wheels, for which they had been born and among which they would die.

A squabbling buzz filled the dining room where the men all gathered at noon. The echo of sawn timber reverberated within those log walls, whose decay and blackness were proof that they, as well as the sawmill itself, dated from the first year of the century. In the distance, large river barges were waiting. On one side of the square, in the isolated, taciturn, antisocial factory dormitory, lived the foremen. These were bachelors who looked as if they had been chosen for their huge frame and sneering contempt for the village as a whole. Quick to anger, hateful, they were like mighty lords banished to Guiana, forced to live among serfs.

Huge barges loaded with timber drifted slowly down the river like a fleet in a procession. And between the men in the sheds and those on the water there was an established rivalry, a certain cultivated animosity which the parish priest tried to assuage in his evening talks, soothing this one, admonishing another, showing everyone the utility of the undisputed voice of experience. Much given to scoffing, the priest had a garden near the tavern, with a fountain, a bed of pansies, and a St. Bernard.

The head foreman was a short, bald fellow called Mólers; next to him came Grundi, a woman-hater, and the strongly built and spiteful Rómola and Bastenone. In their youth they had all been skilled strikers, daring and undaunted, some of them in the South, others in the Chaco and Misiones.

But now they strode around with their big bellies and their strong shoulders, their faces prone to derision, disbelief, and sarcasm.

When Chaves arrived at the sawmill one morning, Mólers eyed him with distrust from his seat in the office.

Mólers was short and bald, the newcomer tall and tanned by the sun, with regular, gaunt features, black hair, and full, quiet lips. He looked like a motionless statue.

Suddenly Mólers lost his temper. "Why don't you answer?"

The other didn't move a hair.

In the heat of his anger, Mólers struck the table with violence. He exploded: "Why don't you answer!"

Without changing his expression, Chaves unsealed his lips and started speaking slowly, very slowly, to say that he had already told him he had worked in a factory in Santa Fe, in a textile mill in Resistencia, and later on in the sugar refinery in Diamante.

"That's no answer!" grunted Mólers, pushing aside the papers that littered his desk. "That's no answer! You all come here asking for a job and you can't even say what the hell you've done. . . . Are you all half-witted or what? You don't even look like human beings. Mummies or mules, that's what you are. And where do you get off with your stuck-up manners? What do you think we need here? Dukes?"

Chaves said he only wanted a job.

"A job!" shouted Mólers. "We're full up with people. Just get a look at the sheds: plenty of noise and no work done! Before, we got much more work done with fewer men. Nowadays they all think they're dukes. . . ."

Mólers screwed up his face in disgust and stood up, after putting an iron weight on the bills. He strode over to the window, which he blotted out completely with his short but stout frame, and called "Ciruela! Luis Ciruela!"*

A swarthy and haggard man appeared at the door: his face was so wrinkled and dark that his surname could have been a nickname.

"Take this fellow to shed two. Then tell 'Golden Boy' to find him a place to sleep. I'll have a word with Rómola."

Chaves thanked him.

He still looked stern and impassive, and the other man, Mólers,

---

* *Ciruela:* plum; prune. [Trans.]

ignored his thanks, as if he had not heard. The foreman followed them out and stood with legs apart, looking at the sun. It was eleven o'clock; a shaft of light tinted the yard with a golden hue, and the humming of the saws filled the air, so that even the brightness of the morning seemed to vibrate.

In the distance, the fragrant wood was dense. Beyond the humming, the air retained that sweet state of suspense where nature still dominated.

Walking with his body tall and slow behind the man who led the way, Chaves thought how cool and beautiful the river must be on the fringe of the wood, with the green land of the opposite bank sprinkled with white houses. He had come that way and his nostrils had caught the smell of the water even before the scent of the musk roses.

In the gloomy and noisy immensity of the shed, a man who had just hung up the telephone receiver came over to them. "You're Chaves?" he asked.

Chaves nodded.

The second man smiled quizzically.

"You'll have to work hard here," he said. "It's no child's play. If you aren't sure you can stand it, you'd better take off while you can."

Chaves stood still and did not answer.

"I might have to give you the sack later on," sneered Rómola. "I might have to request you kindly to get the hell out of here. This is a working island. Here, there's work, exhaustion; more work, and bad tempers. We don't like tourists."

He pronounced the word "tourists" as if it amused him immensely to thus designate a gang of good-for-nothings or loafers.

"Mólers tells me what you can do is still a mystery," he added. "All the worse for you, or the better, maybe, if you surprise us. But don't think you can get away with giving us chalk for cheese. Here we know better than anywhere else what a man is worth."

Chaves kept silent.

"Come this way," said Rómola, walking toward the big whirling buzz saws of gray steel. The floor was practically covered with sawdust. The ghastly, shrill racket obliged Rómola

almost to shout. "The last one who came was a fellow called
Mena. A good-for-nothing. . . . On this third day he turned out
to be a wise guy and Bastenone had to kick him out. Down here
we're peaceful people and we don't like that kind of thing."

They were walking toward the saw which was devouring the
proffered victim: a big white-veined log. "You don't seem to talk
at all," Rómola shot at him, as if only just aware of the fact.

But they were already standing in front of a sallow man in shirt
sleeves who kept his vigorous, grimy arms dangling as if trying to
keep the crusty coating of wool and resin uncontaminated.

"Vigliori," called Rómola with a shove of his chin to indicate
Chaves's presence, "this one will be your assistant. Didn't you say
you needed one? Well, here he is."

"He's half mute. . . ."

The three men almost smiled. But the glance Vigliori cast at
the novice was more obvious; it was a conceited and deprecatory
glance meant to assert his own superiority.

And thus, one Monday morning toward the end of March,
Chaves started to work at the sawmill, a few hundred yards from
the river. A fair-faced young man, nicknamed "Golden Boy"
—perhaps on account of his shiny tidiness or because of his
anodyne, bland countenance—found him an out-of-the-way
room in the house of a certain Juan Girossi, a commercial traveler whose family consisted of a surly wife and an even surlier
mother. It was a whitewashed room, like all the others in the
village, with its small mat, and a night table smelling of urine, a
picture of a saint and across it a palm leaf to be used as a fan in
summer. "This room was expensive and too good for the others,"
laughed Golden Boy in great mirth as he left him with Girossi
near the small window overlooking the woods. "Congratulations,
buddy. You're lucky!"

And as he walked away he added with comic gesticulations:
"I'll show you the tavern any time you like. Just let me know . . ."

"He's an inveterate drunkard," stated Girossi contemptuously
and with unctuous commercial presumption, after closing the
door. "An inveterate drunkard. Stay away from him."

The little house stood on a kind of hillock or mound, from
which one could perceive the stillness of the hills and the tower-

ing tops of the trees challenging the clear sky. The noise of the saws stopped at night, and then began the secret murmur of the river and a kind of mysterious warning or whisper sensitively spread by the gentle gliding of the barges.

On the first night, after taking leave of Girossi and his wife, Chaves stood very late by the window, listening, trying to take in the many sounds of the evening. He began to distinguish their shades, their differences, to pick out each from the whole in its concrete and special resonances. He seemed amazed, carried away by such a wealth of variety.

The next day they gave him a hard job, into which he put all of his effort. At first, the sight of his injured hands produced in him a feeling of sadness and pride, as if he had conquered and was aware of it, of having, through his hands, returned part of the way from a decline, and at the same time of resignation, since in his heart he was convinced that now nothing could ever call upon them to exert themselves to the utmost.

He worked from seven o'clock with Vigliori and no sooner had he received the first instructions, which he had no difficulty in following, than he devoted himself wholeheartedly to doing his share of the work alone. Vigliori, who lived with his wife in one of the houses on the hillside, was a good-natured fellow. Other than his discreet self-satisfaction, he was an honest and perfectly decent man to work with. Chaves was accustomed to another sort of work, more of an administrative nature, and this simple, manual, almost mechanical work was new to him and produced in his mind a kind of remote melancholy, a peace of mind, as if someone else's rest had descended on his tension and relieved it. He finished his job a little before dusk; then his body joined that procession of strong young men who scattered themselves all over the village, taking their strong appetites home with them.

Chaves had no home to return to, no refuge at whose door one hears familiar exclamations and those oft-repeated sentences which go to make up the nostalgic image of the more intimate and tribal parts of our lives. He went for a walk alone, and devoted a long period of time to the contemplation of inanimate things.

At first he had almost no relationship with anybody; except for Vigliori, he hardly exchanged one or two words with the other men; certainly he did not awaken much interest in them either. A chance meeting on passing through a door, the light requested for a cigarette as they walked out toward the gate, the instructions or orders given by the office through a third person were the cause of ephemeral encounters which only left on him the fleeting impression of some face illuminated by the flame of a match or the peculiarity of a tone of voice.

It was only when he began to know the village, to visit the tavern, to go near the river to watch the never-ending work of the barges, that the first questions were put to him. Most of them were founded on idle and mechanical curiosity, and he answered them systematically with his usual sparseness of words. In those long evenings, he did not go to the tavern from habit or from pleasure, but in response to a need, renewed each day, to appraise silently the real proportion and character of things, in the same way that a guest is anxious on his arrival in a new house to capture its general atmosphere, through a knowledge of the landscape of every room. He wandered among garrulous men accustomed to indulging their leisure in the plaza or in the tavern with the laughter and mockery which compensate for the boredom and contriction of their personal lives. He would sit among them at a table in the corner, with a large tankard of beer before him, his black eyes and cigarette glowing. From there he took in everything: their gestures and manner, quarrels and brash remarks, generosity and meanness, with the same open, disinterested attention. Occasionally, one of the customers, drunk or sober, would come over with a glass in his hand and fire one of the usual questions at him. What was his name? Where did he come from? Where had he worked before? Where was his family? What were his plans? Invariably polite, Chaves accepted these inquiries, but his answers were always incomplete, partial, perfunctory, of little help in satisfying the interest of the questioner. They finished by leaving him alone, without persisting, sometimes a bit intrigued, but more often with a vague and captious indifference.

He watched them go away like strangers or, if they showed signs of drunkenness, looked at them as we look at a masquerader who approaches us during carnival in an attempt to plunge us into the tragic and fictitious prattle of one night. Chaves's instinct soon recognized among all those strong and lively fellows a subtle and good-natured man who, even when drunk, spoke with a kind, almost superhuman politeness, a politeness born of such self-denial that it instantly turned into a kind of support, an anonymous, impersonal, inner song. The man in question was a confirmed bachelor, about forty years old, with a high forehead and rapid, darting eyes, called Equerí. He was very popular in the village, mainly because of his indifference to material things and his almost childish, Homeric disregard for danger. During the first nights of April—nights alternately warm and cold, when a sudden gust of wind would blow in from the river, go rippling through the woods, and afterward filter through the houses—as Chaves sat alone sipping a glass of beer, he was approached by that restless man, who would visit all the tables and the bar, never stopping anywhere. Always talkative and rather sharp, he would drop one or two pieces of gossip from the sawmill, or make some harmless joke about one of the foremen.

But Chaves came and went home alone. He protected his solitude like a sacred property which was only trespassed upon when someone approached him and walked with him for a while, and on such occasions Chaves only listened. He refused to talk. After a short time he was known by everybody as a melancholy type and left alone except by a few who soon gave him up with an indolent shrug of the shoulders. However, those who besieged him with questions were more disappointed than the others and came to feel toward him a sort of latent spite, bordering on anger.

Only much later did he come to realize—without in any way changing his gloomy taciturnity—that in a world where no one really receives an answer to anything, nobody will accept a person who never tries to answer.

The first perceptible signs of intolerance appeared a few weeks after Chaves's arrival in the village.

He worked regularly and steadily. His life lacked the ups and downs of excitement. At noon and at nine o'clock in the evening he cooked his meals and then went into the small moonlit orchard to throw away the fruit peel, the eggshells, and other leftover food. And, after rinsing the copper receptacle, he would go for a walk in the woods among the cedars, or stay near the white door of the house, leaning against the wall and smoking. Girossi's wife and mother snored peacefully in their rooms at the back of the house. Chaves was intent on the changes in the air. The sounds of night, always so perceptible to him, were sometimes mingled with other noises . . . voices and shouts coming from the workers on the river.

From the fields came the smell of autumn fruits, vegetables, and the fragrant breath of wild flowers which raised their fearful heads in the night once the terrible din of the day's work was over. Finally, Chaves started to walk toward the river, drawn by the sounds of the river workers, the barges, and the water.

He had been frequenting the tavern when he felt like it, with his usual indifference. The night when the hostile demonstration against him took place, he had been walking for more than an hour along the river, and had gone down to the tavern to drink a glass of beer because the new moon and unusually hot night were an invitation to wakefulness. He went up to the bar, asked for a pint, and listened mechanically to the talk of a group of men standing there. He would not have been able to repeat a word of what was said, because what he was listening to distracted rather than interested him. But in the huge room where the light of three yellow lamps never faded, the group of men went on talking, with sudden changes of pitch; words of protest and insult were heard, first in a muffled voice, then in arrogant tones.

Subconsciously, he was aware that some kind of visitation or concerted action was being planned for that night, a project which seemed to appeal to all of them. But his hearing withdrew even from this vague perception upon which it had been absent-mindedly bent. In a new, wandering movement, his eyes looked slowly around the room, now quite empty except for the group of men.

After half an hour of talk, the men stopped speaking, and with garrulous voices whose pitch showed their satisfaction at what they had planned or decided, with a lot of laughing and slapping of backs, the ring of men opened and scattered against the counter, like a wave breaking and coming into the shore. They all spoke at once, each man calling for a drink. One of them pointed at Chaves with a merry and quick gesture, asked why he was not invited, suggested doing so and, raising his glass and his voice happily, applauded his own idea.

His words met with a dead silence and a pause. And then one of the men, who looked like an agitator, pointed with his finger at the still bashful and bewildered Chaves, and shouted hoarsely and angrily at the top of his voice: "No! Not that one! He's not like us! He never talks!"

Calmly braving the glances of those who were already prepared to take sides, as always happens in such cases, Chaves raised his eyes and looked without animosity or surprise at the man who had just spoken and whose sly expression and taut features clearly marked him as a born troublemaker.

The men, so different and yet so much alike, some tanned, others white-faced, awaited his answer; but nothing came, only the usual patient silence. With gestures expressing mockery or mirth, patience or humor, they turned back to the counter to go on drinking, while the man who had spoken showed clearly by his boastful and challenging attitude that he would be the last to look away and join the others in their drinking.

Chaves paid for his beer and left the pub before the others, as if they had not been there, with his usual cool and contemptuous indifference, unhurried and showing neither inhibition nor irritation at the snide glances which followed him.

His sleep was in no way disturbed by the event, which he didn't judge worthy of consideration. As he walked into the sawmill the following morning, he recognized some of the faces he had seen in the group the night before, but without stopping to think about them in this connection, in much the same way as one might distinguish the color of a particular pebble in a gravel pile.

He worked hard all day long, and in the evening when the end of the day's work at the sawmill was announced, he went down to the small square surrounded by the tavern, the chapel, and the parish priest's small garden, walked down the dusty, sloping street along which were to be seen a number of aproned women who, having interrupted their cooking, had come out to catch a breath of evening air. He reached the riverbank where the vegetation seemed to take pleasure in displaying its variety of species. The slime flowed continuously down toward the river. Trees grew sparsely there—the vanguard of a growth which farther on acquired a thick and woods-like density. Chaves halted at the water's edge and sat down to watch the opposite bank of the river where the houses were grouped in clusters. No lights were to be seen, and only the whiteness of the walls emerged from the dusky greenness of the foliage.

Night fell in the midst of an absolute stillness. The river continued its invisible gliding. On the sloping ground of the opposite bank, among the sparse trees and slanting orchards, small houses joined the larger ones, with a display of verandas and balustrades, as if in a kind of combined action against the destruction which awaits all things. Chaves slowly took it all in with a deep, discerning silence, though anyone observing him might perhaps have asserted that he was not looking but listening, and that his eyes were merely reflecting the different shapes of sound on a transparent April night.

On setting out for work in the morning, he heard a violent quarrel between Girossi's wife and his mother, so that he had no wish to go back to the house until sleep had silenced every human voice. Consequently, he sat there almost motionless for hours, watching how the landscape changed owing to minute but very effective transformations, such as the appearance of a light, the opening or closing of a window, or the luminous trail of a bright ray of light marking the passage of a car along the abrupt and sloping roads of the village on the other side of the river.

He was prepared to face any kind of hostility, or better still, more than prepared. Human animosity seemed to him both useless and futile. The world of man no longer held any fears for him. He simply looked and listened, and what he saw and heard provided him with more than sufficient reason to consider hostility and aggression no more than useless outbursts—a form of stupidity unable to express itself otherwise. As had just happened here, or what had happened before, in the place where he came from, no one tolerated his deep and wide reserve. They considered it an insult, an offense, the conscious sign of a direct and definitive superiority. It was attributed to a kind of calculation loaded with unspeakable, secret, and malignant intentions. They thought of everything except of the fact that he had once spoken.

The person we left behind us thirty years ago and who was called by our own name, what is he to us thirty years later? Another person, of another race? Or perhaps, in some monstrous way, the same, unchanged by time, mutations, emotions.

At seventeen, Chaves was as thin as a post. A staff of chipped wood, hard and black; very black hair; unblinking coal-like eyes; a still, obstinate, thoughtful mouth which never opened except in wonder, and legs as thin as those of a lean horse, but slow, not quick.

He was accustomed to withdrawing systematically into the shell of his silent moods. The world was a battle into which one had to plunge very slowly. There was no hurry. He had been born in a populous city on the Atlantic, to the south of Buenos Aires, and was the second son of a shopkeeper named León Chaves. The eldest son, who had gone into the navy, had been drowned when he was twenty in a shipwreck off the West Indies. The second one, Chaves, grew up in a shop dealing with shells—he learned everything about them—bell glasses full of old-fashioned flowers, lamps, clocks, brackets of ancient bronze. His father, an exceedingly tyrannical man, wanted to ordain him for the priesthood of that trade; the young man answered with a tacit refusal. He didn't want to; he refused to do so. He became a street wanderer, a preyless night leopard, without hunger, who looked at things, thought about what he saw, smelled the honeysuckle. In the presence of people, he withdrew into his shell. He could be reached only through the passageways of his solitude.

When he took leave of his father, after bitter scenes during which the older man did his best to destroy the adolescent, he went about that city on the Atlantic in search of life. Here was the "Blanco y Negro" store, the newspaper *El Atlántico*, fashionable O'Higgins Street, the "Iglesia Metropolitana." On the outskirts: the countryside, the railways, the wheat fields, the universe. He clung to the town, stubbornly reluctant to leave it. An inner voice said, "Chaves, stay here." And he stayed.

He lived in a room he rented from the stationmaster. How far away it all seemed! The vase filled with wild flowers, the crocheted tablecloth on which the inkstand rested, the palm-leaf fan which in winter served as a decoration, the clothes hangers, the big black chest of drawers, the portrait of somebody unknown hanging on the wall and looking tragically corrupted by time. He hardly ever saw anybody. He did not speak. What a life for a young man! Finally, he met Julio Retes.

Both of them started working on the same day and in the same pharmacy. The job was a delicate one. Chaves was full of fears; Julio Retes gave himself airs. Youth often brings together such different characters; this one has to play one role, that one another role. Even when two similar souls establish a polarization by their contact, a primacy is born and the predominance of one or the other inevitably becomes final in worldly terms. The shrewd world selects its best agents, some for their knowledge, others for their experience, or for their malevolence or covetousness. Retes took him to dances; one night, at a dance at the Prince d'Udine Hall, Retes introduced him to a girl. History is reversible; change one light, one circumstance, one tactical maneuver, one landscape, the entire tangential immensity; but in each man a songless Homer lies dormant—or perhaps with song merely awaiting rebirth and liberation. Why, in a world that changes so much, does man change so little? Here lies the trick: life simplifies . . . as a preparation for death.

The girl's name was Pura. She had a cold and distant air, not timid; her attitude seemed to be one of detachment or disassociation from all the common things of life upon which people generally confer an ultimate value. She seemed to lead a life apart, constructed piece by piece especially for her, and not to need anyone at all—neither neighbors, friends, nor lovers. Her large, sullen eyes did not conceal that powerful and exclusive propensity of her character toward detachment and evasion.

Before he knew her, and even for some time after being aware of the violent attraction she exerted over him, Chaves had lived systematically secluded in his wordless world, full of images and external events. He went about sullen and silent, so withdrawn in his dumbness that he seemed to her to have been born to cultivate it; but he was all ears to what the others said. Pura dazzled him; he had never before seen such eyes, such breasts; so much attractiveness. In other respects, her status in life approximated his. In spite of her youth, she worked as a desk clerk on night duty in a hotel. After that first evening at the dance, he invited her for a daily walk, and one Sunday they took streetcar number nine to Villa Harding Green. They lunched there. Then they went walking through the green fields. They spoke almost not at all—merely observed the beautiful gardens, the chalets, and the big fleshy flowers—because they felt bound to each other by a sort of self-sufficing and self-justifying animal sympathy. "We shall come again," said Pura, without a change in the expression of her deep black eyes. And they came back, and they walked again in silence, looking at the beautiful gardens, at the chalets, and at the big fleshy flowers.

In November they became engaged, by an act of solitary decision. He seemed possessed by an eager ardor, and she responded to his solicitude with an acquiescent and almost remote passivity. They were seen walking side by side through the central streets of the old city, tranquil and grave, unsmiling. Within, they were ardent, transported; he more than she, she something less than he. He was thin and dark as a post; she was attractive, elusive, and pale. He was content with letting himself be plunged into the enchantment of mutual expectation while butterflies of desire fluttered around them, pausing now on one, now on the other in alternately vivid spells. Only Pura, in her somewhat acrid loquacity, came to enjoy a complex and cruel game of causing him joy and mental anguish. "You know," she said one day, "I've met a student called Senillosa; he's very clever and very amusing." He found it strange that she, usually so reluctant to accept acquaintances, especially new ones, should feel attracted toward that newcomer, and a strange and unknown feeling, uncommonly sharp and uncommonly painful, overwhelmed him.

During the following days, Pura told him that the student lived in the hotel, that she liked him, that he lent her books, and she referred to him with malicious pedantry, averting her face so as not to look at Chaves, thus seeming to ignore what he thought about it all.

He became hardened, rigid, withdrew into himself, down to the depths of his mutism. He conceived feelings of vengeance and anger he had never known before. And because these new sentiments did not modify in any way Pura's partiality for the student, did not remove the danger which his instinct made him see—nor was there a single factor to alleviate his despair—a strong flood of uncertainty, fear, anxiety, and dread overwhelmed him, and his whole behavior toward the woman he loved and desired underwent a change and became more urgent and more conscious.

It was a difficult and deliberate transformation, a change which required discipline and training, and he applied himself with a melancholy and energetic daring, a decisive resolution, to this new conquest. He thought that any conquest must begin with an appeal, and that the denouement would be proportionally conditioned to the intensity and shape of this appeal. Therefore, he wanted to appeal at all costs, and in order to do so, he spoke.

What a sudden effort—an unexpected volume—of will he had to apply to the new inventions he needed, in order to cast them into the air, like bait, to lure the prey! With what fury and desperate eagerness not to fail did he plunge into words! How he filled his days and his nights with inventions, motives, and theses, things and questions, pleas and pretenses, reasoning and fiction! He had to speak, to speak, to say it and say it again, to tell and retell, in order to wrap Pura in a train of words and bring her back to him. "What's happening to you?" she asked vaguely, noticing a feverish change in him. And without stopping he threw himself into new inventions, straining his imperfectly developed articulation, until he reached a confused though eager and unwavering fluency of discourse.

His young, silent heart struggled with all the energy he possessed. The taciturn one lived in constant search of animated deceptions. And Pura? As if caught in a net, shaken by the novelty of that disquieted and disquieting new spirit which she had kindled in her lover, Pura came back. She came back with wonder and delight. Every evening, when he had finished his work and before she started hers, they would walk along the well-lighted O'Higgins Street, and Chaves spoke with eagerness about everything they saw—the shops, the windows, the jewels, the furniture, the ornaments, the advertisements, the people—sometimes in a broken, faltering way, sometimes quickly and fluently, while she laughed and listened, her own attitude transformed at the sight of manly success which she herself had evoked.

The following winter they were married in a little church of the suburb which had become most familiar to them; and a picture, bound to fade because of its poor quality, showed them on sepia: he with shining hair, she in a white dress trimmed with a bit of Milan lace.

Every time Chaves went back to silence, his native abode, she would become sad, dejected, her mind fleeing, wandering away, and he had to yield to that laughter of hers; and once again, through the power of his will, he set out to entertain her.

Two years after their wedding, they went to live in another summer resort where they also had a town and the sea, but a sea with a wide sandy beach. Chaves sold plots of land belonging to a rather unknown real estate concern. He did not sell much because he didn't speak, sparing his loquacity for his appeals to the woman who lived with him and who gave such an intimate and strange warmth to the old house on the outskirts which they had rented for a hundred and fifty pesos a month. He took advantage of his rounds to build his stock of topics of conversation, suggestions, false allurements; his absentmindedness made him lose a lot of time, and sometimes he would walk for hours and hours on end, deaf to the chime of bells ringing for mass, blind to the billboards of movies and to the invitations of the women who passed, outrageously painted, sadly made up, in the deserted streets where the bric-a-brac opened to passers-by their hungry mouths and their useless offers.

Against solitude and poverty, against wretchedness, against the ineffectual fallacy of possessing something, day after day, night after night, in the old house, taking refuge from cold in the cold dining room, Chaves fought with his primitive and sustaining stock of words. He stopped talking only to devise more things to say. A deep gloom filled the difficult, cruel pauses. And from the bottom of himself, while the hands of the clock approached midnight, while it froze outside, while the wind from the sea blew in the surroundings of the beach, while the anonymous shipwrecks wandered in search of their victims, from the bottom of himself, Chaves fetched up words, narrated, spoken. Sometimes Pura watched him with thoughtful eyes and her heart secretly ached at the sight of that obstinate tenacity.

Thus it was that Chaves came to speak for the first time.

He got up with a slow movement from the river's bank where he was sitting and walked slowly along the shore, following it closely. He had nothing on but an old pair of pants and an old shirt under his leather jacket; and his bare neck and chest welcomed the evening breeze coming from the opposite bank. He bent down, picked up a wet branch, held it in his hand for a short time as he went on walking, and finally, with a pliant and effortless movement, threw it into the quiet river, which received it silently and carried it along. The water gave off a soft swallowing or brushing sound, and from time to time the plaint of a broken branch or a remote and unrecognizable animal cry could be heard. With a slow, simultaneous movement, Chaves threw both his hands into his pockets, found them empty, and decided he had left his black cigarettes in his room. There was no wind, no breeze, the air was as cold as ice. A few steps away he made out the night light of the barge workers' shed. Against the background of the night, he saw the men working steadfastly along in the darkness of the shore. Suddenly, one of them would jump into a barge, a quick ripple was heard as a log was shoved into motion and spun around, then there was silence again. He saw the shadowy men coming and going. The shed and the trees hid the movements of the men on the shore. He could only make them out when they came out in the light of the half moon at the mouth of the river or on the bank, just on the edge of the water. Chaves drew near the barges, stopping in a place where he could not be seen. He stood there watching, listening to the different noises of the work and of the night. The hostility toward him had begun, and he didn't know whether he would be able to remain, because he knew where such feelings of animosity would lead. He wondered if there would be the possibility of doing something in the town on the other side of the river, or whether he would have to start all over again. Things weighed on him, and it was sad to see their recurrence. It occurred to him that perhaps Equerí could arrange it all by checking the aggressive ones at the very beginning; but he loathed the mere notion of telling anybody about what had happened, about his fears, or about his pessimistic forebodings.

He remained for about an hour near the riverside and then took the main road to the town, climbed the even slope of the hill to his house, with the whispering of the river still in his ears.

They had given him the kind of work anyone could do. Now it was his job to apply grease to the saw teeth whenever they cut green logs, so that when the friction made them hot the resin would not slow down the speed of the saw. It was a simple task—so easy that, judging it too simple for himself, Vigliori had asked for an assistant. If Vigliori had not asked for an assistant, Chaves would perhaps have had to go away once more and cross over to the other bank, beyond the river and the larch trees, and ask for a job among the people in the rich white houses.

"More grease here," called Vigliori, and Chaves applied a greasy lubricant to the glistening steel blade.

They did not look at him and he didn't look at the others. He only heard the racket of the saws, the strident hum, and the smooth and natural sliding of the logs, like huge creatures filing by to offer their necks to the blade.

He had no need to remember the old and gloomy house they lived in at the seaside town. It was a house with big, damp and dark rooms, a grandfather clock, an upright piano, many faded pictures, many old curtains, and other things which did not show their own taste but that of the landlord. At the beginning, feeling afraid and full of forebodings in the house, Pura used to go with him on his rounds, selling plots of land. She didn't want to stay alone within those walls where a foreign and unknown spirit seemed to dwell. Sometimes, they would cross the desolate esplanade, with its small shops and coffeehouses, and have tea in some teashop in town, always empty in winter. But business was poor. Chaves did not know how to sell, and he sold badly. He gave up his prospective clients at once, remiss of his words, unwilling to offer those uncouth or ill-disposed strangers the words he was saving for his home.

They spent a lot of time together enjoying a sort of soft happiness. They ate sparingly, and their expenses were so reduced that, when they spoke about them in their evening chats with their neighbors, the latter did not believe them and suspected Pura of wanting to boast about her efficiency as a housekeeper. But they were wrong; it was simply that Pura and Chaves were bound together by a soft and tenuous happiness.

They lived alone as their means permitted, and only on Sundays and holidays did they dress up modestly and call on some of their acquaintances: auctioneers or consignees, a post-office worker, the owner of a drugstore, who brought back to Chaves's mind those years when he worked in a pharmacy. Sometimes they went to the movies, and though Chaves was bored by mawkishly sentimental scenes, Pura followed the action of the plot as if they were real events. Chaves humored her, waited on her, acceded to her smallest wishes, and sometimes felt so happy when they returned home at night from some walk, or, on rare occasions, from a play, that he would shut his eyes in order to feel more deeply the touch of her caressing hand.

After three years of marriage, Providence sent them a daughter. In his pride, Chaves walked for hours in the open air, under the rain, with unseeing eyes. He entered a church and went out again, after having stayed at the back, behind the pews, like a statue. Dumfounded, he gave up talking, silenced by Pura's finger, who insisted that no whisper should disturb their child's sleep. It seemed as if his former loquacity had taken the form of his daughter. Pura did not need anything else. And he used to walk alone for hours, through the town, along the esplanade adjoining the harbor. He started to sell a little better, although his sales brought only a small profit. He reached the point where he began to worry because he owed three months' rent, and he vaunted his silence with arrogance.

His strong, fatherly pride reached its peak when the little girl was four years old and walked around the house, showing her omnipotence with the histrionic gravity of children. She played at dressing like grown-up women, mimicked the ladies' manners, the aristocratic and disdainful bearing of women of rank. Chaves imagined her already as a young girl. And when he looked into Pura's eyes and saw in them the same suspended and noble contentment, he almost wept with happiness, in that house where even the furniture chosen by strangers seemed to become proper and friendly through the influence of good luck.

"Daddy, I want this!" "Daddy, I want that!" "Daddy, I want some water from the moon," and out he went, sweetly driven by the tyrannical charm of the little voice. He could not resist her; on the contrary, he humored and petted her, spoiled her hopelessly; and the little girl clung to him, claiming his constant attention. He left to others the task of withstanding, contradicting, and educating her; it was his business to grant her wishes in the same way that an Olympic god might bestow laurels. And he waited with eagerness for her whims. "You're ruining her," said the mother. "You're doing her a lot of harm." But he listened only to the child, and there was between father and daughter a kind of spontaneous agreement which separated them from the mother and united them in their merry unconcern for whatever she said.

But one day, a strange and insidious illness took hold of the child. She was seized with fits of dizziness and put to bed. She lost her color, and the doctor did not like at all the sudden nephritic complication that arose. Suddenly it was as if everything had completely changed. An unhealthy silence filled the house, and the furniture looked as if it had recovered its former hostile power. The whole house was filled with a sort of fear of life; and terrified, awesome whisperings which did not dare assume the shape of voices surrounded the little bed.

The father would have liked to hear loud voices in the house, but nothing was heard but whispers and murmurs of bad omen. And Chaves's heart was wrung, as if physically clutched by the fingers of the hours; his eyes grew bigger in protest and astonishment, and he answered in a kind of broken trembling when the neighbors came whispering in quest of news.

From time to time the child came out of her coma; then, her father started to talk to her. He tried to reach the deep spot where the elusive life took refuge; he tried to attract its reluctant stream in the shape of answers. But the child merely looked at him as if begging for help or understanding for her aching weakness, from the depth of her small, lifeless eyes. The doctor came and went like an agent of silence.

Finally came the crisis of the illness, when everything in the house seemed to have plunged into hideous waiting and into shadows; the child half rose in her father's arms, and seeing the proximity of his ear, she whispered: "I want a soldier with a red coat, Daddy . . . like the one in the story in the big book. You know? . . . A white soldier with a red coat."

The doctor had left them that morning with an eloquent gesture, the dismal significance of which both parents buried at the bottom of their grief without daring to keep it on the surface, like a heavy stone, thrown in despair into a well, which remains at the bottom with its devastation. Only there isn't a stone. It doesn't exist on the surface. Overwhelmed, they sat in the loneliness of their house, looking at each other, without saying a word. It was Sunday; a strong wind had blown during the morning, and the draft that came in from under the door had raised the first three pages of the newspaper lying on the floor and shaken them several times.

Chaves's heart expanded in a wild hope, as if granting that request might bring about a miraculous recovery.

It was just past the siesta hour, and the afternoon sun was still high in the sky when he went into the street with the joyful promise to his daughter of bringing her what she had asked for. But as soon as he was in the street, he remembered that it was Sunday and not a single shop would be open in the whole town. Suddenly cold inside, he started walking quickly. He walked past closed shops, heading for the center of town where something might be open. He was intent on time, and with every minute that passed he felt he had lost something precious and irretrievable. He stopped at the two toy shops he found and, furiously excited, pounded violently at the wrought-iron blinds. The mockery of the steady and repeated lack of response seemed accentuated by the aspect of the strong iron curtains, which stubbornly remained closed.

He continued walking with deadly impotence, until evening began to fall and he had not found a single open door in all that gloomy area.

He did not walk any more, but started running, his heart in his mouth, when the first lights began to shine. He would never be in time, he would not find anything . . . would not find anything . . . would not be in time . . . Desperate, he finally reached the streets near the harbor, with their bars and shops and their high wooden sidewalks. Looking like a mad dog, the collar of his shirt open, his hair blown by the wind, he saw his reflection in the windows at which he stopped. And the night was already there, with the sharp and oceanic cold from the coast.

He went into the bars, one after the other, looking for anything, some toy left behind or a box of sweets in the shape of a soldier, only to come out again as he had gone in, his eyes filled with vague, blurred images of drunkenly human shapes.

Then, all of a sudden, unexpectedly, at the corner of a street, tied to the pillar of a drugstore, he discovered a white post with something like a round head and an almost human shape, foolishly holding an advertisement for Blondel cocoa. He remembered, he would always remember, the half stick, half-man-shaped wooden doll, its rigid arm pointing at the word "Blondel," with only the top of it imitating completely a heavy human head. With an almost joyful moan, he grasped the puppet savagely with both hands, pulling and tearing it away from the post, like a thief destroying everything in his way under the moonlight.

He ran home madly, frantic with expectation, chilled by the fear of being too late. He crossed the gloom of the hall and reached the dimly lit little room, where the mother sat at the head of the bed, moistening the dry lips of the child with a damp cloth. He rushed forward in wild grief, holding the white, splintered stick with its round human head and rigidly extended arm. The delicate little head did not move; it lay on the pillow, heavy as lead, a fringe of fair hair stuck to the sweating brow. And the childish voice said: "It isn't a soldier with a red coat. I don't want that. It isn't a soldier with a red coat."

Hearing that, Chaves started to speak with desperate hoarseness, in such a strange voice that the mother raised her tormented face and looked at him.

He described fictitiously and incessantly the details that she, the child, must notice and which made a soldier of the doll, a true soldier in a red musketeer's coat, except that the coat had been worn out by wars and torn away so that only a little bit was left, a small dark spot. "This is the way it is; wars are always the same. . . ." He tried to explain with words suited to the ears of the child listening to him: "He was a great soldier. Look at that battle-scarred face, the hardness of his body; the arm has a martial gesture, as if still holding a weapon." He spoke with great eagerness.

But the child went on repeating obstinately: "No, Daddy . . . It isn't a soldier with a red coat. I wanted a soldier with a red coat."

And while he, Chaves, tried to bring her to reason through his multiplied, unreasonable words, his shaking hands holding the puppet, looking like a madman, he heaped up his arguments in a clumsy eagerness to create a delusion from that sad emptiness. But the child, rising from time to time from her coma, opened her eyes only to deny and refute his words until, finally, she lay dead tired, silent and asleep, her small heart beating harshly against the walls of her slumber.

Both father and mother went to sit for a moment in the dining room, he to rest his hurt and haggard eyes, she to drink some cold coffee. But the child awoke intermittently with a start and called; Chaves held his head in both his hands as he did when he was twelve years old, bitterly shutting his ears, trying not to hear the little voice in the next room repeating, in a voice louder and calmer than his own, "Daddy didn't bring me a soldier with a red coat . . . Daddy didn't bring me a soldier with a red coat. . . ."

That small life left them at daybreak. Standing before the window and looking outside, like a marble statue, Chaves received the empty sharpness of dawn without even feeling it—a foggy, lonely dawn in which everything seemed far away. Even the sea seemed to stay at a distance, as if the driver had compelled the world to withdraw and leave them alone with the immensity of their grief.

"Did you notice the way that guy goofs off at the saw? It's the business for him!"

They were all sitting in the sun, resting.

Golden Boy laughed, showing his decayed teeth and black mouth. His legs dangled from the low wall in the sunny court-yard of the sawmill. He turned his head and pointed ironically and grimly at Robles, who kept silent: "Robles says they gave him the business at Viedma . . ." Golden Boy gave a biting inflection to the word "business," and Robles lazily cursed under his breath.

Chaves looked at them from his corner in the shadow where he sat, not joining in the chatter, smoking, his hands crossed behind his neck, his back against a pile of timber.

When they had done with their jokes, the men started walking in groups toward the shed of the sawmill. They were more than twenty. The day before, Bastenone had complained about those who were late at their work after having been strolling about on the premises.

Chaves was the last to stand up and walk slowly toward the shed to which he belonged. He avoided conversation with Vigliori, never taking his eyes off the wheel, alert to any noise, to the slightest sign of warming up.

As he had suspected, the hostility against him kept increasing, although slowly. They aimed some gibes at him which he disre-garded, barely acknowledging the existence of his persecutors. And this indifference irritated them even more.

He continued going to the tavern, to have a drink and a smoke. They would have liked to see him take more than one drink, lose control, give them a chance to attack him. But his demeanor was always the same. He was steadfastly true to himself, quiet, almost methodical, his cold eyes lucid.

One day, as he crossed the square, the slight figure of the parish priest approached him, smiling and talkative, asking some-thing about him, about his life; but he answered nothing or prac-tically nothing, and that with a laconic and stiff politeness, with a civility equivalent to silence.

In the house where he lived, he sometimes met Girossi, who told him something about his last trip "on the road." These were usually tales about gambling or women. Girossi would come and sit in Chaves's room and talk and talk. Chaves would go on cook-ing his meal, doing this or that, walking about the room. He listened to the other man's chatter without uttering a word. Sometimes he smiled civilly, out of politeness, to prevent the other man from asking him any questions.

But the hostility was becoming denser and denser. Every evening, Chaves went alone to the riverside to sit at about the same place where he had first sat, in front of the white houses across the river.

For hours and hours he would remain there, listening to sounds and whispers, perceiving the echoes of the workers nearby and the slow passage of the night.

After the calamity, they started going out together every evening for a walk along the deserted winter boulevard. It was as if a huge and deadly weight had fallen on them, oppressing and suffocating them; they felt apart from one another. Between them lay an abyss which neither tried to cross, but which condemned them equally to a hard, malevolent, animal sadness. Pura had always shown herself resolute in her light-minded moods, but now her face had a markedly bitter expression, caused by the sour and dark sense of the impossibility of starting again. They walked among the shops and hovels, unable to transcend their state of mourning. Sometimes Chaves took her to a motion-picture theater called the Great Coliseum. Once inside, he heard her stifled sobs. Finally, they would leave after an hour in which neither had been able to follow the plot of the film.

He had given up selling and stayed with his wife in the lonely house to keep her company, touching with caressing fingers the objects the child had held, raising the corner of a curtain and peering through the windows at the frozen street. Then came a day when they had nothing to eat in the house, when Pura reacted and asked Chaves to shake off his stupor, because they were both still alive, loved each other, and belonged to one another. Then Chaves rushed into the street, with his hungry jaguar eyes, in quest of people whom life had treated well enough to make them wish to put some money in an "excellent" investment.

They gave him some low lands, easily flooded plots of land to sell, and he had to start lying. He had to praise the height and good quality of that flat land.

He postulated almost verbosely the unprecedented opportunity offered by such places, and one day when he took some tourists to the spot, he surprised them looking at him as if he were a madman; they were astounded at the way he shouted aggressively, standing in a pool of mud, proclaiming the fertility of the land.

Late at night, he would arrive home with his throat dry and his heart full of hatred. His soul shrank from the fraud involved in his work, and he resented his own ineptitude which made it impossible for him to reap the profit of his garrulous deceit, through which he foolishly believed he would be able to smile at what is called "misfortune."

Pura fed him, talked to him, cajoled him as if he were an angry child. And he sometimes felt the urge to go out into the streets and shout the hatred and impotence which were corroding him.

But he could do nothing of the sort, and in the morning he would get up with a dry throat, take the prospective buyers to see the wretched plots of land, surrounded by desolation and tamarisks, and start uttering those incredible speeches, a desperate flow of words to which he shut his ears. Sometimes one of the tourists bought a plot, and he still went on talking for the sake of the company. He shut his eyes and ears, and talked. Then, at the end of the month, he was paid a small amount of money, such a small amount that he felt a great shame for the world and for himself.

But after having stimulated him to return to the battle of life in order to meet their immediate needs, Pura began to decline, as do those who base their efforts on fictitious powers. He noticed that she looked tired and sick, and an incoercible physical tenderness filled him with horror and worry.

Once again he tried the spell of words on her.

Once again his forced inventiveness probed into stores of words. Momentarily, Pura seemed to come back to life, her eyes seemed to shine again, as she listened to it all, thinking as she listened that his words were inspired by his love for her and that his feelings endowed him with uncommon and incredible gifts. . . .

"Some lives are like dark galleries, others like an open field," she used to say, her eyes fixed on the evening street. And she added: "I cherish our gallery! It is so well known to us and so much our own! If the ceiling of our gallery broke open, I would not be able to stand the light. . . ."

He tried to dissuade her, then, to make her understand that what she took for a gallery was only a dark recess such as everybody finds once in his life, some at the beginning, as had happened to them; others at the end.

"No," she insisted, "it is a gallery; and I like our gallery. You also must like our gallery."

Chaves threw himself upon new tracts of words. Once, while talking, he raised his eyes toward the tower of the Cooperative Society Building and got the feeling that the tower was laughing at him. Then he spoke in a milder tone, looking at the plants in the park as if their shoots could plumb the depths of his summer prolixity.

And so seven years passed in which life brushed them without bruising them, as an airplane brushes the surface of the earth with it backwash of air on taking off.

One week followed another at the sawmill. The distant snows, called by the autumn, were already beginning to gather, and the larch trees looked taller and more rigid. Chaves took four dry pine cones to his room, prodigiously shaped and delicately polished by the winds, and he placed them on the table by the pile of matchboxes on the worn-out Persian tablecloth.

Work tired him less and less, or perhaps it was just the influence of the increasing coolness of the weather. In fact, every evening, at the end of the day's work, he walked more and more quickly into his house. Then, taking some dry fruit to eat along the way, he would go out in the evening and walk toward the riverbank.

It was as if, on that chosen spot, he withdrew into himself or into some secret recess, and everything disappeared—everything which would blur his perception of the images, the lights and the noises from the coast.

He thought it would be nice to take off his shoes in the summer and wade in the river. He knew the water must be very cold now. No human figure was ever seen among the trees on the other side of the river. He thought everything must be peaceful over there, among the cottages and the villas. He thought of Vigliori and of Bastenone, of Golden Boy who would greet him from time to time with a mad wave of his hand. Distrust and spite did not diminish. He thought of Equerí, gone off a few days before, to return in June.

And he thought of the rest.

He had spent seven years alone with Pura, in constant anguish and fear that the thread of life would suddenly break, leaving one or the other alone among things. Things! Older and more lasting than birth and death; with their monstrous docility which becomes tyranny, obedient to our hands but authoritative at our death, with power over our disappearance.

What was it which made them leave their house at the port on the Atlantic and go away in search of work? There, they were dying. So they sold everything, said good-bye to everything, to all those tattered things in which their absent daughter was materialized. And like mythical children thrust out, rejected by the furniture, the walls and the rooms, they left one day at dawn, a morning on which the cold wind from the sea blew for the last time on them both.

They began an aimless journey, first along the coast, then farther north. With very little luggage, naked as destiny, they became lighter, nearer to one another through that stripping of impedimenta.

They were guided only by ambiguous information, picked up as they went along—such and such a direction, this and that reference. And his only job was to sell, if he could, products for which he could only show the apology, the printed propaganda.

They crossed lakes and rivers, ridges, moors, zones where drought and want wandered like ragged wretches begging for help. But the people did not ask for anything.

They spent the nights in taverns and hotels where the smell of fried food mixed with the rhythmic and nostalgic echoes of music. They crossed forlorn, dreadful places where daylight caused pain and night brought horror. And Pura cried: "Not here, for God's sake, not here!" And then more roads separating one field and the next; roads which fought the immensity.

And everything they found was different—everything except the sky, which was always the same. And when there was nothing to be seen, he started to talk, because he knew that if it all stopped, or if it was interrupted, they wouldn't be able to start again. Because she was traveling in a languishing mood, plunged in the deepest abstractions, and her changeable temper had disappeared, and all her energy seemed to focus upon asking questions.

Chaves felt that now she was only able to ask questions.

And it was necessary to link those questions with successive answers. The journey was an answer in itself, but the gaps required a thread of monologue which had to last till the journey was resumed. "Where are we going, Chaves?"

They went wherever their fancy took them, to those places where the surroundings could still fill them with delusion. They went wherever she wished, wherever she preferred. "There is nothing I like now, Chaves."

He asserted that she was mistaken, that she liked a lot of things. In their room at the hotel where they took refuge by night, he mentioned one by one all the things she liked.

"No, I don't like it any more. There's nothing I like, Chaves."

Then, in despair, he had recourse to one of his flashes of imagination. He started to talk and to laugh, to exclaim, to tell stories. And she looked at him, smiling, knowing that there was nothing she liked any more except the sound of his voice.

They stopped for some time in different towns, watching the cities and the countryside; then they gave up and left. They went up north and down south, into the interior of the country, into inland zones among high mountains, broad plains and large rivers. How green and full of sap everything was! Then suddenly how pallid! The face of things deceived them. They went on traveling.

They passed through Santa Fe, through Tucumán. Traveling by bus during the night, they perceived the skimming murmur of corn as it was shaken by the wind, as it was cropped; later on, they saw the reeds, secretly set together in an immense community; the large creeks in the mountains and, down below, a

gap, an abyss. And between the gorges and the town, the perpendicular mountainsides covered with bright green, damp,
sprouting fern; and the towns, with their wide streets and their
native, secret, forgotten, provincial people.

Finally, they settled in a small town near one of the large cities.
It was a residential district of houses with long balconies, bay
windows and verandas, which the moon filled with natural light.
The verandas were quiet, in colonial style, primitive, open or
covered with diamond-shaped blue-and-white glass. One large
dirt road coming from the city divided the suburb in two, and
both sides of the place stretched out in depths of honeysuckle
and reed flowers.

At the end of the town, as if the town were its waiting room,
the mountain rose, perpendicular to the main street; it had no
houses, and was covered by a dense and wooded vegetation. It
was a mountain with indistinct paths, infinitely mysterious, infinitely deep, from which the eyes of young deer peered at our
mean world.

Chaves went to the city three or four times a week in a slow
bus, to collect the orders which he had to forward to the firm he
represented. He explained, he expounded, and those men looked
contemptuously at him. Sometimes he took Pura with him, and
while he called on his prospective clients she would loiter about
the shops.

They did not get much money, but it was enough to be able to
live near the mountain, in the small town full of old stately
houses dating from the time of National Organization following
Independence, with their cold tiled halls and their ancient wicker
furniture.

Pura hardly asked anything now: she just looked at things with
a certain deep, quiet attention.

Chaves looked back at those years as if at years when adversity
was suspended.

When he set off down the road, toward the west, on his way
home from the sawmill, it did not cross his mind that he would
find Girossi's wife in such a state.

She wore her glossy golden hair parted in the middle, and was
slenderer and taller than Girossi. Chaves met her in the corridor,

a white towel clasped in her hand, shouting at the old woman sitting by the fireplace in matriarchal stillness. Mrs. Girossi was letting out bitter and scornful cries of wrath because she had just come across a letter from a woman in her husband's coat pocket, written in indecent terms, revoltingly crude, and Girossi was away on one of his business trips and was not at hand to be told what she thought of him. When Chaves entered his own room, the woman followed him, her face upset, pale and beautiful, much more refined and rare than her husband.

Plaintively, she affected scorn and contempt, announcing that she cared little whether Girossi went to bed with as many women as he pleased, but she found it vulgar and despicable that he should go about with those filthy scraps of paper in his pockets.

Chaves had placed himself with his back to the window, and she stood framed by the rectangle of the open door, her lips trembling with exasperation.

Systematically, she repeated over and over again that she did not care in the least whether or not he carried on affairs with whom he pleased.

She turned her eyes toward him, an unusual, malignant glint in them: "If that is the law, all right . . . If he likes other women." She sprang at him, with a kind of icy fieriness in her voice. "I—you see, I proclaim it—happen to like you. If that is the law, all right; let everybody do what his heart tells him!"

He saw her take two steps forward, slender and wan, with her catlike maturity, and advance toward him, not looking at him but at the window, her turgid bosom exposing the dividing line of her breasts through the top of her crimson blouse.

He looked at her calmly, untroubled, taking in her blind spite; and without answering, he lit the cigarette between his lips and waited, self-controlled, for her to speak again and unburden herself of words.

He went to the door and closed it. Turning and staring at him, she said, very near him: "If that's the law, then all right . . ."

Chaves drew a chair up to the table for the woman to sit on; she did so. And so that she could see it from where she sat, through the open window, Chaves pointed out to her the hill that rose yonder, dotted with white houses, covered with many trees and plenty of wild grass between the houses. For a fleeting moment, the woman fixed her big wandering eyes on what he was showing her. And he told her, very gently, how that hill never changed, that tomorrow it would be exactly the same as it was today, and that he wished that she, as a woman, would see herself the next day just like the hill, unchanged, in order to be her own mistress, as the hill was also master of itself.

The woman, drawing her eyes abruptly from the window, in a sudden fit of temper, frantically poured out all her resentment against the absent Girossi, and tears filled her eyes because she had not been able to avoid knowing what she knew, what she would know from now on, and what she would never, never forget.

Her hands were shaking, potentially punitive, murderous, and her gaze brimmed with a sort of glassy unhappiness.

Chaves soothed her with a few words. Didn't she realize that her husband had the unsettled temperament of a child, bragging but tied firmly to his mooring, and that she was his mooring?

The woman cast down her eyes in sudden and confused appeasement. "That's a lie," she flung out.

He approached her in a friendly manner, telling her that he must go now because he had promised to meet somebody, though he would come back.

But he did not come back.

He took his solitary walk to the tavern, and he took in, without pausing as he strolled quietly by, the parson's garden where only autumn flowers were in bloom; then he crossed the square and turned down a side road, not visible from his bedroom window, toward the riverside where the barges were moored.

A considerable number of men from the sawmill worked there now, as a result of recent measures; they looked at him as they always did, their eyes filled with reluctance, distrust, and loathing.

But he did not look at them, only at the river and the great floating logs, and at the houses on the opposite bank.

Sitting down on the ground, he listened to those different, confidential, detachable murmurs.

When at last he went home, after midnight, the women had already gone to bed, and only a soft, rustling sound could be heard, a slithering over water, to which he never ceased to listen.

They would walk as far as the mountain, and Pura looked at everything with close attention, in a quiet manner. Sometimes she would stop to examine plants whose alien, hostile, and unfamiliar blossoms, sheltered behind the strangeness of their corollas, seemed to conceal poison. The houses in that little town flaunted small white-enamel plates over the front doors, with the names of the properties engraved upon them in blue or black letters. These inscriptions ranged from expressions of thanksgiving to whimsies: "Hail Mary," "Sunflower," "Dream Come True." Between town and mountain, narrow white paths wound and interwound, flanked by thorny bramblebushes, which shortly turned into mere green trails running through the woodland.

Chaves wanted to know if Pura liked all that, and she always answered yes. When he was not away on one of his trips to the distant city, he would work in the garden of the house. It was a timber house with a veranda built on rickety pillars; the whole house itself was frail and rickety, but its very frailty made it look enchanted, as if gracefully suspended between the *tala* tree and the *espinillo*. He busied himself in the garden, and Pura called him to eat. The dining room had a flat, gloomy vastness . . . too much wood, too much wicker.

"Will you be staying home today?" she would inquire. And he answered yes. And his answer held the promise of a peaceful day ahead. But she was filled with anxiety at the thought that everything was earned through sacrifice, that he slept badly, restlessly, because he never knew what the coming month had in store. Their income was uncertain and they had never managed to save; this was the cause of Pura's worry.

Chaves manfully put aside these unpleasant topics and showed his sound teeth in a confident smile. And when he did go to town, she would save up for him all the juicy gossip picked up in her shopping at the village stores, at the grocer's—Pinores, who came from Lugo; at the butcher's, from La Victoriosa, who used to tell her tales from Tuscany in a mixture of vernacular idioms, Italian expressions, and universal gesturing.

And while they ate, Pura told him these stories with a smile, to amuse him.

Around the lamp above the table, a cloud of mosquitoes and

moths swarmed, and an incipient peace reigned, in an infinite silence. Only two or three times a week did Chaves have to go away and chatter, doing his best to persuade.

A kind of pale serenity had drifted over them, preserving, as far as they were concerned, the powers of evil in a state of ignorance which is the essence of happiness. Things go on like that until the violent flashlight comes near us and spots us.

Though reluctant to make new acquaintances, as if they were coming back to life after a long seclusion, they became little by little part of the village and of the city. On Sundays they would travel the long distance to the city by bus, arriving by mid-afternoon, stayed there for supper, and then went to the Municipal Theater, where rather fanciful versions of old and famous plays were given; they would follow the performance with close attention, as if the acting on the stage were for their sole and personal benefit.

In the village, their only outings consisted of long walks, in the course of which their remarks amounted to a joyful, shared, and almost childish appraisal. "Either a blessed pair or a pair of murderers," farmer Duran would mutter to himself as they went by his window every afternoon without even a curious sidewise glance into his house, which made his temper so much the worse.

And like the "blessed" or a "pair of murderers," they would climb up, isolated, in between the farms, toward the fringe of the mountain. They celebrated the gentle patter of a startled roe deer fleeing in alarm as a joyous bond with the rest of the world, and felt alien and metropolitan in that furtive contact with the universe of wild creatures.

In the evening, on the veranda, Chaves would relentlessly go back to his willful monologues. Sometimes, sitting on their wicker chairs under the moonlight, with the glow of the milky dust falling upon them, they almost imagined they could reach the sky with their hands.

"Bah!" said a German called Wickers. "I don't like this game!"
He flung the dice down and the group of squatting men abandoned their position and stood up grumbling.

"Just because he is leaving we don't all have to go."

"Yes, let's. Everybody is playing as if in mourning. The betting's half-hearted. Let's go."

The five men got to their feet and, in a bored fashion, started walking toward the sawmill sheds. As Wickers was a friend of Bastenone's, they were allowed to remain in the yard after work, talking or gambling. They went to the tavern daily, their earnings known, so that there was no possible doubt as to who was going to stand the rounds of drinks.

When they reached the little square, they came upon him.

One of them stopped him, saying dryly: "Listen, you. Why don't you go away?"

Chaves managed to avoid being touched on the arm by the man. He inquired blandly why he should go.

The other flipped his hat back with the tip of his finger. "Because you're too grand for this place. You don't fit here. That's why . . ."

Chaves went on walking with the others, in the same direction, toward the tavern.

He merely said that he was working there and would leave whenever it pleased him.

"No matter how grand you are, you have to do things our way here!" said the other, a dwarfish fellow, making his voice sound assured.

Chaves glanced at him with a ghost of a smile, or perhaps not even smiling, his lips half-parted in that peculiar way of his. "You can tell miles away . . . ," the dwarf insisted, with growing insolence.

Another from the group, who looked exceedingly tall beside him, silenced him impatiently: "Shut up! What's the use!"

The narrow door stood open as usual, and they parted as they entered.

Sometimes one gets a warning: a dream, an omen. But quite often there is nothing; only the knife itself, as it falls.

Other times nothing, just nothing.

They had been living there for a considerable time, for quite a long time. Always leading the same kind of life. Never daring to

ask themselves why it was always the same. Afraid to question
themselves, to question everything. An unreasonable fear, of
course, without head or tail to it.

But that fear, was it a warning? It was felt only as a fear. Or
perhaps it was just that life does not let us know beforehand what
it has decided will be inevitable.

They had been living there for some time. How immutable the
town was, how immutable everything was. How can we say that
time goes by? Time is a weariness which we elevate to a position
of dignity.

He had spent the entire week trying to penetrate those gentlemen with words, begging them—that was the exact word—to
buy something from him. Expenses mounted. Life was hard. He
needed more and more. And he had launched a fresh assault of
words upon the gentlemen.

They expected better news.

That afternoon, as usual even on days when he went into town,
they had taken their customary walk. The mountain looked more
filled with mystery than ever, with its secret, hidden, restless
waters. With its elusive fauna and immense, rare specimens of
flowers. With that mass of muted silence which took on disdainful tints at sundown.

She refused to take the first steps uphill; she was unutterably
tired that day, and extremely pale.

On getting back home, just before dinner, she suffered a dizzy
spell and, that night, a slight touch of fever which was gone by
morning.

She got up and puttered about the house, refusing to believe
there was anything wrong with her, and saying: "Don't be foolish, go into town. Last night was nothing; it's over now." He left
for the city, and on his return tiptoed into the house and surprised her lying back in the armchair, in the dark bedroom, with
the window wide open to the summer evening. She sat up then,
trying very hard to convince him that there was nothing the
matter with her except plain fatigue. "But it is a comfort, a great
comfort that you should worry and fuss about me. That makes
me feel better."

He pointed out that if he did make her feel better it was only because she was really sick. And he would call Dr. Rosende that very evening and have her examined. But she insisted that he should not, pleading in her weak but firm little voice, full of authority. And she told him that she had been feeling like this since the beginning of the week, and that if her condition had in no way worsened, it only meant that she would soon shake it all off. Even the sharp pain that pierced the nape of her neck and that nasty bloating of her face and that great listlessness . . . "A listlessness that is surely mental, evidently whimsical . . ." And he knew she was lying because she couldn't stand it any longer.

If fact, after those slight and concealed attacks of fever, on Sunday evening, a great shuddering took hold of her with a violence she was unable to conceal. And all her pretending suddenly collapsed.

Pura trembled, shaking with cold, as her body flamed into fire. Chaves could feel in his heart the chattering of her teeth.

He was up all night, and the first thing he did in the morning was to fetch Dr. Rosende, who lived in one of the nearby houses and who had once treated her for a cough.

Dr. Rosende turned up at eleven, carrying a small black bag. After examining her, he took Chaves aside. "She must be taken to a nursing home now, at once," he said. "I'm leaving this evening for the capital and will be away for several days. This might be typhoid fever."

Chaves saw the doctor out and went back to the room, apparently calm and holding himself very straight, but hardly seeing where he walked.

She was lying flat and limp on the sheet, and he told her that Dr. Rosende, fearing that her illness, though not serious, might be long, advised a nursing home. "No," she said. "I don't want to go to a nursing home. I want to stay here. . . . I want to get well here."

And Chaves thought suddenly that the nursing home was like a big circular house set in the midst of a garden, surrounded by glass panes, like a summer house, filled with corridors, and that the rooms, which had no windows, opened on the corridors and were therefore dark and dismal.

He went to the nursing home and spoke to the director, Dr.

Sins, who told him, his catarrh hacking, that chronic catarrh: "She can stay where she is. I'll come round today and bring a nurse with me."

So she stayed in her big room, upstairs, the most comfortable room of all, so comfortable that it made your heart ache; and Chaves brought her, to fill the glass vase which was normally empty, a bunch of those flowers which grew in all the front gardens of the little town, those mountain flowers so big and secretive.

The old doctor, tugging his pessimism and fatigue along with him, and a redheaded, rather quiet, very kind nurse arrived that same afternoon. The doctor had the night table covered with a white cloth, and little by little, throughout the afternoon, after short trips to the drugstore, the nurse kept covering the cloth with small metal boxes, with vials, with medicine flasks, as if preparing for a long and quiet illness.

Pura made a few feeble attempts to raise her head and look at him; and he, from his chair at the back of the room, smiled at her awkwardness, her inability to do so. "We've never seen the other side of the mountain," her slow and faltering voice would say. "We'll have to see it . . . We still have to see it."

Chaves said yes, but asked her to rest, to sleep. That was all he said; yes, yes. He went out for a walk, to impress the fact upon her that if he could leave her alone it was because there was nothing serious the matter with her. On taking leave, the physician had confirmed Rosende's diagnosis.

Chaves took a short walk, but returned soon, to wait at the door during the time he was supposed to be walking.

Later, he lay down at her side and listened to her poor, feeble breathing; she seemed to be gasping for every breath of air, and he underwent endless agony throughout the night. He did not wish to remember his daughter. He made a superhuman effort to blot her out of his mind. And he stared fixedly at the ceiling, like an exhausted swimmer who, floating on his back, expects help will come from somewhere, and listened to the battle going on in her poor body.

The next day, she showed all the symptoms of typhoid fever. She was given her first cold bath, and as she came out of the water, shivering and exhausted, onto her husband's lap, she looked like the marble figure of the Holy Body in the *Pietà*.

But she still spoke, saying: "The other side . . . We have to see it."

And, trying to deceive her, he uttered sentences of dreadful merriment, though he was tormented by an overwhelming pity that tore him to pieces, killing him slowly, and in his few brief respites he followed Dr. Sins about like a shadow. His face was the image of terror.

After the second week, the worst happened. He was sitting in the dark, early in the afternoon of the day of the highest fever, in his chair at the back of the room. The nurse had gone out for a while. Suddenly, he saw her sit up in a state of violence and excitement, a haggard look in her eyes, and fall into a profound and harsh delirium.

But as the weak voice could wring from that face and body nothing but sounds of transparency, the face and the body convulsed in a mad transparency.

And then he, Chaves, who had done so much talking, springing from his chair, came near her bed with fear and started talking too, calling her wildly and shaking her with a frantic and violent desire to bring her back.

His plea mingled with her chimerically pleading voice.

She was burning, and he shouted at her and called her, holding her arms with his own, fighting like a madman to quiet that raging delirium.

How his words fought against her words. How they confused and hurt each other in this shared lunacy, the one rising in a whisper and the other in promises, caresses, and tears!

His mind wandering more than hers, he resorted to his deepest eloquence, which amounted to nothing or almost nothing; and she held her own ground firmly, terribly, sitting up in bed, burning with fever, gesturing spasmodically, struggling to get away— to go and look at the other side of the mountain which they still had to see. . . .

And neither defeated the other, and in that tragic room where they had embraced each other so often in the equally struggling motions of love, their voices linked and unlinked, while he,

Chaves, almost felt his strength leave him, exhausted and beaten by the harsh, mad strength of that body he thought finished.

And all of a sudden he was adult and old, and then suddenly a child, at times rough or imploring, promising and opulently credulous, struggling on the bed among sheets that smelled of fever, to subdue impending death with words and by mounting on words to ride the death riding in the words.

Pura's head dropped back on the pillows, and in a frenzy of panic he raised himself up, and, impelled by solicitude, bent over her once more, only to realize that her breathing had become exhausted. Then he leveled his voice gently, begging forgiveness and sobbing, in human fear, close to her ear, his head against her burning hair, his eyes on her closed and sunken eyes.

And so, in a sudden outburst, when he no longer expected it, she began to speak again, rapt; and he felt a great panic sweeping over his pain. Getting up, he rushed to the door to see if the nurse was coming at last. But nobody was coming. And only the feverish flow of that voice grew and flourished in that room. . . .

He had the feeling that his words no longer mattered, or would never matter, and he was carried away by one single idea—that there was nothing he could do there and that only something new, sudden, immediate, would save them from imminent disaster. Then he remembered a famous, well-paid, exclusive physician, a Dr. Missoloi, and, opening doors and charging through the air, he set out violently and finally in search of him.

He ran down that wide street as he had run only once before, his hair blowing in the wind and the points of his collar fluttering, feeling nothing but the weight of his own soul. He made his way toward the little shadowy street as if he had been there quite often, though he had never been there.

Dr. Missoloi's villa was so hidden by leaves that you could see the house only when you were already on its doorstep. It was one of the few villas built on brick pillars, wrapped in the cold, rigid atmosphere that sumptuous residences often have. Only the green foliage freely surrounded the imprisoned house.

A nurse with a white cap answered the bell. The doctor couldn't see anyone. The doctor only attended patients up to six o'clock. Unfortunately, the doctor was busy just now. But

Chaves's manner was so pressing, his pleading face so terribly anxious and distraught. It must have been filled with so much anguish that the nurse finally yielded and softly opened the door to let him in. Chaves entered, his heart beating fast and full of anxiety, into those ebony, odorous rooms. The walls of the parlor were covered with enormous bookshelves; there were books from floor to ceiling, imposing, overwhelming volumes. And such a voluptuous, solemn, and wide staircase!

After what seemed a century, Dr. Missoloi came down, turning resignation into self-importance, step by step, wearing a white suit and soft shoes. He himself was very white and his slickly combed hair was white. And the frames of his spectacles were transparent, almost white. Everything about him radiated a great calm.

He listened patiently to that man who wanted to take him away, who spoke in torrents, without any logic, pointing at the door. Then he said: "Please be calm, my friend, be calm. Let's look into the case first."

With vehemence, very quickly, imploringly, the other protested that it was a very urgent matter.

"No, my friend. Typhoid fever! There's time, plenty of time. . . . It's a long illness."

At these words, Chaves stood silent, thunderstruck. How can there be time, plenty of time? he kept thinking. And he answered himself silently: "We must hurry, we must hurry." Then in a loud voice he proclaimed that there was a great need to hurry; and the doctor looked at him, staring politely through his foreboding spectacles: "In the first place, there are two sides to this case," he stated slowly; "the medical side and the ethical side. Each has its own importance. But I must consider the ethical side first, my friend. Allow me to refer to the matter."

Chaves listened, suddenly paralyzed, absolutely aghast. The doctor spread his white arms in a slow and priestly gesture as in expectation of the Advent, as if awaiting the sound of his own words.

"My dear friend, I cannot take up a case which is already in the hands of Dr. Sins, without a special summons from Dr. Sins." (He seemed highly gratified with the rhetorical effect produced

by the repetition of the name, and said it over again with relish.)
"Try to understand. Think it over, consider it. We are not in the
Congo . . ."

Chaves raised his tired voice to say he understood, but he im-
plored him; the case was extremely urgent on account of the
patient's constitution; that afternoon's delirium had terrified him;
he firmly believed something terrible was going to happen and he
wished, as a special favor, on whatever conditions, to bring him at
once, that reputed and wonderful science of his, to her bedside,
so as to conjure away the mortal danger.

"To tell the truth, none of these symptoms confirms a fatal
condition," the doctor said, sure of himself. "They are hardly the
usual symptoms. And, keeping to the point, what is at issue here:
I cannot disregard the ethical side of the case. . . . Furthermore, I
do not even practice any longer; I study. I am called in for
consultations; and nothing else. Can one do everything? Today,
for instance, since three o'clock I have been plunged into the
investigation of a case, a very serious one; and very complex,
very complex . . . quite unusual. It happens to be a tumor; that is,
not a tumor, yet at the same time its process of growth is like that
of a tumor, and of the greatest malignity. . . . Neither Morrow-
Hawkins nor Beaulieu approach this enigma in their works . . .
And I've been searching for the answer since three o'clock, and
I'm sure I will find it."

And seeing that face suddenly before him, that desperate
discomposure, he politely chose to shorten his discourse. "Sit
down, collect yourself. Don't get carried away by an unreasonable fear. Of course, Dr. Sins is getting old and drinks. But
we're all getting old, even if we don't drink."

And he laughed at his own joke, bending his torso—his distinguished torso—before listening to that really tiresome, final
burst of imploring words. Folding his hands, he summed up:
"My friend . . ."

And Chaves, therefore, went away, without anger, without a
word of protest, without saying good-bye, obsessed only with
the thought of his total lack of persuasiveness, of time that was
fleeing, of Pura, with her mortal body perhaps already dead,
alone, and of Dr. Boriel, to whom he could still go.

He had never thought particularly of these physicians, and

now discovered he knew them all by reputation, by their peculiarities, and he recalled with remarkable distinctness everything he
had heard about them in casual conversations.

He crossed the streets, the shady avenues, the long glade of the
woods at the end of which that physician lived, that very famous
and brilliant teller of stories, whose mere presence was required
in the city because "he could heal even with a look."

He saw him suddenly, as he burst into the room and came upon
him: a small, sententious, biblical-looking creature, sitting in his
big study in the log house as if in a zoo, surrounded by a cat and
a dog and a white parrot swinging on its perch, presiding over all
that confusion, all that dust, those piles of very old books and
stacks of heterogeneous objects.

When Chaves entered the room, the doctor, his tongue half out
of his mouth, was bent over his desk, carefully pasting scraps of
tissue paper on the large pages of a notebook.

He raised his eyes and saw Chaves. And Chaves, with outstretched arms, his voice hoarse, his mind in a turmoil, taking in
all that absurd esotericism while hardly seeing it, again repeated
his story of Pura's illness. What pains he took in choosing the
most accurate words, those which could not possibly leave any
doubt; the most descriptive, the most touching! He evoked the
picture, stressing the details and even went as far as to borrow
Dr. Missoloi's words, declaring that this was a fatal condition, a
genuinely fatal condition.

"Fatal?" Dr. Bonel inquired blandly. "Fatal? Then there's nothing to be done." And he added: "That's just as well . . . because I
can't go out."

And Chaves saw in that round face with its two-day-old stub-
ble of gray beard that he was sincere, and that he had one obsession, and that his obsession was his belief in himself, above and
before everything else. "Do you know why I can't go out? . . .
Look . . ."

And the doctor took a small contrivance, a kind of long glass
tube attached to an aluminum container, from a drawer of his
desk.

And he explained, to the shocked amazement of his visitor, that
this happened to be an invention of his grandson's and he must,
without delay, write out a report on this invention because his

grandson had brains but lacked power of expression. That idea which had come to him, that invention of his, was so important— though it still had to be kept a secret—that the name of the family would not be carried into posterity through physicians like himself or through agronomists like his son, but through the fruitful inventive mind of his grandson, who bore the name of— and this he was never to forget, never to forget!—Ernesto Dalmiro Isaac Bonel, his third name, Isaac, not being, as he could undoubtedly see, a mere coincidence, but a kind of prior and positive design of Providence. . . .

A gruff, thick, final clamoring torrent of words came to Chaves's mouth at the sight of such insanity; but he still checked himself, as he would have checked himself for eight or ten centuries from sheer panic of losing the chance that the old man might put aside his whimsies and come with him.

He knew, he told him, that he was a most famous and humanitarian local doctor, quite capable of understanding his haste, a selfish haste but one brimming with pity, just as pity is selfish, to get his generous eyes and his great judgment into contact with that poor sick body. And he brought forth other motives, all gently uttered, contriving with a tremendous verbal effort to control his frantic state of mind. "Tut, tut," said the doctor. "Come and have a drink."

And he stood up and produced, from a cupboard whose top was littered with bottles bearing the greatest variety of labels, that bottle and that single glass, repeating: "Drink up first and I'll drink from the same glass, for my profession immunizes, and if it doesn't, so much the worse. Listen to this—" And as Chaves did not accept the drink, he gulped it down himself without relish or apparent pleasure. "Listen to this: it's not good to speculate on neurosis. Don't let yourself become the prey of fatalistic ideas. My long experience as a doctor has told me that nothing can be cured until full sphericity is reached. For maladies, my friend, are round. Don't believe a word about their being acute: that name is one of a series of empty terms, befitting the hermeneutics of fools. . . . Who is in charge of her? Sins? Well, that's enough. Now allow me to write out my report. Let's make one thing clear: everything that is useful is sacred. Tomorrow I'll come around and take a look and have a chat with you or with Sins, who is a monomaniac; and while talking about my grandson, to whom you did not pay much attention, we shall wait for the illness to close the contour of its own sphere."

That was when Chaves embarked on insults, broke into shouts, and resorted to calumny in a last effort to persuade the old physician. Dr. Bonel paid no heed to this shower of abuse and walked over to the parrot's perch. Standing beneath the bird, he raised a soft finger in a gentle caress. At this, the bird started an infernal uproar, trying to get down from the perch by every means, amid excited flapping of wings and frantic squawks. And the doctor held his finger up to the bird, which hopped tentatively onto this new perch and at last regained its balance.

The physician turned toward that mixture of pleas and wrath: "Dear sir, fortunately these scenes no longer impress me. I have reached a stage where I just ignore such things until they are beyond the turning point. Just like diseases . . . And my advice is that you should calm down and leave, because you are battling against that very calmness and control which you need to help you. . . . Go now and, if you wish, send me news. . . . Today I shall finish this report and then I shall accompany you as much as you wish in your perambulations along those glades of patience. It all comes down to that: don't expect anything further in the case from my science."

With his right hand he put the parrot down on the table, first taking care to protect with his left hand the papers he had been pasting in when Chaves arrived:

"Nor from any other."

Then Chaves turned into a frozen spirit and rushed out, in his hurry clumsily knocking over the furniture in the hall and mistaking one room for another in that provincial village house inhabited by live birds and thoughtful, stuffed palmipeds.

Outside, in the shattered evening, night was falling with a promise of rain. He crossed the glade in the wood, the three avenues, and sped down the wide street, where raindrops were beginning to fall, toward the house, as if everything were a dreadful trick played on him by madness.

He ran up the doorsteps, set foot on the gallery, and, as he crossed the threshold, saw Dr. Sins, as old and heavy as he was, coming down the staircase in his shirt sleeves on his way to the kitchen to boil a syringe.

In the midst of his distress, Chaves's face literally fell with shame, and he said to the noble physician, without an explanation: "Forgive me . . . I made a mistake . . ."

And the physician, lifting toward him a pair of eyes with a look of cowlike, everlasting patience, scolded him as he had scolded so often during his many years of healing and making his rounds: "Where the devil have you been? She is much worse . . . Her heart has failed suddenly . . . Where the devil have you been?"

And Chaves, the eternal Chaves, escorted him to the kitchen, reduced to nothing, mute and mechanical, and waited for the little nickel box to boil, and then followed him upstairs. And he entered the room and saw her. Deep inside him, his heart was wrung with an urge for forgiveness. He felt as if everything within him were torn to pieces.

How lean and stiff she lay there, on the bed; how motionless! The single sheet already molded her wasted figure like a sheath. And close to that face with its sunken eyes, eyes turned back, deep down, inward, already drifting through the most indifferent of indifferences, the flowers, the mountain flowers, the large, secretive flowers had faded prematurely. Whereas she seemed to have discovered, secured and now fully possessed, her secret, the defeated flowers had relinquished theirs.

He stood stock-still, pierced more than she by the sword of death.

Then he sat down to wait in silence, watching for every move by the doctor who, in his shirt sleeves, acted and looked as if he were already dealing with a lifeless object.

And Chaves, addressing Pura from within his bleeding soul, recited, offered, unreeled, surrendered tremendous explanations. . . .

But that evening everything came to an end.

The doctor and the nurse, who had just arrived, departed to make the necessary arrangements which that absent specter, to whom they spoke without getting any response and whom they could not bring back to life, was in no way capable of undertaking himself.

The house was left in almost total darkness.

After a while, Chaves rose and went up to talk to the body. It was already deep night; there was a menace of rain outside, and time sharply went its way.

He began to speak, quietly, very quietly, with the voice of despairing and awed respect; and then, little by little, he raised his tone, infusing it with the liveliness of delirium, summoning Pura, calling her and arguing bitterly and frantically with her in the bitter and frantic urge of madness.

His voice rang out. At one moment a whisper, the next a roar, in the dark, silent house. Ruefully ridiculous and derisive reasoning, unconscious sarcasms, furious and ludicrous promises!

He spoke as he had never before spoken, but as he had spoken since he had known her, as he spoke to her and others, to all those changing and elusive multitudes, in a final intemperate, paraphrastic impulse to turn into transparency the definite intransparency of all.

Sometimes standing, sometimes kneeling, sometimes towering at her bedside like a giant in the reflection of his shadow on the wall, Chaves drowned the night with words.

Fiercely he told her of all they had to see and had not yet seen, of all they had to talk about and still had not! With what rapture and eloquence he described to her the trip they had planned up north, where they would behold together the rugged cleft of the ravines! He told her about the unexpected tasks he would be called upon to fulfill in the future, now that the firm he worked for had been reorganized. What vehemence! How many sentences cried out, shouted, drawn from the man.

At dawn, when the undertakers arrived, they found him still talking, but in subdued and faltering tones like a prayer that wearily flows on and on, or like the mumbling of a monomaniac, beyond object or time, meaning or reason.

That was the way Chaves had spoken that time. And how afterward he had drifted from words into the plains of his own solitude. And how he drifted down, alone, throughout the country, through town after town, southward, until he felt the cold and gazed at the lakes, and peered over the houses at the snowy peaks of the larch trees.

In an instant they were all around him, menacing and dangerous.

There were six of them, perhaps eight; and they were waiting for him.

Cold, peremptory faces, weatherbeaten faces, mouths moved by boredom into perpetual chewing, discontented eyes, heads with bristling hair, nervous hands. All were enraged, all self-important. They all felt the need to be highly enraged, to make themselves feel very important.

Some men came slowly from the bar to look on, and carelessly joined the group. They smiled or yawned. But the majority had grim, set faces; grim by force of habit, the habit of receiving only emptiness from life and from craving to have something more than emptiness. And here was their opportunity, crystallized in the "superiority" of the "gentleman." "Superiority! Pooh! . . ." Alfánaga would mumble all day long, chewing on a stalk of grass. Sometimes, something has to happen. Something violent.

They had been looking for him and he had avoided them. Not for any special reason; he had simply avoided them. He had been searching for other sounds: the river, the gliding of the barges.

They let him alone, and later, when the transfer of men took place, they were at it again; because those who had gone away knew him, and the new ones had only heard of the legend; and myth is what is always most hated. Man is always saved in some way, through some weakness or intention; by myth . . . never.

Wickers tried to make him speak; so did the others. Again and again. They didn't want to be convinced that he could hold out and do as he pleased. What people are most afraid of is that others may not believe in fear. They were afraid he might be able to do as he pleased, and without fear.

The other men's concern annoyed him. He had sought ways for them to ignore him. He had tried by every possible means. During the preceding week he had kept more apart than ever, walking along the bank of the river or losing himself in the woods.

That afternoon as he stood smoking, leaning against one of the posts of the fence, a short distance from the shore, they came and gathered around him in a semicircle, with him in the middle.

It looked as if they would not let him go until he said something.

Alfánaga and Oscar Rosto were the first to step forward, slowly. "We don't want any superior airs around here. We don't want any of that here. . . ."

And the menacing bodies were already upon him.

Chaves, abandoning his support and full of decision, using both his hands, with infinite violence, stuck his palms against those chests and, pushing and shoving them apart, walked past his aggressors. They tottered backward with such violence that the others had to pick them up and push them forward.

"What are you doing?" Mólers cried. "What are you doing?"

He was walking toward them. And when the two men pushed forward by the circle were about to attack brutally, he interfered, shouting: "Knock it off, you bastards! What do you know about anything? What do you know about him? He works like the best! He is a man! Look at his body . . . Look at his arms. . . . What do you know? Good-for-nothing bastards!"

He grasped Chaves's arm in a rage and took him away. They walked past the store. It was deserted. Mólers dropped his hat. Before picking it up he stopped again. In a confidential tone he said to Chaves, imploringly: "Aren't you ever going to tell them what they want to be told? Something . . . anything . . . Aren't you ever going to say anything? Won't you ever talk with them, speak with them?"

The larch trees were beginning to take on a tint of blue shadow from the evening slowly covering them. From the distance came the murmur of the river, the perceptible whisperings of the wood, the delicate brushing of the barges in their slow advance, all the sounds gathered in by the growing silence.

"No," Chaves said.

ANGUISH

I

Near the death of winter, Ana Borel changed countenance. Buenos Aires, stiff from the last cold spell, was wrapping itself in its great robe of bitterness, like a body come to rest at last. The Andean frosts, the furious breezes, the raw wind had ravaged that young face, enlarging her eyes, lashing her, sucking her blood, after having devoured the green of the wild and desolate fields in their course from the Pacific to the Atlantic.

The multitudes in the city showed their ferocious teeth and apprehensive eyes as they walked in silence through the parks or along the banks of the grayish river. An invitation to flight, like that which suddenly threatens capital cities and old arid lovers, hovered over the streets. It was the moment when the fountains in the squares no longer remained unnoticed by the eyes of passers-by and the noises of their waterfalls seemed outrageously sordid and ridiculous.

In a little plaza a few blocks away from the Teatro Colón, in the very heart of the metropolis, a baroque fountain hurled its jet from the mouth of a squalid lion. Since the first frost the fountain had persisted in spewing its precocious monotony at this juncture of deserted causeways and sidewalks. The cold pavement and the feeble jet gave this quarter of the city an air of extreme desolation. The lion, poised like a harpist, with its strong, marmoreal mane, seemed an artifact hurled to the pavement from Señora Savisiano's dressmaking shop, whose windows displayed manikins dressed in suits of vivid colors, rich in tawdry trimmings and ribbons.

It was there that Señora Savisiano had her general headquarters or barracks. "Barracks" and "general" were somehow terms which suited her and without which her true social function could never be told. The little white shop, with its door always closed, its basque curtains, its outer air of enclosure, hid a legion of beings—strongly sexed, although female—whose actions were alternately governed by severe discipline and latent insubordination. Revolt and counterrevolt succeeded one another in the back room of the establishment, in the same rapid tempo as with a band of *condottieri*. Señora Savisiano, with her gestures of a prima donna, as easily given to vociferation as to fainting, moved about, gave orders, and cursed her troops, turning her scornful back, like that of a commanding officer, on their slowness and stupidity.

Blasphemy and complaint, proffered tirelessly and rapid-fire, were her weapons. Señora Savisiano had passed fifty. Her heavy eyelashes done up, bloodshot eyes, cheeks painted a vulgar shade of crimson, her hair swept back in a burst of furious coquetry, when combined with her exaggerated gestures and loud suits, had a particularly screaming effect. She had lost control of her voice, so that her conversation was always carried on at the pitch of a shrill cry. The corrosive action of time on the drab gray of her house and on the sign outside, which read in red letters—*Dresses. Savisiano. Distinction. Elegance*—had simultaneously caused her ruin, brought on a liver condition, and been the source of vexation, fury, melancholy, and even of a vague metaphysical uncertainty. Her flaming-red head was sometimes attacked by terrible waves of anxiety. At such moments, she would put on her hat and rush out into the street. In her wake could be heard the commotion of the opening and closing of heavy doors and bursts of laughter in the shop. The pedestrians, outside, close to the door, heard the scandal, the shrieks and the laughter, the squeals; saw laughing faces appear in the high windows above the faded sign. That hound pack of determined girls at liberty only startled strangers in the vicinity. The neighbors knew well the tempestuous nature of the "children." The señora despised her children, except on those occasions when she outdid herself in obsequious courtesy and would name them, one by one, for the benefit of her clients. Rosa, for example, who was the daughter of a bottle manufacturer from Avellaneda, and had never been in France—nor even in Montevideo—knew no rival for the "refinement" of her made-to-order dresses; and as for Carmen Fide—almost as if she could see the fat slob before her—cut with such polished elegance, with such a hand! But as soon as the customer took advantage of the first pause in her monologue to disappear, the señora exorcized herself, pronouncing under her breath words which, had a correspondingly exact fluid existed, would have destroyed Rosa and Carmen Fide in the most exquisite of agonies.

It isn't possible to speak of Ana Borel without alluding to Señora Savisiano.

Señora Savisiano had something sinister about her, like her house facing the little square with those two dismantled and wretched window displays, and the false luxury of her three adjoining drawing rooms. Salons in which an air of drought, the smell of powder, faded flowers, and old age prevailed; the rooms were somehow of the same substance as her dusty hangers and moldy nickels, like those of a down-and-out magician. The most contradictory objects were grouped together, from the grayish lace edgings of cloth to stuffed birds and artificial roses. Señora Savisiano had succeeded in resembling her vocation, an obscure and sinister vocation which brought her grief and inner pain. She would shout, stamp her feet, persecute her charges. Once these daily functions were fulfilled, she would go for a walk under the

chestnut trees with an enormous greyhound in tow. It was her
only friendship, and the lady, in her severity, would not have
tolerated another. The dog was gigantic and had formerly belonged to a German butcher whose effects were sold at public
auction when he went bankrupt.

Señora Savisiano adored this animal, who fed on blood. Her
small army of dressmakers used to tell scandalous stories about
this relationship. Some of them, the most daring, after having
pinched their cheeks in the effort to achieve a grotesque resem-
blance to the lady, would mimic, in the shop itself, conversations
overheard between the owner and her dog. It seems that she used
to explain theosophy to him. Her violent urge to proselytize
often reached a high pitch; but the dog, who paid little or no
attention to such propositions, contented himself by looking at
her with eyes which would have returned the wildest fanatic to
sanity. The more daring rumors had it that the Señora gave herself up to fits of weeping, lasting for hours and hours, after her
long exhortations to the dog, in the little room bearing the
modest sign: Cashier.

The fact was that Señora Savisiano's establishment was a living
hell. The neighbors did not exaggerate: it was a hell. When the
señora had an urgent order, thirty hands would diligently and
deliberately delay its completion, dragging through the work.
Exhausted and beside herself: her varied sciences were of no use,
spent for nought. "This is scandalous," she would cry out; "this
will take me to the grave! Murderers!" A strong smell of cos-
metics escaped her with her cries. Faced with her terrible and
genuine moments of exaltation, the employees seemed truly contrite. But they were really laughing up their sleeves at her. They
hadn't the least respect for the señora; they despised her. It mattered little that at one time she had dressed queens abroad. Good
queens dress themselves. All they need are brains and slaves.
What had Señora Savisiano done in her life to put on such airs, to
indulge in the luxury of persecuting, screaming, and in general
raging about like a caged beast? Having a husband, becoming a
widow, inheriting a few pesos and setting up a luxurious establishment with a musty smell one had to sample to believe, setting

up an enormous red salon in the style of the Restoration, with
windows with gilt jambs and a big fat column, twisted and heavy,
next to the door with the signature of Edward VII, certainly a
forgery—¡Vaya!—all that didn't give her the right to shout herself
hoarse, didn't excuse persecution or bad temper at any and all
hours, or red wigs. Everybody knew how many portraits Edward
VII gave away and why he gave them away. Small favors without
great sacrifices. No, the hell with her, she deserved to be hated.
"Take her to her grave, murderers indeed!"—nice words for a
lady like that. Let her go to her grave! To a Restoration-style
grave, of course, with the portrait of the big fat heir to the
throne surrounded by flowers and a distorted and stupid statue of
her dog.

"Bitches!" shouted the señora, her bust inclining forward,
from the door of the shop.

This scene repeated and repeated itself. The girls cursed under
their breath, needle in hand, eyes lowered, as if counting the
beads of a rosary. Suddenly a voice would ring out: "You old
witch!" A terrible agitation overpowered the señora at those
moments; her eyes strained beyond their orbits, she clenched her
fists. Her red hair above all that congestion was terrifying. She
chewed unintelligible words. "What! What! Murderers!" The
girls' attitude persisted, slyly, furtively. Until another anonymous
voice shouted, then another, more violent—surely Esther's, who
was the fiancée of a reserve officer in the police department, a
fact which lent her great aplomb—and then others. The scandal
increased in tone and the insults were like grenades exploding in
mid-air, right there, alongside of the red nimbus hovering over
the señora.

For an instant, she remained mute with indignation. Like a
weak dike against the ravages of the sea, her pride opened into
inner caverns, weaker than her eyes, to whose burning was added
the fear of seeing herself impotent and beaten. In those moments
of collapse, her head, a chameleon of tints, as if suddenly abandoned by all that was not austere, simple, and dignified, took on
an unwonted dignity. Those who see themselves tenaciously attacked conceive a vague sense of their sacrificed courage of their

heroic nature. The girls saw her erect figure, tense, statuesque, her entire person bathed in worthy self-esteem. All laughter faded away. The air itself seemed to have hardened.

Then Señora Savisiano lowered her head, resumed her attitude, abandoned the shop with decision, crossed the blue room, and, overwhelmed by a sad and total silence, entered the room where Ana Borel was working alone.

In the early hours of the morning when Ana arrived, the women washing the floors heard her staccato tread. Later, her thin figure appeared through the main glass door, her body just touched by the first maturity which follows adolescence. She had a secret air about her. A hint of inner restlessness weighed on her eyes, violently open, on her slightly bitter mouth, as if her entire being were directed and taken up with waiting for a secret visitor. She threw down the small black hat on a table.

Ana Borel was a fine young woman, of firm and nervous flesh, large shining eyes—too large and motionless over hollow cheeks and high cheekbones. When she looked intently, one wondered if there was a trace of fever in her eyes. Those mature and profound eyes were slow in moving from one object to another. They seemed to speak to people on their own, in a way both timid and compelling.

She had been in charge of accounts for Señora Savisiano for ten months. Her knowledge of English, and her silent, well-disciplined character, in addition to an energetic way of facing difficulties, had frequently placed the tiller of that establishment in her hands in times of anarchy. At these moments, the proprietress would walk back and forth through the rooms, prey to the sharpest theosophic crises, followed by the enormous sleepy dog. But these transports of a spiritual order didn't last long. As soon as the señora saw a luxurious conveyance passing near her door, her greed reawakened, she burned her useless ships, and, shouting, urged on the needles to their utmost endeavor.

Ana Borel was not troubled by any spectacle in that somber establishment. Her life in the store was that of a perpetually isolated guest. Next to the show window, open to the little square, she added up her accounts without once abandoning her concentration, a concentration which tended to heighten still more the high arch of her right eyebrow. Every now and then, with a painful gesture, she would brush the hair from her forehead. The sun seemed to want to break into the heavily overcast sky. It was a beautiful, tightly drawn face. When Señora Savisiano entered, worn out by her struggles, or in search of themes for a monotonous chat, or eager to complain bitterly about her sciatica, Ana wouldn't look up at her. She knew all too well what to expect. She went about her business, coming and going between her desk and the pine filing cabinet. Her indifference earned her the hatred of all who worked in the establishment, but also the growing and perplexed respect of the proprietress.

Her steps in that house of fashion would have seemed strange to an onlooker. Every day, she hurled herself into that sea with her eyes resolutely closed, prey to a sort of fear of being contaminated by a contagious disease, apprehensive, like human flesh near a poisonous reptile. She scarcely exchanged a few words, a smile. Her simple suits contrasted sharply with the specious artifice of the fashion shop. In the afternoon, standing next to the window, mute, profound and somber, she devoted herself effortlessly to watching the pavement without seeing it. The noise of great activity, the growing agitation of the big city, reached her only as a vague rumor carried by the palpable breath of dusk. Responsive to this breath, somehow brought together, her features were transformed, obedient to an overwhelming awareness, a stately invocation, a call. It was a bitter call, sounding the constant certainty of her total sterility. . . . Her features withdrew in an infinitely secretive sense; her mouth accentuated its line of bitterness; her eyebrow held its rigid arch. The city's stirring was like a distant hammering. She remained terribly preoccupied by the voyage her spirit had taken. Her gestures were crisp and alive, as if in response to a whiplash, punished by the need to break constant obsessions. Again and again, with a nervous motion, she would throw back her hair. The first moonlight descended, meanwhile, over her, over the morbid birth of her breast, as intrepid as the breast with which birds attack death against all obstacles. At the same time, like a milk-white clarity, from her forehead came a somber sway as if the serene maturity of worry had silenced the impetuous posture of the flesh.

Minutes, hours passed. Before eating, Señora Savisiano went all through the house, the deserted passageways. In the room where Ana Borel worked, a shock awaited her. In the midst of darkness, the erect young figure stood motionless in the white frame of the window.

II

She was twenty-nine years old. From her delicate body, alive with nerves, escaped that dark clamoring, that shy mystery which goes to make up the tragic charm of certain beauties.

Her infancy had been spent in Olivos, in a white house surrounded by green hedges and abundant trees. Her father was an Englishman, an employee of the railroad, who had brought a bitter character and a pessimistic and sullen sense of humor from the fields of Orpington to the bluffs of the greenish river. Her mother had been a creole of finicking courtesy and indolent gestures. Of her, she retained only a vague recollection: a bronze figure moving gracefully against the background of the white walls. Hour after hour, silent, with her great flounce of white hair streaming in the air, she sat in the wing of the property from where the station could be seen. Ana was eight years old when she ceased seeing her—not knowing that the coffin, whose burnished handles had charmed her, held the last remains of her mother. From that time on, her father acquired a still drier air. He was a man whose goodness had foundered on persistent adversity, and he accepted this death bitterly in the depths of his feeble body and soul. He scarcely spoke to the child, leaving her all day accompanied only by an old Negro servant in the solitary house. She was overwhelmed by sadness after her meager delight over her organdy dresses, her clear chignons; condemned to be alone all day, listening to the prayer-like murmurings, rheumatic complaints, and mumbled words of the Negress. From a distance, she saw the arrival and departure of the trains in between whistles. The neighborhood around her house was without children. It was a neighborhood of hedges, somber parks, and abundant trees. She spent all day in the garden, speaking to the animals, the plants, engaged in strange monologues, waiting always for a reply. Sometimes she would enter the large damp rooms to gaze through old albums. She maintained long conversations with herself on the porch, always giving herself a supreme role—Marie Antoinette, Napoleon, Cleopatra, her imaginary questioner an admiring, subordinate character. She abandoned her girl friends and used to walk alone, speaking in a low voice to a small wooden Christ. The Negress would stop with the bed covers in her hand to watch her. Then, shaking her head, she would go away with a deprecatory smile. It was a sad life. Morning, afternoon, evening. Finally the stars; she watched the Southern Cross moving in the sky in order to develop a tale of fantasy. Her father returned at eight o'clock. Sometimes with a sweet roll, sometimes a picture book, but wordlessly. He used to bring friends. Only then did he speak. These men were hard, foreign businessmen—they all scratched their heads as they came in, laughing loudly, and never took their eyes off each other. Delightedly, she followed the movements of those lips, attended the most extraordinary parties, her eyes opened wide, her mouth agape. But those conversations were terribly complicated and they tired her. The Negress came silently and took her off to bed. The noise of the yelling and chatter vibrated over the mellifluous voice of the Negress. In the high room above, she watched a rectangle of night; from the garden by other paths than those of sight, the smooth discourse of the magnolias reached her, bathing her in joy before she fell asleep.

At ten years of age she left the house in the morning to go to a girls' school. At fifteen she had made some friends, reserved like herself, but too much inclined to secrets; not moved by a natural reserve as she was, but by an insidious secretiveness. She grew somber and alone, like a bush with fine leaves. At eighteen she became an assistant secretary in a commercial house. But basic human resources had been blighted in her since childhood. She made four trips a day along the hedges of Olivos, then by the trains which ran to the capital. She worked as if fulfilling a rite. One day, the vice-president of the company, an obese gentleman smelling of makeup and coconut oil, made a proposal to Ana which offended her. Her mouth showed a barely visible expression of disgust. One week later she started work at the dressmaking shop of Señora Savisiano, facing the little square near the Teatro Colón.

She had no friends, no religion, no ambition, neither hope nor envy; only her silent imagination, her serious and secret ardor. But she was made for religion, for faith, for hope. Her father lived in a perpetual drunken stupor, and they ate in silence. The Negress, in the dining room full of mosquitoes, came and went with difficulty, now so constantly beset by rheumatism that her complaints had become transformed into a permanent grimace of pain on her face. Those two lost souls—the Negress and her father—pained her with an inner ache. After eating, she would go out to the veranda on summer nights with a book. But she didn't read. She didn't suffer. Her absent heart was at peace, friendless, uncommitted. She contemplated the straight terraces, one behind another, their greenery devoured by the black air. She only asked herself, without great urgency, the real significance of four or five words in which the world around her seemed to take pride, and with considerable noise and vanity. The words "love," "happiness," "power" held for her no specific intelligible meanings. Only the first bothered her, but her perturbation—wasn't it merely something physical? The language of the men around her, on the train, in chance meetings, at dances she had attended with the girls from the dressmaking shop, was something fleeting and repugnant, related always to a series of postulates which she tenaciously refused to recognize.

She thought of the world as an order whose echo came to her by underground passages but never directly through human contacts. Nevertheless, it was precisely in the expressions and gestures of a given human face, the furrowing of a forehead, the serious look of a worried man, the fearful vacillation of certain eyes, special happy smiles, the look of expectancy in the lips that listen, which most attracted her attention and toward which all her ardor was directed. After these moments of observation, she was sure that she was alive, concerned, really moving. Everything else was silence for her. She had come across two, three, perhaps four masculine faces which impressed her by some quality of inner experience revealed by their features. But those

visages had gone by, had been confused by then in a flood of
words. For her, the three vortices of the sensible universe were
enclosed by the motion-picture theater, her house, and her job.
Her long, empty days were spent in that colonial patio, where
time was counted only by the growth of the magnolias.

The guests her father brought home to dinner were strange
people, given to drunkenness and loud laughter. On Sundays at
midday, these guests formed a definite group. And among those
present was an employee of the government railway, Benes by
name, young, and on the periphery of the heavy intake of Irish
whisky and red table wine. The dining room was level with the
garden. On Sundays she sat next to the window that opened on a
bed of large hortensias; her father at the head of the table; Benes
opposite. Her father told army stories which were applauded in
chorus by the circle of congested faces, while the warm, midday
air accumulated in the dining room. Only the two young people
were untouched by the general atmosphere. Quiet, with the dignity of a queen, Ana ate slowly without speaking. Benes, serious
and cautious, sought her eyes, accentuating his silence with an
alert complicity directed at her. When it was time for coffee, he
would play with his black cigarette case, making it spin slowly,
by means of light twists on the tablecloth. "This great international abstainer!" yelled Mr. Watkins, a jewelry merchant, his
whiskers moistened with a dew of whisky, slapping him on the
back, with secret condemnation.

Finally, she became accustomed to seeing—on Sundays, then
Thursdays and Sundays, then Tuesdays, Thursdays, and Sundays
—the tapered hands of young Benes, playing with his black
cigarette case on the tablecloth. Somehow, this painstaking activity was for her preoccupied silence, a rest. The neighbors in
Olivos, behind the hedges, had come to notice her when they saw
her returning to her house, attributing all kinds of activities to
her. They commented on the strange beauty and simplicity of
her dresses, as upon the concentration of her impetuous walk.
How could that rapid pace, that mystery, go unnoticed, fail to
awaken suspicion? Meanwhile, in Olivos, every day, every hour,
a *quinta* disappeared, to open the way for a pretentious city
building. The fruit trees, ancient plants, disappeared under the

blows of constant axes; clouds of light-suited architects arrived
from the capital. Under the imposing shade of their own foliage,
the execution of the chestnut trees began.

Benes's gesture in striking small blows with his fingers against
the cigarette case had become converted for her into an inexplicably tyrannical habit. The simple gesture now brought with it a
complete theory of gestures belonging to the railroad employee,
each time more numerous, more specific. The cigarette case
brought with it the image of a fine hand, a hand the image of a
pale skin, of an unpredictable forehead, of a total quiescence
which bathed that man. This aroused her curiosity at first. She
observed him, imagined him placing the black cigarette case on a
dark table in a bare and lonely room. She imagined him moving,
like herself, a shadow on the fringes of a confused world. And
during dessert, the total and brutal rejection with which he responded to the conversations at that table, isolated his figure still
more, lending it strength. He had an unintelligent face, made up
of a little stupidity and a little good nature, with neither characteristic dominating the other. It was obvious that he was particularly attentive in all his gestures. Mr. Alvan and Mr. Stokevom
winked furiously every time he spoke. He measured his own
smile by the expression on the feminine face across from him.

Finally, one day, after dessert, as she was leaving the dining
room in her gray tulle suit, the young man came up and spoke to
her. Nervously he told her that his life had no purpose. He had
spent it uninterestingly under the bitter protection of a widowed
aunt who owned innumerable shares in the Consolidated Bank.
He was vegetating within four walls, dividing his concerns
within the limits of the mechanical acts of getting up at seven
thirty, dining frugally at twelve in an Italian restaurant on Corrientes, going to bed at eleven, and reading the international edi-
torials in the newspapers, or, as his only book, for the hundredth
time, Sorel's *Reflections on Violence*. Frankly, he was an island
and, what was worse, an island adrift. Such aridity needed a great
response. Would she want to help him, to constitute herself as the
object of his faith? The young man's hand scarcely moved at the
end of his limp arm, as if moving from a subterranean world of
essences. The trains arrived noisily at the nearby station, in the

Bajo, sending into the air full of smells a violent furrow of smoke.
The day passed slowly. She didn't take her eyes off the distant
spectacle of passengers, at the foot of the bluffs, grouping themselves in windmills before passing the green path; but a rapid flash
burned the young man's pupils, while his nervous hands began to
acquire, that afternoon, an assurance, a sense of security.

And Ana agreed, and married him. It's so difficult to say no,
when one who faces a life without purpose is confronted with a
prayer.

But her eyes never accepted the supreme joy of nuptials. Her
right eyebrow went up, and like those pupils in the paintings of
the primitives, posed a question directed at the cruel mystery of
the world.

III

The barbershop and the pharmacy, face to face from sidewalk to sidewalk, combined their essences in the atmosphere of
the street next to the house where she and Benes had installed
themselves a year ago. Seaver Street extended its surface for a
distance of a modest hundred yards. It lay in a hollow, joined to
the city by a staircase of ten steps under the light of a tall streetlight. Thus sunken and dark, from sunset on, it seemed to be the
atrium of an ancient tragedy. The owners of the pharmacy and
the barbershop came out to the street in their white aprons, receptive to the humid night air. Benes would arrive at seven
o'clock, waving cordial greetings. Then he entered his house,
from which nothing more than the sign of complete monkishness
reached the outside world. A little light was reflected in the
chancel. Swept by a mean gust of wind, the street was dry,
bony—the skeleton of a street. Exactly one half hour later,
hurrying, she appeared at the top of the steps, her face wrapped
in a white splendor, her eyes absorbed, her right eyebrow sharply
arched. She walked down the stairs with rapid strides, scarcely
responding to the neighbors' greetings. In four steps she gained
her door, inserted her key in the keyhole, and entered. The passage of her black beret was marked by the night air. The two
men in white aprons stood motionless, like petrified guards,

bathed in their balsams and essences, their heads turned toward the door which had just been shut, attentive to the last echo of that step.

The life she led was monotonous. Ana Borel tried to think as little as possible. She fought to throw herself completely into the necessary and habitual acts of each day. Occasionally they would go out at night to the movies; on other nights they would go out to take the air at the municipal bathing pool; on still other nights they went on foot to the Sibarita, to listen to a Hungarian ensemble until a little after midnight. Between themselves they exchanged few words. On the other hand, they were almost never alone. Ever since a few days after their marriage—an event hastened by the death of her father, one evening in the solitary house in Olivos—they hadn't really lived alone. They lived surrounded by a coterie of Benes's friends, the most singular beings in the world. A sort of secret Belgian commercial agent, M. Loubie, a Voltairian spirit, prone to sarcastic gallantries and political jokes; a cripple with a solemn air, Mosalé—Augusto Mosalé— a manufacturer of harmoniums, a man of long-range socialist ideas, all moderation, circumspection and baldness, quick to abandon all his convictions according to the will of his interlocutor whenever the latter showed himself to be energetic; the great Elía, a boy always red with animation, empty and elegant; and Moldes, the secretary of the embassy. An easily explained affinity united the group. Augusto Mosalé found a human echo, too human, in the unctuous complacency with which the great Elía abandoned his glasses on the table of the bar in order to act as animator when their meetings grew dull. He would hum off-color songs requiring choruses, such as "The Raspberries and the Strawberries" or "The Death of the Canary." Then they all woke up, generous and eager to contribute to this mutual, collective happiness. Nearly every night, in the motion-picture theater or in the Sibarita bar, they would get together to laugh with that naïveté characteristic of foreigners in the midst of the stiff gravity of the capital, harassed by the hostile wonder of the occupants of neighboring tables.

Mosalé, when conversation declined, would drone enthusiastically:

Society one day
will change guides.
The Red Ladies obliged . . .

At first, Ana was amused by this chorus of unconcerned and
fervent high livers. "Livers" in the sense of mere visceral animation. She was entertained to see reflected in Benes's eyes the
sprightly content produced by the multiform succession of
themes. But the moment came when she first noticed the fixed
grimace of her own smile in the face of the clangor of those
voices—the Belgian agent's socialism, the jokes of the smiling
Loubie—and, like something palpable, she felt in her mouth the
cold sensation of a fixed expression. The awareness of her own
response separated her from the others. He amused himself like a
child watching a spectacle. In the theater, he would sit with lips
half open, like a child involved in the succession of trivial actions
on the screen. She watched the film gravely, rarely commenting
upon the performance. At each instant, his eyes were absorbed
by the rapid and many-faceted world, while she obeyed the voice
of her inner preoccupation. "What does all this mean to me?"
was the question which never left her.

The city moved swiftly through the white months. The harsh
weather raced along, the universe moved hundreds and hundreds
of miles, while the forecast of a terrible era began to form in
masses of idle, somber men living rejected on the outskirts of the
city, to whom the dawns rarely brought opportunities of victory.
Instead, punctually, they seemed to clamor hungrily for human
sacrifice. By the time the afternoon clouds passed by, they had
collected, above the heartbeat of three million souls, a breath of
exacerbation and discouragement.

Every sunrise, a little unnerved by that terror with which, like
a mammoth spectacle, she saw the crimson marriage contract of
dawn consummated, Ana remained for an instant motionless in
her bed. She did not pass from sleep to consciousness; she came
from insomnia to the day's activity, her eyes fixed on the window
facing her bedstead. Benes slept at her side, and he, who could
never submerge himself deeply in anything, with his frothy joviality prone to adapt himself to all the changing gestures of life,

inconstant in his nature and in the flesh, fell asleep with a rapid
and profound sinking, as if his release of mobility each day were
suddenly overwhelmed at the exact moment of going to bed. She
extended a thin arm, brought to her lips the glass of water, nearly
spent by the night's thirst. With an indefinable discontent, she
looked at the man at her side; then through the window, at the
slow formation of the day. This resolution, this act of perfect
creation—why didn't she achieve it somehow in her life? Could
there be anything more inert, more marked by sterility than her
existence? That sensation stayed with her like a disease. Her
mouth moistened by water, she thought of the days of her marriage as a clear break in a chain of taciturnity; but the inconsist-
ency, the ephemeral aspect of this pause, now made her tremble.
She trembled before those little blows with which he always
played with his black-enamel cigarette case, with his eyes dizzily
jumping from object to object, his tongue from topic to topic,
his dark, coarse skin incapable of a sudden decline. The trivial
regularity of his acts was the passive background of her fears, the
anguish, her secret inadaptability, not visible to the observer, now
came muffled to the surface. Benes looked at her: "You're always
nervous. What's the matter?" With a decisive movement, she
threw back the short tresses hanging in her face, but her eyes and
lips remained motionless afterward. On the other hand, he had
not expected a reply; his words immediately took another turn,
to comment on a sporting event, an international crisis, or a
recent plane crash. He kissed her in the same fleeting manner,
brushing her lips coldly. She immediately looked at him in a
maternal way, with pious seriousness, sad, like someone contemplating the endless frivolous playing of a small child. Play, wasn't
that the law of Jaime Benes, with his good-natured but scarcely
comforting movements, with his purely visual voracity, his frivolous and garrulous soul, and his constant leaving things to go in
search of others. The two young people were by nature inclined
to such different extremes, extremes so radically opposed and
removed from each other, that in less than two weeks after the
modest ceremony in the church in San Isidro, each had developed
something like a state of inner independence. At home, through
the long midday dinners, during mealtimes in the evening, amid

the sound of childish games and the smell of the smoke of the dark chimneys of Retiro, the two seemed antagonistic characters in two different comedies, two unrelated dramas. Jaime Benes was turned toward the world with that impetuous volubility which his eyes communicated in a fleeting gesture: he devoured words. He began sentences and never finished them, eager to treat new subjects, to painstakingly root up new fields of investigation. He was a diffuse man. He was always moving his hands, helping himself as if in that way he were shedding what his rapid lips had not been able to grasp. He spoke, he laughed, he whirled words around, pleased with his incredible dexterity. In the long run, this tired him; then he raised his head slightly with a gesture of pleasure. She remained without moving a feature, her right eyebrow arched and tall, her face pale frozen. And while she remained imprisoned behind the bars of her closed universe, Jaime Benes talked and talked.

Then Ana returned to her fixed idea: her uselessness, her tremendous uselessness.

She saw the passage of time in the senile physiognomy of Señora Savisiano. She also felt it growing within herself, but in the form of a solicitous and horrifying ghost who went about closing all the doors in order to be alone with her. I am going mad, she thought; I am going mad.

She saw the passage of time in the houses, the gardens, and the trees. She saw it growing, hurrying along in its terrible flight from men.

Only in her husband, time didn't seem to move. Nothing seemed to mature in him, everything persisted in a jovial, garrulous, and unconcerned verdure. In fear, she saw him at her side with that absolute impotence of the spectator faced with the gestures whereby the protagonist on the stage destroys himself with his every action.

But she had never learned how to cry. Neither could she speak, and where could one project one's narrow, specific, isolated words in that surrounding sea of loquacity? It was then that her spirit desperately needed to breathe, felt itself drowning. It seemed to her that she was going mad. Coming and going from the dressmaker's shop, she walked the streets burdened with an active, cruel, and constant anxiety. She fought, with her hurried pace not to think about it, to rid herself of her obsession. What does all this mean to me? Do I contribute anything, do they contribute anything to me? What meaning is there in living like this?

One day, the insomnia began. Terrible nights spent in wandering about in her own mysterious malaise. The history of her nights of insomnia had its curious aspect. One night, on leaving the motion-picture theater with her husband, she felt in her mouth, under her tongue, a strange taste of electricity. They had seen *Dr. Jekyll and Mr. Hyde*. They entered a *confitería*, a vast and deserted room decorated in a creamy color. The picture of a woman, arms filled with flowers, advertised fruit syrups. Where the association of ideas was concerned, Benes never tired, but his words were unhinged, irreducible to anything alive and concrete. He took out a pencil with a sharp point and drew heads on the paper napkin in front of him. It was a habit of his. He drew disconnected things, faces, fragments. She, with elbows on the table, let her coffee get cold, resting her face in her hands. Her old silence began to invade her spirit again. Images of the film lasted in her mind. Suddenly, as if impelled by an unexpected force to say something she couldn't predict, she said, in a slow voice:

"These last nights I've had the same dream three times. I would like to know the meaning of this repetition concerning something unmotivated and incomprehensible. It was a dream without people, without a single person, where all I could see was blood. At first I didn't know what these strange nights were: I saw a piece of pavement and a dark, irregular-shaped spot; then a human chest, plain but nothing more than a section, and from that white strip, blood began to flow; then I saw that it was blood. The way it flowed, above all, was something restful, something like a release which I felt increasingly in the dream."

Benes, without lifting his eyes from his drawing, answered: "There are many dreams like that. The fact is, I never have dreams, and I don't find anything enigmatic in its meaning."

Apropos of something enigmatic, he then told something that had nothing to do with the case in point or with his later lengthy account of a case of vivisection, nor with the story a bad-tempered traffic superintendent who directed a section of railroad where he worked. She looked around her. The room remained deserted. The mirrors merged, reflecting large sectors of empty space. She fixed her eyes on those vacuities reflected in the mirror and felt a metallic taste in her mouth. They traveled slowly down Charcas Street, then down Arroyo. Benes observed with pleasure all the recently pruned trees, calculating their future growth; he compared the light given by the new street lights with the darkness of a few months before in this wealthy part of the city. He seemed always to be thinking in terms of statistics. She faced the night with an infinitely sad face, her arched eyebrow pained, her beautiful ardor mutilated. There was nothing which separated them so completely as that spoken monologue. Benes lost himself in a labyrinth of loquacity; she walked along, a clipped echo at his side, with a look of desperation as Benes lost his way in a verbal tangle. They arrived finally at the staircase that led to Seaver Street and their house. She went to bed in silence; from the bathroom she heard a monotonous masculine voice humming a song:

Célimene, Célimene, I am blue, Célimene . . .

The room light was turned off. Lying on her back, she closed her eyes, but at the moment of falling asleep, the silence began to fill with sounds, to become charged, transported in a diffuse but noisy concert. She was not slow in noticing, with eyes wide open, that it was her own echo, an echo emanating from her person, multiplied into a swelling sound. As if disassociated and then harmonically joined, the dark elements of her being came to the surface. Alert to her terrible obsession, she awaited new symptoms, wanted to see the nature of her protest clarified completely. She heard the sound of a secret and inarticulate echo—her echo— recurring physically through her whole body; at first vague, then more distinct. A will to prolong herself, creating, giving of herself, integrating her expectant and receptive femininity, predisposed like a tense bow toward the only human unity from which her fruit could come. Her fruit, her fruit—is it permitted to live without bearing fruit? But could she obtain a fruit of the flesh without first realizing another kind of communion, without allowing her timid spirit to lose itself in another, in order to find itself in a bold affirmation. Obscurely, she wanted to take her silent, secret word to another human climate where it might bear fruit. But at her side Benes was already sleeping, he was sleeping when her mute delirium began in crescendo, like a terrible orchestration. Fixedly, from a few inches away, she looked at that masculine forehead where the lines of the bones could not be made out under an overly healthy skin. She trembled, prey to a sudden chill, frightened before the possible destiny of her flesh, the fate of being unable to conceive a new being born in the shadow of her enclosedness, in the secret of her soul.

Thus she spent the night, devoured by a feverish desire to be in communication with some being in that magic way and without words, with that vehement, silent communicability which is in itself faith and love. This fervid vocation overwhelmed her that night, ended by covering her body with sweat, submerging her in a state of subterranean despair. Each hour brought its special note to her anguish. Suddenly obsessed, she heard herself screaming, heard her silence being broken by strong cries. Then she remained tense, in a great effort to remain mute. She shook her head from one side to the other. Her fingers stiffened, rigid. She thought for hours.

Until finally, at dawn, with a painful slowness of birth, she embarked on her insomnia. She saw clearly the prospect of the new journey with terror, stiff with cold.

The early hours of morning were filled with Benes's songs, those songs of the "healthy" man, under the shower or simply amused, occupied with the practical arrangement of some pieces of furniture. He sang and whistled, inviting her happily to comment on some news in the paper, a kidnapping, or a strange event in Cádiz or Greece, certain that there couldn't possibly exist at that moment, under the happy sun of the morning, any spirit that would not joyfully be in tune with his own. After breakfast, they left together. It was pleasant to pace the fresh sidewalks, breathing in the startled honeysuckles. A few minutes after eight, they said good-bye next to the Plaza San Martín.

• • •

IV

The sunsets were rapid; but that afternoon haste brought its compensation, and a fresh country smell advanced over the asphalt.

A cigarette, more than half stained with red, hung from Señora Savisiano's mouth. Its smoke made her blink. In the large central blue room, suddenly, all noises, all echoes of shop talk had stopped. With her red, crisp-curled hair, the señora was wearing a blouse of her own creation, in which she had attempted absurdly to modernize the outmoded whalebone collar. Erect, one hand on her waist and the other leaning against the edge of the magazine table, with an air of affected majesty, she questioned Ana Borel, while the dog lay sleeping at her feet. The perfume of the last client was still heavy in the air.

"For the last three weeks you haven't said a single word to me. You look tired, and this silence of yours, really! Well, I mean it just isn't right for a girl of your age! I don't want to stick my nose in other people's business, God save me from that, but I can't help feeling something sad in you. I don't know, something like sleeping sickness. What's the matter with your husband? Why doesn't he take you out to the theaters to see things? Or maybe, thinking it over carefully, it's your fault—too little spiritual life, eh? Too little inner life. Believe me, you'd better take the path of theosophy before it's too late."

Ana Borel animated her lips with a smile. She shrugged and continued making notations in a folder. After a pause, the señora, annoyed, tried another tack: "I sent a cable to London ordering the six models of Shar, as you told me."

Ana nodded. The señora walked a few steps, going toward the empty vase which crowned the small cashbox. She picked it up and placed it on the floor, crouching down with difficulty. "A lack of spiritual problems, that's it," she stammered as she got up, her back to Ana.

Then she left the blue room. Two seconds later she pushed her head through the half-open glass door again. "Youth is insolence. One must not depart from the path of universal brotherhood. I could give you a series of lessons. You'd see what a change it would make, you'd see how everything here would be renewed in the light of reason and faith."

"Here" meant on this planet. Ana watched her withdraw sorrowfully, troubled by those eternal ravings. She returned to her work; but soon, the turgid light which came in through the streaming banner caught her eye. The afternoon had become clouded over. A succession of freezing days had left behind them a period of mist and rain; the winter was dying. She considered the atmosphere with a somber air. She felt the penetrating hostility of the weather on the march as it moved slowly along the boulevards, advancing through the masses of humanity like an insidious army. She couldn't wait. She couldn't wait any longer. She passed her hand over her forehead. But was she waiting for something in particular? Wasn't she being invaded by a simple weakness, a state of anxiety? Anxiety, yes, without any doubt whatever: like those slow fevers which at the moment of crisis give the impression of strangulation. She shook her head, her white face drawn. She opened the account book, bent on trying to take her mind off her unhappiness by concentrating on those straight columns of figures. But her imagination continued its subterranean process. The idea of a persistent, nagging hunger would not leave her. An inner hunger, a torture developed years ago, which had gestated in the house in Olivos, beside the footsteps of the Negress in solitude. How many times at the end of the day had she despaired, longing to close her eyes and take off from the steep hill, in Olivos, to plumb the abysmal depths, down to the stones of the pavement. Those stones, that abyss, had obsessed her. To break—to break once and for all—all those unfinished ends of spirit which she carried within her, incomplete gestures, incapable of flowering, that profound multitude of roots of dialogue which were enclosed beyond the flesh by her condemnation to monologue.

With a decisive motion, she advanced and closed the high curtain; she turned on the electric light. Surprised, she noticed the trembling of her hands. Her whole body was touched by that inner shaking. Through the shop door came Rosa, wearing a small violet hat. "Are you going home?" she asked.

Ana began to put the books in the desk, to lock up the boxes. Her hands were trembling but her features were motionless.

Within, she was harassed by one fixed idea: uselessness, futility, futility, futility.

They left together. Rosa watched the displays in the windows, delighted with her nocturnal freedom, satisfied by the luxuries it afforded. Laughing, she asked Ana Borel's opinion about an individual who followed her every day, after having waited for her across from the Teatro Cervantes. She explained that she always got rid of her men before they left her, and as quickly as possible, before they had time to get over their surprise, after she had used them. Since Ana only answered her in monosyllables, Rosa said good-bye and, with an unconcerned wave of the hand, headed for the center of town, losing herself among the innumerable women circulating at that hour, identical in appearance, identical in clothing, identical in morals and soul . . . the young women of Buenos Aires.

Ana hastened her pace. A hand reached out to greet her, offering a newspaper with enormous headlines. She crossed rapidly through a market with gleaming white stands, where the atmosphere was permeated with the smell of fruit and fish. She made an effort to fix her attention on this external spectacle, immersing herself in it; but something too violent to be denied was making headway in the more distant regions of her being. Large lumps beat against her in her mind. She could clearly hear the voice of her husband, sure of his arguments, expounding slowly, as one who has his entire life before him to develop in a slow monotone; and mingled with that voice, like a countersong, the voices of Loubie and Mosalé, one hoarse, the other suave and a little effeminate. Those voices were getting louder, growing in her as she walked, hastening her step, in a tortuous progression, lugubrious, with the insistence of Congo drums. They became louder and louder, until they made her dizzy, until she was physically ill. She began to breathe heavily the street air. The electric lights on the street corner illuminated momentarily her taut face and neck, her nervous hands, her anxiety and confusion, her fleeing steps.

She crossed Charcas Street, then the boulevard, full of people, with its fleet of swift vehicles. She was on the outskirts of a

wealthy, solemnly dignified part of town. The mansions closed
their mouths in an extreme tension of stone. Suddenly she heard
someone whistling behind her and mechanically turned her head
to look. Her husband was walking a few steps behind her, smiling, his shining eyes full of alacrity. He had a young but fragile
appearance, with his convex shoulders, medium build and height,
arms somewhat akimbo. As he did every day, he had just left the
last office on the top floor of an immense building and had come
down the stairs of the institution, armed with his leather brief
case, smiling with his gray-green eyes, full of passivity.

He took her by the arm and they continued walking while he
told about the great to-do the manager had caused that afternoon
at the office. The still layer of humid air pressed down, clamped
between the low sky and the asphalt. In the little square in front
of the Loan Bank, the accumulated silence hovered in the atmosphere as if in wait for victims. A child's cry burst in the lobby,
then another, and others—like the yelps of a young herd possessed by ferocity. She walked with eyes fixed on the sidewalk,
with staccato steps, her hand in her jacket pocket. The luminous
advertisements seen in the brusquely ascending perspective of the
street seemed to amuse Benes beyond measure. She lifted her
head, and a gust of violence disturbed the unsociable expression
of her eyes. As if cornered by the brusque reasonings of the
monologues which were growing in her, her eyes seemed to
tremble with revolt, with an agitation which set her lips trembling slightly as well, hardened her green pupils, pressed her motionless arm more closely against her body. While the rapid steps
of the man accompanied her, she felt the immobility of that arm,
was aware of herself, felt herself growing, turning to pain. One
side of her body felt paralyzed, she felt herself invaded by a
motionless bitterness. But wasn't this a prolongation of the rigidity toward which all her thoughts were tending at that moment?
Rigidity, rigidity. She paid no heed to the blurred letters of the
sign. "Chop suey," he repeated, smiling beside her. But her attention was only upon her obsession. Why did the image of a rigid
bird persist in her retina? She thought about the giant bird in
Prince Igor; the boxes, the theater was full, like a cauldron of
human victims with morbid bosoms and shirt fronts; the audience

was a mass with a thousand faces. She shook her head; it amazed her to think of this, to be able to get away so gratuitously from a fixed idea. Because everything living in her, everything feminine, her lofty forehead, thin throat, thighs, had submitted at that moment to the fixed idea, which she controlled. The pharmacist in white greeted them as they passed. They entered and began to light the brief chain of lights; their steps resounded on the paving stones of the floors until the last corner of the house.

The pharmacist entered his store thoughtfully, thinking ruefully how the woman's face had changed in the course of the winter.

v

She saw him making preparations for the party, watched him moving from one side to the next happily, carrying the bottles. He placed the bottles on the table; then the glasses; the centerpiece with flowers. He stepped back for a moment to observe the effect of the arrangement. Immediately he counted the objects on the table, moving his index finger, without speaking; after which he turned toward her, laughing, assuring her happily that this was going to be a splendid party.

She looked at him with eyes wide open, staring at the white tablecloth and the new chairs, and at the city, immense and cold, through the window. He went to the telephone and ordered something—a basket of dried fruit. Afterward, he turned to look again at the table with his arms folded, satisfied. She had a bitter taste in her mouth and her entire body was possessed by a sensation of extreme fatigue. They went to get dressed. He returned to the dining room in his shirt sleeves, to line up on one side of the table the three bottles of port that he had forgotten at the bottom of the cupboard.

At exactly ten o'clock, the bell rang. Ana closed the door to her room.

"Come in!" shouted Benes, from the table where he was preparing the cocktails.

Monsieur Loubie entered, bringing in the cold with his overcoat, his nose and cheeks livid, badly shaved. He was nearly frozen and could barely smile: "It's a rough night," he repeated, waving his short arms while Benes helped him off with his overcoat. "Just in case," he said as he handed Benes his umbrella. Then he slapped his host on the back before entering to rub his hands. With happy obsequiousness, Benes led him to the dining room and served him a glass of the most expensive sherry, which he had placed strategically in order to serve it early in the evening.

Monsieur Loubie thanked him with eyes worthy of Voltaire, his sarcastic master in political and social science.

"An excellent beverage!" he commented suspiciously.

"Fifty years old and bought at the best wineshop in the *barrio norte*," assured the host.

"The best wineshop in the *barrio norte*," the visitor repeated.

"The best," the other reaffirmed.

Thinking about this wineshop, the recent arrival let himself be served another glass, and to these would have added a third, with cynical complacency, if Benes had not leapt to the door, summoned again by the bell. From the foyer he called, jovially: "Behold the magnate, in person!"

The "magnate" entered the dining room. It was another of the nicknames belonging to the "great" Elía, always surrounded by strange superlatives which had to do with his compulsion for wasting money and an infantile irresponsibility concerning the problems of saving. The three embraced each other with ostentatious manifestations, much laughter, and constant conversation. The great Elía congratulated the host for the sumptuous display on the table, warmed his hands, looked at himself in the mirror, and, inspired by the sherry, unhesitatingly began the story of the bullfighter who died trying to make a pass, kneeling after having drunk fourteen glasses of the best Orvieso. The point of the story was scarcely understood but loudly praised, and all three drank to the health of the victim of the Orvieso. Monsieur Loubie gave a short speech, apparently humorous, but basically against bullfighting in general and indicating his slight preference for the *novilladas* in Mexico, where—he had a somewhat confused idea —they didn't kill the horses. Benes, as he put down his empty glass, took advantage of the opportunity to express his scorn for the latest figures in Mexican exports, figures which he repeated with unusual accuracy, exactly as he had read them two days earlier in the office. Neither Loubie nor the great Elía showed any special enthusiasm for Mexican foreign commerce, and Loubie even went so far as to say, with a sarcastic smile, that he infinitely preferred the *novilladas*. This disconcerted the host slightly, and his brilliant role of chief officer in the king's household suffered a slight eclipse. He repeated in a low voice the overall figure of Mexican foreign commerce, saying timidly: "Nobody thought that we would surpass them by two thirds."

"Really," said Monsieur Loubie.

"Really," said the great Elía, and there was a pause.

The word "really" was left floating in the air, and it was doubtless quick thinking which led the host to offer another drink. But Benes was interrupted, the bottle in his hand.

Ana had just entered the dining room. Her grave and ardent taciturnity had now disappeared under an expression of lassitude, under the faint smile which revealed a row of small teeth. She accepted a glass in her slender hand, but hesitated to raise it to her lips. She listened to the very cordial words of Elía and a tribute from Monsieur Loubie—who was looking at her bosom with the smile of an old connoisseur—on her violet dress.

The latter hastened to ask her if she had read the book he had sent her three weeks ago; it was a love story which took place in the Malay Peninsula. She answered decisively that at that moment she couldn't read novels. The three men laughed amiably.

Mosalé and the secretary from the embassy arrived together at that moment, accompanied by an overdressed woman who arched herself backward convulsively in a fit of laughter. The great Elía was pleased to see Carlota come in. She was a woman of turbulent life, who took her loud laughter, brilliant, ill-chosen luxury, and bubbling personality everywhere she went. But why was she arriving with Mosalé? Elía had thought four days ago that they were disgusted with each other. She herself had told him, in the Águila Bar, about Mosalé's "filthy actions," and had obliged him to comment upon them and judge them. Now they arrived as great friends, and at that very moment, now in the dining room, wasn't Mosalé eying him with suspicion? The great

Elía swallowed a glass of port in his bewilderment. I gave myself
away, he thought. It always happens; take a chance and you give
yourself away. There's no hope for an idiot like me. Carlota
didn't look around; she was looking at him with a malicious and
cynical expression. And then she left Mosalé and approached
him, speaking in a low voice, almost into his face, brushing
against him with her strong scents and her young breath: "The
mouth you like so much will think of you drinking the first
drink." He felt himself bathed in a pleasure that surpassed his
wonder. But already Mosalé had come to find her and was taking
her away, because Benes had opened the piano in the living room,
and the young diplomat was going to delight them all with some
pieces which doubtless had never delighted the pianist, with his
feigned displeasure and his rings from the time of the Viceroy-
alty. The drawing room was rectangular, with a small balcony on
the street, literally poisoned with furniture and curtains. Jaime
Benes had decorated it according to his taste and temperament,
imposing on it that dissipated and colorless verbosity which was
natural in him. An upright piano was squeezed between portraits
against one of the walls, and one could be assured that it was the
only stretch of wall where the decorative proclivities of the
owner had found no plastic extension. The curtains on either side
of the balcony differed ostentatiously from one another. Alongside them was the photograph of a gentleman with a white beard
and a frockcoat, wearing a Masonic emblem in his collar. Everyone had come into the drawing room. Since the ironic Monsieur Loubie was so much taller than Elía, together they seemed a
carefully shaved drawing-room version of the Ingenious Knight
and his Squire. "No, No," the host hastened to specify, "no
tangos to begin with . . . Rachmaninoff's Prelude or something
like that." The secretary of the embassy raised his eyes, striking a
note with his bloodless index finger, and indicated with abject
apologies that he didn't know that prelude and his desire to have
them hear instead a rhapsody from his own country. Augusto
Mosalé began to applaud frantically, not without winking his eye
to the left. Carlota whispered in Ana's ear: "A diplomatic rhapsody." The two were standing, and Carlota was receiving all the
sidelong and restless glances of the great Elía, whose deceptively

intellectual head shone under the chandelier. Raising her arm in the air, Carlota shouted to the pianist: "I protest, I protest! A rhapsody is the only thing that diplomats can't play. It's popular music . . . Play a wedding march!" This crime of sacrilege was received with laughter, but the secretary of the embassy looked at the elegant young woman with a scornful expression in his haughty eyes, and, with an impetuous gesture, let his hands fall upon the keys.

Carlota's shoulders trembled. Ana came forward and closed one of the side doors, from where a burst of cold air was coming. Afterward she returned to her place, her face suddenly blank.

The prospect of having to listen without speaking made Mosalé very uncomfortable. He detested music, which he considered soft and sentimental, made for beings capable of spending their lives forever in an armchair poeticizing the repose of their buttocks, nor would he be bullied into putting on an ecstatic face about the matter. He was a veteran socialist, long hardened against such trivia. His slogan consisted of two words: "organization" and the "future": in the meantime, let's have a good time! Without the slightest attempt at dissimulation, he approached Monsieur Loubie and in a loud voice began to tell that sole representative of social criticism and civic austerity that it was unfortunate that the two of them had to put up with the musical experiments of the young diplomat.

"Loubie, I always prefer historical conversations to music, because one can learn something from them," he said in a ponderous tone which not even the sound of the music could drown.

Monsieur Loubie closed his eyes, pointing with his head to the pianist, like someone who recommends circumspection.

"For example," insisted Mosalé, "it's far better to drag out the rags or great deeds of some national hero than to listen to a rhapsody . . . eh? You won't say no to that, will you?"

"No," Monsieur Loubie assured him, without opening his eyes.

At this instant Mosalé received a glance from Carlota, charged with meaning. Then he slipped into the vestibule and, passing on the outside, placed himself directly behind her. "I was telling him," he affirmed, pointing with scorn to the place in the drawing room where his former companion was standing, "that it's far more worthwhile to talk about history than to listen to these silly concerts. Of course, one can turn one's eyes inward with appreciation; that doesn't require any effort . . . But to talk about Fourier or Napoleon, to tell an anecdote, even if it's only one— well, that's different!"

"There's no doubt about it," replied the elegant woman, "no doubt at all. History is the fountain of supreme wisdom," she added after a pause, with a sententious air.

Mosalé didn't give this phrase the credit it deserved, but he looked into Carlota's eyes and caressed her forearm with a paternally incestuous air. The pianist, his head down, his arms open, had just struck the final chord.

"Bravo!" shouted Mosalé, joining in the applause.

Carlota called the great Elía aside and repeated to him the phrase about history as if she were giving him the solemn key to a conspiracy. Afterward she observed the effect she had produced. Expansive and enthusiastic, he indicated that he was in agreement, entirely in agreement. No doubt about it, history comes from great experience and is the fountain of supreme wisdom.

Running her finger along her string of pearls, she then confided to him: "I've been reading in bed lately about the life of a great man . . . but I assure you I don't support the deluded man they write about. I don't approve of his idea of monarchy . . . Imagine, a monarchist! Even if it were today; but in those days . . ."

Benes appeared with a tray of full glasses. "The red port of friendship!" he exclaimed. "Ana!"

Ana came forward, took two glasses, and passed them. The secretary of the embassy took one and raised it to propose a toast, rolling his eyes at her:

"Thank you; because it came from you. From that great dignity! You're always dignified and serene. You should be called" —and he drained the glass at a draught, to the last drop, holding the liquid for a moment in his mouth—"Elizabeth and not Ana . . . Elizabeth, which means, you know, saturated with God."

Ana's forehead clouded and she said nothing, then ran her eyes over the circle of laughing people, all somehow exulting in their

physical good health, brought together like strange lunatics in a
grotesque forest.

She felt fingers touching her elbow: "You're no longer listening to me," said the secretary of the embassy. She smiled and
begged his pardon. He told her, shrugging his shoulders, that
with him music was something natural and unlearned. Without
any study at all, he could surpass in some performances the most
famous concert artists of the world. "It is," he said, "more a
matter of temperament than a matter of technique, you know."
Temperament, temperament. When he was five years old he used
to sit down at the piano and even then he would strike the keys
with a special harmony, a specious and singular sonority.

He spoke with an emphatic self-sufficiency, leaning on the
piano, his hand negligently resting on one of the empty candelabra which came out of the vertical box like a metallic cornucopia. And the piano itself seemed a species of beast, of passive
black deer, under that confidently dominant arm.

Quickly they all displaced each other in a slow whirlpool drift
toward the dining room. The toupee of M. Loubie sparkled
next to Carlota's resplendent neck, and this resplendent neck in
turn sparkled next to the persistent joviality of the great Elía. It
was a glittering picture, of a luxurious human legion, marching
joyfully toward nutrition. . . . The bursts of laughter of Augusto
Mosalé sounded like a trumpet. The recalcitrant Loubie showed
himself unusually bold at the buffet table, and with a gesture of
extraordinary courtliness he withdrew from the silver dish one of
his favorite liqueur bonbons. He closed his eyes, delighted, while
he chewed it, and then smiled benevolently at Carlota, to answer
the warning which she, pretending to be serious, directed at him
with her index finger. The conversations multiplied their hum in
the midst of the happy clink of glasses. The light from the chandelier watched over the exultant ensemble. Mosalé could hardly
contain his enjoyment. Benes, alert, happily saw the triumph of
his work in Mosalé's pleasure. There was a short but amiable
discussion on the different types of drunkenness produced by
two of the liquors they liked; there were supporters of one and
supporters of the other. Carlota intervened like a provincial
arbiter, saying in a loud voice that the two were equally delicious

and that there was no point in keeping in mind the final results just when they were drinking. Everyone agreed. Mosalé smacked his lips and studied the labels on the bottles. Actually, they were like members of a court-martial at a table heaped high with crimes.

Ana refused the liqueur with a gesture. Her mouth smiled, but her expression, ardent and secretive, was distant. Her thighs were against the table, her body arched backward, her hands in the pockets of her jacket, her right leg slightly bent, her foot resting on the point of her toe. The others were too involved in their own motives and actions to notice her terrible distraction. She fluttered there, beautiful, rough, diffident; a strange, human bird in that climate of death.

She found herself dancing in the arms of the secretary of the embassy, who held her very tightly. All were immersed in lively conversation, and the crystalline sound of the glasses accompanied their voices. One had to laugh, laugh, laugh. Just like M. Loubie, with yellowish teeth and faded skin. Laugh, talk. The atmosphere became charged with the bustle, the smoke, the dust on the floor, the smells, the barbarous breath of the party. Very late in the evening, Mr. Stokevom arrived with his absurd trousers and the child's golden trinket hanging from his vest. Alcohol. The secretary of the embassy returned to the piano, stubbornly punishing the same chord: bang, bang, bang, bang.

She felt the repeated blows in her vitals, in her head. She fixed her eyes on the spectacle without seeing it, trembling before the destiny of so much noisy happiness. Oh, to feel sterile, to dominate an internal wave of terror, a telluric fear, hearing always a frightful, mute scream: to say yes, to say yes, to say yes, and, within, a voice without force, God, God, God.

Elía exploded in a raucous laugh: "Finish it, Moldes, finish the rhapsody!"

VI

The tumult was followed by an infinite silence. The dry atmosphere of the house seemed like that of a courtroom, just after an unjust sentence has been passed, a moment when every-

one is holding his breath. Now they were there, the two of them
alone, at the scene of the party, not knowing what to say to each
other, each secretly occupied by private, mysterious, conflicting
wrongs; he for some little passing thing; she for something dark
and overwhelming, difficult to unravel and confess. They went
over the rooms, putting things in order, without speaking. He
couldn't avoid feeling a certain resentment toward her for her
silence during the party. Nevertheless, this passed like a fleeting
cloud, and he returned to his usual loquacity and laughter, recalling some ludicrous characteristics of Loubie. There were several
spots of alcohol on the floor. Ana went to the pantry and brought
a cloth to wipe them up; her movements were lethargic, as if the
blood had stopped circulating in her veins. Her face was tired
and her head was spinning. He commented aloud on the certain
fate to which Carlota's flirtations would bring her, and showing
how much he'd had to drink, lamented volubly about not having
anyone to bet with on his prediction.

She didn't listen to him. At first, she made a desperate effort to
take care of herself, but discovered immediately that it was useless. She had the sensation that her flesh was burning with fever.
Her head was on fire. She was overwhelmed by painful images,
contradictory, incoherent; her forehead ached. Suddenly she
found herself sitting in a chair in the drawing room, her eyes
fixed on the skirt of her violet dress, while he went on speaking
happily from the dining room, busily gathering up the bottles.

Ana got up and went to her room. She felt her head was going
to explode when she saw herself in the mirror and looked at her
shining eyes surrounded by dark circles. Her hair was in perfect
order. She stood there a moment, looking at herself without seeing, really seeing, anything. Then she opened the bathroom door
and drank a glass of cold water. She leaned her forehead against
the windowpane, feeling the cool condensation of frozen vapor.
In the midst of that flock of incoherent and cruel images, she
would have liked to think about someone, to focus her imagination for an instant on something; but she had nothing, no one to
think about, and she looked through the window and the night
air at the nearest roofs, the misty moon. She was breathing
deeply; her eyes burned, her dry lips were parted, her hands were

cold and contracted. She heard Benes coming up the stairs. He opened the door to the room, whistling, with the afternoon paper under his arm. What in the world could change his good nature, his noisily muffled walk, his blind look?

She lay down in the bed next to his. Her eyes were fixed on the window, which coated with mist the clamor she felt within. She was trembling imperceptibly, an internal throbbing which barely reached her skin. The light went out and she heard the newspaper fall, followed by the rapid and audible sleep of Benes.

She kept her eyes open. She knew now that her mysterious visitor was near. That presence which had followed her for so long was here at last. Lying in wait for her since infancy, every day, on the street, at night, on the hill in Olivos, that face, that ghost with the bleeding face . . . *anguish*. She felt it now, very near her, in the eternal air of the night; invading her in the form of a violent and furious fever which would make her head explode.

Her hands clasped and unclasped over the sheet, her eyes took on a tragic intensity and brilliance. At that moment, her beauty would have terrified any observer. A sob came quickly to her aid, but remained within, and then retreated, becoming diluted as her heart pounded. Like something strange and distant, she felt in her nose the fleeing essence of her hair. Her agitation threatened to overwhelm her. Suddenly she saw the house in Olivos, solitary, somber. This vision was no relief, and it paralyzed her mouth, fixing her lips in a still more bitter expression. Desperately she tried to protect her body and soul, so bitter, so solitary, so somber. But it was beyond her power. She looked around her in terror. Time was moving on. The night was soundless. The universe seemed definitively closed around her. She heard the pounding of her pulse. She was alone. Alone with her futility.

Immediately she was shaken by a tremor, a flood of alienation fell upon her spirit, stiffening it. She sat up in bed with a terrible scream. Its savage violence drained her of strength and voice.

Benes, startled, got up heavily. He saw her raised up in the whiteness of the sheets, her eyes blazing with dry fire and madness.

• • •

VII

A day of fever followed, with alternating depression and delirium. She had moments of clarity and silent calm, exhaustion and wonder. But these were fleeting.

In the morning, a neighboring doctor came to see her, a short, unprepossessing young man with apologetic lips, who didn't hide his confusion. He promised to return, and left a prescription. M. Loubie, who arrived quickly a little before noon, advised against filling the prescription and adopted a serious attitude under his dry toupee: "We must proceed with caution," he said, speaking through his nose. Benes was moving around in a stupefied condition. All through the night he hadn't been able to free himself completely from alcoholic vapors and had attended his wife like a ghost. In the morning, early, he called all his friends. But only Loubie could come before noon. While he waited for him, Benes renewed the ice compresses on Ana's burning head.

What terrified him most was that she didn't close her eyes for one instant. He had never seen a stranger beauty. Her color showed the quality of the anemone, and the dilation of her pupils had something awful and impressive about it. Stunned, dressed in his gray flannel suit, he sat on the edge of the chair, looking at her. From the far end of the room, a great, sunless clarity entered. Occasionally, he would get up and mechanically open the drawers of the bureaus, not knowing what he was looking for. Afterward, he would return to his former position, perplexed, afraid.

She didn't laugh or cry. For brief periods she was rigid. Her hands hadn't stopped opening and closing. The light shone down on the purple wrapper which her husband had ineptly put over her.

Thus passed the morning. Benes walked about the house, went up and down stairs. He couldn't come to any clear conclusion: he only wanted to be in motion. He lined up long rows of used cigarettes on the vestibule table. When Monsieur Loubie arrived, he felt some relief. After noon Mosalé and Moldes, secretary of the embassy, arrived. They were all inhibited and walked around on tiptoe. Moldes constantly lifted his hand to his red necktie with nervous movements.

They didn't know whether she recognized them or not, because her stiff, strange expression never varied.

The fever seemed to crackle in her face and the beginning of her bosom. Suddenly the words of her delirium became coherent for an instant and she shook in a violent seizure. At these moments her beauty was like that of a hungry wild animal, lost in mid-journey.

"I don't scream!" she screamed. "No!"

She looked at them, one after another, her eyes out of their sockets. She seemed to be looking for something in them, to want to penetrate them to their roots, to see something beyond the frightened stupor showing in their faces.

"Cheat! Cheat!" she shouted, shaking. And she repeated the word several times.

Without taking her eyes off of the men, whose faces she didn't recognize, she persisted, strident, dry, bitter: "Silence! Silence!" Immediately she subsided to her former delirious murmurs. With a trembling hand, Benes wiped her forehead with a handkerchief. He was sitting at a corner of the Chinese bureau. In her indistinct mumbling, a jumble of words came tumbling out, and her eyes, captive to some unknown, mysterious logic, were filled with unseen images, with an ardent, suspended anticipation.

The moment when Moldes came forward to offer her a glass of water, she stopped him, fixing her motionless gaze upon him. The strong noonday light seemed to give a curious transparency to her features, to her youthful bronzed skin. A word seemed to be running over her lips without quite daring to frame itself. "A little water," Moldes repeated, "a little water."

At nightfall a great stillness came over her and she went to sleep. The men, preoccupied, went downstairs, and came up from the dining room carrying on their breath the smell of stale cognac. Benes was very grateful to his friends for not leaving. At eight o'clock, he had a telephone conversation with Señora Savisiano. The theosophist on the other end of the line was very upset and promised to visit immediately.

Benes went out to the street door for a moment. The wind

blew his hair in disorder, the collar of his gray flannel coat. The barbershop and the pharmacy—smells of hair tonic and turpentine—merged in the raw August night. The light of the only streetlamp seemed frozen. He felt depression, shock, fear. Dark questions entered his consciousness. What was it, where did it come from, what was the strange cause of this fierce isolation which had come over her so suddenly? He felt guilty of something, stricken by a tragic whiplash, wounded like that streetlight by the night frost. It was true he hadn't really known her. Ana Borel had always been a stranger to him. That restless, concentrated, sad Ana Borel. A stranger. He hadn't even deeply moved her flesh, that flesh which had trembled at the first contact. What should he have done to get closer to her, to penetrate her truth, her body, her soul, all equally closed and diffident. Nothing. Surely nothing. It was fated that he would never reach her. Someone else, perhaps. He had given what he had, his nature, his naturalness. Hadn't he given his nature, his naturalness? Laughter, words, animation, company, constant company, a genuine loyalty. As he thought this he vacillated, then persisted in the same thought—a genuine loyalty. Perhaps she had wanted something different, but he had given her what he had to give, all that he had of himself. He had tried to make sure she wouldn't be bored, always to talk with her so that she wouldn't be lonely. Now this alienation . . . He had always felt a sort of inner tension in her. Hands, eyes, soul. But he had never spoken to her about this. He had tried to talk to her about other things, to give her words, interpretations, themes of conversation. Who could deny this? Now it seemed to him that he had been conversing with her constantly and that she had abandoned him in the middle of a conversation, betraying him in his will to happiness, inflicting something upon him which he didn't deserve. This hurt him terribly, as he stood there in the doorway, breathing in the cold of the desolate little street. It wasn't merely this crisis, but her characteristic withdrawal which had been growing—he saw it clearly now—in her concentration, in her tense reserve, in her special courteous passivity. But these were small matters, flecks lost in the blackness of the night. The big question, the supreme question, did not allow of conjecture. It was directed to the powerful, cruel force which held sway over his gray lapel, the hours and the climate, the night, and the important and insignificant circumstances of human life. It fell on him like a great weight. Where was this going to end? Would she return to health, from her withdrawal? Suddenly he felt a strange wild tenderness for that woman who was lying upstairs with her forehead burning under the ice. He wanted to be near her. To speak to her, to flood her with words, to call her with words, even if she persisted in her absence, in her deafness toward him. Now he could pay his debts.

But a countermelody sounded in his spirit, insistent and demoralizing, and that was the deep suspicion that already the two of them were inexorably separated. Inhabitants of two different worlds, two worlds which had moved immeasurable distances apart, perhaps for eternity.

Overwhelmed, he shut the door and entered the hallway, trembling with cold. In the vestibule he met Mosalé coming downstairs. He helped him put on his overcoat without saying a word. He didn't dare ask him any questions. Mosalé was fat, and it was hard for him to put his arms in the sleeves. "A difficult business, a painful business," he allowed himself to say, scarcely moving his lips. At the moment when Moldes reached the upstairs landing, a short, piercing shriek was heard. Benes went running up the stairs.

Mosalé waited, his mouth half open, his hands paralyzed on the collar of his overcoat, perplexed and silent. Then, as if he heard nothing, he took his cane and his hat, and before plunging into the street, closed the door cautiously, with extreme care, so as not to make any noise.

THE
LOST CAUSE OF
JACOB UBER

I

One thing alone kept people from hating Jacob Uber: the undeniable fact that his entire life was overshadowed by suffering, a suffering so intense that in the end it destroyed him.

A small, thin man, Jacob Uber was very regular in his habits, and prone to worry about what he was going to say before he said it. Actually, he was afflicted like this only in the presence of casual acquaintances, whereas with his friends he was invariably quite at ease. Though burdened with a singular weariness of spirit, in the company of intimate acquaintances he struggled to escape from himself, and in rare moments of bliss he succeeded. Otherwise, this inner miasma had stifled him since childhood.

For years and years, all his yearnings had centered on ridding himself once and for all of this vitiated atmosphere which so

weighed him down. But the wretched man could never sufficiently destroy the evil spirit within to achieve this reformation,
and there were periods when he felt as though he were trailing
his hateful self around much as a serpent drags his cast-off skin. It
was painful, too, to observe how unalterable he considered the
traits of character with which nature had endowed him, and with
what charity he condemned them.

He was a solitary and a very melancholy man. Those who
knew him as he went to and fro through the big city, apparently
engaged in the same pursuits as everybody else, never suspected
anything of the kind. On the contrary, they always thought of
him as leading a very peaceful life, as pleasure-loving, easygoing,
relatively satisfied, even though subject to the usual human afflic-
tions. Beginning with his closest friend, a retired supervisor of tax
collectors and a patron of artists, and ending, for example, with
Señora Folan, who kept the office books up on the seventh floor,
everybody thought that Jacob Uber's loneliness was due almost
entirely to his bourgeois smugness, about which they joked in a
good-natured way even when he was present.

Nothing could be more trivial than the life he led in Buenos
Aires. One got the idea that he meekly conformed to any changes
which might take place in his world, but in other respects went
his own way, for he held a city job, lived in a small house in the
southern ward, was very fond of the movies, and on Saturdays
dined in a French restaurant where he ordered succulent dishes
with such high-flown names as *aloyau rôti aux legumes panachées*,
or *omelette à la Tour de Nisan,* together with a half bottle of
Château-Margaux. For a time he looked forward all week long to
this event; later, he continued to go to the restaurant through
inertia, although he no longer found the cooking especially
tasty.

He was quite young when he first started working for the city.
His father had come from Europe—from Lyons—while still a
boy and had been rapidly assimilated into the Argentine way of
life. He had died of angina pectoris one afternoon, in a railroad
station. Then Jacob Uber, taking advantage of the small patri-
mony that fell to his lot, went back to live in the very house
where he had spent his infancy. In his last few years, his father

had rented the house to a Belgian couple in order that he might spend the income from it on expensive liquors, and so young Uber had been forced to live in a *pension*. Yet when he came back to the tiny apartment, located directly above a carpenter's shop, and quite dilapidated, his heart sank and he had a premonition that bad luck and despair were to be his companions in these quarters.

He took delight in repainting the apartment every once in a while, doing the work himself and always using a new color scheme for each room. The chamber which his father had used, however, remained closed, unchanged, and full of his special belongings: a baroque chest, elaborate candelabra, and mirrors with heavily decorated frames. Once a month, Jacob opened the windows in this room and aired it, then once more sealed it up hermetically.

Up until then, Jacob Uber had been very retiring. He was little given to carousing and was always rather taciturn when he returned with groups of gay companions from the brothel district, where sinister madams had overwhelmed him with insincere compliments. Nor was he interested in dancing or sporting events; at the latter he was always depressed by the brutality of the public and the annoying atmosphere of irritation which hovered over the stadium when a contest came to an end. He did, however, get enjoyment out of his friendship with a number of women who worked in different parts of the city and whom he had come to know in a thousand casual and simple ways.

At the office, he worked obstinately, forcing his mind, by nature given to wandering and dreaming, to concentrate upon his work; deliberately bringing his eyes to rest on his typewriter keys and the banal label: "Shipper A—File C.Y.Z." He had never had any ambition to become an efficient employee but he did ardently aspire to submerge completely the thoughts to which he was prone and which so thoroughly exhausted him. Such thoughts always led him back to dwell on his isolation and soon resulted in vague but unbearable anxieties. His greatest agony was to picture the rest of humanity as dwelling in another world with which he had no tie at all except, perhaps, the superficial bonds of his purely physical life.

Once, just as dawn was breaking, he was forced to take refuge in a café, as if in flight from the streets and the city, and there he stayed, anxious, timid, his heart palpitating, sipping a glass of cognac and watching all the strange people seated around him, here and there at little tables, surrounded by blue smoke and the yellow halo of the lamps. Even among strangers like these a certain warmth circulated, while outside in the streets, at this hour of the night, he felt as though his soul were starving in the midst of a desert.

He always had the sensation of living in a stupor, with his eyes wide open, as stationary as a sea anemone. Mornings, as he was leaving for the office, he would drink in the air and sunshine with a certain sense of elation, but as soon as he entered the stream of people among whom he must spend his day, the very sight of their familiar faces produced a feeling of deep disgust, of total disillusionment, which showed through all his mechanical actions and superficial words. Superficial words! Had he, indeed, ever spoken any that were not superficial, any with real meaning? No. No, he realized that he had never had anybody to say them to, nor any opportunity for using them. He had never confided anything to anybody, never had become sufficiently intimate with any human being to feel like unburdening himself of what he considered the vapid story of his life.

When he was about thirty years old, this sensation of depression began to grow on him. He had usually been free from this type of egoistic preoccupation, but now he began to dwell at length on his responsibility as a man, and on his failure to make any sentimental attachments. For he felt that it was this failure which had shut him off in arid loneliness in a recondite world of his own. He thought of saving in order to travel, hoping that this would amuse him and help him to get away from himself; dreamed of giving up his position and beginning another life in which adventure might have a place. This idea gradually evaporated, however, as if even before he had made the slightest effort to put it into effect he were certain that it would fail. So he continued to bend over his files after his daily walk through the sunlit streets and his frugal breakfast at a cheap bar on Reconquista Street. Stooping over his desk, he would send out reports he had composed without the least thought as to what it all meant, while his eyes lingered on the typist's flying fingers and the anemic, skinny legs showing under her work table. He found himself wondering what this girl, Rebecca, would be like in an intimate situation and what motives lay behind her tense energy. Were there really human beings whose least gesture was not predicated on its dramatic effect, and did not have its origin in some seed of tragedy? Beyond doubt, he was living right among just such carefree people, so different from himself, and he envied them. He envied their ability to live outside themselves, since this made it possible for them to fling themselves headlong into a passionate interest in other people, sights, and things. And all the time he felt that he, on the contrary, was doomed to vegetate among familiar objects—a bed, a restaurant, an *aloyau rôti*, a roomful of lithographs and pictures he had cut out of magazines—objects for which he felt an affection never extended to any living thing. He took a melancholy view of himself as a human receptacle containing its own world, one with no outlets, a stagnant world where one mirage after another moves slowly by. Only his imagination showed any sign of activity. Instead of really living, he merely imagined, creating, in this inner world of his, objects and desires which began and ended solely with him.

On holidays, he would ride out into the country with his friend Lucas Mordach and they would stroll over the wide, monotonous prairies until dusk. Then they would come back to the bar in the station and sit down among groups of peaceful farmers, in winter ordering tea with anise, and in summer one of their delicious ices. Lucas Mordach was a very talkative, sensual person, an unusual fellow, always nibbling on calycanthus blossoms and filling his pockets with fragrant cedar buds. As they walked, his eyes would light up, he would open his mouth and take deep breaths, expressing unrestrained pleasure in the natural odors of the fields and shrubs and broad-crowned trees native to this region. As he walked along by Mordach's side, however, Jacob Uber never took any notice of the perfect form of an *ombú* or the "liturgic color" of the pines except when Mordach's nasal tones called them to his attention; instead he would stroll along flicking his trousers with a green switch, while a flock of images having nothing whatever to do with the landscape kept him company. They were sketchy bits of dramatization, mirages wherein events fitted together in a miraculous way, and vague dreams. He would imagine himself dressed up in farmer's boots, blue overalls with a bib, and a broad straw hat, coming over the horizon toward his own home, where he would be eagerly greeted by a wife and a small son in trousers too big for him, nibbling on some seeds. Over this home and these human beings, however, an omen of tragedy would always be hovering. He saw nothing else. The sun did not shine on this or that tree in the nearby meadows, but only his mirage. The same sort of thing happened whenever he went out to hunt partridges or to fish for trout in Lake Baldivén. On such occasions, his usual companion had a strong, hearty voice to which he would listen without really hearing a word. As they returned to the train he would exclaim, "What a fine day to go into the country!" and later, on the way back, his eyes would stare fixedly at the little houses along the track as they slid dizzily backward.

The powerful illumination of the city at night always amazed him and filled him with vague apprehension. What did he fear? When his surroundings began to lose their reality, he was inevitably overcome by fears of some dark catastrophe which he felt continually threatened him as a raging storm threatens an unprotected orchid. Then he would hunt for some refuge; go from bar to bar, and then from movie house to movie house, without ever paying any attention to what he was looking at except when the drama lent support to his own sophistries, or supplemented the fantasy which held sway over his mind at the moment.

II

His younger years were spent in this fashion and he always retained the feeling that all the world, with its varied phenomena and infinite mutations, had been but part of his own experience.

He finally came to believe that a life of introspection was the most noble and generous existence of all. For what more precious gift could one present to others than the qualities which fantasy and imagination built up within one? This reasoning, however, brought him face to face with that condition of solitide which he could not explain away and which became more pathetic with each passing moment.

Only once had he thought of marriage, of bringing into his mournful abode a cheerful and beloved companion, and he could never exactly understand what it was that happened, why he failed in his purpose. One Saturday night, at a party given by one of his childhood friends, Jacob Uber met Carlota Morel, a tall, blond woman with bright eyes, a kind of blithe gaiety in her manner, a proud carriage of her head, and small hands. She was fairly well educated, gave private lessons in languages, and read Hölderlin in the original. She was not concerned with what others thought about her, and was inclined to laugh off any criticism, in a jovial and authoritative manner. From the very first meeting, he felt that he had made an impression on her, for she talked to him intelligently and frankly about her early life, thus creating a rather sudden intimacy which flattered him. Soon he was inviting her to meet him two or three times a week at the Botanical Gardens or in Lexama Park or some of the other quiet, well-shaded sections of the city. One day she confessed to him, in an anxious mood: "I am not a happy person. I am always doing things I don't mean to. I spend my nights in frightful terror, in a state of apprehension, horrified by the emptiness of my life." Jacob Uber gazed at her earnestly, but answered nothing. He never told her about himself. He thought he loved her, and she saw in him a self-absorbed man, endowed with a quiet, courageous attitude toward life, strong and tender. Days, weeks, and months passed and he went on dreaming about her, glad when he saw her approaching but silent when they met. Finally, it got so they hardly spoke. One night, they entered a sordid hotel and took a room which boasted a large, forlorn bed, a washstand, and curtains of Orléans lace. Throughout the night, like old jaded lovers, they hardly said a word. Once, sadly caressing her hair, he cried: "I can no longer live without you, without this hair of yours which I shall love more and more as it grows white with age." He did not realize why he said just that, but as a matter of fact the idea of turning white with age was to him a symbol of the fading of their relationship, since when she was present she never conformed to the image of her which he set up when he was alone, with this image of her as he would like her to be. When he was with the real Carlota Morel, he yearned for the Carlota Morel his brain had created, the one that had taken shape in his dreams, his companion in solitude, the Carlota Morel who for months had been living in his apartment on Constitution Avenue, even though her voice and her flesh never entered there. Before this exotic companion he was exalted, but when he was with the actual Carlota Morel he felt only a desire to escape, to flee from her and go to the other, the Carlota whom he had created in her image. They returned several times to this sordid hotel, and one afternoon she asked him why they couldn't go to his apartment instead. Jacob Uber remained sunk in thought, avoiding any reply. He was wondering what an encounter between the two women would be like; an encounter in which, undoubtedly, the Carlota of his dreams would flee in horror. That would be a terrible thing to have happen. He shook his head at the very idea, mute, and she never knew why Jacob Uber would not take her to his home. It was easy to conjure up many reasons for his reluctance, and she soon forgot all about the incident.

One day, when they were strolling through a deserted street in the center of the city, they got into a dispute and began to argue fiercely. He could no longer control the irritation which overwhelmed him whenever he was with this woman, who seemed more and more a stranger each time they met. He was annoyed by his own silence in her presence, embarrassed because he never knew what to say to her during their strange meetings. And she was so chilled by his attitude that her mechanical actions betrayed her growing apathy. She walked on in her stately way, dwelling on her usual topics, going over once more the different stages of Hölderlin's progress toward insanity. It was that very night, as they were returning through the silent streets after a movie, that another discussion arose, and she, sensing that he was rebuking her, replied with a dominating gesture which expressed her unspoken defiance. Jacob Uber stopped abruptly, insisting obstinately, a spark of fury gleaming in his eyes, and then turned away and strode off in an abrupt and callous manner. He knew well enough that this was no way to demonstrate his manliness or fine sensibilities, or anything else, for that matter. But it was what he had longed to do, what he had been planning to do for a long time. That night, as he was getting into bed, the sheets felt fresher and he felt liberated from a burden, at peace with the ideal which he had been cherishing. That night as he slept, an odor of apples came to him from the hotel next door, and the aroma struck him as something new, hitherto unknown.

The next day, he felt like a different man. From then on he worked happily, singing and whistling. His sudden alacrity became the butt of sly jokes which his office companions aimed at him, especially Nancel, who stuttered, and so made them all the funnier. He really did feel like another man, happy, freed from the weight which each meeting with the language teacher had imposed on him. Now, almost unconsciously, he gave his full attention to the mysterious companion whom he secretly carried everywhere with him—a beautiful, wealthy woman whom he could evoke at any time, summoning her to his side, drinking in her presence with delight. He adored this woman, who had the physical features of Carlota Morel but who responded rapidly to his will, who glided sensuously along beside him, reserved, dressed in garments of his choice, at any given moment making the precious gesture he felt in need of, and demanded. For a fortnight he felt completely happy, with no sense of remorse or regret. He took pleasure in walking through the city alone or with some of his male friends. As they climbed up the streets to the north of an evening, or traversed the market district in the mornings, he scarcely heard what was going on, for he was far away, creating new worlds for his adventures with that other Carlota Morel. After his five hours of work were over each day he would sit on some café terrace near the Congressional Building, and there he would remain motionless for hours before a glass of beer. Although, as night drew near, the traffic would get very heavy, he was rarely distracted in the least by the passersby. Once in a while his gaze would follow the feet of some man who was walking past, and then he would suddenly look away, his eyes fixed upon the distance.

But all this soon changed. The transformation was so sudden that it threw his mind into confusion. He could never explain it to himself, or define the change, much less interpret the reasons for this new state of mind. Nor could he say exactly when it was that he began to hate the image of Carlota which he had carried about in his imagination, and to revert to the real woman, the language teacher whom he had treated with such despotic brutality. In fact, he felt a profound resentment against himself and a powerful longing for the woman whom he had thrust out of his life but who now became his constant obsession. He kept thinking that he must have been mistaken, that each time they were together in that sordid hotel or in their rambles through the city, he had actually felt real pleasure, genuine satisfaction. This thought robbed him of sleep, overwhelmed him with an inner disquietude; he began to work reluctantly. One day, when the head tax collector—a bald, apoplectic, watery-eyed old man named Señor Olda—called him into his office, Jacob Uber just stood there, sunk in a strange apathy, unable even to listen or reply coherently because he was thinking about the woman he had driven out of his life. Señor Olda looked at him over his spectacles, and undoubtedly noticing that his thoughts were far away, shouted in his hoarse, vulgar voice: "Look here, repeat what I was just saying. These instructions are mighty important and they must be carefully obeyed!" Jacob Uber would have liked to vanish from the scene, just suddenly disappear. He leaned a hand on the edge of the broad desk and smiled vaguely in a manner which certainly made him look very stupid. "Go on, repeat them," the inspector demanded. "I don't quite understand you," Jacob Uber admitted. Then Señor Olda became furious and, raising his eyes to heaven in protest, told Jacob Uber to get out, and began to rave at the number of idiots that cluttered his department.

Jacob was forever getting into situations like these. He came to be known as a strange, absentminded man, for he could never cease blaming himself for his conduct with Carlota Morel, the woman he had treated with such inhuman indifference. He would walk sadly through the streets, reliving their hours together, and feeling that he would give anything in the world to caress once more that smooth head which he had forsaken, that head on which gray hairs were beginning to appear. "How cruel I was," he would mutter, thinking of the moment when she used to appear, a little late for her appointment to meet him at a certain corner, how they used to walk through the streets in the moonlight, protected from the serious difficulties of life by the simple fact of being together; how alert and intelligent she appeared, talking to him about Hölderlin's marvelous life and his pathetic decline into insanity. But he had banished all that from his life, and now all he had was this barren loneliness, an endless, aimless future haunted by these phantom memories. Moreover, he took care never to mention it to anybody, lest he fail to impart to his tale the exaltation, the force, the ardor with which his imagination embellished it. He was so upset by all this that his pallor began to excite pity for him among others. Every night he would walk along the street on which that sordid hotel stood and walk up and down, enjoying in his imagination what had never given him any satisfaction at the time. He would stop and look up at the hotel's front, with its narrow balconies beyond which one could look into rooms strewn with odd pieces of clothing. He could picture himself entering the hotel with Carlota Morel; but now it was always the real Carlota Morel, the tall, blond woman with shining eyes who set his senses afire. Once, he even got up courage to enter and asked the clerk for a room he remembered on the fourth floor, with draped curtains of worn velvet and an advertising calendar on one wall, next to a pretentious copy of an oil painting, and there he remained alone until nightfall, seated in a cretonne-covered armchair, the blinds drawn to shut out the daylight.

This mood lasted for some time. But he never tried to look her up; he was so engulfed in lethargy that he made not a single step to catch up with her. Finally this obsession with old memories began to disappear, and Jacob Uber once more felt free. Strange things kept happening to him in other phases of his life. He was constantly assailed by terrible attacks of exhaustion and restlessness and suffered in silence from causes he could not clearly define. More than once he visited a chapel on the green slopes of the Retiro in the northern part of the city, drawn there by some obscure force, although his mind constantly wandered from the liturgy. Always in a terrible state of indecision, he was incapable of adopting any special faith or of making up his mind as to what he did believe so that he could take a definite stand.

Thus days passed by and he could never find an opportunity to express the general human kindliness that he felt, by some concrete act of courtesy toward another person. A deep-seated, secret yearning made him want to make friends, to create something artistic, but it was all based on purely vague feelings, too broad, never brought to a focus. As a result, his desire for friendship was dissipated before he ever found a friend, and he never experienced any well-rooted, lasting attachment. This continual harboring of desires which bore no fruit, of barren aspirations, tortured him. His affair with the language teacher had taken place when he was twenty-eight and she about thirty-four, but by the time he had caught up with her age, Jacob Uber was living in his house on Constitution Avenue like mere vegetation endowed with a soul, to all appearances unnaturally inert, but, within, continually on the watch. Women were inevitably attracted by his eyes, which were beautiful in a virile way, large, eloquent, and with such depth that they hinted at an earnest and lofty purpose in life. Their gaze, however, was so distant and absentminded that after a while they became merely tiresome and monotonous.

This state of concentration on abstract subjects had become so much a part of his nature that he was always dwelling in his inner thoughts. By the time he was thirty-nine years of age he no longer ate in order to live, but in order to sustain this constant distortion of everything created by his imagination, in which he took a languid delight. At times he would suddenly become aware that he was speaking of these imaginary happenings as though they were real. Once, in a Spanish restaurant, a bank clerk who was eating lunch at a table near his invited Jacob Uber to join him on a walking tour of the northern provinces, stopping at cheap inns and observing the curious folkways of both peasants and townspeople of the region. He agreed to the notion and immediately suggested that they plan to include the old houses along the river and the little baroque churches peculiar to northern Argentina. "We will have to leave before the end of this month if we want to avoid cold weather," the clerk reminded him. "All right, that's fine," replied Jacob Uber with an affable and animated smile. But as soon as he had started off alone along the streets lined with big commercial houses, he began to find fault with himself. Why had he agreed in such a hurry? Why had he raved on in such a puerile way, talking so effusively about a trip he had no intention of taking? He was angry with himself for having indulged so deplorably in the lies which his imagination conjured up. And yet the very certainty that he would never take such a trip made him look away from the world around him—from this avenue with its incessant, violent activity, where every face was stamped with strong determination—and plunge headlong into the thought of those little northern towns, so delightfully cradled under the shelter of broad-topped trees below the peaceful Andean foothills. That afternoon as he worked, his secret thoughts dwelled constantly on such an imaginary landscape.

On Saturday nights he would arrange with some of his companions to dine at a *café chantant* on Florida Street where they would be joined by two or three women of easy virtue but not too promiscuous. One, called Elsa, had sensual lips and untidy blond hair; another was a slender Hungarian with drooping eyelids, who translated stories for an evening paper. Sometimes the group was augmented by two sisters, both divorced, and the sweetheart of a certain politician, a lady with cold, cautious eyes that inspired fear in them all. They would pass the evening talking and laughing. Jacob Uber never gave up hope that he might discover some hidden beauty in one of these women, some spark of the spirit, something capable of elevating her for the moment above the common clay, and capable of inspiring her with faith in her unusual qualities. Days went by, however, and these meetings, enlivened by noisy orchestras, resulted in nothing more than tiresome gorging and indigestion. One by one, the women came to his house and became his mistresses, but it was inevitably a crude, boresome, abrupt and brutal affair in the eyes of Jacob Uber—a *Mene, mene, tekel upharsin*. Just bodies and more bodies, all inhabited by a gray specter, bodies imbued with impalpable death; bodies lying exhausted upon the bed while his own imagination went on its way, creating, withdrawing, separating his being from this other being, dividing the waters from the waters as on the second day of creation, dividing his withdrawn self from the body near at hand, motionless, tangible. He was amazed to find how fleeting was his contact with this flesh, although surrounded by perfect solitude. His distress consisted in taking possession of these women in the flesh without being himself present in the spirit; without being *aware* of the event. His eyes would wander and find no place to rest, like the eyes of a condemned man. Perhaps, if in place of the body which at that moment cast a vague glow in the dark of the room, it had another body—those other lips, laughter, tremors, and voice—the lips, laughter, and tremors of someone other than the woman at hand. . . Then the women would dress over near the door of his father's bedroom, so full of memories and dust, either protesting that he keep away, or not noticing him at all.

He had a vision of himself, a rather terrified one, in headlong flight which had no beginning and no end, divorced from the land, the sky, the air, the water—from passion, faith, and friendship—projecting his entity denuded of all roots into a universe where his spirit sailed along its course, vagrant and passive. Once he stood in absorption, smitten, before an engraving representing the dead Ophelia floating on a lake of white lotus blossoms, as if he realized that this image might refer directly to the inert submersion of his own spirit. Desperately at times he longed to find something to which he could anchor, which would make him take root somewhere, irrevocably—some passionate love, or belief, or order of society—something so far-reaching and profound that it would carry him with it and he would find himself in contact with the rest of the world. But every time, he would recant, escape, refuse to listen to the temptation of a broader, more distant vision, and revert to a kind of stupor filled with hallucinations.

III

It was not until after he had become head tax collector that he showed symptoms of a physical breakdown. He began to suffer nightly from spells of suffocation which would wake him from sleep with a terrible feeling of oppression. Soon this developed into an obstinate heart condition. When Jacob Uber left his office at six he would be overcome by his fear of the suffocating sensation, which he knew was bound to visit him that night, and this continual dread had its effect on him. He began to lose interest in conversation and his meals. The friend who had occupied an adjoining table in the Spanish restaurant, now that he had become aware of Uber's sullen and preoccupied taciturnity, no longer even bothered to speak to him. Yet, once dinner was over, Jacob found it hard to endure his solitude. He would travel any distance to visit his favorite office companions who happened to be alone in the world as he was. While he was at the office, he avoided suggesting that they go out together, in the vain hope of getting along without such companionship at least part of the time. When he happened to run into one of them on the street, however, he preferred to walk along without saying a word. This naturally bored his companion. Again, midnight would come and he would find nobody inclined to wander through the streets with him in this strange fashion. Then he would turn to the districts where traffic was still heavy, where there were crowds and plenty of life—the dock areas, the well-illuminated but evil sections of the city. As long as he did not go to bed, he did not feel so bad; he suffered no crisis, and his symptoms were less acute, confined to a dazed sort of melancholy.

He used to wind up in a café where a strangely fascinating comedienne with a harsh voice sang her numbers over and over again until daybreak. This woman, advertised on the big yellow posters as Lola Cifuentes, wore a black, spangled dress carelessly fastened over her soft shoulders and possessed a certain savage elegance. She sang with eyes fixed, pupils concentrated, standing like a priestess close to the piano on which an athletic, blond Dutchman tried to exhibit his training as a gymnast. Jacob Uber would struggle to fix his attention on the people assembled there, scattered around in booths and at tables, submerged in the heavy atmosphere. But his mind persisted in imbuing the various personalities—men who smoked while they conversed or argued with each other, and showy women with tired faces—with a reflection of his own illness, the complex forms of his own case, the destiny which he had to face. At one moment he would decide that he was getting better, then he would feel sure that there was no way out of his condition, that he was getting worse, that he was done for, that he would wind up, once and for all, in a state of complete loneliness. Meantime, the woman's hoarse voice seemed to blend with the piano, to take on its high metallic tones, its sound of worn-out strings. When the first light of day began to filter into the bar, Jacob Uber would drain the last portion of his small glass of cognac which he had been sipping for hours, and return to his house, where he would fall into a sudden, thoroughly exhausted sleep.

His physician, a Dr. Fogueral, frightened him by insisting that what he needed was a more hygienic way of life and immediate, rigorous treatment. He advised him to enter a quiet *pension* at Palermo, run by a friend of his. Disheartened, Jacob Uber gave up his rooms, put a few possessions in a small white leather valise, and wrote the tax collectors' department that he was forced to ask for a leave of absence because of his health. He was so full of dark thoughts that when he got into a taxi he had hired to take him to this guesthouse in Palermo, instead of giving the address, he absent-mindedly asked the chauffeur: "Is your mistress at home?" as if he were talking to the maid. Then he awoke from his woolgathering and smiled feebly as if to beg the chauffeur's pardon.

As he drove along, he looked back over the city with the sky so high above, at its trees shading the big avenues, and the far-reaching sidewalks. Blobs of light seemed to expand and float through the dusk, breaking forth into great sheaves of red glow which were reflected in the long, straight city gutters by a vague brick-red coppery hue. Jacob Uber saw the afternoon slinking off in all its desperate misery. Above the buildings, over the vast horizontal expanse, he heard a tremendous clamor rising from the multivoiced and cosmic throat of Buenos Aires.

The house at Palermo proved to be white, gleaming, and totally bare of extraneous ornaments. The hostess came out to greet him, sporting a dress rich with black lace but entirely out of style, with too tight a belt, and wide, billowing flounces. Her eyes gleamed in lively fashion above excessively painted cheeks. Jacob Uber followed her through bare, whitewashed corridors.

His room had a window from which he could look far down over a great slope leading to the river. Lights were springing up here and there. The hostess inquired as to what he wished to drink with his meals, and then went on to express her amazement at Jacob Uber's likeness to Lincoln in his youth. She would have liked to linger on for further comments, but her guest's face betrayed his weariness and boredom. She noiselessly closed the door. Jacob Uber opened one of the built-in wardrobes and, taking his extra suit from the valise, hung it up. Then he approached the mirror and stood there for some time, looking at himself. His untidy hair falling in wisps over his forehead accentuated the pallor of his face, already showing the ravages wrought by his bad nights. After this period of self-contemplation, he took out his books and placed them here and there on the tables. Several times he went to the window to survey his surroundings—to watch the dark birds winging their way toward the river, or to examine a nearby weathercock. He was especially interested in the assortment of windows in the houses below— windows with venetian blinds, French, baroque, and Byzantine windows.

The tiled roof of a factory and the cupola of a small church peered through the evening dusk. Far off, a flock of sea gulls wheeled in wide concentric flight. Night was creeping up from the river, advancing to engulf him and all that lay about him.

He looked over the furnishings of his rooms a number of times, and then sat down in an armchair upholstered in faded leather and discolored where the hands of former guests had rested. He felt sad and desolate. He raised his head, resting it on the low back, and closed his eyes, remaining in this position until nocturnal gloom had completely filled the room, admitting only the glow from the mirror in which the moonlight found reflection. He had a painful premonition that something agonizing was about to happen to him; yet he wished to get well, to live, at least a while longer, amidst all that he so painfully cherished.

He had turned on the light and was holding one of his few books when, after a discreet knock on the door, an imbecilic-looking maid entered the room. Her red hair was disheveled, and she had an air of being in a sort of trance. Her name was Ercilla, she said. Then she began to set a small, round table which she moved out of a corner into the center of the room. She left to fetch his dinner and came back with a portion of boiled fish and a bottle of milk. She remained watching him, in a dreamlike state, while he ate, picking at his food as if he suspected it, his large white body slightly stooped over his plate. Uber asked her some questions about the house, and she replied with monosyllables, her hands hanging listlessly against her gray skirt.

Time and again this same scene took place. The long days spent in that house were gloomy, far too gloomy for Jacob Uber. He lay about languidly, not caring when a strip of his flabby back showed through a rent in his shirt. Every third day, very early in the morning, he received a visit from Dr. Fogueral. He was a man of few words who said that he was dedicated to philosophy, but who in reality saw the final reason for things only in the viscera, which seemed to him a labyrinth in the face of which he never stopped being frightened, never stopped wrinkling his brow. Every morning after breakfast, Jacob Uber went out to get a little sunshine, walking through the deserted streets beyond the arid Plaza Italia. He had come to hate the tax collectors' office and never went near it even to pay a call, but these short strolls depressed him just as much. Each tree, each human being, each house showed him how far away he was from them all, and how little communication there was between them and the island on which he lived. What a bitter and difficult period he was going through! He constantly had a feeling that though everything in the world originates and exists through an act of love, he had tried to confine this love to his own little island, thus walling himself in more and more, instead of seeking his salvation through a spontaneous abandonment, a surrender of body and soul. Now he sensed that it was too late, and each time he thought of this a great sob would tear him asunder.

Yet he wanted to live. He took good care of the body which he had always loved so much, so solitary and imprisoned in its own fortress. He followed directions carefully, and while the doctor was listening to his heart through a stethoscope he would scan the doctor's face to see what could be read there. In vain he tried to distract himself. He could not read. Each day, he became more intent on the idea of his own sterility, and would hardly say a word to the hostess during her frequent visits to his room. He spent hours gazing at the lights of the city, at the long rows of windows at the top of the big buildings which differed from each other only in their varying degrees of insolent importance, and at the river. He watched the people hurrying past, bent on their own affairs, while he had nothing to look forward to.

In some streets a great solitude lingered, like some poor creature abandoned by time. The portals of the business houses remained hermetically sealed, watched over by the pallid splendor of the moon. This solitude, created by local atmospheric conditions, took on various forms and stalked mournfully through the streets at night.

At times he was harassed by the idea that the thing he had missed most in life was just the fact that his creative powers had never been fertilized by reality. He would observe the sunlight striking on the stones, or bringing out the green in the leaves, and reflect how apparent was its fertilizing effect on them, while he had never borne any fruit.

This led him to believe that he was no longer of any use, except for death, and a slow death at that, and the instinct for self-preservation which formerly had such a hold on him began to change into something approaching complete resignation. What a terrible transmutation was death! At first he was afraid of it. He would leave his room in search of fresh air, light, human faces, whenever he thought of this death which was beginning to haunt him. But later it seemed to him that he had been passing through an arid land whose only inhabitants were grief and discouragement.

The streets appeared barren and destitute of all color, nor did the faces which he studied in passing show any warmth; even the noisy bars were hostile and cold. Winter was already gnawing at the pallid trunks of the plantain trees, and the city dwellers sought refuge early. He would return slowly through the interminable parallel streets, fixing his attention on the blackened ornaments above the eaves and the regular, hermetic buildings. Finally the man's internal disintegration brought to his face an expression of mingled sorrow and acerbity.

His heart no longer functioned properly. He felt weaker each

day and had to force himself to eat. The doctor had nothing good
to report and merely recommended that he rest and keep as quiet
as possible. But each day he was becoming more painfully aware
that he was withdrawing further from his fellow beings, that he
was receding, gradually disappearing from the scene. He now felt
as if he were no longer of this world, as if his spirit had left its
channel and was wandering without anchor, floating on the surface of his memories.

If he could only get a grip on something stable. But what? One
afternoon, wandering back and forth in his room, he thought of
his old love, the teacher, Carlota Morel. He dwelt with some
pleasure on the idea of holding this hope before him, of still
opening up this pleasant horizon onto a new life; thinking that
when he got a little better he would look her up, that he would
hunt everywhere until he found her—even though she were married and had a family. The essential thing was to get to her and
tell her with passionate urgency all his unspoken thoughts which
otherwise would necessarily remain secret and inhibited. They
could still walk together through the city for a while. Perhaps
she would again relate her tales of Hölderlin. Perhaps he would
be able to see her proudly held head and her lively, sparkling eyes
against a background of invading twilight.

This hope gave Jacob Uber new courage on which to feed. His
face lost its harsh expression, was perceptibly softened. He felt
peaceful, reconciled with himself. For three days he breathed the
air of the city with greater happiness. Every face that his eyes fell
upon—a poor man's, a policeman's, this or that woman's—seemed
to come to life again, to suddenly burst into flower. Everything
in the city took on new vitality, and in some corner of that city
was Carlota Morel, if only he could run across her.

For several weeks he seemed to have entered a new life. He felt
much better, and the doctor authorized him to return home. His
wasted features, angular now and almost ascetic, though still
somewhat wistful, were again visited by occasional smiles. He
was happy to leave, and tipped the maid well. On the evening
before his departure he had a long talk with his hostess. She
appeared in his room, resplendent in lace and ribbons, a whale-
bone-supported collar holding her head rigidly erect, every

gesture replete with vital energy, and exhaling a strong odor of brilliantine and cold cream with each movement she made. She and Jacob Uber exchanged some theories as to the probable outcome of the war which was then hovering over the world and which the lady considered as a divine punishment.

Hostess and maid said farewell to him one sunny morning at the street door, while another boarder, draped in a dark-red bathrobe, watched them from the vestibule. After thanking her effusively for all her kindness to him, Jacob Uber left, quite willing to quit that house forever.

IV

He lived for a fortnight in veritable happiness. Everything seemed to him bright and marvelous. Life talked to him in an unknown tongue. He was even glad to handle once more the dust-covered papers which had been accumulating on his desk in the tax collector's office. His imagination abandoned its prey for the time being, and Uber looked on the universe with fresh eyes. Now he appeared attentive and loquacious with his comrades and invited them to dinner at his house on Constitution Avenue. They drank considerably, and after dinner, in his stammering way, Nancel proposed a toast "to the return of the prodigal." After the feast, Uber accompanied them to the Caucaso, a Russian night club, where all of them cheerfully drank a lot more and let some of the women sit on their laps, pointing out Uber as their host and suggesting that they take turns kissing him. This the women did most generously. Jacob Uber smiled, seated at the head of the table with Nancel at his left and an Irishman, McCormack, completely drunk, at his right. The night club was a square room with tables running parallel to the wall and one long bench inside. In the corner opposite the entrance was the small platform for the orchestra. The leader of the band was a Tartar type who laughed and sang as he rattled a tambourine, dressed in a Cossack costume with two rows of decorations across his chest. The tables were so placed as to leave a space in the center for dancing, and the first of this merry group to enter it was McCormack, who gave the spectators a disorderly, nightmarish exhibition. His legs kept folding under him, and the young blonde whom he had taken for a partner had to use super-human strength to keep him on his feet. Finally, McCormack fell flat on his face; Jacob Uber's companions applauded him wildly, while Jacob smiled without moving. The Tartar leader advanced a few steps and helped the blonde lift up the Irishman, who was as helpless as a stuffed doll. "What a fine party!" exclaimed Nancel. The women, wineglasses in their hands, threw them-selves backward in convulsions of laughter.

Somehow or other, when he had left the party, Jacob Uber felt sadder than ever. He brooded over the fact that he had not joined in more heartily, that he had remained shut up within himself, after all; and he felt again that his sky, his earth, his ties with all the outside world were merely a dark projection of his spirit and had nothing to do with his own concrete and elemental being. Therefore, he reasoned, it was useless to hope to sublimate himself in outside interests. It was useless to seek modes of escape from this sense of self-suffocation which was bound to destroy him. His recent hopes had been mere illusions, as transitory and insubstan-tial as his earlier one had always been—a mere reaction from his physical improvement.

Then he fell into a state of continual affliction. Like a starved body which consumes itself from within, he began to lose all desires. He felt abandoned by all, left alone with his own imag-inings. At times he could hardly hold back his sobs, and since this happened at the most unexpected times, he was forced to with-draw from all contact with other people. He could never confide all this to anybody, anybody at all. What good would it do, besides, to give way to such self-pity?

One December afternoon the crisis arrived. He had passed two nights without sleep, full of anxiety, absorbed in the deleterious effect of his uselessness. He had lost the very last of his desires—his appetite had left him; at dinnertime he merely tasted a little red wine and some slices of black bread with ham. The waiters in the restaurant made no attempt to question him, and he nibbled away in silence. That afternoon he did not return to his office, but took a walk along the shore road, walking for almost three hours, until he felt an immense fatigue invade both body and mind. Finally, he reached the estuary. Walking on along its edge he could see up above him, the green slopes of a ravine, rich in luxurious vegetation—here dark shadows, and there green lozenges of fresher, brighter tints. Within, he bore an awful sense of weeping. And a fear, a fear! But he could not turn back now; never more could he return to the world he had known. He could no longer go back to that realm where he was an outsider and where he felt as if he were smothering in the dark.

As he passed beneath one of the highest ravines, he saw two girls up there, dressed in white frocks, walking arm in arm, their beautiful bare heads exposed to the gentle breezes. He sat down and listened to the distant croaking of the frogs beyond the fields of sugar cane which had been planted between the green ravines along the estuary. Suddenly, as if he heard a voice calling or perhaps because he was overcome by a horrible wave of fear, he got up and began to run, his eyes fixed on the distant horizon, as if entranced. Reaching the edge of the water, he flung himself on into the river, producing a noise like applause in the water, which rose up in agitation around him. Then he swam out on that vast, becalmed sea over which such silence had reigned up to now. . . . He swam, and as he swam he wept with frightful anguish, abandoned to his infinite, forlorn despair. How many times, a mere child, he had swum in that river! Death was one place where at last he could enter and find rest, find something real, inexorably real. Suddenly he stopped swimming and began to shout. His cry echoed far. The water opened for a second, then once more presented to the supreme calm of falling dusk its normally motionless and colorless surface.

THE
HEART'S REASON

With brisk step, Celedonio Montuvio, insurance agent, left behind him, drowsing among the laurels of Olivos, the little white house that would be completely his when he had paid up the coming installment on the mortgage, and leaped aboard the bus coming from Tigre that carried him on his daily trip to the city. He was almost completely happy. A little more and he would be able to retire, and the house he lived in would be his in the full sense of the word. These were the dreams he had cherished for a long, long time, and the fact that they were now on the point of becoming tangible realities filled his soul with an unaccustomed warmth, a kind of diffuse, soothing well-being. He had almost no other worry. The assistant manager of the company, with whom he had always had those sharp, rankling differences of opinion, was now fading out of the picture, the victim of a serious ailment, and as a result the staff had taken on a kind of pleasant relaxation, a new ease. As for the marital difficulties of his sister, Adelina, whose husband—that is to say, his brother-in-law—had given them so many bad moments as a result of his stubborn and aggressive alcoholism, the couple, as by a miracle, had gradually entered upon an era of peace, and on one of their last visits to the house in Olivos they had fairly radiated happiness. His cup held only motives of satisfaction.

Just one thing—he reflected to himself in the bus—though very vague, very insignificant, stirred in the depths of his being, scratching in the corners. It would hardly be worth a thought if it were not for the way the idea persisted like a musical chord that echoes in the ear, keeping alive in his mind the imp of doubt. At bottom, wasn't the idea puerile? Any other man, endowed with more confidence in things than he, would have dismissed it instantly, but in him motives for pessimism almost always took root, and when it was a matter of feeling himself a victim, he was suggestible to the most trifling incentives to gloom. He knew himself too well not to recognize or forget this trait, behind which was hidden an unmistakable element of weakness.

The bus that morning carried its usual passengers—clerks, businessmen, the less successful members of the professions, and those never-failing women who were at the bus stop every day, their faces so determinedly and identically made up, powdered, and rouged that they seemed the mechanized symbol of repetition. He and they had been seeing one another almost every day for years; but they never exchanged a sign or a greeting with him, only that glance of aloof but conscious recognition.

He found it absurd to indulge in the little recurring idea. In spite of the somewhat eccentric tastes he had always ascribed to her, his wife, Alicia, had unvaryingly been the most pliant, the most devoted of beings, and he had nothing but gratitude for the self-effacing patience with which she had suffered at his side the hard moments of their life. From childhood she seemed to have adopted that typical reticence of hers, that ease at silence, at evasion, at those sudden escapes to zones of withdrawal which verged on the disdainful; but these attitudes were undoubtedly related to her knowing herself attractive, somewhat different from other women, set apart from early adolescence by that vivid coloring which attracted so much attention. This gave her a certain air, gesture, or attitude that at times might pass for an affectation of superiority. Perhaps this is why Adelina, her sister-in-law, did not care for her as much as she should, being quick to take offense at Alicia's silences.

But the idea that fixed itself in his mind had nothing to do with that. It was rather the product, he thought, of his tendency to brood, to mistrust, and to a certain excess of observation which, even without noticing it, he repeatedly incurred. Here was the problem: for a long time on Sundays certain friends had been in the habit of coming to the house in Olivos to listen to music and have a cup of tea, with pleasant conversation on inoffensive subjects. It was a custom observed like a ritual, and it afforded both him and Alicia agreeable recreation. The white-walled rooms of that little house, the hospitably drawn curtains on those social afternoons, filled him with that special placidity which being a property owner gives. Among those regularly invited were certain of his office colleagues, good-humored, married people, and an occasional spinster friend of Alicia's; only on special occasions were new people asked, for he was timid by nature and preferred not to perturb the easy, entertaining atmosphere of these Sunday afternoons by the introduction of a foreign element. On some exceptional occasion one of the company doctors was invited, some businessman, perhaps some undefined artist—one who never talks about art and thus does not disturb people with his pedantic pronouncements. He could not recall whether it was in January or July of the preceding year, May or June, that he first asked Valentín Bordiguera to the house. It might have been in January; it might have been in July; he had not made a mental note of it because the character of the new guest was conducive to anything but taking him seriously. He was a client of the company, and was believed to be a bachelor of excellent position who did very well for himself and enjoyed amusing people. He had been introduced, along with several of the agents, by old Villaza, the first to know him, and some of them liked to join him at his nocturnal diversions, in which Bordiguera lavished wit and drinks, and was quick to pick up the check. Celedonio Montuvio could not recall why he had first invited Bordiguera to his house;

perhaps it was vanity, that powerful tempter, which moved him, so that a man of Bordiguera's tastes would not lump him with the other company employees as being poor, improvident, and should know that he was the owner of this white house where, on Sundays, there was music and Alicia passed her well-considered judgment on this or that book she was reading. She had always had a certain leaning toward literature, though she did not often discuss it; to be sure, she had not found him particularly receptive; they did not care for the same books; and when, in their early days, on two or three occasions she had given free rein to her enthusiasms, she had grown progressively disheartened in the face of the assurance and emphatic positiveness of his opposing judgments. He would laugh at these differences of opinion, at the exclusivism of her tastes, and finally they came to avoid the topic of their reading, which on his part were popular treatises on economics, and on hers, books of poetry or drama. Besides, Alicia felt no need to communicate her thoughts; she always seemed sufficient unto herself, and only at times some phrase dropped in her presence brought a sudden fleeting gleam to her eyes.

It gave him pleasure to see her receive their guests, with her charming figure, tall and stately, her well-bred gestures, her unvarying, attentive courtesy, that courtesy in which a certain reserve could be felt, but which for that very reason was so quick, so intentionally alert.

It was her duty to portion out the milk and tea in the delicate china cups, select the records, talk with the guests on such down-to-earth questions as the price of sugar or the rate of growth of the laurel and the acacias. Montuvio never could understand her reason for suddenly locking herself in her room on Sunday nights, claiming that she was tired. A kind of depression or neurosis would come over her, and he, alone downstairs, would eat his supper of fish or pudding, still listening, after a whole afternoon of music, to the Ninth Symphony or the delightful harmonies of *Così fan tutte*.

For many months, friend Bordiguera was one of the visitors at the house in Olivos. It was necessary to get this matter of "friend" straight; he was never really that to Montuvio; as far as the latter was concerned, Bordiguera was one of those persons clearly defined on the surface, but evasive in their intimacy, with whom positive, solid bonds of affection are rarely established. Montuvio looked upon Bordiguera rather as a pleasant diversion, and had brought him into his house on this account, as well as because of that faint aura of attraction the prodigal and the rich possess for the middle class. Montuvio, therefore, observed with satisfaction the ease and distinction he displayed at the house in Olivos on Sundays, the pleasure he gave to his agent friends and their wives, the delicacy and refinement of his conversation, the ductility of his opinions.

From his armchair in the parlor, leaning comfortably back in his chair beside Osorio or Carlos Lagos, Montuvio found enjoyment in seeing, beyond the corner of the screen, which was opened wide on Sundays, his wife chatting with Bordiguera. In the beginning, it afforded him only satisfaction, the sight of his wife discussing, as it seemed to him, refined matters with a refined person, the same satisfaction he derived those Sundays from seeing the pleasure with which the guests consumed cream cake or the admiration aroused in the visitors by the transparency of the starched linen curtains or the good taste and beauty of the rooms on the first floor, with their delicate opalescent lamps and mahogany Victorian furniture. It was not until one day, when he noticed that his wife and Bordiguera quickly tended to initiate a conversation between themselves, that he asked himself, without attaching much importance to the idea, almost absent-mindedly— as almost absent-mindedly he was enchanted by the whole scene: "What would they be talking about?" He looked at them as he asked himself the question, and saw them there, at the end of the dining room, standing together beside the arch of the window, absorbed in one of their characteristic smiling conversations. This time the question quickly faded out; but it came back to him. For, the next Sunday, and still the next, they showed the same haste to withdraw, to become absorbed, they alone, in those topics which were peculiar to them or captivated them. One night, after they had dined alone and Alicia had not gone upstairs to lock herself in as usual, Montuvio asked her, smiling and affable, curious, really interested, what she talked about with Bordiguera. Alicia answered him without hesitating: "We always talk about literary works, about books." And her reply left him bewildered because he could not imagine how it was possible to talk so much about so many indifferent printed pages.

One of those Sundays, Montuvio experienced a strange feeling. He had always shared with Alicia a careful concern for their guests; they waited together for them to finish one thing and offer them another; they divided between them the work of passing trays, serving the refreshments, attending promptly to their wishes. But that day, when two hours had elapsed since tea, and the moment had come for the sherry aperitif, Montuvio, following his custom, went for the bottles, and as he prepared to fill the glasses he noticed that Alicia, instead of being at his side helping him, was talking in the garden with Bordiguera. As a result, he suddenly felt himself in a strange, awkward situation, with a tray in his hand and a task too great to perform; for several seconds he stood without moving, looking at himself from within himself, as at some downtrodden creature burdened beyond his powers.

At that moment Alicia entered, radiant. "Shall I help you?"

And without a word, he handed her the two glasses he held in his hand.

He did not think about the matter again, but there began to form within him something like the remote, bittersweet echo of a haunting, nostalgic phrase. He looked at his hands and noted that they were the hands of a solitary, and that Alicia had no connection with those hands. But he quickly brushed aside these vapors or broodings and turned resolutely toward his work and his affairs, which were proceeding in a highly satisfactory manner.

Only some days back, three days before, suddenly, the idea had filtered into his mind. It was an idea he fought against, but there it was. As he came into the house, he had seen Alicia hang up the receiver—stealthily, it seemed to him—and get up from the telephone in a strange manner, maintaining a silence toward him that struck him as hostile, aggressive. "God," he asked himself, "God, is that what she's up to?" And this *that*, which he could not bring himself to put into words, was an unfaithful, intimate relationship with Bordiguera. He had noticed a number of strange things—certain starts, certain gestures, more elusive, more mysterious than ever, not to mention the fact that she went out nearly every afternoon and he did not know where she went. But aside from this, the thought was so absurd, so obviously the figment of his suspicions, for his wife was dignity personified, with her self-control and poise; and besides, apart from these trifles, what reason or concrete cause did he have to harbor a single doubt?

And that very morning, as he was leaving the house, when he just happened to ask her in the dining room what she was doing that afternoon, he was amazed at the impatience in her tone, the curtness, the rudeness, almost:

"What do you think I'm doing? Things I have to do. Errands. Chores."

"But what chores?"

"What would they be? The usual things."

He finished dressing and left to catch his bus. He was almost completely happy. The bus sped along over the macadam, past playing fields and suburban houses. If only he could have cast out entirely that shadow of a thought. He had only reasons to cast it out; but why didn't it go? Isn't the idea a logical principle? Then why did it keep rasping at his soul? There in the depths, a depth so deep it did not even seem his.

He asked himself this in the bus, full of concern for himself; and, to clear his head of cobwebs, he fixed his eyes on the route, marking its every feature. He knew the way by heart and could anticipate no surprise, except, at most, the appearance on some terrace of a new face or the evidence of a new coat of paint on one of the familiar gables.

Suddenly he gave a start: it was not the lightning flash of intelligence, but the upsurge of intuition. By what right was he placing himself above the evidence? It was apparent that his wife was up to something. It showed, not only in the reticence of her behavior, but in a manifest, marked need to be alone; for some time she had not asked him, as she used to do, to hurry home as soon as he could; it seemed almost as though she did not care whether he came back or not, and that lack of warmth, which had always been a part of her, was now more evident and emphasized. The week before, a most unusual thing had happened, and that was that she got back to the house in Olivos after he did, at nearly ten o'clock. And it had annoyed her beyond

words, almost throwing her into a rage, when he called attention
to the time, even though he did it very gently and tactfully. He
had seen her buying stationery, too, even though she was nearly
always remiss about letter writing to the point of being practically a mute from the epistolary point of view.

Then, what was going on? The question aborted in his mind,
unable to emerge or develop. There it stuck, encysted. And to
the question clung stubbornly, in form not mental but plastic,
visible, sensory, the image of Valentín Bordiguera.

He experienced a kind of disgusted shrinking, an instinctive
feeling of revulsion, but no corresponding recoil of repudiating a
base suspicion.

He reached the corner of the avenue which was his stop, without having been able to rid himself of this viscous, degrading
feeling. A vague residue of anger, a gray humiliation, contributed
to his disturbance. He had the feeling that he was stumbling
across a bewildering terrain where it would be impossible for him
to find an opening leading to the light.

A few steps brought him to the large marble building of the
company, and slipping into the elevator, he rode up to the floor
where he had to pick up some papers to check on a policy that
was coming due. He set about the job half-heartedly and irritably, jerking and tearing out sheets from the typewriter, which
stubbornly refused to strike the right letter or failed to hit
the *p*.

At noon he went out for lunch in the company of his annoyance and his disturbance. As a rule he lunched at a restaurant
there on the square, in a kind of artificially lighted basement
decorated with fish tanks and bad frescoes. He had no desire to
enter into a conversation with the waiter, and he quickly ordered
a cold plate and the fruits in season. He saw Rodas, a pompous
agent of the company, at a table, and the sight filled him with
such exasperation that he avoided speaking to him. He stood the
menu up in front of him against the water pitcher and pretended
to be studying the long list of dishes. But his imagination was in
the house in Olivos. Alicia would be having lunch at this same
time, comfortable in her solitude, no doubt at ease about the hour
when she would be going out, her plans complete and her spirit

satisfied. She had the whole afternoon to herself, the whole long afternoon, and she did not have to be back until eight or nine, her secret hermetically sealed within her, cloaked in the memory of her private, invulnerable acts.

By three or four in the afternoon she will be in Bordiguera's flat, Montuvio thought. The precision of the idea provided him the opportunity to refute it with equal precision. It was no longer a matter of nebulosities, hypotheses, confused conjecturing. It was a question of an act. And that act—was impossible.

He calmly peeled his fruit. No, that act was impossible. A kind of animation, born of a clear-cut sense of relief, came over him, and, calling the waiter, he made a jocose remark having to do with a couple who always came to the resturant and about whom he had spoken with him before.

"No, it's impossible," he said to himself on the way out. In his mouth was the taste of coffee, and along with the taste of coffee, the taste of such a palpable, satisfying comfort. It was a sunny afternoon, warm, the square once more full after the lull of midday, and leaden-hued pigeons promenading their bulging crops along the cornices of the buildings. Montuvio crossed two or three streets with the laudable intention of winding up once and for all that long-drawn-out business with the manager of Varas Rey, who was reluctant to sign up for even a third-class policy. But the manager was not in. He would not be back until five. Montuvio, promising to return, descended again in the black cage of the elevator. Only when he reached the ground floor was he seized, openly, by that need, that inclination or drift, really unjustifiable, which was not yet a plan.

An idea is one thing, the newborn tendency seemed to insinuate, and facts are another. An idea cannot be completely done away with until it is confronted with reality itself.

He started walking quickly to his destination, to spare himself the shame of thinking it over. He had plenty of time. Bordiguera's flat was near the Plaza de la República; it was in the second of three houses, all alike, in a street that ran east and west and was filled with shops and motion-picture theaters. Montuvio crossed the streets with the nervousness of a student at examination time or an actor making his debut, and as he stole a glance at himself in the show window of a photographer's studio, he noticed that he was pale, with a greenish pallor, and that the shadows on his face did not come from needing a shave but from his bad color.

In his heart he knew he would not be satisfied until he had seen for himself. On more than one occasion he had been the plaything of his ideas. What he liked was the practical, the visible, that which left no room for doubt. This sudden need for spying —this base, shameful action—would have been unbearably humiliating to him if he had not considered it, as he did now, in the light of the exigencies of his very makeup. So he accepted it as a natural demand of the deepest fibers of his being; the least praiseworthy, perhaps, but the most human.

It did not take him more than ten minutes to reach the block where the apartment building stood; on one of those floors Bordiguera had his bachelor establishment. All the way, Montuvio felt that vague fear inherent in every test we undertake, still safe as we embark upon it, but from which we may emerge utterly routed. Naturally, there contributed to this, in a heavy, dragging, almost visceral manner, the needless and absurd nature of the proof to which he was lending himself; and yet no power in the world could now have persuaded him not to carry it out: on the contrary, any obstacle that might have suddenly arisen to prevent him from keeping watch over Bordiguera's doorway would have aroused his anger, a confused but virulent, savage, almost animal protest.

Now he had to see. Once admitting conjecture, could he reject the supreme proof, that which the eyes give, the evidence? He felt a strange mixture of disgust and sadness as he passed on the opposite side of the street, the door of the apartment house. The wide, dark foyer stretched deserted toward the elevators. Montuvio walked by. He stopped just before he reached the corner, in the entrance of one of the narrow doorways, from which he could comfortably watch both the house that had become his preoccupation and a long stretch of the street. Across from where he stood were the two show windows of a shop with Chinese goods; in the windows were displayed, on two male manikins, two Asiatic garments of pale blue, of silk so thin that the creases seemed additional, designed pleats; on the floor of the windows, beside these dynastic vestments, was an assemblage of small jade dragons, curtains of painted straw, an old scepter, and two tiny pairs of black sandals.

Montuvio, after taking his position in the doorway he had chosen, prepared to wait. He carefully observed the shops alongside the Chinese store, but none of them could compare with it in age and attractiveness. His eyes rested for a few minutes on its exotic variety. But at once, quickly and by degrees, as though borne on the mingled stream of a single current of thought, of a single liquid flow, the idea came to him of what would happen if Alicia, at a given moment, came out of that house. The conjecture began turning into anger. He acquired a feeling of the assurance and the superiority it would give him to have the proof in his hands if the fault did exist; and this feeling hardened and exasperated him. It was as though he said to himself: "Now I've got you; you are in the trap; you can't flee from deceit into evasions, but straight into me, before my eyes." He felt reassured, and thought that he could wait for hours without moving from the spot.

He remained thus for some time. People passed by, brisk, objective, without worries of the kind he had, all ostensibly free from intimate problems; he alone had that matter to settle. His gaze clung to the show windows of the Chinese shop, but within him the wheels turned without stopping in the effort to put pressure on his memory to give him some point of support for the possible presence of his wife at Bordiguera's house. He recalled gestures and smiles. He recalled himself; he saw himself alone and wronged by the amatory complicity of Alicia and Bordiguera; and a sour, nauseating hatred brewed in his liver against that witty talker, with his honeyed glance, his refined manners, whom he had once brought into his house. After the first quarter hour of his vigil, a restless, gnawing impatience began to grow in him, a kind of feeling as though he himself had invited misfortune, and that now he could escape neither the fact nor the consequences of having given it origin.

When nobody came out of the house by half past five, he began to think, cautiously and with precarious relief, that undoubtedly there was no one in Bordiguera's flat, not even Bordiguera himself, and that perhaps the sensible and manly thing to do was to consider the proof complete, and rid himself, with a normal disdain, of suspicions, base ideas, and shameful imaginings. But this was instantly followed by the thought that, now that he was here, if he waited a little longer he would be even surer of how childish, unwarranted, and insulting his imagining had been.

Thus he began to wait more calmly, firm in the conviction that nobody would come out of the house. The longer he waited, the greater his satisfaction. He could stay there until eight or nine; perhaps until he saw Bordiguera come in at dinnertime. Yes, perhaps even this was possible. Filled with a sense of calm and assurance, he left the spot where he had stationed himself and leisurely crossed over to the Chinese shop, where he stopped to admire the objects exhibited there. He found them impressive, extraordinary as a whole and in their details, the expression of a subtle, alien civilization in which he would have been unable to live even for an hour. Then he crossed back to his observation post. Killing time with a certain impatience, he tried to find something on which to fix his attention on that side of the street; but there was nothing but the meaningless window of a dry-cleaning establishment and a monotonous list of professional signs tacked in the corner of an old doorway. He went over to read one of those signs.

At that moment he had his back turned to the house he was watching, when his instinct suddenly warned him, making him turn, startled and confused: Bordiguera was coming out of the doorway of his house, and with him was a woman, a slender woman wearing a light dress and light shoes. He saw them from the distance and barely had time to hide; poking his head out, his heart thudding heavily, he looked again at the woman. Meanwhile Bordiguera hailed a cab and they got into it. They were hidden from view for a fraction of a second by the car, which started off quickly toward the intersection, passing before Montuvio's very eyes. . . .

God above! He saw it so clearly. His heart stopped beating. He stepped back, as though dodging a blow from the flat of an ax. His face felt white, his veins white, as though they had no blood.

The automobile passed and disappeared in the distance. Montuvio, with the weakness that follows a shock, took one liberating
step into the street.

The person who had just come out with Bordiguera was not
Alicia. Thank God! The man was not having an affair with his
wife. He had had the proof at first glance, in a lightning flash,
when he saw her standing on the sidewalk, and then as the features of the woman who had entered the cab with Bordiguera
whirled past him. It was a thin face, very delicately modeled,
very pale, whose features he could not describe exactly, and she
was wearing clothes that were loose and too light, which somehow gave the impression that she was a foreigner.

Montuvio felt a kind of glory, as though all his blood vessels
had dilated in a burst of instant well-being. A kind of shame of
himself came over him at the same time, bringing with it happiness and a strange, impulsive feeling of sympathy, almost of gratitude, toward Bordiguera. He would have thrown his arms around
him, glorified him, at that moment. And his mind flew to the
house in Olivos, bringing him anew the vision of a happy, noble
home ruled over, as never before, by the decorous figure of his
wife, innocent of all suspicion and above suspicion itself. It
seemed to him that he would have to tell her about it that very
night, mingling his account with a tacit plea for forgiveness.

As it was summer, the afternoon sun was still high. A bright
golden haze outlined the outer edges of the buildings, luminously
dividing matter from space. The city glowed; day's transit was
reaching its peak. Montuvio drank in the light. He would have
called his house at that very moment, but at this time his wife
would be somewhere not far from him, on streets like these. He
thought he had plenty of time to call on the manager of Varas
Rey. Happy, self-assured, buoyed up, he started down one of the
streets; with light step he crossed the square. Even the elevator
operator seemed a witness and a friend.

The manager of Varas Rey, with his Herculean shoulders and
his unexpectedly small, ironical mouth, received him more coolly
than on other occasions. He was alone, slouched in his chair, in
his office, similar to the five hundred other offices of the marble,
presumptuous, glowing building. "It's like this," the manager

began. "It's like this . . ." And for the seventh or eighth time he monotonously expounded his reasons for not wanting to take out insurance, for preferring not to take out insurance.

"It's not right for me to saddle myself with more expense now," the manager argued, excusing himself with a shrug of his expressive, powerful shoulders.

"But of course," Montuvio burst out. "You are absolutely right. Forgive me. I am not going to insist." And he laughed, mouth and spirit. "Absolutely right."

He finally took his leave, reiterating excuses. He would have given a medal to the stubborn manager; he would have asked forgiveness on bended knee for his intrusion, for his importunacy, for his insistence. He went out, tripping over his own excuses.

What did all this matter to him? Happiness rained on him. He admired his wife. He felt that a new life was beginning. In a few more months the house in Olivos would be his. That evening he would have dinner with Alicia, he would open the windows to the cool of summer, the house would be an abode where the noble calm of peace reigned. What more could he ask? Bordiguera could continue coming to the end of time; as sure as his name was Montuvio, a suspicion would never again cross his mind. God, if we are the rulers of our reason, why are we not the rulers of our reasoning? Why do we allow our inner garden to be profaned by wild birds that do not belong there?

He looked at his watch; it was half past six, and he did not intend to go back to the office. What for? The vast afternoon was ripening. A bluish gold vied with the breezes. The best thing was to feel free, to watch the people, to stop before the show windows, to loiter among the hurrying throngs. He walked for about an hour, visiting the shops full of luxurious objects; he read the stock-exchange quotations, looked at the women going by, stopped before stores selling the things that appealed least to him; but then a vague boredom began to assail him, a certain lassitude. What could he do? He thought of Gambrinus's beer garden, which he liked so well, and set out for it.

It was a big, dark beer garden, shadowy, wainscoted in somber wood, with imposing Bavarian steins and railings and bluish glass separating the small booths. The only light of day that entered the place came through the high skylight. And from a hook hung newspapers printed in barbaric, undecipherable, Gothic characters.

Montuvio seated himself at one of the tables in the main room and ordered his usual bock. A sensation of rest and infinite coolness came over him. On the table stood a dish of pretzels and a little white jar of mustard.

He began to recall his day, slowly, from the start: the conversation with Alicia, the bus trip to the city, the building up of his doubts, the bitter lunch, the vicissitudes of his spying, the anxiety, and, finally, the surprising revelation. The scene had acquired the swift illumination of a flash of light. In seconds it was over and had disappeared. Nevertheless, he had had more than enough time to take in the woman's appearance, her clothing, her features, so different from Alicia's. He had had time to see Bordiguera's amatory solicitude toward her. As the car passed him, they both were laughing: she leaning back a little against the upholstery, Bordiguera attentive, gay. The woman was wearing a very light dress, white, almost cream-colored, and a simple hat, turned up a little—a hat that covered only one side of her head. How Montuvio had stared at her as the car rushed swiftly by! He would not have been able to recall the woman's features; he knew only they were not Alicia's, with a kind of illumined and general knowledge, revealed, above specific knowing. His eyes had clung anxiously to this lightning flash as it passed; it was not she; that was enough. He had seen enough.

Montuvio took a swallow of his beer, and it suddenly occurred to him that he might take something home with him that evening —chicken in aspic or a baked ham, both favorites of Alicia's. For a long time he had been coming in empty-handed; he had not noticed it before, but now he did. We all have a responsibility for those shifts of wind that come up and gradually change, becloud our relationships. The delicate shades of courtesy are always important; a feeling we trample on or offend in another may suddenly turn into a bitter poison, a wound, a corrosive acid. Alicia's sullenness might well be owing to a series of unconscious provocations on his part, subtle provocations, muted, subliminal, those which begin and develop insidiously, secretly, like a mortal disease. His eyes wandered over the room, which was cool and dim. He looked at the black railings and the plants. A mental breeze brought him once more, as a result of his lassitude, the image of the woman he saw come out with Bordiguera, the image of the automobile, and of the liberation the scene had brought him. Step by step, the i   began to grow in him that there was just one thing that was odd. He turned the question over in his mind. How could he explain the fact that he was absolutely unable to recall the woman's features clearly? Perhaps it was owing only to the speed at which the car was traveling, his great confusion at the moment, the need to obtain the negation of one set of features before being able to take in clearly the lineaments of another. The fact was that all he saw was a specter that was not Alicia. Aside from this, aren't all specters alike? Especially if the clothes they wear define them as being of one sex, which in turn separates them from other specters. That was not Alicia's face, nor her dress; no. To be sure, all women make themselves up alike; Alicia was blond, like the woman in the car. But why hadn't he looked more closely at her features, why didn't he know definitely what they were like? Montuvio put his glass down on the table. Had he seen right?

Suddenly, a kind of disquiet, a malaise, took possession of him —an inexplicable mental distress that had arisen against his will. He was a hopeless fool! Tormenting himself with doubts! How could he ask himself such a question? He had seen with his own eyes, with his own eyes. Not another's; *his*. And that woman *was not* Alicia. Different features, a different person altogether. And then that dress. Though Alicia did have a white dress. A white silk dress; only it was put away until now, until summer. Montuvio scoffed at himself. He had always been an easy prey to conflicting impressions.

But behind the scoffing—which was in his favor—remained the doubt, which   s against him. Against all his will, his mind kept turning thi   s over. He raised his eyes and saw the people, the few who were talking in the beer garden, and a fat, plain, blond woman who was arguing with two Germans. She did not look like the woman in the car, either. But just what was the woman in the car like? He tried to think, and his memory made a feeble, vague endeavor. He could not get beyond a woman's face, a generic face, no matter how hard he tried. But it was not Alicia, that was clear. Even supposing there could be confusion about the dress, the features were clearly different, the whole appearance. What he had had was not an impression, it was proof. Naturally the light, as it fell, could modify the peculiarities of a face, if the coloring, the shade of the skin, were similar. But what was the sense of such reasoning, since the woman was another, definitely another. Proof is not an impression. The evanescence, the rapidity of an impression can change it, deform it; but they cannot change or deform proof.

He called the waiter and ordered another beer. His head drooped; he was tired and much less happy than he had been moments before. He was accustomed to this kind of rage or disappointment at himself, which often attacked him—this cruel confusion that had darkened many moments of his life. Almost with fury against himself, he called up in his mind an image: the moment when he had been standing opposite Bordiguera's house, and the categorical assurance with which he had distinguished from his wife the woman who came out. He clung to the vision, struggling to give his mind the grip of a claw. But his mind was not a claw, and little by little there began to issue from it threads of arguments, evil suppositions, contradictory factors that he could neither contain nor suppress. He was a fool. Why this doubt? Was it possible that he had not seen clearly?

Allowing himself to be swept along by a succession of recollections which superimposed themselves on the events of the afternoon, he realized that there had been a reason for his going there to spy. It was evident—the word his mind selected frightened him—that there was something going on within Alicia. And the automobile which Bordiguera and his friend had passed in was going at a speed that made only the most dizzying impact on the eye. Dizzying? Naturally, producing dizziness. Was it possible that he had been misled by this dizziness? For a few moments he was morally crushed by the idea, and then another motive came to his mind: the remote, intimate suggestion that his desire not to recognize Alicia had led him to twist even his visual impression. Impression? But wasn't it proof that he had, which had nothing to do with an impression? Now it turned out that they were the same thing. He sat there actually gripped by fear, and it took him several minutes to recover.

With disgust, almost with revulsion, he thought that the color of the woman's hair could have seemed, from a distance, the same as Alicia's; and if he recalled the white dress he had seen her wear the summer before, he could not honestly refrain from doubt. Who would not be confused by a rapid vision? A certain face, a certain figure, could it not suddenly seem another under the influence of certain psychic conditions in the observer, and changes caused in the image by the angle of vision? Maybe the woman who had not looked like Alicia to him was Alicia herself. Why not? Could he trust, absolutely, a vision that was relative? Could he even hold fast to an image that he could not reconstruct in memory, that he could not describe? And, on the other hand, the other impression was alive, the other intuition, the other idea: the shadow of that inner conviction which had led him to think, gradually and insistently, that there was evidently something between his wife and Bordiguera. But why was he mixing the proofs like this? Yes, he was mixing them; he couldn't help mixing them, he could not resist this inner prompting; and now the two proofs, the inductive and the visual, were struggling for supremacy, and he felt with a vague terror that little by little the first was getting the upper hand.

In the last analysis, in point of certainty, in a clear, trustworthy manner, he knew nothing about the woman he had seen come out with Bordiguera. It might have been any woman. Even Alicia. Even any other. Any other, like Alicia. "Let's see," he asked himself, and he tormented and baited himself like a witness under examination, "let's see: how was she different, how was she another?"

The question left him overwhelmed, unable to find an answer. And it began to seem to him clear, possible, capable of proof that he had been deceived by the fleetingness of what he had seen, and that the woman, in effect, might very well have been Alicia.

A great agitation seized Montuvio, and a troop of contradictory ideas filled his mind. Had he once more suffered a deception? Had he? Was this conceivable? He could not be sure. He wasn't sure of anything. He would have given anything to turn time back to the moment when he saw the woman come out with

Bordiguera, anything to detain that moment now beyond proof, to whose veracity he could not swear. The most fanstastic and counterpoised ideas throbbed in his head; he was like an over-wound watch; there seemed no floor under his feet, or body about his fainting spirit; his pulse began to thud violently, and a wave of his former hatred toward Bordiguera and of rancor and bitterness toward his wife jarred his soul.

He got up with uncontrolled violence, almost upsetting the mustard jar, the dish of pretzels, and the stein on the table; turning toward the counter, he stumblingly made his way to the telephone. He swiftly dialed the number of his house in Olivos, and for a moment, not breathing, he waited for the sound of the ringing to be interrupted by the lifting of the receiver. But the isochronous insistence of the ringing went on without the slightest change, threatening to become eternalized in its unanswered repetition.

Montuvio went back to his table. It seemed to him that he was seeing the scene of the afternoon, the woman coming out of Bordiguera's house; but the one who emerged in his mind now was his wife; it was his wife, but not on that account was the impression that remained of the other woman changed. Had there been another? The images matched. He could not swear that they were different. Nor that they weren't. Were they one or two? One thing was as possible as the other, and he had no way of proving it; he saw himself at the center of a fixed uncertainty.

He was blasted by a chill despair, a quivering frenzy brought on by his impotence to decide between the allegations of his reason and the embers of his memory. Not one detail of what he had seen stood out bright, separate, clear, determinate. He knew just as much as before he had taken his stand across from Bordiguera's house. He was as ignorant as when he had gone there. And much more bewildered, much more impotently lost.

He tossed a handful of change on the table and blundered out to the street. And there he stood, he, Celedonio Montuvio, insurance agent, his back to the door of Gambrinus's café, not knowing what to do or which way to go, his lower lip hanging idiotically, terrified, paralyzed, as though struck by lightning.

THE
SHOES

RETURN THIS SLIP IN BOOK

IF CANNOT SUPPLY - REASON:

☐ Out of print. Order cancelled.

☐ Not yet published, will send when issued, expected publishing date _____

☐ Out of stock. Order cancelled.

☐ Other reason. Order cancelled.

HOLDING ORDER FOR FURTHER INSTRUCTIONS. DO YOU STILL WANT?

☐ Item is part of this numbered series.

☐ Price is substantially greater than your estimate. Price. _____

☐

☐

☐

Traces of sultry summer weather still hung oppressively over the streets on the day that Federico Morales suddenly caught sight of that imposing pair of shoes in the smart window of the importer Capistrano.

It was a beautiful pair of walking shoes, brown, bordering on the red, well fashioned and delicately stitched, with tapering toes: unquestionably the work of a master craftsman. They were displayed on shining shoe trees, over which hung a ticket flaunting the word: IMPORTED.

As if done on purpose to create the maximum effect and avoid anything that might outshine them, they were displayed all alone in the window, with only a few ties hanging unobtrusively in the background, doing duty as a curtain or backdrop.

Federico Morales had nothing to do on that Saturday and had been strolling about aimlessly, devoting his two-day holiday to getting figures, calculations, and employers out of his system. He stood dazzled in front of the pair of shoes which seemed to him to symbolize all that is unattainable and far beyond our means.

First from one angle and then from another, like someone in a famous museum examining and appraising a masterpiece, turning his eyes slowly from right to left, with the thoroughness of an expert, he took in and weighed the shoes with his eyes, and, lost in wonder, felt suddenly the deep thrill which heralds the birth of desire, the onset of covetousness, the almost diabolical signs of the craving for possession.

The use of the word diabolical is not exactly accurate, for in that look of desire there was more of timidity, sadness, and modesty than of any potential aspiration toward power, or of the feeling of hatred for all that stands in our way, which is how the instinct of possession usually makes itself manifest in human beings.

In this case there was the fact that Federico Morales was a man of modest means, poor rather than rich, who, like his wife, was used to not allowing himself great ambitions or expenses beyond a moderate, not to say humble, standard of living. He earned no more than the average clerk who is placed above the underlings but below the chiefs. And what he had just seen before his eyes was, without a doubt, an article of luxury, meant, like so many other things, only for those who could afford them.

Far from leaving the window of the importer Capistrano, as he should have done under the circumstances, he persisted in his pleasant occupation of contemplating the magnificent pair of shoes, and even allowed himself the shadow of a dream of somehow becoming their owner.

As it was a Saturday afternoon, the shop was closed, and he could not ask about the price, but everything pointed to its being very high, almost certainly beyond his reach, for, apart from its being a very expensive shop, one of the most fashionable in the city, the fact that there was no price tag clearly indicated that the goods were matchless and that they would cost, as the saying goes, a fortune.

Federico Morales still lingered at his observation post, refusing to withdraw his admiring glances. Ah! the perfect design, the symmetry of the instep and the finish of the soles, the distinction of the whole! But at last he wrenched himself away from the window and set off, a little melancholy, as we feel when we have to take leave, because we must, of a scene which for some reason or other has entranced us and which we should love to go on admiring forever.

He started to walk down the Avenida Santa Fe. Fragments of his life flashed through his mind, and instead of looking at other windows that might perhaps have tempted him with other things, he started to analyze himself and his way of life. He began to consider all that shaped his present life, long devoid of anything that could have made for joy or gratification. He had been married for ten years to the daughter of an old chartered accountant, now retired; he had no children; he was accustomed to normal, sober habits, and did not cherish impossible ambitions or wild fancies. He spent the whole week waiting for Saturday and Sunday to arrive, when he sometimes went out with his wife or else met some of his friends, for the rest of the days only offered him those biblical duties which, since the beginning of the world, have filled men's lives with melancholy and hard work. It is not a good thing to call work melancholy, but it is the right word in this case because, by nature, he tended to color with somber hues all those things which in other people's lives are routine, gay, or even positively happy.

He found some satisfaction in the fact that he was not an ordinary clerk. His refined tastes, his willingness to interpret and discuss lucidly the leading articles dealing with politics, his flair for guessing accurately the outcome of world affairs—his good sense, in short—had won for him a fair share of consideration; while his friends, for the same reasons, used to come to consult him whenever they met with any difficulties. The fact that he had turned his home—a small interior flat on the ground floor of a new building on the Calle Charcas—into a pleasant place to live and visit, with an excellent record player bought on the installment plan, together with many fine records (Ah! those Beethoven sonatas and Wagnerian themes) with which he regaled his closest friends (who always felt themselves raised above their usual level by what the invitation implied and meant) on Monday and Thursday evenings. These sessions had certainly contributed to increase the good opinion in which he was held. He was not particularly attracted by books, but he had at one time read a ponderous treatise on economics, and that perusal, recalled again and again for many and varied reasons, had been the means of providing him with a long string of conclusive quotations and of exerting on those who were not aware of it a certain hypnotic, superstitious attraction.

It may have been his quotations or his somewhat artistic tastes, perhaps his sympathetic nature or his good moral qualities, which had been the cause of his being elected secretary of a local cultural society, a job which naturally put him in touch with other people in different walks of life.

The distinction did not turn his head. He had relatively little self-conceit, and his lack of arrogance, total lack of opposition to the ambition of others, made everybody regard his modest prestige with favor, his prosperity and comfortable life without animosity. Least of all could he have excited jealousy; nobody was readier to withdraw—as a result of natural modesty—in order to allow others to take the limelight. At home with his friends, he would sit back and enjoy himself when someone started trying to be brilliant or original, something he was always ready to applaud.

He had always wanted good things, but had never had any valuable possessions. For years his comparatively limited income had prevented him from purchasing things other than those strictly necessary to his household and in accord with the average bourgeois tastes of a married couple of modest background. He had so far done little more than recall and comment on the good things he had seen or thought about with his wife and fellow workers, all this wistfully perhaps, but also in a sane and unselfish frame of mind. Seldom had he had any whims, and the few he had entertained had made their appearance and vanished with the same pleasant rapidity. He had never shown any signs of resentment, and all his friends did their best to dispel his occasional spells of silent moroseness which were mere fleeting shadows in his life.

He had few close friends; in fact, only three of them shared his intimacy, and this number, by reason of his nature, was not likely to increase. An insurmountable bashfulness, a sort of awe for anything new, limited Morales to the circle of his old acquaint-ances and kept him to his old habits. When he felt the need to share with somebody else anything that excited or worried him, he turned to those friends: Suárez, a music critic; Bordabehere, a retired bank clerk; and finally, Celaya, a cunning old fox, who was inherently skeptical, talkative, and sententious. They were his advisers and in turn received advice from him. He showed a steady, benevolent preference for these three men and no oth-ers.

His wife was not very exacting. She was practically free from the complaints and demands which become unbearable in the routine of married life, and contented herself, apart from the domestic tranquillity and peace people are wont to call love, with visits and telephone calls to the group of friends that numbered among them Suárez's wife and Bordabehere's sister, and their lives followed their course uneventfully in the midst of a lifelong, uninterrupted game of canasta. The women met, now at this one's house, now at the other's, for their silent card games, and the only variations introduced were when a current topic was brought up and became either a subject of criticism or of simple discussion.

After having walked down the Avenida Santa Fe, Morales turned into Charcas and reached his house while it was still light.

Leonor was not yet back from her usual canasta, the maid was out doing her afternoon shopping, and the apartment was im-mersed in the characteristic quietness of holidays.

As usual, he went to the record player, and, choosing at random one of the records in the pile, he lowered the needle, releasing the flow of music. This time it happened to be the second part of the Seventh Symphony, and he began to walk aimlessly from room to room, stimulating his mind by his idle pacing. As a matter of fact, he really had nothing to complain about. If happiness is a momentary absence of worries, a calm spot where no unplesant surprises spring up on you, then he was undoubtedly happy. The company was doing well, and with the passing years he received periodical, if moderate, increases in salary. A few days before, he had written for new lists of records and leaflets dealing with household appliances. Remembering he had brought two pipes to clean from the office, he went to the bedroom for them and began cleaning them in the bathroom, while his ears were filled with the strains of music he had already heard hundreds of times.

It was funny that he liked the shoes so much. Few things excited him. Few things took his fancy. With the passing of years his desire for new things had been pared down to virtual non-existence. And indeed, it was really as if he had always deliberately tried to protect himself from any change in that direction, for, as has been said, he looked on everything that was not a part of his routine as somehow likely to disrupt his life.

He was about to finish drying his pipes when he heard the sound of the back door as the maid came in, the click of the light switch, and the rattle of pans in the kitchen. The record player continued to function and he heard the low thud of the record falling and the brief pause until the next one took its place automatically. He was so used to it that he could hear all the other sounds as well.

As usual, Leonor came back at eight, quickly opening and shutting the door, as if she were always late, when in fact she always arrived half an hour before dinnertime. But one of the characteristics of her temperament was a certain nervous restlessness completely without cause, and she seemed to bring back with her a sort of useless haste, whose permanent characteristics were well known to Federico. Sometimes, smilingly, he had asked her what the hurry was, and Leonor, not understanding, had stood there, bewildered, as if the haste she had been asked about had been the wrong dress put on by mistake.

From the bathroom, he asked her if she had brought the newspaper with her, and she answered that she had left it on the hall table. After he had put away his pipes, Federico picked up the paper and began to look through it. He read systematically, beginning with the comic strips on the last page, then going on to the sensational news the evening paper always stressed in screaming headlines. At first Morales had considered them too large, but as time passed, they had lost all extravagance in his eyes.

That evening he did not tell his wife anything about the shoes. Of course, he thought of them when he was in bed, as soon as the light was out, but like somebody taking leave of a pleasant dream.

The next day, Sunday, as they wandered in search for a convenient movie, and had passed a few shops, Leonor stopped to look in the windows. He could not refrain from telling her, lightly and even with indifference, about his find of the day before, in the window of the shoe store. He laughed as he described them, and was surprised when Leonor immediately encouraged him to buy them. It is true that she had always encouraged him in the few and moderate fancies he had had for things that might be bought, but he was surprised and pleased to see how quickly and naturally she had done so this time, placing considerable emphasis on the question: "Why don't you buy them?" Just as quickly, he felt obliged to parry the suggestion.

"But do you realize how expensive they are likely to be? Don't forget they are imported."

"Bah!" she said. "They can't possibly be as expensive as all that!"

As a matter of fact, he thought, she's probably right. They'll cost a little more than the usual price of ordinary shoes, but perhaps the difference won't be too great. But on thinking it over, he decided it was out of the question. Prices were high enough as it was, and should never be beyond the bounds of reason.

Feeling pleasantly cheered and hopeful, he paid for the tickets at the box office and entered the darkness with Leonor. They liked the front rows best and they headed for them, practically groping their way in the dark, only slightly aided by the tiny flashlight carried by the usherette.

That night they laughed and talked for a long time, and the next day, as soon as he left the office (where he performed his duties dreaming about what was to follow), he made for Capistrano's shop. There they were, the fabulous shoes, in the left-hand window, scintillating under the lights. He looked at them thoroughly and with renewed delight. To the remembered details he now added some new ones concerning the character of the line of stitching around the top of the shoes.

Without further ado, he entered the shop, at once determined and diffident, still troubled by the fear that the price might be too high. A fair-haired shop assistant in a light-brown Prince of Wales checked suit came forward at once, his hands crossed affectedly on his chest, smiling, unctuous and servile. From the inside, Morales pointed out the pair he wanted.

"I only want to know their price . . ."

The assistant looked at the shoes, and with a still more unctuous smile: "The British-made?" he queried, and he indulgently added the amount: "Only three thousand."

Morales nodded, insincerely, hiding his confusion and embarrassment.

"Three thousand?" he repeated in the voice of somebody coming back to earth with a thud.

"Three thousand, and cheap at that. You know, high quality, foreign materials, handmade . . . the very best. Believe me, all things considered, the price is most reasonable."

"Well, many thanks. I'll be back," Morales murmured, disheartened. And he left the shop without even glancing at the window where, a few minutes before, he had stopped, uplifted by his admiration and desire.

"Three thousand pesos," he kept saying to himself as he hurried away. "Three thousand pesos," and the three words had an absurd, farcical resonance in his mind, where bewilderment still persisted. "Three thousand pesos." And the very clear idea that he could never call these shoes his own was the only lucid concept his confused mind was able to grasp.

God had willed they should not be his. And, really, what on earth had made him entertain such a dream, without rhyme or reason, like an adolescent? He ought to have known that in this shop the price for such an article would necessarily be extravagantly high. He told himself to forget all about it, turned his eyes to the spectacle of the crowds, and unwillingly let himself be caught up in the whirlpool of the Calle Florida.

As he walked, he kept seeing shoe shops right and left, normal shoe shops with ordinary, familiar prices, 150, 200, at most 250. . . . And the scoundrels had asked three thousand pesos without turning a hair.

It was exactly the amount of his monthly salary, no more, no less. And nevertheless there must be people who bought such things and thought no more about it. As a matter of fact, it was only fair to say that the shoes were marvelous and that a piece of workmanship of that kind deserved to be paid for handsomely. He had never seen anything like it before. The quality, the finish . . . Those who could allow themselves an item like that were indeed to be envied.

He walked on, thinking as he did so that he had never really had any whims and that he had never overindulged himself. He had nearly always thought about Leonor only and he had given her, from time to time, an expensive, valuable, special present. . . . But he had always willingly denied *himself*, and the thought gave him a sort of pride, a sense of peace, a bittersweet feeling of renunciation and disinterestedness. He had almost made it a rule, and a very good rule it was: you can do for others what you cannot do, or can hardly do, for yourself. Yes, it was a good rule, and he had always stuck to it.

Perhaps if he was liked, it was just because of this. Who could help noticing how unwaveringly, how steadfastly he had adhered to that rule for years? Leonor herself, no doubt, without saying so, thanked him for it. And this made him feel better, for, on that score at least, nobody could find fault with him.

That night they had an early supper because they were expecting the Suárezes later on. Federico did not even mention the shoes at dinner. Leonor described her afternoon game, a stiff game of canasta she had played, accompanied by sighs on the part of her partner, her equal in skill, against such a superior team that they always seemed to be cheating.

After dinner, together with the Suárezes, always so ceremoniously punctual, they listened to a new record, a symphony which had just been delivered to Federico.

It was a pleasant evening. Really the orchestra had no rivals; it was sublime. And having heard the record, the four of them agreed. They discussed it over a cup of tea, their ears full of the sheer wonder of it. What a purity of tone, what conducting, what a group of virtuosi, what force, and also what softness when it was melodically necessary. Suárez, carefully choosing a page in his morocco-backed notebook, wrote down the number of the record and the name of the recording company. It was only when they were in bed, alone after the pleasant evening, in the warm intimacy of the bedroom, the lights still on, and feeling shy at the mere thought of the subject, that Federico mentioned the much-admired shoes, his visit to Capistrano's, the price he had been asked, and his discomfiture. He mentioned it with a smile, making fun of it, as if it were all a joke involving the shoe shop, the assistant, the situation, and even himself in the same absurd incident. What an expression he must have worn on his face on leaving the shop! If people could always see what is happening inside one, life would be unbearable. How ridiculous one would look! And the worst of it is that trifles affect us as much as important things. What a rotten gambler he would have made, he who showed his feelings so plainly on his face! It reflected his inner emotions so clearly as to cause him real distress at times.

Leonor was not of the same mind about the shoes. She did not approve of his renunciation, his selflessness in giving them up. On the contrary, to Federico's surprise, she said, quite calmly and naturally: "And why shouldn't you buy them if they are as nice as you say? You've never bought yourself anything worthwhile. We could save on something else. Or pay for them by the month. . . . Couldn't you pay for them by the month?"

He answered at once, earnestly: "No, no! Not in that kind of shop!"

"Well, if you can't," she insisted, "why don't you ask the assistant to hold them for you by paying a deposit, and then buy them at the end of the month?"

He resumed his humorous attitude, dismissing the subject as absurd, and tried to change it at once by talking about the record they had just bought.

But Leonor did not give up, and, in the same calm, deliberate voice, she insisted again, this time bringing forward a new argument: Hadn't he still some money left in the bank? Only last month, after making the final payment on the vacuum cleaner, he himself had told her so. She remembered the amount left over and thought it was more than enough for him to gratify his present fancy.

Federico then snapped at her saying that it was foolish even to contemplate such a preposterous expense. They ought to stop thinking about it, even if only on principle. Only a Croesus or a parasite could afford such fancies. And since he had always been a man of normal habits he was not going to make a fool of himself now.

Leonor held her tongue, stopped arguing, but something inside her refused to be convinced, persisted in believing she was right. Perhaps she was thinking that the poor man had never indulged himself and that he was leading a life devoid of fair and just gratifications, melancholy in its moderation, moderate even in its melancholy.

The next day, Federico was busy. After work he went to the office of the cultural society, and, together with the president, went over some papers, gave his approval, and signed them. Then he walked through the city streets to post a few routine letters. He was so engrossed in thoughts about what he was doing and what he had to do during the next few days that he hardly noticed the people hanging about in the streets at that hour of the night. He had always performed his duties faithfully and scrupulously. Even after he had performed them, they had a way of revolving in his mind in quick succession in the form of worries and preoccupations. And yet, at the same time, he was somewhat inclined to daydream, thereby acquiring his reputation of being absentminded. "Morales is always in the clouds." "Absentminded Morales." And they would hand him something he had left behind: a piece of paper, some notes, or a bit of scented soap he took to the office to wash his hands with before leaving.

Two or three days later, without knowing why, he began to feel sad. It was a dull feeling, as of something missing, a certain unfathomable, abstract nostalgia, a kind of gloom, a weariness he felt when doing what he did every day. "But I am leading my usual life and I have never been tired before," he told himself whenever he became aware of these feelings encroaching on his mind. Nevertheless, he was depressed and tired easily.

Leonor noticed, of course, as she noticed everything, and she soon told him so, asking what the matter was.

"There's nothing wrong with me," answered Federico. "Nothing." And he seemed to be examining his soul to see if what he felt could really be so plainly noticeable already.

"There's something the matter, I know."

"No," he said again, "no, nothing is wrong. Why should there be?"

But the truth is that he *was* sad and didn't do things with the same zest.

At last, one night, Leonor said to him: "I know; it's the shoes."

"What?" he said.

"Yes, and you are sad because you didn't buy your shoes."

"How silly!" he protested. The image of the shoe-shop window with the coveted shoes exhibited there in all their splendor flashed through his mind. "How silly!"

The truth is that he had forgotten them. Or at least his conscious mind had. You give up what you cannot afford, but the renunciation leaves a longing behind. The latter part of this thought left a bitter taste in his mouth and he turned it over in his mind at the table, before Leonor, calmly and humbly, as he always did. "If you don't buy them you are a fool," Leonor said bluntly.

He laughed at this and thought it all absurd and ridiculous, and left the table somewhat like a child who has been reminded of something that had distressed or saddened him long ago.

Next day, Bordabehere had dinner with them. He was glum and dull as never before. He smoked three fat cigars in the course of his visit and never said a word. He was beset by boredom. We are annoyed when we have nothing to say. Federico brought up the topic of high prices. His friend agreed, sprawling on the sofa, in the process of digesting, boa-like, his chicken and rice. In the end, he got ready to go, but took his time getting into his raincoat, helped by Federico. Finally he left.

Federico did not sleep well. He was upset and worried, and the next day, in the afternoon, giving way to an impulse he could not resist and didn't feel like resisting, he walked past Capistrano's shop; once there, he glanced longingly at the pair of shoes which still lorded it over riding boots and shoe trees.

Disheartened, he forced himself to draw away from the window, going back the same way he had taken when he had first come to the shop and seen the shoes. Again the Calle Florida engulfed him in its whirlpool, and he let himself drift, lost in the crowds, disturbed and annoyed.

He ate his dinner with no appetite at all, silently, passively listening to Leonor chatter away, neither agreeing with her nor contradicting her.

The next day, after an hour or two at the office, he decided to leave early and, walking mechanically, as he had done the day before, he made for the bank where he kept his savings account. He asked for his balance sheet at the counter and, after having examined it carefully, returned it, left the bank, and walked very slowly to the underground station where he took a direct train to cover the short distance to his house.

"I'm going to buy the shoes," he announced point blank as soon as they had sat down to their usual cold meal. And as she did not answer at once, engrossed as she was in adding some figures on the back of an envelope, he repeated, "I'm going to buy the shoes."

She applauded his decision, happily, though a little distractedly, because her figures hadn't come out right. Having unburdened himself, he ate, with more appetite than the day before, the eggs and ham and the usual quince jelly. His mind was so full of that pair of shoes, so shining and so beautiful, that the most ordinary and trifling things now appeared radiant and beautiful because of the reflection shed on them by his decision and its object.

He had made up his mind "just like that," in a direct and natural way, and had just disclosed it without stressing or magnifying it, but with a certain inner feeling of calm and peace.

He went to bed feeling unusually happy; he was unutterably relieved, and his fancy ran high. His earlier feeling of exhaustion had vanished. He slept well that night.

He worked the whole morning and part of the afternoon as if compelled to hurry by something inside him. He felt at once disturbed and lighthearted, efficient, and ready to answer good-humoredly and willingly the questions his fellow workers put to him about different aspects of their work. Their minds were, on the whole, sluggish, and they assailed him with questions on the more insignificant details of the most ordinary business matters.

He was sometimes impatient with them, but that morning he was in high spirits and answered readily.

At six o'clock, no sooner had he finished working than he made straight for Capistrano's shop. He had thought it over and had come to the conclusion that, with what he had saved the year before (when his economies had been bigger than he had anticipated because of the brief, cheap holiday they had taken), he could well afford to make this lavish expenditure. Furthermore, he was influenced by the argument that the effect of liberated impulses on our minds is good, improving our behavior by giving us the peace and serenity that ought to be at the bottom of our permanent efforts and sacrifices.

In high spirits, he crossed the pavement, leaving the business section behind, and walked past the shopwindows filled with temptations until at last he reached the street where Capistrano's shop was located. He entered the shop, erect and without hesitation, though not without first having made sure—out of the corner of his eyes—that the coveted shoes were in their accustomed place.

He tried them on, with nervous movements, assisted by an incompetent, insignificant assistant—not the one who had waited on him before—who gave stupid answers to his eager questions about the name of the model, the trademark, where exactly they had been made, whether the manufacturer was an old firm, and how long the shoes would really last. No doubt the assistant did not share his curiosity and did not seek to satisfy it fully either, for his answers were polite but perfunctory, full of the freezing superiority with which presumptuous assistants give explanations beyond those necessary in a routine sale. As a final answer, he pointed out with his chin—he had one of the shoes in his hands— the perfection and elegance of the stitching, and proceeded to put the shoe on Federico's foot with the aid of a sort of long spoon made of horn, inserted where Federico put his heel, so that his foot might slip into the exquisite leather just as fingers do into a glove.

Federico got up and balanced himself, first on one foot and then on the other, observing the shoes in a mirror standing at right angles to the stool where he had sat for his fitting. He then stood still for a few minutes, assuming the attitude of a connoisseur, studying the effect produced by the coveted pair of shoes, and found it was really stunning. He took a few steps, walking carefully on the linoleum with the slippery new soles, and with his mouth he made a sign of silent approval which was answered by the assistant with a superior muttering, as if he were saying: "*Now* are you satisfied that I was right? I have nothing but contempt for you amateur shoe critics with your middle-class comments and your timid hesitations! A good shoe is a good shoe, and that's that!"

Federico examined the prodigious pair of shoes a moment longer—from heel to toe and side to side—took a few more steps in them on the waxed floor, cast a few inquiring glances right and left to ascertain the prices of the other goods displayed in the expensive shop, and at last asked whether he could pay for them by check. He immediately made it clear that he would take the shoes with him, as he did not want any alterations made. He did not want rubber heels or anything else that might alter their original shape. He paid for them and tucked them under his arm, well wrapped up inside their elegant cardboard box on which a red label, printed in the best type, was prominent. And, in possession of his treasure, he began walking the same streets as on former occasions when he had returned home, but not without experiencing a certain pride, odd in him, an inner sense of superiority of which only he was aware.

As soon as he reached home, Morales, at once proud and a little ashamed of having spent so much, showed Leonor the admirable pair of shoes. "They are really nice," said Leonor, who used the word "nice" whenever she was unable to find some other sufficiently laudatory word.

Carefully and reverently, they examined the coveted pair of shoes. Federico put them on the shelf over the fireplace so that they might be seen, from a convenient distance, in all their beauty and uniqueness. And in point of fact, their superb and unusual color was such that it was indeed unlikely that any rivals would appear to outshine them. "You can wear them next Sunday to go to the Olsens'," Leonor suggested. The Olsens were a Danish married couple, very fond of music.

But Federico kept silent.

He did not wear them that Sunday. Instead he removed them from the mantelpiece and placed them in his wardrobe, among shirts and undershirts, where shoes are never kept. Something forbade him to put them on. He had a premature feeling of pity, almost of sorrow, for the harm that use would do to the pair of shoes which, in Federico's eyes, were like a jewel or even something miraculous. And two weeks passed without Federico's having worn them.

It was only on the Saturday following those two weeks that he made up his mind to show them to his friends. He gave in to the impulse of showing them off before the first spot, the first blemish due to wear, marred them. And, on that Saturday, after dinner, before they devoted themselves to music, yielding, not without diffidence, to a hint from Leonor—or rather, to her audible prompting—he showed Bordabehere and Celaya the splendid objects he had acquired.

He took the shoes to the living room and, silently, they examined them with curiosity and unfeigned astonishment. The price was not mentioned. The external qualities of the shoes were solemnly praised, and Celaya, holding them to the light with the tips of his fingers, raised them above his head, just as is done with a diamond or a picture. Finally, the praises ended.

"How much did they cost?" asked Bordabehere, who was highly inquisitive by nature.

"They were expensive," said Federico, but avoided the topic by going on to talk about the decadence of craftsmanship, which usually gives us only vulgar, inelegant, and mass-produced goods.

"All right, but how much were they?" insisted the inquisitive Bordabehere.

And then, with a certain constraint, a certain trepidation, Federico Morales answered him.

"Three thousand pesos!" And Celaya jumped as if he had been stung by a bee.

Bordabehere flung himself back on the sofa as if collapsing from excitement, horror, and shock.

"But they are extraordinary," pleaded Leonor. "They are so lovely . . ."

"Extraordinary though they be," Bordabehere disagreed, "they cannot be worth as much as all that!"

"That was their price," repeated Federico, "and they are worth it if you think they will last you a lifetime."

"Lifetime my eye!" shouted Celaya. "It's robbery, that's what it is; sheer robbery!"

"Sheer robbery!" echoed Bordabehere.

And, frowning, the two visitors looked at each other, shocked and indignant.

Federico picked up the shoes, took them to the bedroom, and, carefully and lovingly, put them away among the shirts and handkerchiefs. When he went back to the living room he found Leonor arguing with Celaya and Bordabehere.

"He shouldn't have done it," Bordabehere reiterated. "He shouldn't have done it!"

Federico, smiling bashfully, explained that he had allowed himself this one and only unreasonable extravagance.

"He has indulged himself so little," sighed Leonor.

"He certainly splurged this time!" said Celaya ironically. And his mouth showed his intense disapproval.

They spent the rest of the evening listening to music, talking about the well-known music, discovering new aspects they had not noticed before.

That night Federico went to bed somewhat embittered toward Celaya and Bordabehere. He could not forgive them for trying to dampen his satisfaction. The shoes were simply extraordinary, and they should have admitted it wholeheartedly.

But the dismayed comments, the disapproving silences irritated him. He found that people will always object, even though their objections are really less justifiable than what they object to.

That Saturday, as they had been asked to dinner at the house of a friend of theirs, an assistant manager married to a very interesting woman, Federico wore his shoes for the first time.

He, as well as Leonor, dressed with extreme care. They began their preparations at seven o'clock. All the lights were on and they went from place to place, from bedroom to bathroom, in search of something or other: the shoehorn that could not be found a misplaced mirror, or a knife to open a bottle of eau de cologne. When he had donned the trousers of his blue suit, Federico, in his shirt sleeves, put on the virgin shoes and examined himself in the wardrobe mirror, squeezing himself against the bed in order to see better. Then he proceeded to pull up his suspenders so that the cuffs of his trousers would not come down too far and hide his shoes. They did not look so perfect when contrasted with blue, but in themselves they were magnificent, the best shoes he had ever worn, and the most comfortable.

Feeling happy, he went to the hall where Leonor was filing her nails under the light, and, moving noiselessly, he stopped in front of his wife so that she could appreciate wholly and fully the effect produced by the appearance of the brand-new shoes, whose technical merits, as it were, she was able to comprehend and appreciate to a limited degree only.

Humming a tune, Federico finished dressing, examining himself again from all angles in the mirror, satisfied with himself as never before, except possibly on the occasion when, for the first time, at the age of seven or eight, he had put on a sailor suit with a wide sky-blue collar and a white ribbon, with a whistle on the end of it, which wound its way down to a tiny breast pocket.

Finally, at nine o'clock, they arrived at the home of their friend, the assistant manager, to find the other guests already there. Immediately Federico could feel and value the impression made by his appearance, and especially, of course, by his shoes, on those kind, receptive minds. Aware of the signs of respect and grateful for them, after shaking hands, almost without saying a word, he tended to be self-effacing, for he wished to hide behind his shoes, which attracted the gaze of everyone: an unequivocal proof of silent and devoted reverence. Of course, nobody would have dared to say anything in praise of so trivial a thing as a pair of shoes, but nevertheless it was very pleasant to enjoy the secure feeling of wearing such matchless objects. Modest as he was, he had almost never paid any attention to what he wore, but at that moment he felt an odd, rewarding pride. He did not think he was more important than he really was, but he did feel that he was more pleasing than usual, therefore better able to practice that form of generosity which consists of showing our friends our best side, even when that side is symbolized by mere material things.

That night he ate heartily; he was much more loquacious and brilliant than usual; he related anecdotes at random, and repeated witticisms he had heard from others which, under other circumstances, he would not have dared to repeat or imitate. His right-hand neighbor was a satirical, lively, bespectacled spinster with skin blemishes, while on his left sat his host's mother-in-law, a good-natured lump of flesh. The food was excellent, the wine exquisite. The assistant manager was a man who liked to display every sign of prosperity he could command, and his dinners were famous for the excellence of the food and the late hour at which they ended.

When coffee was served in the living room—where the hostess kept her holiday souvenirs and the manager certain questionable family portraits—Federico sat down beside his host's mother-in-law on the center sofa; and as he let himself sink into the deep cushions he felt that, with his legs slightly apart, his feet would be seen flaunting the shiny pair of shoes. He then withdrew his legs a little, as if suddenly overcome by a feeling of modesty and shyness, and let the objects of his pride be appreciated only by observant and discerning eyes. Shy and modest by nature, he couldn't help feeling a little embarrassed by his impulse toward excessive ostentation, which tends to harm rather than help and is offensive rather than pleasing.

A few minutes later, partly because of the wine, partly because of the delight he experienced when appearing at his best in the presence of other people, he felt blissfully happy. His host and the other guests were talking a short distance away, seated on sofas and chairs. Leonor, with the help of quick gestures full of meaning, was holding a conversation with a bald man in a green tie, who looked like a diplomat and who answered her in the pompous manner some officials affect; he himself was sitting comfortably on the sofa with the now silent host's mother-in-law, conferring his blessings on the scene, for this was indeed a happy evening for him.

They returned home and went to bed late, kept awake as they were by the many things they had to tell each other, and, next day, Federico went back to work full of a naïve optimism. It was strange that so slight an encouragement as a pleasant evening should have changed his frame of mind so thoroughly and given him a happiness and lightheartedness none of his fellow workers could help noticing.

For two evenings in succession he went to the premises of the cultural society and worked by himself, efficiently and steadily, until late at night, with the happy image of the shoes deep inside him. He had cleared up a few bills, methodically made a list of things that had been suggested, ordered the purchase of a lamp, and complained, in stern terms, about the price asked for another piece of furniture they had decided to buy.

At that time he paid a few more calls, wearing the shoes, enjoying the feeling of innocent self-confidence with which he was so strangely filled.

One afternoon, he entered Gath and Chaves's to buy a pair of brown socks to go with the new shoes—a pair of moderately priced socks. He asked Leonor to go to a movie after supper, and even propounded a theory on the difference between the motion pictures and the theater, which, he believed, was slightly favorable to the movies.

It was only a week afterward that the sturdy and pompous Oropesa, on meeting him accidentally at the office door said, point blank, with an ironical, insolent air: "So you've bought yourself a three-thousand-peso pair of shoes . . ."

Federico blushed, and the only words that came to his lips were: "Who told you?"

"I don't know, someone . . . Soriano or Molina Viana."

Evidently the news had spread.

Federico smiled. "One can afford a whim now and then."

"Well!"

"I liked them."

"They must be truly grand . . ." His comments fairly dripped with sarcasm. "Going this way?"

"No. That way," said Federico, nodding his head in the direction he was going.

"Well, then, see you tomorrow."

Oropesa waved good-bye.

The same night, while they were drinking anisette at the Three Billiard Balls, Oropesa brought up the subject while he was talking with Berdina, the salesman.

"Have you heard about Morales?"

"What?"

"He's bought himself a three-thousand-peso pair of shoes."

"You don't say!"

"Just like that."

"His monthly salary, no less."

And Berdina pursed his lips, in a gesture of astonishment, almost of reproach.

"I hardly know him," he said, "but I have always felt him to be a little silly."

"Silly? Him? He knows what he's about. He never misses a trick."

"What do you mean?"

"He's a smart cookie."

"Three thousand pesos for shoes!"

"It certainly is something!"

"Of course, there's the firm angle to it . . ."

Berdina was puzzled and vexed. He lifted his eyebrows. "What firm?"

"The firm he's working for."

"What's that got to do with it?"

"Nothing directly, perhaps. But relations with employers are tricky things . . ."

"Hold on. Don't get things wrong. A fool is a fool. That's all there is to it."

"I was only saying . . ."

"Don't be silly!"

Later, Oropesa talked it over with Celaya. "Yes, I know," Celaya said. And then, troubled, before changing the subject, he added, "Well, it's his funeral. . . ."

The story of Morales's purchase began to spread. There was a lot of talk about the shoes, first in fun, then with an undertone of reproach, finally with jealousy and anger. His business associates busied themselves with this topic with an odd passion, for until then they had not really taken much notice of Morales except to praise him mildly. Now the beginnings of actual hatred were noticeable. Apparently John Cahin had said: "It's an affront to the others to buy a pair of shoes like that." In the meantime, Federico paraded as much as he could, naïvely, and with an innocent pride, the shoes that were his delight.

The first time the board of the cultural society met, after a long interval, everybody glanced down at Morales's feet. However, he was not wearing the new shoes. The members were disappointed. They had all wanted to have a look at them, to ascertain how much real basis there was for all the talk. When the meeting opened, Riguera said to Morales, rather irritably, "Young man, we have not come to any useful decisions for weeks. And there are so many things waiting to be settled."

"It's not *my* fault," Morales protested. "There was nobody here last week, and the week before we were only two."

"But now nearly all of us are here."

"All right, sir, let's get going."

Morales, somewhat annoyed, performed his duties. The atmosphere was not pleasant. Riguera still seemed intolerant and Morales did not answer him willingly. When they were leaving, Riguera said to young Perez: "I don't know what's the matter with him."

"Since he bought himself those shoes they say he has become a little uppish."

"Well! Well!"

"A pity; he was always such a nice fellow."

"It's just one of those things. Maybe his wife had something to do with it."

"No. He's got a slightly swelled head, that's all."

That he had a "swelled head" became a hackneyed phrase from then on among the people in Morales's office and those in the cultural group. Some of them still laughed when they talked about the shoes: "They must be made of pure gold!" "It's beyond me!" "They must be out of this world!"

Naturally, Morales never wore his shoes to the office nor to the board meetings. He saved them.

He put them on when Bordabehere and Celaya came to his house one evening, together with a German, to listen to a prelude. Bordabehere and Celaya could not keep their eyes off the shoes. They looked at them again and again, but in a friendly fashion. And not only did they praise the prelude highly, but also attacked the port and cakes as if they were ambrosia. They applauded a good-natured jibe Morales aimed at the German.

And, half-smilingly, they continued to look at his shoes, his resplendent shoes, so well-stitched, so well-designed. Princely shoes, to be sure! A rich man's! What else, when they cost so much? Three thousand pesos!

But at the office, a far less friendly attitude prevailed. At first his associates merely said to themselves: "Three thousand pesos certainly isn't chicken feed!" But now, having recovered from their surprise, they said: "He must be out of his mind!" And you could almost see their disapproval and annoyance choking them.

They simply could not stomach the fact that he had bought such a pair of shoes.

The snowball grew bigger. A month later, about a hundred of the office clerks had heard about Morales's shoes.

When he entered the office they began to look at him as one looks at a freak or at someone suspected of being up to no good.

"It's wrong to spend money like that, I tell you. . . . In times like these . . ."

"You're quite right. It's wrong."

"And by the way, where do you suppose all his dough comes from?"

Somebody answered: "Skip it. What's that got to do with it?"

"What do you mean, 'skip it'? I have a right to express an opinion!"

"Not when it tends to cast suspicion on an innocent man."

True enough, the origin of the money was irrelevant in this case. He was honest, no doubt of it, but nevertheless how do you account for the fact that he bought himself a three-thousand-peso pair of shoes? How indeed! His co-workers were genuinely distressed because they could not solve the problem by branding Morales an embezzler. They had worked side by side with him for years, and he was known to be honest and reliable.

That was part of what worried them. They could not simply say, "He's a crook," and let it go at that.

"All right, he is as honest as you say he is," they agreed, "but why the shoes?" What about that? Yes, why the shoes?

One cannot lightly defy people's conventional ideas. Never again would they say, "Morales is a harmless dreamer." No, Morales had dared. He was not merely a harmless dreamer. He had had the audacity to ignore completely their ideas as to what was proper conduct for a man in his position.

And was it not effrontery, a slap in the face, to have bought himself such an article, a costly luxury? Outrageous! It was not to be tolerated. Somehow, they had to make him aware of their annoyance and disapproval.

And as a matter of fact, as knowledge of the matter spread more and more widely, certain signs of annoyance and hostility were manifested openly.

It was not exactly envy, but rather something subtler, more complex, more intricate. It was a sort of mania for leveling, the vindictive will and fury to retaliate on the part of those who resented Morales's shoes, who could not accept them and blamed them for the connotation of potential defiance they held for them, for the unbearable provocation ascribed to their importance and, above all, for their obvious, glaring superiority. You cannot hate, or envy, a hero or a saint; we accept the fact that we are incapable of surpassing them; but there are certain other qualities and values that we feel exist deep inside us, and when these are made manifest in people who dare to exhibit them without consulting us or caring about us in the least, they kindle in us a sort of wrath based on an obscure feeling that we have been relegated to an inferior position. This is what was happening to Morales's fellow workers and not a few of his friends. The annoyance was present, and the hostility.

And the annoyance and hostility began to show themselves in different ways. At the board meetings of the cultural association, which had in the past been so peaceful, there was a feeling of uneasiness and latent discord. The uncooperative Riguera became still more uncooperative. Others followed suit.

Things were definitely not going well at the board meetings. Of course, in the evening, two or three times a week, Federico was able to shake off his worries when they met to listen to music, either at his house or elsewhere. He dressed more carefully when going to the theater, and he matched his splendid shoes with the suits Leonor took care to keep in perfect order. They bought seats in the gallery of the Colón to listen to an unforgettable Suor Angelica. Afterward, they treated themselves to a delicious chocolate at the Cosechera.

But the unfriendly tendencies did not decrease. Far from it, as Morales noticed with surprise. The board of the association even rejected part of the yearly program he had so painstakingly and carefully drafted before submitting it for their consideration. He felt confused. And when he left the premises, sometimes alone, sometimes with Bordabehere, he could not help experiencing a feeling of wonder and bewilderment which he was very careful not to mention to his wife. "How strange," he said to himself again, "how strange!"

And so it was, and stranger still when he noticed that even when they chatted together before and after the meetings, his friends addressed him laconically, with a marked lack of cordiality, and in certain instances he noticed an underlying tone of mockery or derision for which he could find no valid reason. Though he did not show it, this hurt him.

For hurt he really was. They had always behaved so differently. They had always shown a liking for him. They had tacitly approved of his conventionality, his conduct in not setting himself up as better than they were, his eagerness not to stand in anybody's light, his lack of conceit, his fondness—in short, for decent, standard conduct, which quality is balm to ordinary minds. And now they had become so bitter, so intolerant. What had he done to them?

His attitude did not change, however. On the contrary, he tried to be more cordial, more outgoing; he made efforts to talk more, about more things, and more affably; and even tried to win goodwill by redoubling the care he took in his dress, and by putting on the new shoes more frequently. This had no favorable effect whatever, and indeed seemed to have the opposite result. He noticed one or two sly smiles and malicious looks, and these had an exceedingly distressing effect on him.

Among other things, he was accused of being stuck up and a

fop. The more he wore the shoes he liked, the less they tolerated him.

When Bordabehere and Celaya visited him, they began to argue with him about anything and everything. "No, that's impossible. . . ." "Of course not. . . ." "You're all wrong about that." Or else they maintained a sullen, sour silence.

The resentment spread and grew: a bitter, deep, incomprehensible resentment for Morales. All this half-suppressed ill will constituted a sort of sword of Damocles forever suspended over his head.

How could he dissolve or, at least, mollify it if he didn't even know its cause?

In order to shake off the painful effect this foolish and malicious behavior had on him, he would put on his shoes and wander about after dark, absorbing as he did so the luminous blessing of the city: happiness and brightness, reflecting happiness and brighteness. . . .

But the atmosphere grew worse.

Gordillo, one of the clerks, met Sirvent, another clerk. The traffic of Corrientes was flowing past them amid much tooting and blaring of horns. After having discussed several subjects, public and office affairs, Gordillo, sugaring the pill with a smile, asked: "Have you heard about Morales?"

"What about Morales?"

"About the shoes . . ."

"No. What happened?"

Gordillo told him about the purchase.

"You don't say!"

"It's the truth!"

"Well, well!"

And Sirvent and Gordillo sniggered in unison.

Sometimes they discussed it in this way but at other times they spoke about it in a harshly puritanical manner. "Such conduct is positively immoral."

"It's not only immoral, it's an insult to the rest of us!"

Bonfanti and some other good-natured person ventured to be broad-minded:

"I don't see what's wrong with it."

"What's so extraordinary about it?"

There was always somebody to answer, fairly exuding venom: "What's *wrong* with it? Say, fellows . . . Listen to this! He's asking what's *wrong* with it! What d'you know?"

And "What d'you know" was as good as saying that the previous speaker was an idiot.

In February, Morales found out that a new candidate had been nominated for the secretaryship which he held. The new candidate's many backers said they had discussed the matter thoroughly and decided it was a bad thing for one man to hold the post too long.

And besides, they said, Morales has been neglecting his duties. He is more concerned with being dressed up like a swell than performing his duties faithfully.

In April, they ousted him from his post. Riguera succeeded him.

And Leonor, once more, had to persuade him not to attach more importance to a matter than it really possessed. "We all have enemies and this time yours have the upper hand."

"Enemies?" he asked himself rather seriously and reflectively. He had always done the right thing by all his co-workers. That is, if doing the right thing consists of acting in a harmless and kindly fashion. Enemies? Who and why?

He was more thoughtful than sad.

He found more time to devote himself to music, and after office hours he was able to stroll about the city streets, looking at the windows in front of which, like a child, he loved to stop and examine the displays.

In the evening, he went out quite a lot with Leonor. He did not wear his best shoes so often because he had noticed slight signs of wear at the tips and he didn't want them spoiled. He went to the theater and was more sensitive, more receptive than ever before, more sentimental perhaps. He talked less, and was more wary of addressing his friends, as if afraid of a snub. Was this man, or perhaps that one, the enemy Leonor meant? He no longer felt at ease with them, and he greeted his friends with a certain timidity and as though he were slightly startled at meeting them.

One afternoon about this time, as Federico Morales was walking toward an important concert hall after having had his valuable shoes shined at one of the busiest corners of the city, he encountered a group of men who greeted him with a "Hi, Morales," and long, inquiring glances. They were talking as he passed by, but they stopped talking to look at him long and hard, from head to foot, so as to be able to judge for themselves, and later speak authoritatively with regard to the splendor of that notorious part of his dress.

"Now that's what I call luxury!"

The sentence was pregnant with sarcasm, almost as much so as the following one: "Not even the Maharajah of Kapurtala has shoes like that!"

They stood there laughing, treating the whole thing more as a joke than as a cause for ill will.

Other people, however, were more resentful. For instance, the new members of the board, who felt superior and vindictive, were full of jealousy and burning with resentment. They were young firebrands, denizens of an aggressive bohemia, bull-necked, dirty-shoed advocates of untrammeled behavior and even physical violence. When somebody there recalled Morales, mentioning his work, they burst out simultaneously with contemptuous remarks, and interrupted each other in order to abuse him the more roundly. They could not tolerate a man they branded as a vulgar bourgeois not worthy of mention by important self-respecting people like themselves. No, you have to be thoroughgoing and inexorable; you cannot tolerate superficial upstarts.

"Moreover," said Torres on one occasion, wiping his mouth with a napkin after having had some pie at the counter, "we must put an end to this sort of people and their criminally gay way of life." He liked the phrase and he repeated it. "And their criminally gay way of life."

"He's right," asserted the gloomy Cardini, "quite right."

"True," said the scowling Roque, "one hundred percent correct."

And Torres's opinion, and Cardini's opinion, and scowling Roque's opinion made their way into other people's minds. In a very short time Morales was hated by almost everybody. It became impossible to mention him without noticing disapproval, reproach, intolerance, and resentment in the air.

"These depraved characters are harmful," Torres kept on saying. "They contaminate, they corrupt people."

And he always found a Cardini or a scowling Roque to think he was right, to approve of his judgment, and to congratulate himself because, suddenly and easily, he had placed himself on a higher plane than the culprit. Then they strutted like cocks and their comments dripped with self-righteousness. They were at once the victim and the sacrificial priest.

They often discussed the shoes Morales had purchased. Time and again they mentioned them with righteous indignation, and the phrase "Morales's shoes" became commonplace whenever they referred to anything ostentatious. The burning hate they harbored grew and accumulated.

Naturally, all this gossiping, like an all-pervading cloud of filthy smoke, reached the manager's office, and although at first the company officers ignored it, they were forced, little by little, to yield to the majority opinion and compelled to do something about it. Morales had already been convicted in the court of public opinion.

"But he has always been an excellent employee," they mumbled at first.

To which the others viciously replied that he was a scoundrel who defied honest men with his unforgivable frivolity, and who set a bad example because he was the living proof of a life based on the cult of luxury, extravagance, and ostentation inherited from the odious and dissolute privileged classes.

At first, the managers were puzzled; they did not know what it was all about or the why and wherefore of a story that, when all was said and done, rested on nothing more substantial than an expensive pair of shoes. They were puzzled and undecided, but they were soon conquered by the apparent common sense, the inflexibility, and the heroic and patrician air of the Catos who had been delegated to acquaint them with the matter by dropping hints whenever they saw a chance to do so. They ended by accepting the condemnation without understanding it, and played their special roles in it by looking suspiciously and distrustfully at

Morales. God help the man who is talked about. The snowball will grow and soon he will be buried under the monstrous growth.

Gradually, Morales came to feel that there was something seriously wrong. Initially, the attack had found him unprepared and unguarded; he felt only disillusioned and somewhat sad. But as he needed very little to feel at peace with the world, he found it easy to soothe his feelings in the peaceful atmosphere of his home, and in his usual meetings with Celaya and Bordabehere, despite the fact that they showed themselves every day more inexplicably cynical, ironical, and rude. But later on, it began to worry him. He asked himself again, and this time more searchingly, the same questions he had asked himself when things had been so unpleasant at the meetings. What had happened? What did they blame him for? What did they accuse him of? Why did they hate him? Why did they all seem to bear him a grudge?

He avoided talking it over with Leonor, and he only did so, cautiously and shyly, with Bordabehere, on an evening when they were left alone in front of the radio while Leonor, Celaya, and the ladies were playing canasta in the next room. Bordabehere only smiled, sat back, and said casually: "You're imagining things . . ."

It was only after a while that he admitted: "Well, the truth is that they perhaps find you a little changed toward them, perhaps a little more self-centered, self-important and vain."

"Vain?" ejaculated Morales. "Vain?"

And the question lingered there, like an echo, deep inside his mystified heart.

Yes, he thought, perhaps they see in me a certain ostentation, a certain new and superior attitude, a certain pride. . . . They may consider themselves slighted.

Morales remembered his blameless life, his unfailing politeness, an inherent politeness stemming from genuine good will, and accompanied by a gentle feeling of happiness which he experienced while living at peace with his neighbors. No, it could not be any change in him. Bordabehere was hiding something. Something worse, something occult was at the bottom of it all. The subject haunted his thoughts and caused him acute worry and pain.

The crucial point was reached when one of the managers summoned him to his office. He was a short, rather awkward man with a ruddy face, and he received Morales affably, politely, even deferentially, but with a certain restraint. He was smoking a cigar that was as black, twisted, and short as he was. He offered Morales a chair in front of him, on the other side of the desk, and came straight to the point. He wanted to ask him to retire. Of course, the pension was not very big, but it was close enough to the amount of his monthly salary, and carried with it none of the disadvantages of a job. "But why?" asked Morales. He fidgeted in his chair; he was disturbed, ill at ease; what he was most interested in was in knowing why. His face became pale and he seemed to shrink into himself. Had he perhaps done something wrong without realizing it? The manager, smilingly, rejected this supposition: it was only in the interest of fairness that they wanted to open the way, systematically, but little by little, and without discrimination, to the newcomers, the young employees, the young blood. And he, as manager, had taken it upon himself to ask the old employees, one by one, to leave their jobs open to the new ones, as a realistic approach to life demanded. It was in no sense a negative or unfriendly policy, it was simply part of a general plan and as such ought to be favorably received and not misconstrued.

Federico left him without having uttered a word of complaint, and went home, his eyes and his spirits clouded. Leonor was in the kitchen, preparing the coffee they had every evening at seven. Morales, his face drawn, told her what had happened, and what explanation the manager had given. She listened to him without a change of expression, seemingly indifferent, but really because of the serene strength she hoarded for moments of need. "What will be will be," was her only answer. As for him, though he uttered a protest against what had happened, he showed no bitterness, and his protest was aimed at nobody in particular. He felt himself to be the victim of some kind of spell, caught in the midst of an ominous game obscured by equivocations, a game which defeated him even though comprehension of it eluded him.

"What can they have thought up? What crime do they accuse

me of?" the wretched man asked himself as he paced up and down the length of the room.

Leonor put the steaming coffee on the table and sat down to drink it, without a sign of being upset. "It's useless to ask yourself why. There are things which apparently have no cause, like illnesses that appear suddenly like a bolt from the blue. Don't bother looking for the cause. There's no point in it. And besides, what for? Either you can do something about it or you can't."

But he still wanted to know what was wrong, from whom or what all the trouble emanated. Where did it all come from? He felt he had a right to know. Leonor probably knew and wouldn't tell him.

"I?" she said. "I don't know anything. What I believe is that there's a pack of scoundrels in your company. A pack of rascals. That's what I think. And they hate you because you are different."

Federico let himself fall back on the sofa, thoughtful and downcast. What was the good of the many years spent in self-denial, in working steadfastly from morning till night, in trying hard to be useful and to help, rather than hinder people?

"And don't you think I'm right?" asked Leonor. "You must stand up for your rights. The world is full of dishonesty and ill will. A kind of man who does not harm anybody should be an object of sympathy, because everyone takes advantage of him." And her anger showed in her eyes. "Do you know what's happened? You've been too good, and you cannot be like that. People want you to be like them: malignant, so as to fight you on their own level with brass knuckles. That's what they want."

Federico remained where he was for a little while, depressed and downcast, and then, by an effort of will, he got up and began to prepare the clothes he intended to wear that evening.

"Where shall we go?" asked Leonor.

"To a movie."

"There are only sad ones scheduled for tonight."

"Never mind. Let's go anywhere."

They went "anywhere." "Anywhere" turned out to be a theater in the city where they had to wait in line to get in. The line moved forward . . . Federico sighed several times, heavy-hearted and hurt, tired, defeated. They waited in silence for the line to move on and eventually found themselves inside. The film was tedious and long, indeed almost endless. Toward the end, however, he began to take a little interest in the plot and gave it gentle and condescending attention. But before long they were again in the street, in the crowd, in the devilish stream of traffic that made it so difficult to move.

He found the long Calvary of the succeeding months particularly unbearable, for the only thing he had begun to look forward to was the first installment of the pension he had applied for. In a very short time he had learned to protect himself from, and ward off, the others' hostility, for he had become sensitive to it. He never spoke unless he was spoken to. When somebody did speak to him, it was with a sort of piercing irony resembling the peculiar tone of voice people use to address a man who has done something wrong but has managed to escape being punished for it. As if they wanted, without saying so, to show him that they were in on the secret. He made the acquaintance, however, of one of the company's new clerks whom he treated affably, lavishing on him, by way of friendly conduct, what he could not give the others since they were definitely determined not to accept it.

Leonor, without his knowing it, had an enlightening talk with Bordabehere. Bordabehere was embarrassed and confused. He did not know what to say, and he hesitated, fumbling for words, alleging that he didn't know what had caused all this ill will toward Federico. He looked secretly pleased, however, at having something to say at last, at being able to compensate, by means of factual knowledge, for his total lack of imagination. And at last he admitted that he knew the cause of all the trouble: it was the purchase of the three-thousand-peso shoes that had outraged everybody. "Don't you see? It shocked them."

"But who publicized it? You, Celaya, Suárez?"

"No, nobody. The story spread by itself, that's all."

"But *somebody* must have started it."

"No, not at all. It's just that things get noticed. You know . . . And then they are discussed. Your husband's purchase startled and shocked a lot of people."

He said "a lot of people" as though he meant to include himself.

Leonor, disgusted, left him. She felt the whole affair was based on gratuitous malevolence, and was a foolish, inept, and highly unpleasant injustice done to her husband. She thought that at the bottom of it all lay a certain occult hate, ever present in the hearts of the dissatisfied, and always striving to find somebody on whom to vent itself. The truth is that the dissatisfied hate themselves, and vent their self-hatred by being hateful to others. This thought made her feel a little better, although she was still upset.

Federico noticed that on entering and leaving the office they looked and looked at him. Some practically made a career of it. He felt these looks heavy on him. What lay behind them? For all one could tell, they were looks and looks only, though they certainly seemed serious enough. Apart from this, nobody paid any attention to him. They hardly ever said anything to him except to answer yes or no, so as not to leave him without any answer at all. And, in this case, when they answered him, they still looked . . . stared at him.

The result was that, more than ever, he concentrated his attention on his silent routine and in fulfilling his duties during the time he still had left to work with the company on his own special job. He suffered because of his wounded self-esteem, his abused goodness, the atmosphere full of hatred that surrounded him, and the way people who had been friendly in the past now cut him dead.

In the course of the following months he found himself becoming more and more remote from his co-workers, until they seemed like an unfriendly race of alien beings. He had become remote, just as men who are about to die become remote from other men, with this difference: that, more than ever, he felt life's call, still enjoyed little things, although there was a deep-seated bitterness in his heart.

He limited himself to talking to the most modest, obscure people—a shopkeeper with an honest look in his eyes, the man who sold newspapers and flowers, the girl with curly hair in the candy shop; and he found that none of them had become infected by the general ill will, but that, on the contrary, they showed him a kindly, if superficial, human sympathy. And as goodness is a thing likely to spread quickly, his home benefited from it and more and more frequently he came home to Leonor with inexpensive boxes of chocolates, magazines, a bunch of tulips or dahlias, and an occasional jar of guava jelly.

They went on seeing Celaya, Bordabehere, and Suárez, but the spell of friendship had been broken. They avoided certain topics; others brought about embarrassing and annoying silences; they disagreed more than ever on the interpretation of music; and when Federico wore the shoes (of which he naturally took the greatest care) he thought he saw in the others a sort of uneasy astonishment. Federico once complained: "It is as if I were wearing a stolen diamond."

But from Leonor he didn't get any answer beyond a shrug of the shoulders with which she systematically showed her contemptuous indifference toward the Bordabeheres, the Celayas, the Suárezes, and the rest of the fauna at the office.

As the year drew to a close, the time for retirement, fixed for the winter, drew nearer. They had to think of curtailing their expenses and renting a smaller house. They did not find it an easy thing to do. In July, they had begun house hunting, without any satisfactory results. It seemed impossible to find anything in the city. When November came they made up their minds to rent a house in the suburbs, in Temperley or Banfield. Leonor could not stand apartments.

As a matter of fact, the search for a new house had done them both good, especially Federico, who, simply because of it, had begun to feel younger. He told Leonor, and she commented, "But you *are* young."

When he looked in the mirror hanging over the fireplace and saw his hated face, he realized that he was actually still young and didn't look at all like a man about to be retired on a pension. He fixed the knot of his tie with nimble fingers, decided that green contrasted pleasantly with his light-colored suit, and then serenely sat on the sofa to discuss a newspaper clipping with Leonor, the houses they still had to see among those advertised in the suburbs.

In a way, he was beginning to feel much less bitter.

Surprisingly, he discovered that even though they were unaccountably dead set against him, the others could not harm him in any way. He was stronger because, even if they had rejected him, there was one thing from which he was not excluded, and that was justice. And the others, all of them, however powerful they were, could not prevent him from living his life, the life that God, in spite of them all and above them all, grants just men. Though he well knew it was a sin of pride to consider himself a just man, he felt happiness welling within him, a happiness greater than the pain the others with their ill will had inflicted on him.

He left the company without saying good-bye to anybody except the manager who had broached the subject of his dismissal and the new employee he had singled out and liked, and who, no doubt, because he was a new man, had not been influenced by the prevalent ill will; it sometimes takes time for evil to do its work of corruption.

They moved into the house they had recently rented, a three-room villa in a district devoted to houses of that type, far away from everything, and sparsely built up, except for the rows of villas which stood there rather forlornly.

But they arrived with a new spirit, if you can apply the term "new spirit" to the desire and need to forget recent widely diffused pain, and soon the three rooms were filled with their old furniture and they could listen alone to the music they had listened to before with the others. The symphonies sounded different on the carpetless polished floors; the record player seemed better; the sounds were amplified.

But the house was so small that, as soon as Leonor or Federico started walking about, they bumped into doors and pieces of furniture, and they both found it innocently amusing as they had found the interludes of love amusing in the days of their honeymoon.

One of the worst winters they had known reigned outside with its retinue of winds; in and out of the villas the cold winds blew incessantly, now hissing, now growling hoarsely, now roaring. In the evening the wind dropped and the stars came out, and in the silence they heard a neighbor's dog barking.

When, on their first Saturday night in their new house, Federico took the clothes out of the trunks, and, in preparation for Sunday, put his favorite shoes on the white deal shelf, erect and formal-looking on their handsome, sturdy shoe trees, a smile played about his lips. "Aren't they just beautiful?" he asked Leonor, who was putting on a dress she had just ironed.

"They are the loveliest shoes in the world," she agreed. (She always liked to use the word "lovely"; it made her feel more sure of herself and more refined.)

Then, going to the tiny hall, she opened the front door to get the daily paper which was sticking out of the mail box. For a moment she looked at the landscape and felt the winter cold on her face; then, with a bittersweet feeling in which there was so much that was unconfessed, so much faith and compassion, and so much melancholy, she closed the door against the icy air, the long dark rows of houses, the starry sky, and against evil as it roamed freely over the surface of this world.

A Note about the Author

Eduardo Mallea, by general consent the foremost writer of fiction in contemporary Argentina, was born in 1903 in the Argentine city of Bahía Blanca, where his father was a noted surgeon. He received his education in Buenos Aires, first at the Colegio Nacional and then at the University, where for two years he studied law. He published his first book when only twenty-three (1926). Since then, he has contributed very widely to periodicals in Europe and America (including *La Nación* and *Sur*, both of Buenos Aires) and has published a long series of distinguished books. He received the Buenos Aires Municipal Prize for Prose in 1935, the National Prize for Literature in 1937. He was introduced to readers in the United States in 1942, when the Houghton Mifflin Company published *Fiesta in November* (reissued in the present volume) in a collection under that title. When Alfred A. Knopf issued Mallea's novel *The Bay of Silence* in 1944, *The New York Times* said of it: "Here at last is a South American novel that challenges comparison with good contemporary writing anywhere." Mallea, who has traveled extensively and who lived for some time in France, now resides in Buenos Aires.

January 1966

A Note on the Type

The text of this book was set on the Linotype in Janson, a recutting made direct from type cast from matrices long thought to have been made by the Dutchman Anton Janson, who was a practicing type founder in Leipzig during the years 1668-87. However, it has been conclusively demonstrated that these types are actually the work of Nicholas Kis (1650-1702), a Hungarian, who most probably learned his trade from the master Dutch type founder Kirk Voskens. The type is an excellent example of the influential and sturdy Dutch types that prevailed in England up to the time William Caslon developed his own incomparable designs from these Dutch faces.

Composed, printed and bound by
The Haddon Craftsmen, Scranton, Pennsylvania.
Illustrations printed by
Halliday Lithograph Corporation, West Hanover, Mass.